THE AUTUMN TREE

TONY J FORDER

A DI Bliss Novel

"Every leaf speaks bliss to me,
fluttering from the autumn tree."
Emily Brontë

tonyjforder.com
tony@tonyjforder.com

For my family.
To those whose presence continues to bring joy into my life.
And to those no longer with us.
Because family is everything.

To Karen
With very best wishes.

ONE

I'M GOING TO DIE!

As he crouched over the lifeless body so cruelly exposed by the naked glare of a single LED floodlight, Jimmy Bliss saw the young woman's final thoughts reflected in her sightless eyes.

I'm going to die. And there's nothing I can do to stop it happening.

He knew then that she had stared into the cold, dark heart of her assailant. That in a moment of awful clarity, she had realised what was about to happen to her. If the jagged fingernails and bracelets of discoloured flesh around both wrists were anything to go by, this slender woman who looked to be barely more than a child had fought hard to fend off her attacker.

To no avail.

At the end, she had most likely accepted the horrific inevitability of her fate. Where passion and anger had once burned, now sorrow and fear formed a misty glaze over both corneas. Bliss felt sick to his stomach knowing that the last person those eyes had rested upon intended to end her life.

His preliminary analysis over with, he stood upright and arched his back until he felt it pop. He took out a mobile phone from the inside breast pocket of his black leather jacket. Snapping photographs at a murder scene had become a source of controversy between the police and the public, but Bliss did it anyway. An establishing shot from each end of the tent. Then from both sides. Followed by two close-ups of the victim's face.

When he was done, he tucked the phone away again before stepping back outside the white tent fringed with a narrow hem of blue. A thin layer of frost lay on the ground, compacting in the rapidly decreasing temperature. Tendrils of mist coiled and danced in the frigid air, masking the illumination provided by dozens of additional floodlights surrounding the tent and the sealed-off crime scene. A single tree, growing well away from its closest neighbours, loomed over the forensic tent as if desperate to possess its contents.

Bliss made a beeline for the crime scene manager, Magda Nowicki, who was waiting close by for him to finish his own inspection. 'Thanks for allowing me a quick shufty without having to get suited up,' he said. 'It seemed like a waste of time for no more than a few minutes.'

'No problem,' Nowicki said. 'We got everything we needed beforehand, so there's no issue with cross-contamination. You're done with her?'

'I am.'

'Good. The body snatchers are here and I still have to bag and tag her.'

Bliss thanked her again, then went to find Detective Inspector Kennedy, the somewhat brusque detective he'd spoken with upon arrival.

He was still walking towards him when the man said, 'You recognise our victim?'

Bliss frowned. Little more than an hour earlier, he'd received a phone call from Kennedy, who worked out of Cambridge police station, close to the centre of the university city. He'd requested

Bliss's assistance on a new murder investigation, but had insisted on providing a full explanation of the circumstances only when Bliss arrived at the crime scene. It had taken him a little over forty minutes to drive from his home in Peterborough to the Hinton chalk pits on the south-east outskirts of Cambridge. There he was met by the DI and a younger man who hovered close by but made no effort to introduce himself.

Bliss had no need of a second look in order to answer the question, but his senses had been on high alert since arriving at the pits. He was wary of the two men who looked to have taken charge. They made for an uneven pair; Mr Cagey stood tall and solid, while Kennedy was short and doughy. The older man, overweight and losing the battle to keep his hair, the younger trying a little too hard when it came to his appearance. The only thing they seemed to have in common was their fixation on Bliss, having watched him like a couple of hawks from the moment he'd stepped out of his car.

He shook his head. 'I don't know her. I may have seen her somewhere before. Perhaps we've even met. But she's not familiar to me.'

'Are you sure about that?' the reticent one asked.

Ignoring him, Bliss instead turned to DI Kennedy. 'What made you think I would recognise this girl? Why didn't you just text me her photo? Or did you drag me all the way over here just to see my reaction when I laid eyes on her for the first time?'

'You always this edgy, Bliss?' the younger man said before Kennedy had a chance to respond. He carried his weight well on a large frame, but Bliss guessed he had little more going for him than his physique. The look on his face suggested he had assumed command of the discussion, and that did not sit well.

Bliss barely looked at the man when he spoke next. 'Until you do me the courtesy of giving me your rank or position, that's DS Bliss to you.'

Mr Cagey shrugged as if it were of no consequence. 'I'll try to remember that. Consider it a lesson learned. Meanwhile, why don't you tell us why you are being so unhelpful?'

'Are you refusing to give me your name and rank?'

'I don't have to. This is an informal chat. For the time being.'

Bliss heaved a sigh and this time turned to face the man. His expelled breath fogged the gap between them for a couple of seconds. 'Thank you, chaps,' he said, looking between the two men. 'This has been fun. Let me repay you both by dragging you out of your homes in the dead of night for no good reason sometime soon.'

'I wouldn't leave if I were you, Sergeant.' This time it was Kennedy who spoke up. His tone was firm but not unfriendly. 'It won't take much for us to make things more formal. I don't think you want that.'

'Not with your form, certainly,' his companion added.

Bliss's head jerked up. 'Form? What do you mean by that?'

The man's snort was derisive. 'You really have to ask? The fact that you're currently outranked by DI Kennedy here doesn't give you a clue?'

Bliss had no argument. The price for his behaviour during a prior case, and his attitude towards a senior officer in the immediate aftermath, was being subjected to the indignity of a probationary period during which time he'd also been demoted back down to Detective Sergeant. It was one he'd been willing to pay at the time, but he couldn't yet work out why he was being given a hard time here and now. He chose to push back.

'Yes, I have to ask,' he said in a flat, even tone. 'Why don't you tell me more?'

'This is not your first time being…' the man let his words trail off, cheeks pinking.

'Go on, finish that sentence,' Bliss told him. 'This is not my first time being interrogated? Was that what you were going to say? You slipped up there, didn't you, Lurch? But at least we're getting somewhere.' He paused, slowly switching his gaze back to Kennedy. 'This is not some informal chat at all, is it? And you didn't ask me over here to offer advice on that poor girl's murder. I'm being interviewed, but without caution or representation.'

'Hold on a second,' Kennedy spluttered. 'That's not what this is at all.'

Bliss stared hard at him. 'Bollocks it isn't. Let's start again, shall we? And this time, I'll take charge. I'll give your friend here one final opportunity to tell me his name and give me his rank. Then *you* can tell me why I am here, or I will leave. Don't test me on that, Inspector, because I'm not in the mood for more of your stupid bloody games.'

The DI gave his companion a sidelong glance. Shrugged and nodded. The younger man inclined his head and said, 'I'm an investigator with the NCA.'

Bliss had already guessed as much. 'What kind of alphabetti spaghetti are we talking about?'

'I'm with ERSOU,' he said, pronouncing the acronym as a single word. 'Specifically, MSHTU.'

Bliss knew the Modern Slavery and Human Trafficking Unit well. Attached to the Eastern Region Special Operations Unit of the National Crime Agency based in Bedford, Bliss had spent some time posted there himself, working organised crime. Not all investigators had previous police service experience, and Bliss assumed this man had not long stepped up from being a trainee.

'And your name?' Bliss asked.

'Glen Ashton.'

Whatever the situation, Bliss understood the NCA were involved by invitation – meaning DI Kennedy was ultimately in charge. He turned to his fellow detective once more. 'I think we've had enough pratting around, don't you? Let's get down to why you wanted me here tonight.'

Kennedy took a beat before speaking, while Ashton shuffled from foot to foot like an impatient toddler. All three men were wrapped up well against the bitter night air: thick jackets fastened to the neck, scarves protruding to protect their throats. The DI shivered once before speaking.

'Our naked young woman was probably strangled within the past twenty-four hours. So far we've been unable to identify her. We found no bag, no purse, no phone, no jewellery; nothing except her clothes in a pile beside the body. She has a couple of tattoos on her back, but they're generic and of generally poor quality. However, I did find a couple of business cards tucked away inside the lining of her bra. One of those cards was yours, Sergeant.'

Bliss felt his eyebrows arch reflexively as he nodded. 'Okay. Well, although most of the time I forget, I do occasionally hand them out. If you thought I might be able to help ID her, that would be one thing – but that's not why you brought me here. We could have done it at the mortuary. You were keen to see my reaction in the place where she was found, and you didn't believe me when I told you I had no idea who she was. I have to assume there's a good reason why.'

'There is,' Ashton said, taking over without waiting for permission from Kennedy. 'On the reverse side of the card was something hand-written. A single phrase: *Get out of jail free!* I'm betting that means something to you, because I think you wrote it.'

Bliss felt a jolt as if he'd been kicked in the ribs. He had only ever written that line five times. Five separate cards, all doled out on the same occasion. He put his head down for a moment, catching his breath. 'It does. And I did. But tell me, what did you take it to mean? Clearly you suspect me of something, or I wouldn't be here and you wouldn't be all attitude.'

Ashton nodded, looking Bliss up and down. 'This card tells me you are on the take, DS Bliss. I think you hand them out to young girls in return for something or other, telling them you'll work some magic to make sure they walk should they ever get in trouble with the police. We both know you have a fondness for brasses.'

Bliss kept his eyes cast to the floor. 'Investigator Ashton, that's going to be the one and only time you get to accuse me of being on the take. Or talk to me in that way. You do it again and I'll knock you spark out.'

The NCA man bristled and tensed. 'I wouldn't make idle threats if I were you.'

'There's nothing idle about it. I'll turn the other cheek when it comes to most accusations, but not that. Never that. Do you understand me?'

Ashton said nothing.

Bliss looked up, his anger bubbling under. 'Don't go thinking you can intimidate me with silence. You're not Jack fucking Reacher. You're a wet-behind-the-ears NCA investigator who's trying to climb a ladder before he can even walk.' He turned to glare at DI Kennedy. 'I have to hope you're better than this, Inspector. For that poor girl's sake. This was all Ashton's idea, right?'

Kennedy shrugged and gave a sheepish nod. 'I would have gone a different way. The connection was too flimsy for my liking.'

'And too bloody obvious. What kind of shit cop criminal would I be if I handed out business cards bearing that message to people I wanted sexual favours from?'

'The thought did cross my mind.'

'But we can't say the same for Rain Man here.' Bliss hooked a thumb at Ashton. 'And now I think about it some more, why exactly is he here?'

'Taking into account her flesh tone and bone structure, our victim looks to be of Middle Eastern heritage. Judging by the clothes she wore and the tramp stamp, there's the distinct possibility of her having been a sex worker. You know as well as I do that combo sends up a trafficking flare these days.'

Bliss rubbed a hand across his face. He glanced over at the tent covering the young woman's tiny, doll-like body. The PVC structure looked lost and somehow fragile, as if cast adrift upon a landscape as bleak as anything he had ever seen. It was no place to be remembered by.

'Which brings us back to my business card, and why she had it on her,' he said. 'All right, I'll tell you about it. *Them*, to be precise.'

Ashton choked down on a laugh. 'Oh, so there's more than one? Why am I not surprised?'

'Bloody well listen, will you?' Bliss snarled at him. 'You might even learn a thing or two. A few years back, my team rescued five trafficked young women from a transport container at RAF Wittering. They were close to death by the time we found them, but those we did find all survived after they'd received medical treatment. I wrote that message on the cards I gave each of them. And yes, I wanted them to know that if they got caught up in anything unsavoury, they could call me. I made a joke of it by writing that phrase, to lighten the mood. But there was nothing offered in return, and you suggesting otherwise turns my stomach.'

'So why tell us you didn't know our victim?' Ashton asked.

Bliss sighed, his breath escaping in a dense cloud of vapour. He closed his eyes, still seeing the naked form beneath the tent. 'Because I don't. I gave out five cards to five young women. Girls, really. But your victim wasn't one of them.'

'You said this thing at the RAF base was a few years ago. How can you possibly be sure this isn't one of those girls?'

'Because they were minutes away from death when we found them. Having spent days in conditions you can't possibly begin to imagine and would almost certainly not have survived.'

Ashton hiked his broad shoulders. 'I still don't understand.'

'What a shocker. Maybe you're able to experience something like that and forget all about it afterwards. Me? I remember their faces. I'll never forget them. I also kept myself informed as to what became of those young women. That poor creature under your forensic tent is definitely not one of the five young women we rescued that night.'

'Then why did she have your card on her?'

Bliss took a breath. 'That's precisely what I intend to find out.'

TWO

IT WAS 7.00AM, AND Bliss found himself sitting on a bench in a long corridor sipping weak vending-machine coffee alongside a bleary-eyed and disgruntled DCI Warburton. Cambridge police station, an anonymous four-storey building adjacent to the fire station and opposite Parker's Piece park and garden, was not unlike every other older city centre nick. Filing cabinets lining up like suspects around the perimeter of open-plan work areas, each of which was separated into individual bases; overlapping posters depicting actual suspects adorning the walls as if they were abstract works of art; interview rooms created from little more than blank square boxes, designed to be dour and uninspiring; bland, squeaky hallways with discontent brewing behind every door; canteens serving tasteless microwaved food and vending machines spewing out hot drinks you wouldn't wish to inflict on the drains.

'Here we are yet again,' Warburton said, looking as if she was trying hard not to scowl at him. 'What is it about you and the past?'

'It's not by design,' Bliss protested. 'They came to me, remember?'

'Indeed they did. And do you recall why, Jimmy? Because it's their case. Yet here I am, having been woken at stupid o'clock, because you want to take it from them.'

'The victim had my card in her possession. That means she belongs to us.'

Warburton swallowed some of her own insipid drink. 'And yet, as you've already admitted to DI Kennedy, she isn't one of the five girls from your previous investigation. The card on its own proves nothing.'

Bliss sniffed. 'I'd argue it proves just enough.'

'You'd argue black was white if it meant getting your own way.'

'That's as maybe, but whoever the victim is, she was clearly close to one of ours. Her having my card is all the evidence I need of that.'

'Even if that were true, and even if we could prove it, I'm still struggling to find an angle here for the discussion I'm about to have with DI Kennedy's boss. I'm not seeing how a girl you don't recognise being murdered on another team's patch becomes our case, Jimmy. Sorry, but I'm not.'

'And we won't end up with it, either, if that's your attitude going in.'

His DCI rolled her eyes. On the tail end of a sigh she said, 'It has bugger all to do with my attitude. Some of us have to graft within the protocols and procedures. Give me something to work with and I'll support you.'

Bliss put his head back and blew out some pent-up frustration. 'The fact that she had one of those cards and might well be a sex worker tells me there's a connection to our case against Lewis Drake. My team and I rescued those young women from his clutches, boss, and in the process we disassembled Drake's trafficking operation. We never got him to talk about those who came before – the girls and women he'd sneaked in and out of that airbase before we caught him. But what if this victim is one of them?'

'What if she is? How do you imagine we can tie her in when we can't speak to her about it?'

'We do what we do best. Investigate. If she entered this country courtesy of Drake, then even though he's banged up, he may still have something to do with her murder.'

This was mostly wishful thinking on his part. Lewis Drake ran a scrapyard in Peterborough, the business nothing more than a front for his illegal operations. There had been six women in that container flown into RAF Wittering on a transport plane. One managed to escape. Her liquefied remains were later discovered in a barrel of acid on Drake's property, but so far Drake's legal team had successfully thwarted all attempts to charge him with the woman's murder. In fact, a member of his staff had already confessed to snatching the girl, killing her, and disposing of her remains. Nailing Drake for a different murder would go some way to compensating for missing out on the one Bliss knew the man had at the very least ordered.

'You ask so much of me, Jimmy,' Warburton said, shaking her head. 'You send me into battle with my opposite number, but provide me with no weapons.'

'I'd argue my own case if I still had the rank.'

'Yes, well, we all know whose fault that is. Be grateful you still have a job at all.'

Bliss let go of his irritation. 'I am. You and Superintendent Fletcher went in to bat for me, and I won't ever forget the debt I owe you both. And neither will the people I'm still able to help in whatever time I have remaining in the job. Just like this poor victim we have here. Little more than a kid. If this is Drake's work, he deserves to be collared for it. If not, there's a distinct possibility that whoever slipped into his shoes when we put him away signed off on the job.'

Warburton sighed. 'And you know all this how?'

'I don't. I feel it in my water.'

'You sure that's not old age and a dodgy bladder?'

'Forgive me for saying so, boss, but you're starting to sound like Penny.'

'DS Chandler is a wise woman. And a saint to put up with you. Look, Jimmy, I hear you. I understand. But do you really want the responsibility? Or should I say – do you really want it to be the team's responsibility?'

'It's not a matter of want,' he said softly. 'Call me old fashioned if you like, but to me it's more a matter of duty. That girl had my card on her person. That card ties me to her, whether or not I'm part of the team investigating her murder. But you're right about one thing: I do feel responsible. So let me do what I can to find the bastard who strangled her to death.'

Warburton acknowledged his plea with a dip of her head. 'There's still a budget to fight over, Jimmy.'

'Then use that as one of your arguments in there.' He nodded towards the office door to their left. 'Our case, our budget.'

'And have Superintendent Fletcher all over me demanding to know why.'

'No problem. Remind her it's the right thing to do.'

She clenched both fists and raised them to her forehead, letting out an exasperated groan. 'You'll be the death of me, Jimmy Bliss. Of my career, at least.'

He grinned. 'So you'll do it?'

'You knew I would.'

'I hoped.' He thought about it for a moment, then nodded. 'Yeah, I did know it. Not because you're a soft touch, either. Truth is, you're a good copper and you do the right thing when it needs doing. I realise this is a long shot. I'd be stupid not to. Our victim might not have been a brass at all. Even if she was, she could still have been killed by a punter. Plus, there are plenty of parasites like Drake out there running young girls. I get all that, boss. But her having my card tells me there's a possible connection. I have to follow up on that.'

The office door opened and Kennedy's DCI beckoned Warburton in. She got to her feet, smoothed down her trousers, and buttoned her suit jacket. 'I'll give it my best shot, Jimmy. But don't sulk if they keep it for themselves.'

Bliss put a hand to his chest. 'I'm insulted.'

'You're immune to insults. All that experience you've had, I expect.'

'Perhaps. But thanks, boss. I know you'll work something out.'

***

To say he sulked on the drive back would be an overstatement, but Bliss was not an entirely happy man. Cambridge had handed over the investigation with great reluctance, but not before attaching a couple of unwelcome strings. The first compelled Bliss to report to DI Kennedy once a day – and at the first indication that there was no connection to Lewis Drake or whoever had replaced him in the trafficking business, he was to hand it all back. The second was harder to stomach: the NCA liaison, Glen Ashton, had been assigned to the investigation to work with Bliss and the Major Crimes team based at Thorpe Wood in Peterborough.

Bliss's natural instinct had almost persuaded him to lodge a complaint. Having been an NCA investigator himself, he understood their expertise could often make the difference in trafficking cases. But Ashton was too raw. Bliss regarded himself as Marley's ghost, and the investigator merely the set of chains he was compelled to drag around as a penitence. Having to pander to the man was a big ask. But he was immensely grateful to Warburton for having fought for his right to run the case. Settling for what he had was ultimately the best approach.

The Major Crimes Unit morning briefing was over by the time he arrived at HQ. Earlier, he'd messaged Detective Sergeant Bishop, who was acting up as DI in preparation for making the move on a full-time basis. Explaining his tardiness, Bliss also mentioned he hoped to be bringing back a live one. Quite what the team would make of it, he had no idea. The unit had a number of cases on the go, but nothing as pressing as murder. He believed any mention of Lewis Drake and the young women found in the transport container might swing matters his way.

Only Chandler, Bishop and DC Ansari were in the squad room when he eventually made it upstairs. He glanced at a wall-mounted whiteboard on the way in, which told him DCs John Hunt and Phil Gratton were out pursuing enquires on another matter. DCI Warburton was not in her office; he doubted she had made it back from Cambridge ahead of him. He also assumed that when his boss did get in, she would head straight upstairs to discuss the case with Detective Superintendent Fletcher.

'How's it going, boss?' Chandler asked. 'I gather you might have something juicy for us?'

Bliss threw a glance at DS Bishop. Officially, the acting DI was currently Penny Chandler's direct supervisor. As a squad, they had agreed early on that nothing much would change after Bliss had been reinstated at a lower rank. Bishop would effectively act in his stead when it came to attending meetings, stepping up as deputy Senior Investigating Officer as required, as well as addressing the day-to-day management of the unit and the administrative burden of the role. As for running operations, they continued to regard Bliss as their leader. Bishop had been the first to suggest the arrangement, but still Bliss wondered when the time would come for his DS to step forward to ask to be referred to as the boss.

It hadn't happened yet, so Bliss was happy to continue. He explained why he'd been dragged out in the early hours of the morning. He noticed his colleagues' heightened interest when he mentioned the business card.

'No,' he said, shaking his head. 'It wasn't any of our girls. But she had the card, which might indicate she was close to one of them. I threw Lewis Drake's name into the mix, hoping the connection would make all the difference in how the case was eventually assigned. DI Kennedy was not overly impressed, but he understood my line of thinking.'

'Any idea which of the girls gave up her card?' Bishop asked.

'No. All five went through the NRM. One of them later changed her mind and decided to be repatriated. Of the other four, one absconded from her temporary residence – I don't know why she ran, but perhaps she thought her case wasn't strong enough to win. The remaining three had also applied for asylum and were eventually accepted for refugee status. Perhaps the girl who chose to go back home gave her card to another trafficked young woman. I'll be contacting the three whose details we have.'

Ansari whistled. 'You found all that out this morning, boss?'

'No,' Bliss said. 'I've followed their progress since the day we found them in that container. I've previously spoken to the three who obtained refugee status. I know how to get hold of them.'

The National Referral Mechanism was often the starting point for young people trafficked into the United Kingdom. As a body, it was capable of quickly establishing a 'reasonable grounds' decision in favour of the applicants, followed by a 'conclusive grounds' finding and eventual residence permit if things went their way. An appeal for asylum was also often made at the same time. In many cases, circumstances changed for those not wishing to return immediately to their own country. But the process could also make allowances for victims of trafficking to reside on a more permanent basis. Bliss had followed this process all the way through for the women in the container, offering documentation and his own sworn testimony to their status as trafficked people.

'Do you ever sleep?' Chandler asked him in almost child-like wonder. 'Or do you have access to more than the twenty-four hours a day we mere mortals are allowed?'

'I do sleep. Us old folk need less of it, that's all.'

'You want to run with that?' Bishop asked. 'You and Pen?'

Bliss nodded. 'Makes sense.'

'Good. Meanwhile, Gul and I will follow up with the pathologist and forensic bods to see if we can nail down an ID on our victim. TOD and COD as well.'

'When you speak to Nancy, make sure you ask about lividity.' Nancy Drinkwater was the city's head of pathology, popular with the team.

Bishop regarded him with surprise. 'You think our victim might have been killed elsewhere and moved?'

'I think we ought to consider the possibility, yes. It's been bloody cold out, the past couple of days, and even if she was a brass I don't think she was there to meet with a punter. It could be a body dump. Also, I couldn't tell if what I noticed on her skin was blood pooling or bruising. She was discovered lying on her side, so it's something to note.'

'Who found her? Is there anyone working on that?'

'Locals. There were plenty of places to hide her over at the chalk pits, but our victim was left out in the open. A jogger found her, and the discovery was witnessed by a woman walking her dog. Both were interviewed and cleared. I might want to meet with them myself, but DI Kennedy was satisfied they were legit.'

Bishop considered this fresh information. 'Okay. It's early days, so let's stick with our current actions for the time being. If we need John and Phil, I'll rope them in as soon as they both become available. How about the NCA? Where do they fit in?'

Bliss remembered Ashton, and winced. 'Ah, yes. There's something I forgot to tell you all.'

THREE

B LISS REALISED HE AND Chandler ought to wait for Glen Ashton to arrive before heading out, but the problem was he had taken an instant dislike to the young man, and it was this that won the day. The way Bliss saw it, the NCA investigator was attached to the case, not directly to him or his role in it. He also didn't particularly want the man intervening in the interviews he had planned, given their nature and sensitivity.

He made three calls to numbers stored on his personal mobile phone. All three were answered, and after a series of brief conversations, he had successfully arranged appointments with each of the young women he'd spoken to.

Parastu Mazdaki lived and worked in Leicester, little more than an hour's drive west. She led educational tours for school-children at the National Space Centre. During their previous conversations, she had claimed to be happy with her life and expressed no desire to return to Iran. She had fled her homeland along with many others to escape political upheaval, but had been abducted at gunpoint by traffickers in Turkey two days after arriving in Gaziantep. Hers was one of a million or more such unhappy tales, and Bliss was pleased to have played a small role in helping Mazdaki find sanctuary in the UK.

Against all odds, Bliss had found a space in the visitors' car park at the National Space Centre. It was a short walk to the entrance, where they showed their warrant cards and obtained a visitor badge each on yet another lanyard. They were early and Mazdaki had been delayed, so they took a look at the exhibits and used the unexpected free time to catch up.

Penny's relationship with a man Bliss referred to as Shrek was going from strength to strength, and with her once-estranged daughter currently studying at Cambridge University, his friend was as happy as he'd ever seen her. The change had shaved years off her. She looked at peace, and a glow had returned to her face.

'How about you and the Bone Woman?' Chandler asked. 'You haven't mentioned much about her of late.'

He shrugged. 'Not a lot to mention. We're still seeing each other off and on – though perhaps more off than on.'

'Any particular reason for that?'

'Not really.' Bliss left it at that, hoping Chandler would do likewise.

He and Emily Grant had a relaxed personal arrangement, with no commitment to anything other than spending time together when it suited them both. She had backed off recently, the two of them having argued over an issue he was dealing with outside the job. He didn't feel up to discussing any of this with his colleague, so took the conversation in a different direction.

'How are you and the rest of the team coping? Anybody having any problems with the situation? Can't be easy on any of you with me and Bish having swapped roles.'

Chandler pursed her lips before responding. 'Nobody that I'm aware of. I'm fine with it. Not sure how much the others would say to me, given how close you and I are. As far as I know they're all getting on with their work. It's an odd situation, I grant you. But I think they'd all prefer to deal with that if it means you're still with us in the team.'

'That's good to know. I can't say it's not been awkward. Bish seems to be taking it in his stride, and I've accepted it's the way things have to be. I'd rather still be based at HQ and suffer the occasional humiliation from those who don't care for me than get transferred out.'

'I still say you got a raw deal.'

Bliss shook his head. 'No. They were right, Pen. I was bang out of order. I went against procedure, which was bad enough. But to bad-mouth the Chief Super... that was me being the worst version of me. If I have to put up with dropping back a rank and having another few months of therapy, then so be it.'

He hadn't always been honest enough to admit when he was wrong, and the learning curve was sharper than he'd imagined. Having carried out illegal surveillance on two fellow officers during a major case over the summer, he'd behaved like a spoiled child when caught out and grilled by his bosses. If not for strenuous appeals on his behalf by DCI Warburton and DSI Fletcher, he'd probably have been shipped out of the city for a second – and final – time. To remain in Major Crimes at Thorpe Wood, he'd had to accept demotion, and had done so without a second thought the moment the offer was put to him.

'I still can't believe you kept in touch with those women we rescued,' Chandler said, pulling him back into the moment. 'Yet another side of Jimmy Bliss most people never get to see or hear about. Not even your closest friend, apparently.'

He laughed. 'Don't sulk, you soppy tart. I told nobody, not even Emily. It's a private matter. You can't tell me that finding them in that container and thinking they had to be dead when we threw the doors open didn't touch you emotionally.'

'Oh, it did. Very much so. You weren't the only one in tears when we realised all five of them were still breathing. Never occurred to me to keep in touch once it was over, though.'

'That's just it, Pen. How over is it? We put away a lot of people involved in that operation, even that bastard Lewis Drake. But you and I both know he's the kind of vermin who won't be happy letting that go. He might not be prepared to let them live during his appeal.'

'He'd have to find them first.'

'Yeah, and we both know how easy it can be to get information if you have the right amount of money or favours to offer in return. I decided to keep in touch to keep them updated on how it was all progressing. That's all.'

They paused in front of a display case containing various types of space suit. Bliss had never been much of one for the planets and space travel, other than the many Hollywood versions.

'Still no idea where our absconder might have gone?' Chandler asked.

He shook his head. 'Not a scooby. I doubt we'll ever find out, either.'

The Somalian girl had disappeared after spending six months in the care of the state. Her refugee status was not as unequivocal as the others'. There had been discussions at all levels in relation to her trafficking story; specifically, whether she had volunteered to be taken in order to find a better life in the UK. Bliss had tried looking for her, but came to the conclusion that she had vanished into the Somalian community, probably in London.

'Which leaves us with an Iranian and the two women from the Ukraine.'

He nodded. 'Yeva Savchuk and Marta Lsenko. Did you know Yeva means *to breathe*? She told me that herself during our first real conversation. Said she had to remind herself of it while she and the others were struggling for air in those final few hours. Repeated her name over and over again, using it as some kind of mantra.'

'They're an amazing bunch. I'm not sure I would have lasted as long as they did in those conditions.'

Bliss recalled finding the young women and wondering how they had managed to survive. 'Me neither.'

Chandler narrowed her gaze. 'You admire them.'

'Don't you?'

'Of course. Who wouldn't? But it's more obvious with you. Almost as if you're… proud of them for having managed to stay alive in such atrocious conditions.'

'I suppose I am. Finding them and saving them from certain death created a connection – one I find hard to let go of.'

They fell into silence as they continued walking around the exhibition, before Chandler spoke again. 'You remembered their names. Off the top of your head.'

Bliss gave her a sidelong glance. 'What's your point?'

'It astonishes me how you do that. You rarely – if ever – take notes, whether it's a briefing, a meeting, or an interview. I often wonder why.'

Bliss nodded. 'Then I'll tell you. Provided you answer one of my own questions first.'

'I can do that.'

'You always used to save your own note writing until those same briefings, meetings, and interviews were over. But since Mia's been gone, it's as if you and your notepad are inseparable. And you tap the pen on its cover the way she did. Are you aware of that, or is it a subconscious thing?'

Chandler ran a hand across her hair and fussed over her braided ponytail. 'It's deliberate. It was Mia's little quirk, but now that it's mine, I feel closer to her somehow. I find it comforting. I thought others might, too.'

'It is.' Bliss nodded appreciatively. 'We do. That was a good call.'

'So now you. Why do you hardly ever take notes?'

Bliss shrugged. 'Testing myself. I used to note stuff down, back when we first worked together. But my condition occasionally leaves me with brain-fog. My mind gets a little muddled and my concentration can be difficult to keep on track. So I work off what I hear and take in at the time, and I try to remember it all, hoping the focus will keep me sharp.'

'And how often does that work out?'

'Not as often as I'd like. But the things I absolutely need to remember do seem to stick. Doing mundane tasks like food shopping, or the laundry – even eating – not so much. But I reckon that's a fair trade.'

'All of which you've told your therapist, right?'

Bliss snorted. 'What do you think? She doesn't tell me anything I didn't already know. In return, I don't tell her anything I don't want her to know.'

Chandler shook her head and threw him a sour look. 'That sounds like a healthy arrangement. Not. And a complete waste of time.'

If ever a sniff could be derisory, such was the one he gave at that moment. 'I got something from it when I first went, but not any longer. Therapy isn't what I need. But attendance is mandatory, so I go. I find having some down time with my music or in the garden watching my fish does more for me than spilling my guts to a relative stranger.'

'It helped you before. Why do you think it's not working this time?'

'Because there's nothing in my past or present gnawing at me; if anything, it's the future that gives me cause for concern. My

CRA applies in less than two years' time. That gives me less than eighteen months to decide if I want to apply for an extension.'

Chandler's eyes widened and her voice rose an octave. 'Decide? That suggests there's a decision to be made. I didn't think wild horses could prevent you from extending your time in the job, Jimmy.'

Bliss grunted. 'If I thought it'd be unopposed, I wouldn't have to think twice. Do you actually think DCS Feeley is going to agree to my staying on?'

'His won't be the deciding vote. Nor the only voice heard. The others will look at your record and...'

Bliss jumped in on the pause. 'Yeah. Exactly. They study my record, and what do they find? "This man clears cases... but hold on, what are all these black marks against him?"'

'Don't do yourself down. The good you've done more than outweighs the bad.'

'I think so, too. I'm not convinced they'll see things the same way, though. Not when presented with a way of showing me the exit door.'

'Have you considered taking retirement and signing up as a consultant?'

'Considered, and rejected. First of all, they'd get to choose when to use me, and where. I want to stay on in Major Crimes at Thorpe Wood. If I can't have that, I might as well walk. But the real kicker would be being a civilian, having no powers of arrest, and not being out on the streets with you lot. I'd be stuck taking witness statements all day. No – give me my music, my fish, and my boat over that option, thanks.'

Chandler was quiet for a few seconds. A huge globe filled the space ahead of them, groups of people posing for photos around it. When she spoke next, her voice was soft and considered. 'I notice you didn't include Emily in that list. Twice you've mentioned relaxing with your music and your fish. You spoke about your garden, and this time you included your boat as well. But not Em.'

Bliss breathed out heavily. 'Pen, I know you two have become friendly. You conspired with her to put the two of us back together again, so you feel as if you have skin in the game. But a square piece needs a square hole for a reason, and I'm still not sure that's what we are to each other. Not that I'm saying we're over; that's not it at all.'

'Fair enough. You clearly need to work that out between you. I won't interfere.'

'You? Not interfere? That'd be a first.'

She nudged him in the ribs. 'Sod off! I can sit back and observe when I have to.'

'I'm not convinced about that. Anyhow, all that shit is for another day.'

'As is your future in the job. I don't believe for one moment that you intend to walk away without a fight when the time comes.'

He puffed out his lips and waved it off. 'All of that is ahead of me. I'll be prepared.'

'Without seeming as if I'm interfering moments after I said I wouldn't, what does Em have to say about it? I bet she'd rather you pulled the plug on this life.'

'We haven't discussed it. It's my concern, my decision.'

He was staring at a region on the globe, but Bliss could almost feel her eyes roll as she snapped back at him, 'For goodness' sake, Jimmy. What is wrong with you?'

'What? I don't know what you mean.'

'Don't give me that old cobblers. You need to grow up, old man. And fast. If you don't, you might let her get away. You do that, and I guarantee you'll regret it.'

'This is you not interfering? I'd hate to think what you might say if you weren't leaving it alone.'

'Oh, balls! I only said that to shut you up. Jimmy, If you and Em are going to have any hope whatsoever, this is one of those discussions you have to have. Together.'

He shook his head. 'It's a decision *I* have to make about *my* future. What's so hard to understand about that?'

This time she turned to confront him. 'You're not a stupid man, Jimmy – not *that* stupid, anyway. If you don't take Emily into your confidence over a matter that's going to have a direct impact on your future when you reach compulsory retirement age at sixty, what do you think that will tell her?'

'I think–'

'I'll tell you what it will say to her: that you don't see her as part of that future.'

'You can't answer your own questions, Pen. You're supposed to wait for me to reply.'

'I didn't need you to reply. I was making a point. Let me tell you something – and please, for once do me a big favour and bloody well listen. You make that decision on your own and when she finds out, Emily will walk out of your life forever. Is that what you want?'

'You don't know that. You can't possibly know that.'

'Is it what you want?'

Bliss took a breath. He checked his watch and saw they were late for their meeting. Eventually he said, 'I don't know what I want. Okay? I really don't know.'

Chandler nodded. 'Then perhaps that's all the answer you need.'

FOUR

THEY FOUND MAZDAKI WAITING for them at a table in the Boosters café attached to the Soyuz lounge.

She stood to greet the two detectives, offering a shy smile. 'It is good to see you, Mr Jimmy.' Her eyes sparkled, and to his astonishment she wrapped her arms around him for a moment and laid her head against his shoulder. Small and slight, the young woman wore western clothing and nothing to conceal her hair.

'You probably don't remember me,' Chandler said, accepting a brief embrace. 'I'm DS Chandler.'

'Miss Penny, yes? Of course I remember.'

Bliss found the café's garish red seats an assault on the eyes, but the rocket and capsule parts suspended from the ceiling more than made up for it. He fetched them each a drink, arriving back at the table to find the young Iranian describing the various pieces on display around them. The three spent a few minutes idly chatting, but as Mazdaki was on a break, the conversation quickly became more formal. When Bliss mentioned the business card, she flashed a wide grin, dipped two fingers into her purse and pulled out the one he had handed her more than two years ago. It did not bear a single crease.

'I would never give this to anybody else,' she said. Her features became more earnest as she clutched it to her chest. 'It is a precious item. It reminds me there is kindness in this world.'

Bliss was touched by the comment. His aim in passing out cards had simply been to provide a means of requesting his help directly should they ever need it. He had not foreseen the possibility of it becoming some kind of talisman to any of them.

Parastu Mazdaki had spoken no English at all when Bliss and Chandler first attempted to interview her, in a quiet hospital room after the Iranian and four other young women had been treated for a variety of conditions resulting from dehydration, malnutrition, and oxygen deprivation. They had gleaned all the information they required via an interpreter, and upon leaving the ward four days later, Mazdaki had been driven away to an undisclosed temporary location in the city. She now spoke the language with confidence.

The two detectives learned that she had a boyfriend, who lived not far away from her flat in Belgrave and was studying architecture at De Montfort University. She was enjoying her life in the UK and had no desire to return home, despite missing her mother and two sisters. She told the two detectives that she had neither seen nor heard from any of the other young women with whom she had shared the transportation container since they parted ways.

Her face creased suddenly as she spoke. 'It is not something I enjoy remembering. In those few days which felt like many more, I fought to stay alive, but did not care if I died. I wanted both, if you understand?'

'I think I can,' Bliss told her. 'We can never truly comprehend what you and the other girls went through. However, we can imagine.'

'So you know why I can never let go of this card.'

It wasn't a question, but it had him nodding all the same. 'I think I do. Which makes me wonder why one of you did give theirs to somebody else. Perhaps she was going somewhere new. Away from here. Somewhere she would no longer need it.'

Mazdaki shook her head. 'Even then, you keep it close. To remind you, yes?'

'Clearly not all of you felt the same, Parastu. Our having the card in our possession proves that.'

'They would have to take it from me. And only after a fight.'

Bliss thought about that possibility. It had been crouching there in the back of his mind, where it was darkest. Yet he suggested something quite different. 'What about if somebody else needed it more than you did? If they were in some kind of danger, maybe. Would you give it to them then?'

'No. I would perhaps share the details. Your name. Your number. But I would never willingly hand over that card.'

The woman's simple, flat statement made Bliss feel as if he and Chandler were on a fool's errand. There was a better than average chance that the card belonged to either the Somalian who had absconded, or the girl who chose to return to her home country – most likely the latter, because she would have no need of it. He was okay with that, provided the card had been willingly passed on to somebody else in dire need. Not that it had done their victim any good.

Chandler and Mazdaki chatted for a while as Bliss became contemplative, but it soon became clear they would find nothing here to take them further. Both detectives received another hug as they said their goodbyes.

Bliss was quiet as he drove back to Peterborough. He'd remembered Mazdaki from the night in the container, and from the hospital afterwards. She was the only one of the five who spoke no English at all, and her detachment from the others had been noticeable. Even trapped inside that steel box with other young girls who each shared the same degradation, she had been alone.

Having been repeatedly raped and abused along the way by the men who took her, the young Iranian's resolve had eventually been beaten out of her. The last thing any of the women were told before the steel container door clanged shut to seal them inside was that they were headed for a life and a destination where they could expect much of the same on a daily basis.

Bliss had often wondered why, if they believed that was all life had in store for them, any of them had fought so hard to live. Each of them had clung on so desperately, when it would have been far easier to give up, to succumb to their conditions and slip away. He assumed it had to be hope that kept them going. Hope was not something in which he was a great believer.

***

Yeva Savchuk worked as many shifts at Frankie and Benny's as the owner would give her. By the time they arrived at the restaurant, Chandler had made an update call to Bishop, and Bliss had taken a rather irate one from DCI Warburton. Apparently they disagreed on Glen Ashton's role; Warburton wanted him to shadow Bliss and Chandler. For the first time, Bliss thought he might be able to use the demotion to his advantage.

'With respect, boss,' he said. 'Surely any NCA involvement needs to be at SIO level. That's either you or Bish as your deputy. It's certainly not me any more.'

After accusing him of being a slippery bugger living too close to the edge for comfort, his Chief Inspector relented and told Bliss to report to her the moment he arrived back at Thorpe Wood. He yearned for the days when the unit's DCI had made use of her assigned office space on the floor above Major Crimes. Warburton's predecessor, Alicia Edwards, liked to remain close to the Superintendent. Her replacement, however, had cleared out the squad's break room and settled herself in there, making it almost impossible for Bliss to hide himself away and remain unseen.

It was lunchtime, so they both ordered food. He opted for a chicken wrap, while Chandler went for the Mediterranean salad. Savchuk joined them when they were close to being done. Tall and slender, fine blonde hair tied back in a long ponytail, the young woman was all smiles. Her skin shone with vigour. When Chandler brought up the subject of her partner's business card, Savchuk held up a finger and walked away from their booth. They watched as she disappeared beyond a door marked *Staff Only*. For a moment, Bliss wondered if she might make a run for it, but she returned seconds later with his card in her hand.

Twisting the little white rectangle between her fingers, she spoke unfalteringly about that night on the airbase and about her recuperation and life since. Other than Marta Lsenko, her fellow Ukrainian, she knew nothing about the young women she had shared a container with. Lsenko had become a friend, she explained. The two had worked together at the restaurant for a short time, but the physical demands and type of work had not been to Lsenko's liking. She'd lasted no longer than four months in the job.

'So what's she up to these days?' Bliss asked. 'How is she making a living?'

Savchuk wrinkled her nose and turned away. Her strong cheekbones glistened and her full lips had become a thin slit. Eventually she shrugged and faced them again, folding her arms across her chest.

'I do not like to say. Marta, she try to talk me into same thing. She say I make a lot of money doing what she does.'

'Yeva, is she a prostitute?' Bliss asked softly.

'No. She… is escort. She has photographs on website. She meet with men and pretend to be girlfriend, yes?'

Bliss nodded, not wishing to point out the obvious. 'But you don't want to do that?'

She shook her head and gave a little shudder. 'No. I not like showing myself off in photograph. Nor to men. They ask you to wear… not much. Sexy things, you know?'

'Lingerie,' Chandler suggested. 'Stockings and suspenders, that sort of thing.'

'Yes. This. I tell Marta I will stay here and do what I do. Soon I am manager. I live okay. I tell her I have no need of this thing she does.'

'Do you know if she still has her card?' Bliss asked.

'I think yes. But I am not so sure.'

Bliss huffed out a sigh of frustration. Already he could see this was going to be a dead end. Locating whoever had given their victim the card was essential for forward momentum. His team thrived on such impetus, and learning which girl had given up their card would have been a great start; his money was still on the one who elected to return to her homeland. He thanked Savchuk, wished her well, paid the bill and got out of there. The young woman gave him a peck on the cheek before they left, thanking both detectives once again for rescuing her and the others. Bliss brushed it aside – it was his job, after all.

'Am I wrong, or is this a complete waste of time?' Chandler asked as they walked back out to the car. 'I mean traipsing around to visit them. You could have asked about the card when you called them.'

Bliss acknowledged her observation with a slight dip of his head. 'I could have. But I wanted to see the cards for myself. Any of the girls might have lied to me for one reason or another.'

They were early for their final interview, so Bliss called ahead. Lsenko asked him to give her half an hour; he suspected she was entertaining a client. It took them less than ten minutes to reach her flat in Hampton Vale, close to the Moorhen pub. Bliss parked the pool car a little way up the road so they could covertly observe the entrance to her property. Nobody emerged while they sat there.

'Unless she threw her punter out of the door the moment she put down her phone, I guess she wasn't busy after all,' Chandler said. There was no judgement in her voice.

The pair got out of the car, walked up to the door, and rang the bell. A buzzer sounded, the lock shot open with a loud *thunk*, and they let themselves in.

Marta Lsenko was by far the most striking of the women they had rescued. Same high cheekbones as her friend Yeva, but where Savchuk had an athlete's build, Lsenko was all soft curves. She wore a pink leisure suit that was more tasteful than it sounded. Damp hair hung in thick strands over her broad shoulders. Bliss's eyes were drawn to her eyebrows, which were so arched she looked to be in a permanent state of shock.

Within two minutes, their host had also produced her card. She leaned down to hug Bliss before showing it to him. 'You gave me this life,' she said. 'You and Penny. I won't ever forget you.'

A dark cloud entered the room to squat over Bliss's head. Was this what he had rescued her for? To endure the same indentured slavery she would have been forced into under Lewis Drake? He wondered if the agency Lsenko worked for was part of that man's organisation. How ironic that would be.

The woman was open about what she did for a living and why. She had worked as a prostitute back home in Ukraine from the age of fourteen. As with all organised crime gangs, the one that ran her in the town of Donetsk was harsh with its girls, often brutal. But she had a wild streak her masters were unable to contain, and they had sold her on, a chattel to be haggled over. There she had lived in a single room that functioned as her entire home. A life of squalor and unhappiness. Here, Lsenko told them, she had a whole apartment to herself, and only ever saw the men who controlled her very existence when it came to handing over their cut of any cash she received. Provided she earned them twelve hundred pounds per week, whatever she made above that figure was hers to keep. Given her obvious allure, Bliss imagined she was a popular girl all round.

'Show me your dead girl's picture,' she said at one point. 'I check out competition, look at how I am able to improve my own advertising. If you think she did what I do to make a living, I might recognise her.'

Bliss immediately picked up on what she had said. 'Your own… Marta, please tell me you don't run your own business on the side.'

She gave a coy smile. 'I would not tell you this. It is illegal.'

'You might be surprised. The law is a bit muddy regarding the services you offer.'

'It is? Then this is good, no?'

'No. What I mean is, if the people who employ you to escort for them and them alone get to hear of it, they will make you suffer. They'll hurt you. Not so badly that you can't work for them, but they will hurt you. And they have long memories, Marta. You must be more careful.'

Lsenko regarded him as if his concerns were unwarranted. 'I want to have nice things. I have good clothes, I drive and have nice car. I can't do all this with what I make from escort agency.'

'So you run your own ads. Online?'

'Yes. Of course. How else?'

Bliss nodded. How else indeed, in this increasingly digital age. He took a breath. 'Marta, I can't tell you what to do or what not to do. It's none of my business. But the world you live in is a dangerous one, and you will make it more so by working for yourself on the side. My advice: stop it. And stop it now.'

While they had been talking, Chandler had taken out her phone. Earlier in the day, Bliss had sent her the crime scene photos via WhatsApp, and now she edged forward in her seat to show Lsenko the screen. She had selected the least intrusive shot, one that clearly revealed their victim's features in the best light possible.

After studying it for at least ten seconds, Lsenko nodded her head and jabbed the screen with one of her perfectly manicured fingernails. 'I do not know her name, but I do recognise her face. She is not with my agency. She work for another that supplies escorts here in Peterborough, but also in Cambridge and Huntingdon.'

Bliss felt the heavy thump of a dead weight striking his heart like a clapper on a bell. Just when he'd least expected progress, it seemed they had a breakthrough. 'Do you remember which agency?'

She shook her head. 'No. But is easy to find.'

'You definitely don't remember her name, though?'

'I never knew her name. Not her real name.' She picked up her own mobile, which had been sitting on the arm of her chair. Her thumbs flashed on it for a couple of seconds. Then she nodded to herself and handed the phone to Bliss. 'See, here. With my agency I am Rebecca, not Marta.'

The online page she showed him contained four photographs in addition to her assumed name. In the first she wore a full-length evening gown, looking both striking and elegant. In the second she reclined on a sofa, wearing black nightwear that left little to the imagination. In the third she wore white lingerie while lying across the foot of a bed. In the final shot she was standing upright and completely naked, turned side-on to the camera while looking back over her shoulder.

Bliss handed the phone back to Lsenko, who smiled sweetly at him. 'Here I am Marta, you see. There I am Rebecca. On your girl's site, she is Honey.'

FIVE

U PON ARRIVING BACK AT Thorpe Wood, Bliss asked Chandler
to update the rest of the team before joining him in the Sex
Crimes unit. Officially, the division no longer existed and worked
under the banner of the Sexual Offence Investigation Unit. Unof-
ficially, while the squad ran investigations ranging from sexual
abuse to rape, it also provided intelligence support for the NCA
in connection to local prostitution rings.

Bliss and the squad leader, DI Angie Burton, had once enjoyed
a brief fling. It had ended amicably and they remained friends as
well as colleagues. He knew her experience would be useful in
finding a way through the sleaze and grime he was set to encounter in tracking down the woman they currently knew as Honey.

Burton was sitting at the far end of the room talking with two
members of her team when Bliss entered. He stood, waiting to
catch her eye, before taking a seat at the closest free desk with a
computer terminal. He didn't bother trying to access any relevant
sites, as he knew his network credentials were invalid on this
equipment. Given the graphic nature of the material this team
often had to analyse, the system was locked down tight with every
keystroke monitored, to protect the user as much as the service.

A couple of minutes later, Burton came to sit down beside him. She had the kind of face you could hopefully still describe as being pretty without getting a rap over the knuckles for it. Her smile was warm and genuine, if a little weary. 'And how are you doing these days, Jimmy?' she asked. 'Playing by the rules, I hope.'

'Don't I always?'

They both laughed.

'How is it you don't seem to age?' he asked her. 'Do you have a painting of yourself tucked away in an attic?'

'Oh, I age. Believe me. I can't sit or stand without farting these days.'

'Well, something is working for you. On the outside, at least.'

'That's my healthy lifestyle. I've kicked out all the bad stuff. Besides, you're not looking too shabby yourself, Jimmy. What's your secret?'

'I enjoy all the bad stuff.'

Burton shook her head at him. 'Always the contrarian. So, what can I do for you?'

Bliss laid it out for her. 'I'm working a murder. Young woman strangled to death in Cambridge. There's a good chance she was an escort. Probably working for an agency covering the whole county.'

'Off the books as well?'

'Most likely, yes. Though I'm not quite sure how that works.'

Burton had Bliss shift over so that she could sit in front of the widescreen monitor and keyboard. After logging on, she opened up a browser and navigated to Google. 'You can search for escorts here and it will give you a whole range of options. The most common results come back for *Vivastreet*, *Adultwork*, *UKescorts*, *Ukadultzone*, and *Friday-ad*. More sites are springing up all the time, but these few usually cover all the main agencies and independents. All of them will include adverts for agency escorts. Do you have a name?'

'Honey.'

'How sweet. If your victim is known as Honey on her agency website, chances are she won't be using the same name as an independent. Let's find her first, after which we can expand and dig into her a bit more.'

Burton's fingers flashed over the keyboard. On the first site she quickly navigated her way to the Cambridgeshire area. 'What colour hair does your victim have?' she asked.

'Dark brown, maybe even black.'

'Okay. On here she'll be classified as brunette. Slender frame?'

'Yes. She was petite.'

'Okay. I can include that as a sub-category. Let's search there first. Do you have her photo on you? Only there's a possibility we'll encounter more than one girl using that same name on different sites.'

Bliss dug out his phone and accessed his crime scene photos. Burton looked through them, then back up at him. 'This is what you call playing by the rules, is it?'

He waved the rebuke away as she tapped at the keys once more. 'It doesn't go against policy. It's not the taking of photos we have problems with – it's how they're used afterwards.'

Her first search threw up twenty-three results. She glanced at him. 'If she's multi-agency she may go by a different name again, so stop me scrolling if you spot her.'

Twice he asked her to pause. Two of the girls looked a lot like his victim, but they were both far more busty.

'You got twenty-three hits for slim brunettes?' he said. 'That's depressing.'

Burton nodded. 'It's big business. A lot of money to be made. Even the independents charge around eighty per hour. Imagine what the agency rate is.'

The fourth site they visited gave up Bliss's victim. Burton clicked on the young woman's photo, which took them to her profile page. On the wide screen the images were sharp and detailed. Bliss held his phone close to the largest of them, comparing the two.

'It's her,' Burton said.

Bliss agreed.

A more revealing array of photographs was available, but Bliss noticed none of them showed her fully naked. He asked Burton about that.

'These agencies are allowed to exist because they claim to be selling escort-only services. Nothing illegal about that. They're careful not to include any shots we might be able to use to argue against that claim. So a woman in lingerie is fine, because for some reason a businessman visiting the city and wanting a date for the night needs to know what she looks like in her underwear. But one nip-slip and we could be all over them. It's the indies who reveal all.'

Bliss was about to ask more when the unit door opened and Chandler entered the room. She was closely followed by Glen Ashton, and the NCA man did not look at all happy. He zoned in on Bliss and stood with both hands on his hips, legs spread wide.

'Is this what you call inter-agency cooperation?' Ashton said. He jabbed out a finger. 'You struck a deal. That deal is the only reason you have this case, and I'm part of that deal, whether you like it or not. Am I making myself clear, Sergeant?'

Bliss took the steam out of it by pausing before he responded. 'As it happens, you're in danger of making a bit of a berk of yourself, Glen,' he said in a neutral tone. 'When you enter someone else's squad room and you've never met them before, it's customary to introduce yourself first before you start barking at people.'

He let it go there, allowing a chagrined Ashton to shake hands with Burton. The two exchanged names and greetings.

When things were just awkward enough, Bliss continued. 'Before you so rudely interrupted, we were making some progress in identifying our victim. If you want to play nice, drop the Superman pose, pull out a chair and watch in admiration along with me and Pen as DI Burton here weaves her magic spell over the internet.'

Ashton remained on his feet, but narrowed his stance and allowed his hands to fall by his sides. Chandler pulled out a nearby chair for herself. Burton was busy with something, but Bliss was lost trying to follow her.

'What are you doing now?' he asked.

'I've copied Honey's photos, which I'm feeding into a little piece of software we have. What this will do is send out a request across the net, searching for exact matches of the same image. If we're lucky, we'll get some hits for sites on which she appears as an independent.'

Burton knew her stuff. Less than five minutes later, she had produced an extensive list of links to other websites. 'Many of these will be doubled or even tripled up, because the site may feature the same image two or three times. But I mentioned both *Vivastreet* and *Friday-ad*, and she appears on both. Let's check them out first.'

The first proved to be the most useful. On *Vivastreet* their victim called herself Bunny and the profile listed her as an independent. In addition to an array of more explicit photographs and video clips requiring a paid subscription, the details given revealed two things of note: the area in which she lived, and a mobile phone number. This arrangement, Burton revealed, was standard. If you were a potential client, you'd select the service you wanted, and for how long. Then you called the number from your own phone – only mobile numbers were accepted. At that point you arranged a date and time, and would be given the full address.

Bliss was interested in the area – the Woodston district of Peterborough. Their victim being based in the city gave him additional leverage in respect of keeping the case local. He was storing her contact number in his work phone when he noticed something in her bio.

'It says there she's new to the area. If that's true, I don't understand how she came to have my business card on her.'

'Don't be fooled by that,' Burton told him, swivelling in her chair to face him. 'To us that's a major red flag; it tells me this is not a truly independent advert. Also, there's a good chance it means this woman was trafficked. They get moved around the country every few months, which is why they are listed as being new to the area. You see an awful lot of those ads on these sites. Also, the ones who say they've recently returned to the area throw up the same red flag. It means they're on a cycle, moving from place to place.'

The information chimed with Bliss's thoughts so far. Without any further discussion, he dialled the number on the page. It rang five times before voicemail cut in. The outgoing message was impersonal: a generic provider asking the caller to leave their name and number. On the off-chance, Bliss did so.

'We never found her phone,' he explained. 'Somebody might hear it and think I'm a genuine caller.'

Burton shrugged. 'It's worth a shot. If you like, I can trawl through this lot to see if I can find a genuinely independent page for her. If you're thinking of contacting the agency and requesting her details, forget about it. Obtaining her information through legal means will take months, if you get it at all. Depends on who owns and runs the agency.'

'See if you can find me a local one, will you, please?'

'There will be one. There always is a local outlet, even for an organised crime operation. They like to have close control over their properties, girls, and clients.'

'This is where I could be of some genuine use,' Ashton said. The anger he'd carried into the room with him had dissipated now that a familiar task was at hand. 'I'll run a check through our own database as soon as I know who to look for. We might even have this victim in our records somewhere. If I could have one of the images, I'll send it through to my office and have someone run it by facial recognition.'

Burton agreed to send him the best facial shot, and he gave her his ERSOU e-mail address.

Chandler, who until this point had merely been observing, leaned forward and pointed at the screen. 'If this girl has been trafficked, we must assume she is being watched closely. I noticed the fake independent page said she does in-house calls only. To me that suggests they don't trust her enough to meet up with clients in their own homes or at hotels. So why are they okay with putting her out as an escort?'

'Escort clients are more closely vetted,' Burton told them. 'Plus, whatever the girls offer their clients is written off as purely a physical act between two consenting adults, and of no interest to the agency. You can see from her dodgy independent profile that she's clear about what's on offer, and with clients simply calling in to make arrangements, the people controlling her want to make sure she doesn't stray. When these same girls take on truly independent profiles, you can usually spot them because they pixelate their faces and expose more of their bodies.'

Bliss was nodding, taking it all in. 'If you come across a completely indie page for her, let me know what her mobile number is on there.'

'Why, what are you thinking?'

'I reckon the number I have is a corporate one. They monitor her voicemail messages and either make the arrangements themselves or tell her which ones she can and can't accept. If she has her own profile somewhere, I'm willing to bet it's her own phone she uses.'

They left Burton to it. Bliss trusted her work ethic enough to know that she wouldn't take a break away from the job in hand until she had visited every link relating to their victim. Angie was not only a great cop with wonderful instincts; she also cared.

On the way out, Ashton leaned down and said to Chandler, 'So you're his bag man, are you? That must be a tough task.'

'Don't you mean bag woman?' Chandler said, smiling sweetly.

Bliss snorted. 'Bag lady, more like. Complete with a scrap of cardboard to sit on and a smelly dog by her side.'

Chandler gave him one of her looks before turning to Ashton. 'For your information, I'm nobody's anything. I'm DS Chandler to you. Penny, if you're around long enough to be accepted.'

'And you'd be wise to take note,' Bliss said, making his way past them. 'Our Pen has a mighty right hook.'

Ashton straightened to his full height. 'Oh, I think I can handle one little 'un.'

'Be it on your own head if you try, old son. I mean it. Many a jaw has foundered on the rocks of DS Chandler's knuckles.'

The Major Crimes squad room was empty when they got there, so the three huddled together around Chandler's desk. Bliss had been thinking hard during their walk over, and he was now keen to explore a number of possibilities. 'That agency Angie came up with rang a bell. I seem to recall *EZEscorts* being listed as one of Drake's companies.'

'Who is this Drake?' Ashton asked.

'He's the local scumbag we arrested for trafficking after we rescued those girls from the transport container. I'm pretty sure that site is one of his, in which case I know where to pay them a visit.'

'Where is he?'

'Banged up in Belmarsh. We still want to nail the bastard for murder, but we did manage to get him for a number of other things. He's appealing, of course. Using the system as you might expect.'

'And meanwhile his organisation continues unaffected.'

'Pretty much. Somebody obviously stepped up in his place, but we're uncertain as to who. Mind you, he's as powerful inside as he was out. The only thing he doesn't have is his freedom.'

'As you rightly pointed out, I've not been in the job long. Even so, I've encountered a few like him.'

Bliss appraised the investigator. Ashton had angered him with his attitude when they met at the crime scene. He had shown his inexperience, coming across as cocky and more than a little condescending. Much as Bliss had been at his age.

He decided to give the man a second chance.

'You and I got off on the wrong foot, Glen,' he said. 'I suggest we put it behind us and work together. Your ERSOU systems and contacts could be a huge advantage to us if this is even close to what I suspect.'

'What would that be?'

'The two most likely paths to follow on this are that she either fell victim to a client who went too far, or that she got caught operating outside of the organisation and they decided to put a stop to it – permanently. I'm thinking the latter is the most likely.'

Ashton considered that for a few seconds. 'I'll make a few calls. If DI Burton has sent me that image, I'll forward it on and we'll see if our victim is already in the system. I'll also pull up anything we have on Drake's operation here.'

He left the room in a hurry just as Bishop and Ansari stepped back into it. 'Blimey, he's keen,' Bishop said, jerking his head back towards the door.

Chandler nodded. 'He's just a pup. Throw him a bone and off he scampers.'

'He's raw,' Bliss said. 'But then we all were, once.'

'Difference is, we were aware of it,' Ansari muttered, dropping into her chair with a groan. 'He already thinks he knows it all.'

'That's the NCA for you. The moment they started comparing the agency to the FBI, it got people thinking about it differently. Including those who work for them.'

'That include you, boss?' Bishop asked. He grinned as he, too, took his seat.

Bliss ignored the verbal slip; the fact that his colleague still thought of Bliss as his boss was only natural. But if he wanted to make the temporary step up a more permanent move, he would need to start showing everybody – Bliss included – that he was in charge.

'I always hated the comparison,' he admitted. 'The NCA have to be able to move into any area in the country and work hand in hand with the locals without it resulting in any sort of pissing contest. Trying to rebrand them as the UK's version of the Feebs can only decrease the chances of that. I've been there, seen it in action.'

'That why you welcomed Ashton with such open arms?' Chandler said, stifling a grin.

Bliss glared at her. 'Don't even go there. You weren't with us last night. He behaved like a dick. He gave it the big one and had bugger all to back it up. He may be one of those investigators who likes to think of himself as a Bureau man, and if that's the case then I see it as my sworn duty to knock it out of him.'

'Is that what they meant by tolerance back in your halcyon days?'

'It had a different meaning. In this job you don't need, or want, to merely tolerate people. You don't even need to like them. But you do need to respect them. If someone steps out of line, they have to be taken down a peg or two.'

'If anyone can do that, it's you.'

Bliss knew Chandler was baiting him. He decided to bite. 'Bloody well right it is. If your colleagues act like tits, you have to call them on it. I did with you.'

She squinted at him. 'I never acted like a tit.'

'True. You never had to act.'

'Are you saying I *was* a tit?'

He shrugged. 'A bit of one. At times.'

'So says the biggest tit of all.'

'Any chance we can stop talking about tits? You'll have me up on a sexual harassment charge next.'

Chandler grinned. 'I don't think so. I reckon you'd enjoy it too much.'

This brought a smile to his face. He winked. 'You better believe it. Come on, let's get to work.'

SIX

T HE THREE-STOREY END-OF-TERRACE HOUSE in Orton Malbourne was firmly on every Peterborough copper's radar. The
top two floors contained four bedrooms in total, which meant
four working girls turning over punters day and night. The girls
took time out and made snacks and refreshments on the ground
floor, at the rear of which was an office dedicated to the running
of this specific aspect of Lewis Drake's organisation.

Before knocking on the front door, Bliss issued a warning
to Ashton. 'If you get the urge to speak out while we're inside,
ignore it,' he said. 'I mean it. Pen and I know these people. These
particular people, I mean. Remember, we're here to learn something from them, not get in their faces.'

Ashton raised both hands. 'This is your show, Sergeant. But
in my defence, I'm not quite as green as you make me out to be.
I do know how to do this job.'

Bliss arched his eyebrows. 'We'll see.'

A human wrecking ball answered Bliss's second knock. The
man who filled the doorway was so tall and wide, Bliss thought
they must have to remove the windows to hoist him in and out of
the house. Not all of his bulk was muscle, but there was enough

of it to intimidate beyond the sheer size of him. A shaved round head and sunken narrowed eyes were the icing on a daunting cake.

'Afternoon, Igor,' Bliss said pleasantly. The man's real name was some Slavic collection of mismatched consonants, but Bliss had never managed to wrap his tongue around it. 'We'd like a word with Nicola.'

Igor fixed him with a piercing gaze that lasted longer than was comfortable. Bliss followed suit. It was like staring at the weathered, implacable face of an ancient gravestone. Finally, the doorman grunted something unintelligible and made his way back inside, leaving the front door wide open.

'What was that?' Ashton asked.

'One FBU,' Bliss replied, stepping up into the passage.

'A what?'

'Fucking Big Unit.'

'Believe me, you don't want to know,' Chandler said, following Bliss inside. 'Be sure to get out of his way if you see him charging towards you.'

'Was leaving the door open his way of inviting us in?'

'Yes. That's Igor being polite. That grunt you heard is him at his most gregarious.'

Bliss remembered the layout. A galley kitchen stood to the right, opposite a lounge in which the girls often relaxed, watching TV or chatting in between clients. At the far end of the hall there was a toilet and shower room, and to its left the office. He entered without knocking, his colleagues close behind.

A mature, inoffensive-looking woman by the name of Nicola Parkinson regarded them from behind an ostentatious solid oak desk. It was squat and sturdy, like a pit bull, and she looked almost lost behind it. With her short copper hair seeming to bracket her round cheekbones, Bliss was always struck by how cherubic she looked.

As usual, the spell broke the moment the woman opened her mouth.

'You cheese-rimmed bellends go around in threes these days, eh? I hope for her sake that you two strapping men team up on DS Chandler every chance you get. I'm betting she doesn't get her oats any other way.'

'Now now, you old trollop,' Bliss said, casually propping himself up against the wall to his right. 'That's no way to speak about one of Peterborough's fairest maidens. I told you last time what I'd do to you if you kept up those levels of abuse.'

Parkinson tossed him a look of disdain. 'Wash my mouth out with soap and water. Yeah, I remember. I dared you to go through with it, and you backed off. Like all you tossers do in the end. All mouth and no action.'

'You're showing your claws early today, Nicola,' Chandler said, no inflection in her voice. 'What's up? Menopause? I hear women your age suffer badly when that hits. Or do you have unexpected staffing problems? You one down today, are you?'

'What's it to you?' Parkinson shot back without taking her eyes off Bliss. 'Go and put the kettle on, there's a love. Let me and the boys have a natter.'

Chandler remained where she was. Bliss eased himself away from the wall. The changeable weather conditions were playing havoc with his chronic illness. The Ménière's disease affected his balance, and rapid fluctuations in the barometric pressure made his stability less predictable. The high squeal of tinnitus raged inside his head, its acuteness often a trigger warning of an impending vertigo attack. He wasn't about to show this woman any sign of weakness, though. Not if he could help it.

'Is that it, Nicola?' he asked. 'You got it all off your ample chest? If there are more insults you want to hurl, we can wait you out. But if it's all the same to you, I'd rather not. My visits here always seem to coincide with me feeling the need to scrub myself raw under a scalding hot shower.'

'I could help you with that if you like,' Parkinson said, with a wide grin that only accentuated his earlier impression of a cherub. 'Unless DS Chandler objects. I wouldn't want to trample all over her territory.'

'Even my worst enemy wouldn't wish that on me. So how about we cut out the crap and get down to business?'

She heaved a long sigh and eased herself back into the chair. 'If we must. But if you're here to ask me any questions about our perfectly legit business, I'm going to need to call our solicitors first.'

'I think we can avoid that,' Bliss said. 'We're not here about your little knocking shop.'

'Massage parlour.'

'If you say so.'

'I do say so. And so will our brief if I have to make that call, Inspector.'

Bliss decided not to correct her; they'd already wasted enough time. 'Let's move on. There's no need for your brief.'

'Fair enough. All the same…' She picked her mobile up off the desk and tapped the screen. A few moments later, a young man entered the room. He was of no more than average stature, yet the room seemed a lot more crowded with a fifth person in it. 'You remember my lad, Troy? He'll be sitting in to witness what is and isn't said.'

Troy Parkinson said nothing. He moved to stand at the back of the room, eyes narrowed but taking everything in. Bliss gave him a courtesy nod, then turned back to the woman behind the desk.

'We're here about a young girl you might know, Nicola. Goes by the name of Honey.'

Parkinson gave a long, exaggerated shrug. 'Doesn't ring a bell.'

'Don't play stupid games, you stroppy cow!' Ashton snapped. His voice was loud and bounced off the walls. He took a step closer to the desk, looming over it. 'She's one of your girls. She's on your fucking website. You know who she is, so stop dicking us around.'

Parkinson's gaze was icy as she shuddered theatrically. 'Ooh, scary. I can see why you need that third wheel, Inspector Bliss.'

Ashton's face became a picture of twisted rage. He turned to Bliss, whose features told their own story. 'That was useful, Glen. Thanks a million. But if you could go back to being mute, as we discussed, I'd treat it as a personal favour.'

'What? So you're happy being fucked about like this? By someone like her?'

Bliss glanced at Parkinson Junior to make sure he wasn't looking to get involved. He reeled in his temper before returning his gaze to Ashton. 'Perhaps you and I have different ideas when it comes to remaining silent, Glen. We probably need a chat about that – afterwards. In the meantime, you need to understand that Nicola and I are simply going through the motions: I talk, she postures. We're old foes. It's how we do things. Let me emphasise that for you. It's how *we* do things. Am I making myself clear?'

The NCA investigator was clearly infuriated. He rubbed a hand across his mouth before turning away towards the window. Bliss took a beat to compose himself. Then he switched his attention to Parkinson once again. 'Sorry about that, Nicola. Can't get the staff these days. Which reminds me… where were you with remembering our girl, Honey?'

She stared him down before teasing out a sigh. 'I think I know the name. Not sure about the girl. What did she do? Get caught hooking? If that's the case, we'll fire her immediately.'

'No. Afraid not. Sorry. She got caught being dead. Strangled to death, to be precise. Sometime yesterday. Found her body way out at the chalk pits outside Cambridge. Any idea why she would be over there?'

'If she's one of our escorts, she might have been with a client.'

'That was precisely our line of thinking. I was hoping you could tell us who, where, and when.'

Parkinson tightened her gaze. A smile teased her lips. 'Oh, I'm so sorry. You know I can't give out confidential information relating to our clients, Inspector. Not unless you have one of those pesky warrants.'

Bliss played along. 'I know you're not supposed to, Nicola. And we both care about you and your legit business being squeaky clean. All I'm saying is, couldn't you help us out this one time? We're not looking to throw the cuffs on anyone. We're talking about a murdered young woman, most likely one of your own. Surely you can bend the rules a little bit to help us out.'

'Sorry. No can do. If I bent the rules for you, I'd have to do it for everyone who needed a favour. It wouldn't be right.'

So far he'd been happy to go along to get along, but her flippancy was getting under Bliss's skin. 'Not right? Being murdered isn't right, either. Even a hard-faced cow like you can see that, surely? How about this: you bring her records up on screen, then take yourself off to the loo for five minutes. Your lad can step out, too, if he likes. That sound any better?'

Parkinson put her head back as if considering his suggestion, but after a moment or two she slowly shook it. 'Nope. I can't risk it. You know how it is.'

'For crying out loud!' Ashton snapped, swivelling hard and squeezing his fists tight. 'This is fucking ridiculous! I've never heard anything like it before. Arrest this bitch and throw her into a holding cell. Don't let her walk all over you. It's embarrassing.'

This time Bliss didn't have to wade in. Instead, Chandler moved to stand between Ashton and Nicola. 'Shut the fuck up, Glen! In fact, get the fuck out.' She pointed towards the door. 'Go on. Go! Go and sit in the car. Play with some crayons or something. Whatever pleases your tiny mind. Just fuck off out of here.'

Ashton stared down at her with round, wide eyes. 'You can't be serious. Are you yanking my chain?'

'Don't talk so daft. I wouldn't yank *your* chain if it was the last one on earth.'

Bliss laughed. He couldn't help himself; Chandler in full flow was an impressive sight. 'I'd do as she says if I were you, Glen. You'd be better off feeding your balls into a bacon slicer than taking on our Penny when she's in this frame of mind.'

A seething coil of fury, Glen Ashton stormed out of the office. Seconds later, the house reverberated to the sound of the front door slamming.

'He doesn't play nicely with others, does he?' Parkinson said. 'I take it he's not one of yours, Inspector?'

'NCA,' Bliss said, as if that explained everything.

She nodded as if it did, too. 'I'm sorry you've had a wasted trip,' she said. 'I'm also sorry to hear about Honey. I genuinely don't know her. She's not one of our low-rent girls, otherwise she'd have been in and out of here a time or two.'

'You're sorry, but you won't tell us anything?' Chandler said, unable to hide her disgust.

'I can't.' Parkinson sat up straight, as if commanding an office of respect. 'You had to have known that coming in.'

Bliss caught his partner's eye and gave her the nod to continue. He liked it when a flame was lit beneath her.

Chandler gave it some thought. 'All right,' she said eventually. 'I know we're not going to get a client's name from you. But there is something you can give us – something that means I won't have to send in our clean-up crew to hassle you and the girls for the next five nights in a row.'

'I'm listening,' Parkinson said.

'I don't think it's breaching any sort of confidentiality if you at least tell us whether Honey was booked out in Cambridge yesterday. No need to mention precisely where or who with.'

'That's it?'

'That's it.'

'And then you'll bugger off?'

'And then we'll bugger off.'

With a huff that was more for show than due to genuine annoyance, Parkinson leaned forward and started typing on her open laptop. She made a few clicks with the mouse, scrolling down a page. When she looked up, Bliss thought he saw a look of genuine relief. 'As it happens, we do have a girl by the name of Honey. But she was not booked out in Cambridge yesterday.'

'That had better be the truth, Nicola,' Chandler said. 'I mean it. I'm done fucking around with you.'

'It is. And for what it's worth, she wasn't booked out at all yesterday. In fact, she's not worked for us in almost two weeks.'

'Is that unusual?' Bliss asked. He'd noted a momentary frown flicker across the woman's features. 'For her to go that long without a booking?'

'Let me check… yes, extremely unusual. She did a fair bit of work for our agency, as far as I can tell.'

'Could she perhaps have taken time off for personal reasons? A holiday, maybe?'

'If she did, she doesn't appear to have told anybody.'

Bliss thought they'd got what they came for, which was all this woman was going to give up without a warrant. 'If you learn any more, you will contact us, won't you?' he said.

Parkinson didn't bother to respond.

'Fine. We'll leave you to your grief. Our condolences on your sad loss.' He turned to Chandler. 'Come on, Pen. Neither of us wants to see Nicola here weeping and wailing.'

As he reached the door, he paused. Looked Troy Parkinson up and down. 'You must be so proud,' he said. Still the young man remained tight-lipped.

'Yeah, and fuck you, too, Bliss!' Nicola screeched as they left the room.

In your dreams, he thought. *And my nightmares.*

If they thought the air was frigid outside the car, it was frostier still inside. Fuming, Ashton said nothing, yet said so much at the same time.

Chandler was the first to tackle him on it. 'You think we were hard on you back there, Glen? If so, you need to think again. Rethink your entire career, maybe. Before we went inside, Jimmy politely told you to say nothing. You were there to observe. You couldn't do that, though, could you? You had to let go of your frustrations. Thing is, the way you went about it could have made Nicola back off so far we'd never be able to speak to her again. You could have hurt us, Glen. Me and Jimmy. The MCU. Not you, though, because you're off somewhere else as soon as we have a result. Nicola Parkinson is no CHIS, and she's a mouthy mare, but if you dig hard enough you can often find a way through her defences. What little she gave us, we may never have got had you stayed in the room.'

Bliss finished the explanation. 'We know our murder victim was not supposed to be anywhere near Cambridge – at least, not on official business. And we already know she did only in-house calls as a semi-official sideline. It's not a lot, Glen, but it's something. It was the only something Nicola was prepared to give up, and we could have missed out.'

He took a breath as he started the engine and waited for warm air to demist the windows. 'Glen,' he said, more softly. 'I know when you hit the NCA and hear all that FBI bullshit, it makes you feel as if your shit don't stink. Well, it does. I was older than you when I did the job, and had been there since SOCA knocked down the barriers. When it comes to people like Nicola Parkinson, I'm not saying there's never a time to shout at them, lie to them, do whatever it takes to get information from them. Sometimes she makes me so angry I stand there shaking like a dog taking a shit. But you have to know *when* to give in to that rage, and that takes more experience than you currently have. Okay?'

Ashton seemed to accept the rebuke well, but he remained quiet all the way back to HQ.

SEVEN

ESPITE THE LOW-DOUBLE-FIGURES TEMPERATURE, Bliss was sitting in the garden with the sliding doors pulled wide open. A Samantha Fish album spun on the turntable; 'Watch It Die' had just ended. He reflected on the lyrics, and idly wondered if the singer's plaintive voice echoed what he'd been doing: sitting back and watching while his relationship with Emily withered and died on the vine. The next cut along, 'Try Not to Fall in Love With You', was never going to get him out of his funk. He tried hard to focus on Fish's playing style and the soulful tones she wrought from her guitar.

It had been a while since he had listened to music while gazing at his garden, his eye caught by the pond and its fish swimming in lazy patterns; in fact, he probably hadn't done it since before the crazy shit with the 'slow slicing' case back in August. His mind had been too unsettled in the turbulent weeks and months since, an inability to relax not helping his cause with Emily. He realised things were not right between them. And that it was mainly his fault. She perhaps saw him slipping away in the long silences between their infrequent conversations, and he wondered if she would stick around long enough to watch him fall.

The moment the song reached a quieter section, Bliss heard thumping coming from his front door. Expecting one of his team to start complaining about having to wait outside in the cold, he instead found DI Burton standing on his doorstep. In typical Angie style, she didn't wait to be invited in; brushing past without a word, she marched straight down the short passageway and into the living room at the far end.

'Bloody hell!' She wore a heavy overcoat but still hugged herself and rubbed her arms. 'Were you born in a barn?'

'A stable,' he said. 'As all great leaders are. Anyway, quit your whining and tell me why you've so rudely interrupted my peace and quiet.'

She smiled. 'Your moment of bliss, you might say.'

'You might. I never would.' He crossed the room to slide the doors closed, then went to the sound system, levered the stylus off the vinyl and shut it all down. 'Is this about our victim, Ange?'

'Yes and no. Where were you earlier? I tried several times to find you.'

'We had a house call to make. After that, Pen and I were stuck in a meeting with Bish and Diane.'

'Fair enough. Duty calls. Anyhow, I eventually found your girl's true indie page. Calls herself Autumn on there. From what I could tell, she's been running it for at least a year. It's not at all subtle, either. About the only thing she doesn't offer is bareback.'

'Does anybody these days?'

'Well, some girls are still willing to screw without a condom, provided the man can provide a recent clear HIV and STI test.'

Bliss shook his head in bewilderment. He told her about his conversation with Marta Lsenko. 'Sounds to me as if having a sideline income outside of the agency has become a common practice for these girls.'

Burton nodded. 'Things change rapidly in this business. And

yet, somehow they stay horribly the same. It's still tomming around at the end of the day, only now it's tiered. These escort agency girls operate at a completely different level from your usual brasses. They're meant to look good all the time, so they have to agree to regular drug tests, there's no smoking allowed, and their alcohol intake is kept to a bare minimum. They need to be both classy escorts at a restaurant and dirty whores in bed. Many have regular clients who buy them gifts and treat them extremely well. They're a bit like mistresses, in some ways.'

'So the complete opposite of how they treat girls at the lower end of the scale.'

'Entirely. Those poor women are still kept supplied with drugs and force is used to keep them hooking, not to make them secure. Compared to them, these top-rate escorts lead a pampered life.'

'So why the need for that bit of extra income on the side as well? Pure greed?'

'For some, perhaps. This Lsenko girl sounds as if she may be one of those. Others... I think they do it for that spark of genuine liberation. A token gesture of defiance aimed at the people who run them.'

'A gesture that can get them killed.'

She wagged a finger at him. 'That's the other side of the coin. If this isn't a punter gone wild – which it still could be, I'll remind you – then I suppose you're going to be looking long and hard at Drake's organisation.'

'Funny you should say that.' Bliss outlined the result of their visit to the house in Orton Malbourne. 'It's where the investigation took us,' he explained. 'I wouldn't be doing my job if I turned a blind eye to what we know is going on right under our noses. You should have heard Ashton banging on about it afterwards. He couldn't understand why we allow them to operate out in the open like that.'

'Ashton?'

'Our ERSOU liaison.'

'Oh, him. He's young. He'll learn.'

'He'd better do so fast. At the moment he's a fucking massive albatross and my raft is in danger of capsizing.'

'Ignore him.' Burton snapped her fingers. 'No, in fact, don't. Do the exact opposite. Use him, Jimmy. You know you're on dangerous ground working this while Drake's appeal is ongoing.'

'Fuck Drake!'

'Thank you, but I'll give that a swerve if you don't mind. And I'm thinking more about the CPS and the various legal niceties involved. What you're doing quite legitimately as part of your new investigation could be regarded by others as harassment. Working something against him and his business enterprise while they are adjudicating his verdict and sentence is not something they are going to welcome.'

'Which is tough. They're going to have to get over themselves. I go where the case takes me. You know that better than most, Ange. You'd do the same.'

She nodded. 'You're right. I would. But I don't have a gazillion beady eyes watching me closely, waiting and perhaps even praying for that one final slip-up.'

Silence hung in the air between them for a few moments. Bliss hiked his shoulders. 'I like it that you care about me, Ange. I do. But I can't ignore this path we've gone down.'

'I'm not saying you should. But you have an NCA investigator at your disposal. Use him. Have him run this down. I sent him the images, so he'll be chasing those up anyway. Have him do your donkey work for you. You do the thinking, you come up with the strategy. But when the time comes for action, you press his button and if there's shit to wade through, you let him get his shoes dirty.'

Bliss laughed. 'You always did have a lovely turn of phrase.'

'Am I interrupting anything?'

Bliss and Burton snapped their heads around. In the doorway stood Emily Grant, one hand clutching a shopping bag, the other holding her door key. Bliss had not heard her come in. He made the introductions as each woman took the measure of the other.

'I've heard a lot about you,' Burton said to Emily. 'You're an anthropologist, is that right?'

'These days, yes. Forensically speaking. And you work with Jimmy?'

'Not as such. I'm strictly sex crimes; we consult with various units as required. In fact, it's been a few years since Jimmy and I last worked together.'

'But you are at the moment, I take it?'

'Sort of. Not sure how much my team and I will be needed. I think he wanted to pick my brains, that's all.'

Emily looked around. 'Has he even bothered to offer you a cup of tea?'

Burton smiled. 'I'm sure he would have got around to it eventually. I've not been here long.'

'In that case, please do take a seat and make yourself comfortable. You two continue your chat and I'll put the kettle on. Tea or coffee? Or I've got some of those instant mocha drinks if you prefer?'

'The mocha sounds good. Thanks.'

When Emily stepped out of the room, Bliss felt Burton's eyes drilling holes into him. He met her gaze, which widened. 'I see she has her own key. Must be serious, Jimmy.'

He shrugged. 'I wouldn't read too much into it if I were you. With my hours, it makes sense for her to be able to come and go as she pleases.'

'Oh. I got the impression… you two aren't living together?'

'No. It's a more practical arrangement this way, that's all.'

Burton nodded as if she didn't quite know what to believe. 'Either way, I'm pleased you have somebody. I always thought you were one of the loneliest souls I ever came across – even when you had people all around you. It's good for you to have someone close in your life.'

He shrugged. 'It's relatively new.'

She grinned. 'As effusive as ever, Jimmy. You just can't stop spilling your guts and banging on about your feelings, can you?'

Emily came into the room carrying two mugs. She handed one to Burton, the other to Bliss. He smelled his favourite Earl Grey tea. 'Are you not joining us?' he asked.

'No, you two go ahead. I've got dinner to do, and I'm sure there are things you need to discuss that I ought not to hear.'

Bliss shook his head. 'We were pretty much done. Ange came over to update me on a new case so's I'd have additional information for the morning briefing.'

Emily nodded and smiled. 'How thoughtful. I was beginning to think the rest of your colleagues were mythical. Anyhow, you two don't mind me. Dinner in about an hour, Jimmy. That okay?'

'She likes me,' Burton said when the kitchen door closed. 'You can tell.'

Chuckling, Bliss said, 'You being here took her by surprise, that's all. I don't get many visitors.'

'Oh, I think it's more than that, Jimmy. We women have a sixth sense about exes. Your lady friend took one look at me, sized me up in an instant, and knew without doubt that you and I had once had a fling.'

Bliss did not argue. He'd seen something pass across Emily's gaze the moment it alighted on Burton: an immediate suspicion, which put her on high alert. He nodded. 'You may well be right. And if so, she's bound to ask me about you later.'

'You want my advice?'

'I sense I'm about to get it no matter what I say.'

'You've got good instincts. Listen, be honest with her. You and I had a moment. That was it. We've seen each other around the nick on many occasions since. We get on well, for which I'm grateful. You're a good friend, but there's no lingering spark. Tell her that and she'll believe you.'

'Em is not a jealous woman.'

Burton laughed. 'Oh, Jimmy. How can you still be so naïve? You don't have to be a jealous woman to feel jealous. You only have to see the opposition.'

'But there isn't anything between you and me anymore – you said so yourself. So what has she got to worry about?'

'That there *was* once a you and me. She knows we must have been attracted to each other at some point in the past, which means we could be again in the future. The here and now aren't always relevant when it comes to sex, Jimmy. Emily knows – or at least is pretty certain – that a woman you once slept with is here in her territory. And was here with you, alone, when she arrived home. That's why she's in the kitchen. There's no way she can look at me or talk to me without thinking about the things you and I might have done together.'

Bliss took a deep breath and blew it out slowly. 'You women are far more complicated than I give you credit for.'

'Which is why you'll always be the weaker sex. But don't worry. I'll drink up and go. And don't make the mistake of waiting for her to ask you about me. Tell her. She'll feel more comfortable having it out there.'

Bliss was about to reply when his personal mobile rang. He checked the screen and frowned. 'Sorry – I have to take this.'

He slipped out into the garden and walked across to the far side, where a bamboo bridge crossed the narrow part of his pond.

As if they sensed his presence, the koi began to gather close by. He spoke for less than thirty seconds, the conversation causing him alarm. When he went back inside, he said, 'I have to go. Sorry. Thank you for the info, and for… well, the life lesson. I'll tell Em about us when I get back.'

Burton got to her feet. 'Is it the case?'

'The… no. Something else. You take your time with your drink. I'll say goodbye to Em.'

This was not how he wanted to leave it, but the information he had received gave him only a narrow window of time in which to react. At least it would take Emily's mind off Angie Burton, because the reason he was headed out again was the one that had kept the two of them at loggerheads for the past fortnight.

EIGHT

Vesuvio's italian restaurant and pizzeria was located in one of several unassuming brick-built units along Eastgate Mews in Whittlesea, a small fenland town six miles east of Peterborough.

Bliss abruptly shook his head and walked silently past the man who tried to seat him. He hadn't gone there to eat. Instead, his eyes scoured the diners. He spotted the man he'd been told he would find sitting at a table with a mature redhead. The two were enjoying their main course, a glass of red wine poured for each of them. The woman leaned forward attentively as her companion spoke. She had one of those curious faces that at first glance seemed plain, yet the more you looked, the more attractive qualities emerged. The man had his broad back facing the entrance and he reacted with surprise when Bliss approached their table from behind, pulled out a chair and sat down to join them.

Ignoring him, Bliss turned to the redhead. 'Good evening,' he said. 'I'm sorry to drop by unannounced. I don't want to spoil your enjoyment, but believe me, it's better to do that than allow you to ruin the rest of your life.'

'Do we… do we know each other?' Her voice had the cadence of a local fenlander.

'No. We've never met before. But tonight is your lucky night, because I'm here to do you a massive favour. Especially if you have young children. Do you have young children?'

The woman's mouth flapped open a couple of times. She narrowed her gaze and stared hard at her companion, who said and did nothing.

Bliss waved a hand. 'It doesn't matter. I don't need to know your name, nor where you live. Neither do I need to know if you have kids you love to bits. You don't know who I am, and that's fine, too. All I need is for you to listen to me. Can you do that?'

The woman inhaled quickly and sat back, uncertain and fearful. Her eyes were fixed on his, and Bliss knew he had her full attention.

'I have no idea how well you know the man you're here with this evening, but my guess is that this is your first date. Believe me when I say it also has to be the last. In fact, cut it short right now. Leave with me if you like – or before me, if you prefer. But whatever you do, walk away and never so much as speak with this man again. I know you must be scared, wondering what on earth is going on. But you do not want this man in your life. Not now. Not ever. Because the man you're sitting at this table with is pure evil.'

While he'd been talking, the woman's breathing had become increasingly laboured. She was having trouble gathering herself, coping with the intrusion. As she was bringing herself back down from her near panic attack, Bliss became aware that a figure had appeared by his side. He looked up to see the staff member who had initially attempted to seat him.

'Is there something wrong here?' the man asked, switching his focus between the woman and her companion. 'Something we can help you with?'

For the first time, Bliss faced the occupant of the other chair. 'Tell him, Neil. Answer the man. Is there something wrong? Am I causing you problems?'

Having already set aside his cutlery, the man whose meal Bliss had interrupted sat back in his chair and folded his massive arms. Despite the seasonal chill, he wore a polo neck T-shirt, with a perfect snug fit to show off those powerful-looking biceps. Anger creased his acne-flared face, but he remained silent. He glared at Bliss, not taking his eyes off him. Bliss smiled, looked up at the member of staff, winked. 'We're okay here, pal. This nice lady will want her coat, though.'

'Neil?' the woman said, her darting eyes suddenly more fearful. 'You told me your name was Robert. What the bloody hell is going on here?'

Bliss shook his head. 'He didn't even tell you his real name? I'm so sorry. I realise you must be terribly disappointed. It's not your fault, though. Whatever else happens, don't blame yourself; you did nothing wrong. But pond life like Neil here can't help themselves. He gave you a false name – you have to wonder what else he lied about. Worse still, why did he lie at all? Think about that and be grateful you found out early on. When you get home, if you do have kids, give them a kiss and a warm cuddle and take comfort from knowing you've all had a lucky escape.'

The woman did not need any further persuasion. She stood, threw a withering look at her date, and marched towards the door. Bliss kept his eyes on her as she pulled on her coat and hurried out of the restaurant. She risked one backward glance before taking off along the pavement.

Bliss picked up the woman's glass of wine and took a sip. Nodded and smacked his lips. 'Not bad,' he said, 'for what I'm guessing is the house plonk. I doubt you splurged on anything more expensive than that. I make no apologies for ruining *your* evening, Neil. I thought that pleasant redhead would be better off knowing you're a wrong 'un before she discovered for herself how wrong you can be.'

Neil Watson was only of average height, but he was squat and muscular. He worked as a physical trainer, and had clearly developed his body to the point where his physique alone might easily intimidate others. His reaction to the intrusion puzzled Bliss, though. It wasn't anything like he had expected. Watson was known to have a temper and not slow in finding it, but he appeared to be taking this in his stride.

Bliss decided to probe a little deeper. 'What's the matter, Neil? You not up for a barney tonight?'

'I'm working out the precise wording of the complaint I'm going to make against you,' Watson said. It was the first time he'd spoken since Bliss had interrupted, and he was more composed than he had been during their previous meetings.

'You off your 'roids, Neil? You got a piss test coming up? Is that why you're so placid tonight?'

'Like I said, I'm too busy thinking about how I'm going to fuck you over in other ways.'

'I'm impressed. All that thinking must have worn you out. And by the way, *what* complaint? When the staff intervened you said nothing, and clearly your date for the night won't be saying anything, either. All I did was join you at a restaurant table. Hardly crime of the century, is it?'

'You know what you're doing,' Watson said. 'And you have no right. I don't want you here. I didn't ask you to come. This is harassment.'

Bliss feigned surprise. 'It is? Well, you're entitled to your opinion. Of course, I'll have a completely different story to tell. And I don't see your date backing up your version, do you… Robert, was it?'

Watson said nothing for a few seconds, but something seemed to click. 'How the hell did you know we were here? Are you following me? If you're following me I'll bloody well have you for that as well, Bliss. You see if I don't.'

Bliss spread his hands and grinned. 'Hey, when you sat down at this table I was back home contemplating a nice hot dinner myself. What's more, I have two witnesses to the precise time I left.'

'So you have someone doing your dirty business for you? Another piece of filth like you, no doubt. You can't get away with this, Bliss. Harassing an innocent man is wrong. It's illegal. And sometime soon I'm going to make you pay for it.'

Bliss leaned forward, aware that their discussion was drawing unwanted attention from other diners. 'Was that a threat I heard, Neil? Sounded like one to me – or close enough, at least. I don't think you ought to be doing that, old son.'

'I wasn't making a threat. I was saying you can't treat me this way without there being consequences.'

'Consequences?' Bliss felt the flesh on his face pull taut against the bone. He dropped his voice. 'You don't know the meaning of the word. It sounds abhorrent coming out of your gob. If there was such a thing in life as consequences, Neil, you'd be banged up with all the other child killers.'

For the first time, Watson stirred. He sneered at Bliss, his nose and mouth twisting in fury. 'You can accuse me all you like, but that don't make it true. Julie told you lot what happened to Harry. She told the court what happened to Harry. That's why she's inside and I'm out here.'

For a moment, Bliss was almost persuaded that the man believed it himself. But he remembered the crime scene photographs, the video footage of the interviews; both had featured in a TV documentary. He shook his head. 'You and I both know that's not how it went down, Neil. Just like you know I'm never going to let it go. You are the kind of man who beats and eventually murders his stepson. I am the kind of man who puts scum like you in prison. You think you got away with murder because your other half covered for you. I'm here to tell you that ain't happening. I'll get the truth out of you, Neil. One way or another.'

'You might want to think twice about pushing me, Bliss. If you think I'm capable of doing that to a kid, imagine what I'd be willing to do to you.'

Bliss figured the redhead would be well clear of the area. He got to his feet and stood looking down at Watson for a few moments. 'I understand what you mean, Neil, but there's one thing you should bear in mind.'

'Yeah? What's that?'

'I'm not a seven-year-old child. I can fight back. And that makes all the difference in the world to a coward like you.'

He replayed the entire conversation over and over again in his head as he drove home. He knew he was finally getting to Watson, even though the man had so far resisted reacting. The muscle-bound thug was coming to the boil nicely, though. Bliss felt sure it wouldn't take much more to have him bubbling over the edge.

The first thing he did when he got indoors was to apologise to Emily for leaving her in an uncomfortable situation. 'I don't know where my head was. Leaving the two of you together like that must have been awkward for both of you.'

'It was certainly unexpected,' Emily said. 'I think she drank up so quickly the mocha scalded her mouth.'

'I'll talk to her about it tomorrow. She came over to do me a favour, and that's how I repaid her. And I'm sorry if you felt uncomfortable. I had only a narrow window to do what I needed to do, and as usual I wasn't thinking clearly.'

'I don't suppose you're going to tell me why you dashed out of here – even though you do owe me an explanation in addition to the apology.'

Bliss hung his head a little. 'We agreed not to discuss it any more.'

Emily's eyes grew concerned. 'So it was him again – Watson? Not work?'

'Still work in my book,' he said. 'Just a different approach.'

'But not sanctioned work, Jimmy. Not an actual case.'

'Not yet. But like I said… we agreed not to talk about it again.'

She nodded and went into the kitchen. He followed her and fetched himself a beer from the fridge while she put the oven on to heat up his dinner. Without asking, he topped up her wine glass that was sitting on the side.

'Do you have questions about Angie?' he asked, popping the cap off his bottle and taking a long hit. 'Because whatever she and I once had, it was fleeting and it's long over. I like her as a person and a colleague, but that's all she is to me these days. And the feeling is mutual.'

Emily took a sip from her glass, one elbow resting on the other hand that she had draped across her stomach as if protecting it from something. 'I'm not that insecure, Jimmy. But yes, I could tell there had been something between you, and I wondered if you would own up to it.'

Bliss raised a weak smile. 'My relationship with Angie is one thing you don't have to worry about, Em. And all the other shit will work itself out.'

'And what if it doesn't?'

'It will.'

'So you say. Is it okay if I worry about you in the meantime?'

He nodded. 'But there's no need. I'm going to take care of it.'

After taking another sip of her wine, Emily leaned back against the counter. 'One of these days, Jimmy, you're going to realise how little comfort those words offer.'

NINE

Bliss rose early the following morning. After he'd showered and dressed, he texted Chandler asking her to pick him up as he wasn't feeling at his best. He explained that he wanted to take a look at the crime scene in daylight and was ready to leave. She arrived twenty minutes later, and seemed pleased to see the flask he carried out to the car.

'You know what pisses me off?' he said as he slid in beside her.

'Literally everything?'

'Besides that.'

'Besides literally everything?'

'Yeah.'

'That doesn't leave a lot of scope. But please enlighten me. This ought to be good.'

'I caught five minutes of a documentary last night, about Shoreditch and the changes there over the past couple of decades. Back in the day – my day, to be more precise – that area was full of faces. Mean, ugly, shovel-faced bastards who'd choke a kitten with one hand to prove they weren't gay. These days it's full of hipsters. Weedy nerds with their Guy Fawkes beards and heavy-rimmed glasses they don't even need. Surviving on muesli, tofu and mung beans. What the fuck happened while I wasn't looking?'

'It's called progress, Jimmy.'

'It's called the end of days. Where was all that gentrification when I was a kid? Oh, no, our kind were supposed to be happy with our outdoor khazis, coal fires, cold baths, and the rats having a knees-up in the basement. Get a few warehouses and office blocks redeveloped and suddenly everybody wants to tart the place up.'

'You're only jealous.'

'Bloody right I am. When I think of the squalor we lived in and what passes for poverty these days... ah, forget it. I woke up in a shitty mood.'

'I take it all is not well chez Bliss?' Chandler said.

He grunted. 'I don't want to talk about it. You keep your attention on the road.'

Bliss waited until they'd passed the Norman's Cross intersection before telling Chandler what was on his mind.

'Our victim was moonlighting. That definitely put her in a dangerous position. Angie confirmed our suspicions last night. She also suggested we consider using Glen Ashton to pave the way if we go after Drake or his organisation – have him and ERSOU operate as some kind of buffer. What do you think?'

Chandler gave him a knowing look. 'I gather you'd like us to be on the same page when we get back to HQ?'

'Ideally. The idea has merit. It would be better if any further sniffing around came from somewhere other than us. Plus, if ERSOU are involved, not even the defence can claim harassment. The CPS will have kittens as per, but they have to know we can't stand aside if this young woman's death is even remotely connected to Drake and our case against him.'

'Even if she did work for his organisation, you'll have a hard job making anything stick when it comes to him personally.'

'I know that, Pen. Impossible, probably. But the more ammunition I get, the more likely we are to keep hold of the case. If all roads eventually lead to Drake, great. If not, we still get to solve it.'

'It could work out quite well, having Ashton and ERSOU do the spade work. If it goes nowhere, we've lost nothing. If Drake is responsible, we swoop in and take it out of Ashton's hands. I like it. That Angie is a shrewd one. When did you speak to her?'

With some reluctance, Bliss told his partner about the first part of the previous evening. He also mentioned Emily's reaction to Burton's presence. 'Ange reckons Em came over all protective. What's your take?'

'No question in my mind. If she's anything like me, Emily probably picked up the scent while she was still turning the key in the lock. About that, by the way – am I right to take it as a good sign?'

Bliss tipped his hand one way and then the other. 'Don't read too much into it. Like I told Ange, Em having my front door key has more to do with practicality than any long-term commitment on our part.'

Chandler slipped the car onto the A14, and Bliss poured a cup of hot filtered coffee and passed it over. He let her take a couple of sips before picking up where he'd left off. 'It's an arrangement that suits us both. Her having the key. It doesn't mean anything more than that.'

Chandler arched her eyebrows. 'And Emily knows this, I assume?'

'Of course.'

'Then there should be no problem.'

'Forget about it,' he said, dismissing the matter. 'It'll sort itself out one way or another. Let's get back to our victim. I was wondering where we go next if we come up short on an ID.'

'We can't all go around hammering square pegs into round holes, Jimmy.'

'I know that – give me some credit. But what do we do in those circumstances? I'm hoping lividity together with the evidence gathered at the scene will tell us if she was killed at the chalk pits or strangled elsewhere before being dumped. Hopefully it's the latter. The more time she spent in her killer's company, the more likely it is that we'll pull some fibres off her clothes. I looked at her shoes and her feet, and I saw no sign of scuffing or abrasions on the heels of either, so I don't think she was dragged anywhere. The spot where she was found is a good hundred yards away from the closest track where you could bring a vehicle. She was no heavyweight, but that's still one hell of a carry.'

'Igor could probably do it one-handed.'

Bliss flicked a finger at her. 'That same thought went through my head.'

'Or there are two people involved.'

'Another possibility, though less likely.'

'But why Cambridge? Why the chalk pits? If our girl lived and worked in Peterborough, why not dispose of her over at Ferry Meadows, or in the river? Bretton Woods, even. Anywhere close by? Why all the way out there?'

He nodded. It didn't feel quite right. There was more to this murder than they were seeing. He fell into contemplative silence.

'You okay, Jimmy?' Chandler asked after a while. 'Other than your health today, I mean.'

'Yeah. Why d'you ask?'

'Your lousy mood, for one thing. You also seem a bit more preoccupied than usual lately. A little bit more solemn. I thought it was probably the whole demotion thing, especially knowing how close you came to losing your job altogether. Now… I'm not so sure.'

He shrugged. 'Even someone as shallow as me pauses to reflect occasionally, Pen.'

Chandler dipped her head in his direction. 'See? That's what I mean. Usually you'd make a joke of it and shoot something back at me. This time you took it the wrong way. Jimmy, you know you can tell me anything. Is it this misunderstanding between you and Emily?'

Bliss shook his head.

'What, then? Is it the job?'

'It's nothing in particular. I'm off my game, is all. I'll be fine.'

'If you say so. But we need you at full throttle. Our victim needs that you, not this you.'

He almost opened up. If there was anyone he could speak to about the things that bothered him, it was Chandler. He knew he could say anything to her without it affecting how they worked together. Without judgement. And if there had only been one thing on his mind, he might have relented and told her. But there were so many concerns spiralling around inside his head, he could hardly make sense of it himself. He wouldn't know where to start.

His harassment of Neil Watson was something Chandler would disapprove of. She'd call him all the names under the sun, but she would also understand. As for Emily, he had no idea where to even begin. His feelings were complicated, his emotions more so. For some people they were one and the same, but not to him. He thought of feelings as being based on a more rational thought process – something for him to cling to when the world went awry. Emotions, however, were beyond his scope of genuine understanding. He was aware that he had them; he also understood that he had no control over them whatsoever. That knowledge made him feel uneasy.

'You're right,' he admitted eventually. 'I have been distracted. I've always allowed my job to spill over into my personal life, but not usually the other way around. I can't be effective if I allow that to happen. I need to be able to think straight.'

'Good. I'm pleased to hear you admit it. I miss old Jimmy.'

Bliss sighed. 'Old Jimmy has moved on to become ancient Jimmy. At least, that's how it feels. Defunct. Soon to be put out to pasture.'

Chandler huffed at him. 'So that's what's bothering you. You're still thinking about the end.'

'I've seen the future, Pen. And it's pretty bleak. I was thinking about our Lingchi case back in the summer. Specifically, my poor attempt at chasing down our suspect, which ended with me falling arse over tit on the ground by the railway track.'

'You didn't fall; you dived to grab hold of him.'

'And missed.'

She scoffed at that. 'Not entirely. You grabbed hold of his foot. His shoe even flew off, remember?'

'Terrific. That counts as one of my great arrests of all time: a fucking shoe. I might as well become a cobbler. Then there was the humiliation of watching Gul, who started off twenty yards behind me, actually managing to collar our man.'

'You slowed him down, Jimmy. If you hadn't, he might well have got away. You're just feeling sorry for yourself because retirement is drawing closer. You need to snap out of it. There's a good few months before we get there. A good many cases. You're no use to us at this moment if you're too busy with the future.'

Bliss regarded his friend thoughtfully. 'When did you become so wise? Has to have something to do with my influence. Stands to reason.'

'I was astute long before you showed up. A case of having to be. But you don't need the likes of me telling you what's what. Get your head out of your arse and back in the investigation.'

'Is that any way to talk to a senior officer?'

Chandler switched her grin to stun. 'But you're not. Not at the moment. We're equal rank. Which means I can talk to you any way I like. You better not forget that, old man.'

'Balls! I knew you'd have the last laugh.'

'You should have taken better care of me while you had the chance. Now we're on an even footing, and I have a bloody long memory.'

Bliss huffed. 'Yeah. You and every other woman I've ever met.'

She threw him a doubtful look. 'You spoken to Sandra since we got this case?'

Sandra Bannister was a reporter for the *Peterborough Telegraph*, which ran crime features both online and in its print edition. Bannister was the senior of a two-person partnership. She and Bliss had come close to dating, but he'd pulled away at the last minute. Their relationship since then had been ambiguous, with neither truly getting to grips with how to balance their professional association with what might have been. In truth, Bliss was not allowed to discuss investigations with the journalist, but she had provided useful information in the past and would do so again. This time, however, he had additional news for his partner.

'No. I expect to hear from her today if I don't call her asking for info. However, she did give me a bell last week. You remember that book she wrote on the Burnout case from 2005?'

'You mean the one you starred in and yet somehow managed to emerge without a stain on your dubious character?'

'That's the one, yes. Well, she's approached me with a proposition.'

'The bitch! Does Em know?'

He smiled. 'Behave yourself. No, she has two ideas in mind. She's considering writing a novel, and wants to use me as a consultant. She also told me that if I ever decide to write an auto-biography, she wants to be offered first refusal on ghost-writing it.'

'Ooh, get you! You'd be better off going with JK Rowling, though. I reckon your life story would come out about as factual as Harry Potter.'

Bliss frowned, feigning hurt. 'Why d'you say that?'

'Because there's no way you're going to sit there for hour after hour talking about yourself. Jimmy Bliss banging on about Jimmy Bliss? Honestly, does that sound like you?'

'Not especially. Plus, there's too much I couldn't say.'

'And too much you wouldn't want to say. Without either of those, what are you left with?'

She had a point. 'Okay. The consulting doesn't sound like a bad idea, though. That can't get me into too much trouble.'

Chandler sighed and shook her head.

'What?' he said, shrugging.

'Have you met you, Jimmy?'

TEN

'BLOODY HELL!' WAS THE first thing Bliss said when they reached the crime scene. The taped-off area had shrunk, but the tent was still in place despite the body having been removed long ago.

'What is it?' Chandler said, looking around in alarm.

He shook his head and smiled. 'Oh, nothing. I noticed the tree by the forensic tent the other night. I couldn't make it out properly in the LED lights. Seeing it in daylight… it's breathtaking.'

Though the season had taken its natural toll, there remained a significant number of leaves on the tree. In the pale early morning light, set against a watery blue sky, the warmth of its vivid creamy yellow colour held Bliss captive.

'It's a field maple,' he told his colleague. 'Normally they're green and red, but come this time of year they change to this. I only know them because they're related to the acer family. I thought about getting one in my garden, but the mature ones were too pricey.'

'It's lovely,' Chandler said absently. Bliss knew she did not share his affection for certain plants and trees. 'Looks a bit like one of those pot plants you have.'

He nodded. 'The autumn moon. It's what I opted for when I decided against the tree.'

'You think our victim being either killed or dumped here means something? The tree does stand out from the others.'

'I'm not sure if there's a ritualistic note to it. Trees do feature in mythology in relation to death; I think the cypress is most closely associated with it, though. As for the maple, it's popular in Celtic mythology, and also thought to repel demons and evil spirits. But I don't think one murder victim being found close to a maple tree establishes a pattern.'

Two uniforms had been left to protect and preserve the radically reduced crime scene. And to make sure nobody stripped down the tent and made off with it, Bliss thought, as he wandered over to the closest of them. He introduced himself and asked if the officer knew the area well or lived locally.

'Couldn't be more so,' the young constable replied, after giving him her name. 'I live in Cherry Hinton. I come over here all the time with my kids, and to walk the dog.'

'Perfect. My oppo and I were talking about the tree. That maple standing alone, over by the tent. We were wondering if there might be any significance attached to the body being left almost beneath it. Do you happen to know if there's anything special about that one? Does it have a colloquial name? Any history you know of?'

Constable Stevens bit her lip before shaking her head. 'I don't think so, sir. Not that I've heard. Not regards any history, at least. We've always called it The Autumn Tree. It seems to be the first to turn but the last to shed its leaves.'

'Yeah, maples do cling on. So nothing noteworthy otherwise?'

'Sorry, sir. No.'

Bliss shrugged. 'Not to worry. It seemed a little off to me, her being dumped right there. It's quite a distance from the path.'

The young constable seemed surprised. 'I think we assumed the victim had been murdered right here, sir. Like you say, it's a fair old hike from the closest spot to park a vehicle. It seemed logical to us that she walked here with her killer. Are you certain that's not the case?'

He wondered how much to reveal, thinking about what might get back to DI Kennedy. But PC Stevens was keen, not content with kicking her heels and looking to keep warm. 'Not certain,' he admitted. 'Just one of the theories we're looking into. We'll know more after the PM.'

'We heard Peterborough had taken over the investigation. Personally, I don't care who has it, provided they find the bastard responsible. If she was a prostitute, she must have known the risks, but she didn't deserve that.'

'Nobody does. And we'll do our best to find her killer. Rest assured, I'll bust a gut the same way I would if she were royalty.'

PC Stevens appeared placated. It wasn't a great deal of fun manning cordons, and the majority of her time would be spent in thoughtful solitude. Bliss was delighted by her attitude of not caring who got the arrest, as long as somebody did. Clearly she was focussed and keen on a successful outcome.

'If you hear anything relevant about the tree, please do get in touch,' he said. Ironically, he had not brought any business cards with him. He motioned for Chandler to join them and asked her to hand Stevens one of hers. Bliss's phone rang at that moment, and he walked away, leaving the two to chat.

He was unsurprised to see Sandra Bannister's name on the screen; she'd be looking for an angle all of her own. 'I've got nothing for you,' he said in place of a greeting. 'It's too early.'

'So, you confirm you and your unit are working the murder at the chalk pits?'

Bliss smiled to himself. This was one he could let her have. 'I can confirm that, yes. But that's all you're getting out of me.'

'Oh? Only I also heard ERSOU were involved.'

He wondered how she had acquired that snippet of information. 'Did you? That's interesting. I don't suppose you'd like to give me your source?'

'You know what, I think I will. Just for old times' sake. It's all extremely hush-hush, but… the NCA have it on the news page of their website.'

She didn't have to laugh; he could hear the amusement in her voice. 'Oh, how droll. Okay, so… Yes, we have an ERSOU investigator working with us. We'll see which way this blows before knowing if they'll attach more to it.'

'You're looking at an OC connection, though.'

'Looking at. Don't know for sure.'

'You're being extremely guarded today, Jimmy. Is someone listening in?'

Bliss raised his eyebrows. 'Isn't that a good question these days? But let's assume not. No, I'm with Pen, but she can't overhear. The fact is, we're working hard to prevent Cambridge taking this back off us. The crime scene is on their patch and there's a DI Kennedy champing at the bit, waiting to snatch this case out of my hands. I can tell you this much: ERSOU are liaising because the victim is an escort and therefore possibly trafficked. So, yes, there's a potential organised crime connection, as you suggested. If our investigation leads us to conclude that she was killed by a punter, it goes to Kennedy. If it has anything to do with her employers, we get to keep it.'

'And your money is on…?'

'Too soon to call. I suspect it will stay with us, but I should know much more by this time tomorrow.'

'Does that mean "Get off the phone, Sandra, and wind your neck in"?'

He laughed. 'You can read me like a book.'

'Which reminds me. Have you given any thought to our previous discussion?'

He winced at his careless remark, having not intended to encourage her further. He liked the fact that they were on friendly terms again, but he did not enjoy being backed into a corner. 'I have. I'll let you know for sure as soon as I've made up my mind. But I have to tell you that I'm leaning more towards the consultancy angle.'

'Okay. If that's what you prefer. I'll give you some more time to think about it. In the meantime, I'll get back to you later today to see if there have been any developments in the case.'

'Don't waste your breath,' Bliss told her, realising as soon as he had said it that he had wasted his own. Bannister could sense something brewing, and she was not about to let it go.

He and Chandler said goodbye to PC Stevens and started heading back towards the Ford Focus. Their route forced them to climb a steep rise, eventually working their way through knee-high grass as they skirted the chalky surfaces below. The largest pit, to the east, had not been quarried in almost forty years. At almost thirteen hectares, the site had long been established as a Site of Special Scientific Interest, and therefore protected land for conservation.

'It's quite something,' Chandler said, casting her gaze out over the desolate-looking scrubland.

Bliss grunted. 'I think you'd probably need to be a botanist or a rambler to truly appreciate the beauty of the place. To tell you the truth, it doesn't hold a great deal of interest for me.'

'Except for your maple tree. Don't forget that.'

He stopped walking and turned to look back the way they had come. Peering through some dense gorse, he was still able to see it. From this angle it did not stand out at all, but he would take away with him the first sight of it. There appeared to be no legend attached to the tree, but in that moment Bliss had felt its presence deep inside and knew he would find it difficult to let go of the memory.

ELEVEN

THE NEWS FROM GLEN Ashton and ERSOU was good. Their facial recognition software had thrown up three potential identities, one with a 98% probability rating. He quickly explained that after he'd forwarded the original photograph to his office in Bedford, it was scanned and enhanced at the same time. The software transformed the image into digital data by applying an algorithm, and the data was subsequently compared with records previously captured in its database. The fact that the system had spat out more than one result told them it wasn't infallible, but he was confident they had their girl.

Unlike Bliss, who continued to rely on whiteboards, markers and hard copy, Ashton had commandeered the e-board and brought up the NCA photo on the screen via his phone, courtesy of a Bluetooth connection. He arranged the NCA image alongside an official crime scene photograph. Satisfied, he turned to the group.

'They're the same,' he said proudly. 'We have the victim in our system.'

Bliss studied each image in turn. He struggled to tell the two faces apart, but the clincher was a small mole above the left eyebrow that could be seen clearly in both photos. He exchanged nods with Chandler and Bishop. 'So who is she?'

For a moment, Ashton looked as if somebody had stuck a pin in him to let the air out of his lungs. He moved from a state of pure elation to one of dejection in the blink of an eye. Hands resting on his hips, he shook his head. 'I'm sorry, but we don't have an answer to that.'

'What?' Bishop unfolded his arms and drew himself upright from the desk he'd been perched on. It was like watching a flower bloom in super-fast motion. 'You have her in your system but you don't have a name for her? How's that even possible?'

'Oh, no. We do have an ID. Larmina Nuri is the name she gave us, only it's not her real one. Let me fill you in. She was never brought in or questioned as a suspect, only interviewed as a witness. Evidently, our investigators suspected her but didn't have nearly enough on her at the time. They eventually managed to speak to her in connection with an escort ring for especially young girls, and we secured surveillance photos of her at the time. But she was in our hands for less than an hour, half of which was spent going through the motions. At that point, a rather expensive solicitor arrived on her behalf, and we were unable to detain her further. Our investigation continued, which is how we discovered that the name and contact details she provided us with were false.'

'So after all that we're no further ahead than we were before,' Chandler said, following a sigh that bordered on a groan of disappointment. 'The only ID we have on our victim is fake.'

Ashton seemed to reinflate. 'That's not quite right. It's true to say that we learned nothing from her directly. But like I mentioned before, we looked into her in greater detail afterwards. Using the same techniques your own DI Burton uses, we scoured the internet for her face. We got many hits. Several, you'll be

interested to hear, were associated with your man, Lewis Drake –
his business interests, at least. But she was also on the books of
at least one other agency, and most likely worked as an independent, too. We may not have her real name, but we did set up
an operation to get closer to her. Earlier this year, in fact. One
of our investigators booked a massage service using the contact
details provided right there in her genuinely independent profile.
Which means we have both her mobile number and the address
she gave him. Which is right here in the city.'

Bishop pumped both fists. 'Yes! That's what I call progress.'

'Is it in Woodston?' Chandler asked. 'Her address?'

'No. Bretton. Why do you ask?'

'Her agency address lists her as living in Woodston. But that
address is most likely connected to Lewis Drake. This one is new
to us. Intelligence we didn't have before.'

A hubbub of excitement spread around the room. It was a
sound Bliss enjoyed hearing, and seeing wide smiles on the faces
of colleagues was immensely gratifying. He did, however, have a
follow-up question. 'This solicitor who represented our victim.
Do you know who sent him?'

Ashton shook his head. 'No. But he was from Fraser and
Gooch. A Cambridge-based firm.'

Bliss felt his lips twist in disappointment. Unless Lewis Drake's
organisation had switched solicitors or added to their legal roster,
the representation of their victim had nothing to do with the
man or his operation.

'No matter,' Bishop said, rubbing his hands together and
taking charge. 'We'll follow up on that. First thing we need to
crack on with is our victim's phone and address.' He turned to
DC Ansari, who sat alongside fellow detective constables Hunt
and Gratton. 'Gul. I want you to do the honours tracking down

her mobile provider and pulling all the records we can lay our hands on.'

Ansari winced. 'That ought to keep me tied up for the next week.'

'I know it's a pain in the arse. But at least the RIPA forms have templates to work off these days.'

'I was thinking more about the provider. Some of them are great to work with. With others it's like trudging through a combination of mud, treacle, wet cement and quicksand.'

'Just get the ball rolling, Gul. I'll bring in some uniforms and a couple of civilian workers if necessary. Once you've completed the requests you can hand it off to one of them.'

'Yes, boss.'

Bishop turned to Bliss and Chandler, who as usual stood next to each other. 'You want to take the girl's home address?'

Bliss did, happy not to have to slog his way through Regulation of Investigatory Powers Act forms as Ansari was about to. But he also knew that Bishop had to be eager to prove himself. 'By rights, this should be yours,' he said.

'Why don't the pair of you go,' Chandler offered. 'I'm sure I can make myself busy here. I have John and Phil to help.'

Bishop readily agreed. 'That sounds good. If you could run the office for me, Pen, so much the better. We're still waiting on access to the crime scene photos and video files. Also, if you could call pathology and ask what time they expect to do the PM, I'd appreciate it. If it's early and the boss and I are not back, you get the pleasure of assigning who attends.'

Chandler groaned and hung her head. Nobody ever wanted to be selected to attend a post mortem, and handing over the shitty end of the stick was an unpleasant task. Alongside her, both Hunt and Gratton did the same, knowing they were the most likely candidates.

'What about me?' Ashton asked. He stood by the screen, its glow illuminating his face. 'How would you like the NCA and ERSOU to follow up?'

Bliss appreciated the investigator's fresh approach. He'd had the stuffing knocked out of him over the past day or so, but he seemed to have learned from it and was looking to be treated as part of the team. Bliss felt a little bad about what he was now going to do, but it was for a good cause and so he didn't miss a beat. 'I think if Penny and our team take the solicitor and also follow up on the other escort agency as well, your time would be best spent working the Lewis Drake angle. Maybe his organisation didn't spring her, but she's on their books and so it's a valid thread to pursue.'

'You don't think your local knowledge is better suited?'

'I reckon it might have the opposite effect and actually hamper us, Glen. We may be too close. A fresh eye – at least to begin with – could be what this needs.'

Ashton frowned. 'I haven't got to go and visit that vile dragon we spoke to yesterday, have I?'

Bliss chuckled. 'Who, Nicola Parkinson? No, I'll spare you that. We may want to take a look at Igor at some point, but Pen and I know them, so we'll handle them as and when.'

Without the need for further instruction, the team split and set about their new areas of the investigation. Bliss caught Bishop's eye and said, 'Can we have a word? In your office?'

'In my… you mean your office?'

'Not at the moment it isn't.'

In silence, the two left the major incident room, walked along the corridor, pushed through the door leading into the Major Crimes Unit and went on into the office close to the near corner. The room was small and cluttered – pretty much as Bliss had left it. Both men remained standing. Bliss thought his colleague had lost weight recently; Bishop's ill-fitting clothes hung on him more than usual, his creased shirt partially untucked. His appearance had not smartened up in line with his new role. Something Bliss would have to mention.

But something else caught his eye, and before saying another word, he marched across to the far end of the office. On the wall was his Bliss Pissed-ometer, a joke cardboard thermometer dating back to his first posting to the city. It was intended to gauge his mood, the joke being that its settings never climbed above grumpy. He reached up and yanked it off the wall, drawing pins springing out, scattering over the carpet like a shower of confetti.

'I think this has had its day,' he said. He crumpled it in half and stuffed it into the wastepaper basket close to the desk.

Bishop wore a look of concern. 'That was a bit drastic, Jimmy. I realise the situation has to be hard on you, but this'll be your office again before you know it.'

'I'm not so sure about that, Bish.'

'What? That you'll get it back or that you'll want it back?'

Bliss looked down at his feet. 'Either. Both. But the fact is, it's not my office any more, and we all have to adjust to that.'

'Okay. So is that why you wanted to have a word with me in here?'

'Primarily, I wanted to speak to you out of earshot,' Bliss said. 'I think we've reached that stage.'

'This still about the change in our respective roles?'

'What else? Bish, I think it's about time you stepped up and became the boss in more than name only. I accept your reservations, and I understand your argument about this possibly being a temporary adjustment. On the other hand, we both know it could go the other way; for all I know, what's happening here could be a stay of execution. Whatever the outcome, I can take care of myself. You need to think about you. You've wanted DI for some time. You've completed the first three steps in the promotion framework. Acting up in my place is a great way to achieve your work-based assessment.'

As he spoke, Bliss recalled a similar conversation he'd once had with Mia Short. Neither of them knew at the time how temporary her assignment would prove to be.

After a brief pause, Bishop said, 'Of course it is. But you know I have my misgivings. I want the salary hike that goes with the job. Who wouldn't? I want to lead my own team. Who doesn't? But equally, I don't want to be the kind of DI the job description currently says I should be. Nor do I particularly want to leave this team.'

Bliss empathised with his friend's dilemma. The job had changed in so many ways over the years. If he had been coming up in the modern era, achieving the rank of Detective Inspector wasn't a promotion he would be craving. Even so, he and Bishop had different demands upon them in terms of family and a structured future.

'That's understandable,' he said. 'But look at it this way, Bish: I'm as good as on probation for a further four months. At the end of that period, either I'll be gone, my probationary period will be extended, my demotion will become permanent, or I'll be back at DI. If it's any of the first three options, you'll have your own team right here waiting for you. If not, you'll have a bigger choice to make.'

His colleague winced. 'I don't even want to think about some of those possibilities, Jimmy.'

'I know. All I'm saying is, use these next few months wisely. You and I may not like it, but you are the boss at the moment. You're a DI, and I'm a DS at your disposal. Nobody should still be referring to me as the boss. You're too good a bloke to come down on the others for it, so I'm going to step up. I'm going to make it clear to all of them that you get tagged as the boss in future. I'm at the same level as you were and Penny continues to be. That's it. That's how I want it. And frankly, that should be how you want it, too.'

Bishop heaved a heavy sigh. He looked uncomfortable with the arrangement, and was probably disgruntled at his big opportunity having arisen for all the wrong reasons. Bliss recognised how unusual their position was, but the big man was due his time in the spotlight. And while everybody still thought of Bliss as the team's leader, he would cast too large a shadow if he did not act to prevent it.

'If you need anything, even if it's just to talk or ask questions, I'm here for you, mate. Don't worry about how I feel. I brought this on myself.'

'Fair enough. I'll accept all the help and advice I can get. How about I start with an easy one?'

'Of course. Fire away.'

'I'm deputy SIO on this case – albeit closely monitored by DCI Warburton. I know how the policy book works, but how significant are they in reality?'

Bliss smiled. 'Ah. You may have heard them referred to as both CYA and FYA books. That's because a senior investigating officer has to think about covering their arse when they complete the policy book. If they don't, the powers that be might use it to fire their arse instead.'

Startled, Bishop said, 'They're that critical? I assumed they were another box-ticking exercise.'

'Not at all. Look, make notes on any old pad as you go along. Even on Post-its. As many as it takes to jog your memory come the end of shift. That's when you take your time piecing them together to include every decision you made. Only... couched in such a way as to make sure you emerge smelling of roses in the event that shit hits the fan afterwards. Remember, Bish, the details in that book get fed back into the HOLMES database, so your single aim has to be not to fuck it up.'

Seeing his colleague's face turn ashen, Bliss smiled and said, 'You'll do fine. Can I offer one more piece of advice, though?'

'Of course. Anything.'

'Get yourself a new whistle. Tuck yourself in. Put a shine on those shoes.'

Bishop looked down at himself, smiled sheepishly and nodded.

'Shall we see about our victim's home address?' Bliss said. He found Bishop's steady gaze. 'Boss?'

TWELVE

I T DIDN'T TAKE LONG for Bliss to discover the details of their victim's landlord. Built by the Peterborough Development Corporation in the 1970s, Bretton was the city's first major township of new council housing. The property Bliss and Bishop visited that morning had exchanged hands on several occasions since being purchased under the right to buy scheme, and was currently owned by a housing entrepreneur born and raised locally. As was the case with many similar properties, what had once been a single house had since been redeveloped into two individual flats with shared facilities.

Tim Beaumont had initially been amenable to letting them look at the ground floor flat, provided they obtained a warrant. Speaking to him on the phone, Bliss had agreed, but in exchange he expected to be given copies of all of the landlord's relevant safety and insurance certificates relating to each of his properties. They'd compromised on a thirty-minute inspection with no need for paperwork either way.

Bishop took the keys from the man and told him to wait outside until he and Bliss were done. Beaumont did not argue.

Once inside the property, Bliss was surprised at how spacious the accommodation was. The original dining room had been converted into a bedroom, and was twice the size of Bliss's own. The living room was again much larger than his. He mentioned the generous proportions to his colleague.

'That's why these properties are so sought after,' Bishop said. 'Especially compared to some of the homes being built over in the Hamptons. These early PDC places have huge rooms, plenty of cupboard space, and come with parking bays. It was a big step up for many of those who moved here. Nice houses… until they weren't.'

Bliss knew what he meant, and corrected him. 'The houses are still the same, Bish. It's the people who made the area what it's become.'

Bishop nodded absently. 'I remember my parents being on the waiting list, before they got offered a place in Werrington. It was the same deal there, with the huge rooms and built-in cupboards. Before that we were squeezed into a poky little place in Woodston, so it felt like a palace to us when we finally moved in. Mum and Dad are still there, though I know my old man wants to move when he retires. He's had enough of the place.'

Bliss remembered the home he'd grown up in: a tiny two-up, two-down in east London. Bethnal Green in the sixties had a far from uniform architecture. The Bliss house stood in a street spared from the Blitz bombing campaign, but if you turned one way at a junction you might well encounter prefabricated homes; turn in the opposite direction and it would be new-build estates. Many old-timers from the area believed the Luftwaffe had done them a favour, but Bliss had only fond memories of the house he grew up in.

Whatever the relative merits of spacious living, their victim seemed to live a reasonably spartan life – apart from the clothes she chose to wear. Her wardrobe was choked with garments, either hanging or folded neatly on shelves, numerous shoes and boots arranged in pairs beneath. Other than her attire, the bedroom was curiously lacking in personality. No paintings on the wall, no photos in frames, no cuddly toys, no shelves laden with knick-knacks collecting dust. On a chest of drawers, Bliss found a single bottle of perfume, together with a bag of makeup and a double-sided mirror. He found the top drawer crammed with sexy lingerie, the next overflowing with more regular underwear, and the final drawer full of tights, socks, and jeans. Nothing personal. The bed was made, he noticed, its patterned duvet wrinkle free.

Meanwhile, Bishop had been searching the living room. From what Bliss could tell when he joined him, this room presented more of the same. Not that such conditions were unusual. In his experience, working girls tended to live in one of two ways: either they adorned their home with all manner of things cute and pretty, putting elements of their personality on display as if this might somehow obfuscate what they did for a living, or they surrounded themselves with the bare minimum because such a place could never truly represent a home to them.

'This flat is clean,' Bishop said, putting voice to the exact same thoughts Bliss had been having. 'And I don't just mean the lack of obvious personal items. There's nothing at all to suggest anybody was living here. None of the usual documentation, no bills, no invoices. It's as clean a place as I've seen.'

'Too clean.' Bliss nodded. 'I agree. Other than her clothes, there's bugger all here. I'm beginning to think our victim didn't live here at all. This was a habitat to entertain men in, and that was it. A place of business. No more than that.'

'But didn't she already have one of these? The place in Woodston that was mentioned on the escort agency website?'

'Yep. But we also know she spread herself around.'

'So we're no wiser.' Bishop shook his head and cursed beneath his breath.

Bliss understood his frustration – but one thing had occurred to him. 'Not quite. I had half a mind that our victim might have been murdered here. But I see no sign of that, do you?'

Bishop glanced around. 'Nothing obvious. But if she was strangled, that wouldn't cause a great deal of mess. Whoever did it could have cleaned up after themselves.'

'Judging by the marks on her wrists, I'd say she put up a struggle. She didn't go quietly. You look around and this place is pristine. You can still see the little furrows in the carpet where it's been vacuumed recently. Who would hang around to do all that after killing somebody? Not to mention having to cart her out of here unseen.'

Bishop huffed through his nose. 'You said it. Pristine. We agree the place is far too clean. Perhaps that's because it was all done afterwards.'

'I'm not ruling it out. But like I said, who is going to…' Bliss broke off, catching hold of the thread Bishop had thrown out there. 'Fuck it! Let's have him in here.'

Bishop stepped back outside to fetch Beaumont, the man surly and resentful as he stood between the two detectives. Bliss gave his colleague the nod before returning his gaze upon the landlord.

'Mr Beaumont,' Bishop said. 'Did you send in a cleaning team, or did you take care of the place yourself?'

The man tried hard to look bewildered, but overplayed his hand. 'What are you talking about?' he asked. 'I don't know nothing about nothing.'

Bliss clicked his tongue against his teeth. 'I fucking hate double negatives,' he muttered softly.

Bishop continued to confront Beaumont. 'Maybe you looked the other way while somebody else cleaned the place out. If that's the case, you did nothing wrong, sir. You have nothing to reproach yourself about. That said, what you choose to do now, what you opt to tell us *now*, will dictate your immediate future.'

Once more, Beaumont went for perplexed but missed by a long way. 'I have no idea what you're getting at. What are you trying to suggest went on here?'

'I'm not suggesting anything, Mr Beaumont. I'm saying somebody cleared this place out and cleaned it up in the process; trouble is, they did too good a job. Either you allowed them to do it, or you commissioned the job, or you did it all yourself. Whichever of those it was, I have questions for you. You can answer them here and now, or you can answer them after you've been held in a cell for a few hours. Your choice entirely.'

Bliss waited for the bluff to play out. Most civilians were clueless when it came to the detaining of a person for questioning. The only way he and Bishop could compel the landlord to accompany them back to HQ was to arrest him. He could agree to go with them or decide to settle things immediately, as Bishop had mentioned. Equally, he had every right to walk away and there would be little they could do about it. Fortunately, Beaumont's increasingly relaxed stance told Bliss he was ready to talk.

'I had a call from my tenant on the top floor. He said there were people he didn't recognise downstairs, walking in and out of the flat. I asked him if the tenant was with them, and he told me he hadn't seen her in several days.'

Neither Bliss nor Bishop had so far mentioned their victim by name. They had agreed on the strategy during the drive over, hoping that either Beaumont himself would mention it, or that they would find documented evidence. This was the moment to draw it out of him, Bliss felt.

'What's her name?' he asked. 'The tenant of this flat, I mean.'

Beaumont looked uneasy. 'Come on,' Bliss urged him. 'It's a simple enough question. What's your problem?'

'She told me her name was Nuri. She had all the required documents to that effect, even a bank account from which she paid her rent every month by direct debit.'

'That all sounds above board. I'm still not seeing your difficulty.'

'It's just that I overheard her talking on the phone one day and she called herself by a different name entirely.'

'I see. And that was?'

'Majidah. Majidah Rassooli.'

Bliss looked at Bishop and nodded once. He left the two men to it and stepped out of the flat, moving into the kitchen where he could not be overheard. He called Chandler and she picked up on the third ring.

'What's up, boss? You and Bish enjoying your jolly boys' outing?'

He grinned. Her upbeat nature almost always made him feel better. 'Remind me to have a word with you about that afterwards. Things have changed, and we all need to move on. But it can wait until later. I have a new name for you to run through the system – hopefully a real one this time.' He gave her the name and asked her to pass it on to Glen Ashton too, together with a request that he run it by his people.

'Is that all?' she asked.

'For the time being. We got that from the landlord. He was telling us about a few people being here at the flat yesterday. Seems they were cleaning up and clearing out. What with that and us traipsing all over the gaff, I don't think there will be any pickings for CSI, but you'd better call them out to this address anyway. I'm doubtful, Pen, but this could be our original crime scene.'

'Will do. Oh, and boss…'

'Yeah, I know. Don't call you Pen.'

He cut the connection before she could respond. He knew that would irritate her, which brought out another grin.

Back in the living room, Beaumont had decided to sit while Bishop grilled him hard. Bliss said nothing, listening to his colleague's technique. The interview stage could be a trying one for all concerned, but Bishop was good at questioning people. The aim from the police side was to run through a list of events and hope to catch the suspect in a lie. If that happened, it would be used against them as the interview progressed. The hardest part was knowing what to ask and what to hold back. Bliss liked the way Bishop wrung so much out of the landlord while saying so little himself.

Beaumont claimed to have encountered three men and a woman. Each of them had carried black bin liners out to a waiting vehicle, tossing them into the boot. Beaumont had also seen a bucket of cleaning supplies going the other way. The men claimed not to speak or understand English well enough to have a conversation with him, so the woman had done all the talking. She told him the young female tenant had been taken by the Border Force, and that she and her companions were simply gathering together some personal possessions and leaving the place as they would wish to find it.

The landlord's story had the ring of truth to it. Bliss thought about the wardrobe and chest of drawers crammed with clothes, and the makeup on the dressing table. He wondered why they'd been left untouched. But he was more interested in Beaumont's compliance at the time.

'So, let me get this straight,' he said. 'At no point did you lay eyes on the girl who lived here, yet for some reason you were quite happy for these strangers to clear out her flat?'

'I didn't think burglars would be cleaning up after themselves.' Beaumont seemed pleased with his reply.

'And neither did you think of giving us a bell, apparently. Yet you had no evidence to confirm they were doing any of it with the permission of the young woman who lived here.'

'I told you. I didn't think there was an issue.'

'Thinking is clearly not your speciality,' Bishop said. 'That much is obvious. But even you can't be that dumb. You must have known you'd be leaving yourself wide open to all manner of legal repercussions if your tenant arrived home to find her flat cleared out while you'd stood by watching them do it.'

'But she wasn't coming back, was she? She'd been snatched up by the border cops.'

'Which didn't necessarily mean she'd be detained and deported, even if it were true.'

For the first time, the man appeared edgy. 'Are you telling me it's not true? She isn't being held by immigration?'

Bishop made no immediate reply. Bliss said nothing, either.

After an awkward silence, the man seemed to crumble. 'Look, I'm sorry. All right? There were four of them and only one of me. I was being straight when I told you how it happened, and about what they told me. But yeah, of course I knew it was dodgy. I've had these foreigners come and go like this before, and they don't clean up after themselves that way. I'm not saying they all leave the flats like shitholes, but they certainly don't send in cleaning crews behind them.'

'So you knew it was off, but you stood aside and allowed it to happen anyway?'

'Yes. It wasn't something I wanted to get involved with.'

'Did you get any names at all?'

'No.'

'How about the registration plate of their vehicle?'

'No. I didn't think to look.'

On a hunch, Bliss pulled out his phone. Seconds later he was showing the man a photo of Nicola Parkinson. 'Is this the woman you spoke to?'

Beaumont barely glanced at the image before shaking his head. 'No. That's not her.'

'Are you sure? Take another look. Closer this time.'

Again the man shook his head. 'It's nothing like her. The woman I spoke to was much younger. A blonde.'

'So what did you think was going on?' Bishop asked him. 'Or didn't you care at all?'

'Or did they give you something to look the other way?' Bliss suggested. 'Is that why you're so nervous?'

Beaumont looked between them. Finally his shoulders dipped. 'I asked about the damage deposit and who I should return it to. They said I could keep it. That's all, I swear.'

'And you didn't regard that as a bribe to turn a blind eye?'

'No.'

Bishop snorted. 'You're either a plank of the highest order, Mr Beaumont, or you're bent. Either way, we're not done with you.'

The man's face screwed up so much Bliss thought he might cry. 'Are you arresting me?'

'Did I say that? No. I won't be placing you under arrest today, sir. But I will be authorising an investigation into you. I will also expect a fully detailed statement from you, and if you haven't presented yourself at Thorpe Wood police station by noon tomorrow, I will send officers out looking for you. I can assure you they won't be as charming as myself or DI – DS Bliss here. I hope I've made myself clear.'

The landlord gave a sullen nod. 'I didn't do nothing wrong. Not knowingly. What happened to her, anyway? To Majidah? Can you at least tell me that?'

Bliss regarded the man closely; he searched for a spark of humanity, but saw none. He knew then that Beaumont had most likely used their victim's services, and that what he was attempting to pass off as concern was merely fear of discovery. He took a step towards him.

'It's none of your business,' Bliss said. 'But you'd better hope we don't end up making you our number one suspect. Because if that happens, *you* become *our* business. And believe me, that's when things start to turn ugly for you.'

Before leaving, they spoke to the upstairs tenant, who had little more to add to what they already knew. He'd heard movement from downstairs, and from his window overlooking the street had spotted bags and other items being taken into and from the flat below. His involvement ended when he contacted Beaumont, and he had no memory of the vehicle they were using. He confirmed that he had not seen Rassooli in days; he'd assumed she was visiting family or had gone on holiday.

When they were back in the car, Bliss continued to fret about what they had learned. 'You know what bothers me most, Bish?' he said.

'The keys?'

'Precisely. Whoever cleaned up had keys to the front door and the flat.'

Bishop nodded, but when he spoke his tone was one of caution. 'But not necessarily hers,' he said. 'I can guess what you're thinking: they let themselves in, so they must be connected to our killer. But her agency are bound to have their own keys. It could be them who were here.'

Bliss wasn't so sure. 'Except that Beaumont told us she paid for the flat every month from an account in her fake name. Doesn't that suggest it was her flat and not one of theirs?'

'Maybe; maybe not. It's rented, so they have no financial inter-ests in the property. All they have to provide is a place for her to work out of. Instead of paying it themselves from a source that might leave an accounting trail, they let her keep the rent back from the money she earns provided she pays it into her bank and back out again. I'm betting that's what we'll find when we check her account.'

Bliss gave it some thought. 'You're right,' he said. 'But if that's the case, that still leaves us with an unanswered question.'

'Which is?'

'How did they know she wasn't coming back?'

THIRTEEN

THE TEAM EXCHANGED UPDATES ahead of lunch, each throwing something new into the simmering pot that was Operation Phoenix. Bishop related his and Bliss's experience at the victim's flat. They discussed the matter of the keys, and how their use left the team struggling for more answers. A connection between the murder and the agency running Rassooli from that flat had to be given serious consideration. Bliss was happy with the outcome, convinced Lewis Drake's organised crime gang were responsible.

DC Ansari had got as far as discovering the provider of the mobile phone number used on their victim's independent web page. As anticipated, her request for access to stored data was met with a tepid response. She had subsequently completed and submitted the necessary procedural forms.

Meanwhile, Chandler had chased forensics and also spoken with Nancy Drinkwater about the post mortem. It was scheduled to be her final PM of the day and, as the pair had suspected, DCs Hunt and Gratton were given the unenviable task of attending. The Cambridge crime scene manager, Magda Nowicki, had willingly provided access to the forensic files, details and media. She also gave a verbal report over the phone, which pleased Chandler as the informal terminology made for better understanding. Nowicki had seemed eager to confirm there were no obvious signs of rape, though she wouldn't entirely rule out the possibility. She was confident the cause of death would prove to be manual strangulation. The lack of prints indicated the killer had worn gloves, and fibres collected from the scene had been sent away for further analysis and testing.

'Oh, and she also found minute traces of chemicals on our victim's skin,' Chandler said, having to consult her notebook before reading them off. 'Benzyl alkyldimethyl chloride, and something called cocamidopropyl betaine.'

'Did Magda know what their use was?' Bliss asked.

'Cleansing agents. Most likely some form of disinfectant, but less harsh than pure bleach.'

Bliss thought back to the naked body lying still beneath the forensic tent, the victim's flesh stark and pure. 'But they would irritate the skin nonetheless, yes?'

'Very much so. Which would explain the emollients, emulsifiers and aloe vera that were also detected, as were some minor abrasions. Our victim was most likely scrubbed down with the disinfectant and shampooed afterwards.'

'Sounds thorough.'

Nodding, Chandler said, 'It does, except you have to wonder why they bothered with the shampoo. Magda is still researching what she found, but it looks obvious that whoever killed our girl was making sure they left no forensics on the body itself.'

'Did you remember to ask about lividity?' Bliss said.

'I didn't have to; Magda beat me to it. She told me there was insufficient evidence to confirm your theory that our victim was killed elsewhere and dumped at the chalk pits. But she went on to say that she also expects our pathologist to conclude that the body was moved after she was killed.'

'In other words, our victim was not killed in the exact spot where she was discovered, but could still have been strangled in or around the chalk pits.'

'That was the gist, yes.'

Bliss felt a little kick of adrenaline. This information might be important, though he wasn't quite sure how. His thoughts drifted back to the flat in Bretton. Hopefully their own CSI unit would find something to suggest the murder had taken place there, but the clean-up had been thorough. Strangulation was not a messy method of murdering somebody, other than the potential leakage of bodily waste.

He turned back to his partner. Chandler was explaining that she'd brought in DC Ansari to run down the second escort agency while she herself spoke to Fraser and Gooch, the firm whose solicitor had rescued their victim from her ERSOU grilling.

'They were not particularly forthcoming,' Chandler admitted. 'Other than confirming representation of our victim, they offered nothing else. Oh, and they point blank refused to tell me who'd contacted them to request their presence in Bedford that day.'

'What name did they have for her?' Bishop asked.

'Larmina Nuri. The name she gave both ERSOU and the landlord.'

'Makes sense. Clearly that was the name she stuck with when it came to her agency work and its repercussions.'

'I'm getting nowhere fast with this second agency,' Ansari told them. 'Seems to be a string of them all under one umbrella, but they appear to be based in Armenia. I'm still chasing up a more local contact so that we can at least speak with them – my main problem being that the contact details on their various websites have so far proven to be false.'

Glen Ashton had not yet returned to HQ. According to Chandler, he'd initially attempted to gather his information over the phone, but had eventually relented and driven down to his own offices in Bedford. His absence made it easier to talk more freely.

'What's your gut telling you?' Chandler asked Bliss. 'Was our victim killed by a punter, or is there more to it than that?'

Bliss felt the pressure of expectation. Ashton being out of the room allowed him to open up without running the risk of having the case taken away due to a lack of evidence connecting the victim to Lewis Drake. Even so, the team were looking to him for guidance, and he had to be honest with them.

'I think a punter flees the scene immediately after he kills her.'

'I agree,' Chandler said.

'The presence of those fluids on her skin points to her having been murdered by somebody with time on their hands, which suggests they were confident of not being disturbed. It also reveals a cold and calculated mindset in taking anti-forensic measures. I believe she was disinfected and washed down, driven out to the chalk pits and dumped, then whoever did all that later summoned up a cleaning crew for her flat.'

'But does that necessarily mean Drake was involved? Or anyone else from his organisation, for that matter?'

Bliss shook his head. 'No. But neither does it rule out the possibility, so we have to look closely at them. Our victim – let's call her Majidah Rassooli until we know for certain otherwise – worked for an agency run by Drake's operation. It puts them and him in the frame. I suggest we hold firm on that to keep this investigation under our control. But we also know she tommed for at least one other agency. As a working hypothesis, we could say there's a good chance that one of her employers caught her moonlighting and decided to take her out. It explains how the agency knew to clean out her flat. The only thing that doesn't quite work for me at present is the location of the body dump.'

Bishop nodded his agreement. 'It's a problem. Why leave her out in the open to be found? Why not bury her or weigh down her body and throw it in the river?'

'Perhaps she was left that way as a warning?' Ansari suggested. 'To the other girls, I mean. "This is what happens if you step out of line."'

Bliss decided it was a genuine possibility. 'That's a good thought, Gul. It's also another avenue for us to explore. We could speak to some of those other girls, ask if there's been a general warning recently about them hooking on the side.'

Ansari put her next question to Bishop. 'I don't see them talking to us, do you, boss?'

After the slightest of pauses, he responded positively. 'They might choose not to talk. But they won't be able to stop us noticing the split second of fear in their eyes when we ask the question.' Bishop's own gaze switched to DCs Hunt and Gratton. 'John and Phil, you two can pick up on that action. You can have the delightful experience of dealing with Nicola Parkinson this time.'

That lightened the mood. There was some chuckling from those who'd had the dubious pleasure in the past. But even though Bliss disliked the woman intensely, he at least had a rapport with her. He thought he and Chandler might squeeze more out of the situation. However, the look he got from his partner when he volunteered their efforts in place of the two DCs almost shattered his resolve. When the team broke for lunch, he did his best to pacify her, but she was not happy with him. Eventually he gave up trying.

Halfway through their break, Bliss took a call. He carried his hot chocolate out of the canteen and moved towards the stairwell, seeking privacy. Thirty seconds later he texted Chandler to tell her he was going off site for a short while and that she should wait for him in the squad room. He booked out a pool car – which raised a few eyebrows, considering he already had a vehicle assigned to his name – drove the short distance to the city hospital at Bretton Gate, found a parking space close to the emergency care entrance, and showed his warrant card at the reception desk. He gave the name of the patient he was there to see. Having checked the details on a monitor, the young man behind the desk provided him with clear directions.

As he turned away, Bliss almost collided with a couple of paramedics. He apologised, without paying them too much attention.

'Mind how you go with those dodgy ribs, Inspector,' one of them said.

This time he did look up. The female paramedic was staring intently at him, but Bliss could not place her. She was smiling, waiting for a response. When it became obvious none was forthcoming, she put the smile on full beam for him. 'And there was me thinking I'd left a wonderful memory of our time together forever embedded in your heart. Tell me, Inspector, how many times *have* you been stripped to the waist and treated by a vivacious young woman while your car slowly disappears into a lake?'

Bliss couldn't help but laugh. Even for him, what she had described was a rarity. 'Kelly,' he said, nodding to emphasise his certainty about who she was. 'How are you doing?'

'Still in at the deep end. You?'

'Steering clear of lakes. I'm pleased to say I haven't needed bandaging for a while.'

'Shame. I'd be happy to help when you do. Always good to keep your hand in.'

'I'll remember that.'

Her partner dipped his head. 'Do you two need a room?' he asked.

Kelly smiled but kept her eyes firmly on Bliss. 'I don't know. Do we need a room, Inspector?'

Bliss knew she was teasing – only, he didn't know for sure how much of it was a joke and how much of it she might follow up on if put to the test. His response ought to have been the same whatever her intent, but for a moment he found himself teetering on the edge. Laugh it off, or take it further? He'd sensed an interest from her when they'd met, but that was a long time ago and things had moved on a great deal – for him, at least. He glanced down at her left hand, saw no rings. When he looked up again their eyes locked, and he knew she had noticed. He felt almost as bad as if she'd caught him peeking down her top.

'Which is the more polite answer?' he said, hoping to climb back out of the deep hole he'd dug for himself. 'Yes, we do need a room, or no, we don't?'

'The second is more polite,' Kelly said, her gaze not shifting, 'but an awful lot less interesting.'

He took a deep breath. For the first time in as long as he could remember, he had no clue how to respond. After an awkward pause, Kelly touched his arm and said, 'Have I embarrassed you? I do apologise. Me and my big mouth.'

'No.' Bliss shook his head. 'Not embarrassed. Just… caught unawares. I'm a little bit distracted. Bit rusty, too. Sorry.'

She nodded. 'That's fine. I was only being playful.'

'Good. Of course you were. That makes sense.'

'On the other hand, I'm sure someone as resourceful as you will know how to find me once you've thought of a more honest answer than the polite one.'

Bliss swallowed. Kelly had to be ten or twelve years his junior, and he didn't even know her surname. Could he be reading her so badly? Had he lost the ability to talk to women and reliably understand their intent? A fog of confusion hung over the manner in which men and women regarded one another in the current social climate, but he'd take some convincing that appreciating a woman's body as much as her mind and her talent made him a sexist. Pretty much every loving relationship began with physical attraction, and to his mind the human race was doomed if that ever changed.

'I have to run,' he said eventually. 'It was good seeing you again.'

'You too. Don't leave it so long next time.'

She flashed the smile once more before heading off with her colleague. Bliss was left to stand and shake his head. What had that been? Another tease, or an invitation to call? He pushed out a breath and told himself off. He was being foolish. A middle-aged man coveting a younger woman was one of the oldest stories going, and he had fallen into the trap of misreading the paramedic's easy-going nature and bubbly personality.

As the thought came and Bliss watched her walk away, Kelly glanced back over her shoulder. He raised a hand to say goodbye. She flashed that smile again and did the same.

Continuing along the corridor, Bliss mentally chided himself all the way to the treatment area. A flirt was just a flirt, a wave a wave. He found the bay he'd been told to look out for; its curtains were open. The man being treated by a nurse and examined by a doctor caught sight of Bliss and rolled his eyes. Not wishing to interrupt, Bliss waited outside the cubicle. Almost ten minutes passed before he was allowed to speak to the patient. He pulled the curtain around to afford them some privacy.

'Was this Watson?' Bliss demanded.

The man – with a swollen eye socket, deep red marks surrounding it, and three ugly lacerations to his face – was Edward Barr, known as Teddy to everyone who encountered him. An ex-cop working as a private investigator, Barr had been hired by Bliss to keep an eye on Neil Watson. It was he who had made the phone call the previous night, having followed the target to the restaurant in Whittlesey.

Barr nodded. Even the slow and slight neck movements caused him to wince. He set his chin as though unwilling to say more, but softened it again after a moment of reflection. 'I thought he might be going to pay the woman a visit. He was behaving oddly, walking around the streets in circles but at the same time consistently edging towards the same general location. I have to assume he knew I was there and had been looking for a good spot to jump me, because when he turned into an alleyway and I followed, he got the drop on me. Sad to say I didn't manage to land a single blow of my own. He threw himself at me, knocked me to the ground and it was all over from that point. Well, you've seen him. It would've taken a crane to hoist him off me. He gave me a good hiding, told me to stop following him or next time it would be worse.'

'He's a big unit,' Bliss said. 'Even in your prime, you'd have struggled. Don't beat yourself up about it, Teddy. Watson did enough of that for the two of you.'

Barr gasped in pain as he laughed. 'Stop it, you evil bastard. It bloody well hurts when I laugh.'

'Sorry. Couldn't resist. Has it been reported? It should have been, if you were found unconscious.'

'No, nothing like that. I wasn't going to bother, but I got a bit dizzy so I came here under my own steam.'

'Are you going to report it?'

'If I do, I land you in it, Jimmy. I don't want that.'

'Sod me, Teddy. He assaulted you. He has previous. It's a chance to bang him up.'

'Yeah, but it's my word against his. Nobody saw a thing.'

'You can't know that for sure,' Bliss said. 'Just because nobody came to help doesn't mean they didn't see what happened. The fight could have been witnessed from any of the surrounding buildings. You tell me where and I'll check it out before you speak to uniform.'

Barr took a moment before responding. 'I'm telling you there was no one around, Jimmy. I checked the windows myself while I was pulling myself together. Nobody saw us, so there's no reason to report it. It won't go anywhere.'

Bliss saw the sense in that. The only reason to report the offence was if they had a better than average chance of it resulting in a prosecution. Without a corroborating witness, that was unlikely, especially given the circumstances.

'All right. But if you think of anything we can use against him, let me know.' He lowered his voice. 'Tell me something, Teddy. You already planning payback? Thinking of having a few friends pay our Mr Watson a visit, maybe?'

'Something of the sort, yeah. Why?'

'Any chance you could leave it until my bit of business with him is over? A dish best served cold, and all that?'

'I was thinking of waiting anyway. I don't want him being taken down a peg without me being part of it.'

Bliss chewed on his bottom lip. 'I'm sorry about this, Teddy. It's my fault. Me going in there after him last night gave the game away. He knew he'd been followed, and stupidly I made a point of insisting that it couldn't have been me. He must have been keeping an eye out for you today. I should have thought to warn you.'

As uncomfortable as it was, Barr gently shook his head. 'Nah. This one's down to me, Jimmy. I should have been more aware. Other than his bulk, he's an average bloke. I thought I could follow him without him noticing. Plus, I turned into that alleyway blindly. I should have held back, taken it in before strolling down there like I owned the place.'

Bliss asked for the precise location and nodded when Barr told him. He knew the area quite well and was certain he could find it if he had to. He was starting to get riled up about the assault when Barr stuck a hand out to tug at his sleeve. 'Let it go, mate. I'm not up to talking about it, if I'm being honest. Especially with the boys in blue. Knowing my luck I'll get a couple who recognise me, and this is hardly my finest hour. Besides, neither of us wants to bring you into it. And let's face it: if I don't, then Watson will if he's pinched. The truth is, I got careless. He'll get his, in time. What you want him for is worth far more than my little embarrassment. So, do us both a favour and focus on that fucker.'

Reluctantly, Bliss agreed. A reprieve for Neil Watson, perhaps. But he was determined to make it a temporary one.

FOURTEEN

A S BLISS STRODE INTO the station from the car park, he heard his name being yelled out. He looked around to see a uniform bounding over. Police Constable Barry Griffin, all rosy-cheeked youth and Bambi-limbed vigour, had won Bliss over with his infinite enthusiasm and dedication. Griffin gave boxing lessons to a group of young people who lived close to the edge and were in danger of taking the next step into the abyss. He had asked Bliss to volunteer a couple of hours a week, helping out with the coaching. Initially sceptical, Jimmy had caved to the point of saying he would think about it.

He hadn't, of course. He'd completely forgotten.

'Well?' Griffin asked. His body was on the move even when standing still. Eagerness gleamed in his eyes. Somehow to let him down would be akin to booting a puppy up the arse.

'Two hours a week, you said?'

'Three at most, if we include setting up beforehand and cleaning down afterwards.'

Bliss shook his head. 'That stops if I agree to this. If I'm going to help train these youngsters, we do it the right way. Those we coach do those jobs in future. It's good discipline.'

'That's terrific, Jimmy. See, you're already contributing. I said you'd be perfect for this.' He was beaming all over his face. 'All right. Two hours during the week, and maybe the odd Sunday morning.'

'Woah, hold on a minute. You never said anything about weekends. Or additional hours.'

'Just the odd occasion, sir. When I'm on duty, that sort of thing.'

Squinting, Bliss couldn't help but admire his colleague's sheer cheek. 'You've got some neck, Barry, I'll say that about you.'

'My mother always told me if you don't ask you don't get.'

'Mothers are wise. Generally speaking.'

Griffin gave a wide grin. 'So you'll do it?'

'I'm going to have to see what kind of shape I'm in. I do some stretching exercises, but nothing strenuous. I haven't worked a bag or a speed ball in ages. And I certainly haven't stepped inside a ring in decades. I don't want to embarrass myself, so let me do that and I'll get back to you.'

'No problem. You will get back to me this time, yes?'

'I will. And I'll commit on a trial basis. But you have to understand: if I'm balls deep in a case, I can't always walk away because people are expecting me somewhere else.'

'I appreciate what you're saying, sir. But *you* have to understand that if we tell these young people we're doing something, then we have to do it. We can't ever allow them to question our commitment, or our word. That gives them an easy way out, and it's not what this club is about.'

Bliss regarded him thoughtfully, admiring the young officer's outspoken nature and commitment. 'So, what you're telling me is that if I'm in, I'm in all the way?'

'That's about it, sir. One of us has to make it. Every single time. We let these kids down, we lose them.'

'Fair enough. Count me in.'

'I knew I could, sir. Next Wednesday evening if you want to do a spot of training in the gym. Seven till nine, at the hall we spoke about.'

'I'll be there,' Bliss told him, heading towards the stairs. He knew it was a serious obligation once accepted, but he supported the idea. It had worked for him, providing an outlet for testosterone-fuelled aggression. And as for signing up as a coach, he'd had no real choice in the matter. Not supporting Griffin had never been a viable option; you just don't kick puppies up the arse.

When he entered the room, Bliss noticed Ashton had rejoined the unit. The NCA investigator sat alone at a desk close to the e-board, tapping away at a laptop. Ansari, Hunt and Gratton huddled together at another desk opposite. Meanwhile, Bishop and Chandler stood poring over an open folder containing a bunch of documents clipped together.

'Sorry I'm late back,' Bliss said. 'I had to nip out to attend to something personal. I'll make up the time.'

Bishop's cheeks flushed red as he looked up from his reading material. He appeared stumped as to how to respond. Awkward moments like these were bound to arise, Bliss reflected. But he'd been right to make the apology. It was giving the man his due respect.

'No problem,' Bishop finally said. 'You put more than your fair share in every day. I think we can let this one go.'

'No revelations while I've been gone?' Bliss asked.

'Not so as you'd notice. Glen managed to dredge up some fresh info on that other escort agency. Looks as if it might be another of Drake's, masquerading as an eastern European outfit. It genuinely is based where it says it is. What's more, we're still coming up short trying to find a local contact.'

Bliss thought about that, and knew what his next move would be. 'You thinking we should pose as a punter and give one or two of their girls a bell?'

'That's precisely what Penny and I were talking about when you came in.' Bishop indicated the folder sitting on the desk, and gave it a spin so that the information it contained was the right way up for Bliss to read. 'These are some of the young women we're considering. For the time being, we're looking at those most likely to be English, or at least potentially born here. We don't want to waste a setup on a girl who's fresh off the boat and barely able to speak the language.'

Nodding, Bliss said, 'That's a good shout. I'm still thinking about giving Nicola Parkinson another go. That all right by you?'

'Sure thing. We can take care of the rest. Perhaps by the end of the day we'll actually have some idea where to focus our resources.'

'Yeah. That's always the tough part. Sometimes you get too many leads, sometimes not enough. Most of the time you get what we have at the moment: a pile of odds and sods that don't amount to much, but need following up on anyway.'

Bliss was about to suggest Chandler grab her jacket when something occurred to him. In the rush to follow up on how his own business card had come to be with their victim, he'd completely neglected the other card that had been discovered inserted into the lining of her bra. He looked up, spotted the person he needed to talk to.

Carolyn Miller had been assigned as the case exhibits officer. As an adaptable civilian worker, Miller had experienced a whole range of investigation-related roles. She worked alongside police officers and other civilians, gaining an overall insight into each case and their differing operational methods. Bliss knew the woman and appreciated her diligence and sharp mind.

'DI Bliss,' she said, looking up from her monitor. The accompanying smile was genuine. 'What can I do you for?'

Pulling a pained expression, he reminded Miller of his demotion. 'But don't worry about it, Carolyn, because we can easily overcome that by you calling me Jimmy, as I've always asked you to.'

She put a hand to her mouth and blushed. 'Whoops. Sorry. Yes, perhaps sticking to Jimmy will prevent me from putting my foot in it again.'

'It's not a problem. Honestly. What I'm after is a piece of evidence that would have come in from Cambridge. Two business cards were found secreted in our victim's clothing. One of the cards is mine. It's the other one I'm interested in.'

Miller raised a finger. 'First thing this morning I removed the evidence from the storage area and locked it away in here so that it's available should anybody need it.' She took out a key, unlocked the desk drawer and pulled it open. After rummaging around for a few seconds, she took out a plastic evidence bag and handed it across the desk.

'Cheers.' Bliss smiled and checked the seal. Nobody had signed it out since it was originally stuck in place.

'Are you going to need to open it up?' Miller asked.

'I'm not sure. Let me find a better light and I'll see if I can make do.'

Chain of custody had to be followed at all times. If he opened the evidence bag he would have to seal it again, before signing and dating the inspection of the material it contained. He moved to stand beneath a ceiling light strip, examining the card through the clear plastic.

Similar in size to his own, the card felt thicker, heavier, and clearly more expensive. It was matte black, with two words in shiny black print on the front: *Dark Desires*. The reverse side was also black, only this time Bliss saw a series of letters and numbers written in gold coloured ink.

EE

Enter in A1

DP575

He looked over at Ansari and called out to her. 'Gul. Our victim's phone provider – I don't suppose it was EE, was it?'

'It was, yes. Why, d'you have something?'

'Maybe. Come and take a look at this.' Bliss showed her the card, the writing on the back. 'I'm thinking this Dark Desires might be an exclusive escort agency. If this writing refers to our victim's mobile number, this may provide a new connection for us. Problem is, I have no idea what the rest of it means. Perhaps some kind of access code related to the account? I don't know. Any immediate thoughts?'

Ansari took a breath and shook her head. 'Not off the top of my head. I can tack it on to my request, see if it makes any sense to them.' She paused for a moment. 'Actually, this may be something they can tell me outside of RIPA. I can ask them if it's a generic code, not attached to a specific number.'

'Good. Do that for me, please. See if you can get me an answer by the time I get back from visiting dear Nicola P.'

The DC gave a mock shudder. 'Rather you than me. That woman makes my flesh crawl.'

Bliss nodded. 'I know exactly what you mean.'

He gave the exhibits back to Carolyn Miller and chivvied up Chandler. Trapped inside his sergeant's car as they headed over to Orton Malbourne, he was at her mercy and expecting a grilling. Which was precisely what he got.

'So where did you disappear to earlier?'

'I had something personal to attend to.'

'A meeting?'

He flashed a sidelong glance. 'Personal. You did hear that bit, yes?'

'You and I don't keep secrets from each other, Jimmy.'

'Yes we do. Of course we do.'

'Only the deeply personal stuff. You didn't say that.'

She kept it up all the way there, and despite his heart sinking at the thought of another verbal sparring match with Parkinson, he was glad when they arrived at their destination.

Igor must have been running an errand or having a day off, because another man opened the door to them this time. The regular doorman's replacement was equally tall, but nowhere near as wide. Nevertheless, he looked mean and fit and capable of virtually anything. His bushy beard looked capable of sustaining nests and shelter for all manner of woodland creatures. After showing them into the office, the man stepped out again – all without uttering a single word.

'I suppose you call that one Fritz,' Bliss said.

'Why Fritz?' Parkinson asked, playing along from the same chair behind the same desk.

'It's a popular misconception that Frankenstein's lab assistant was called Igor. His name was actually Fritz.'

'Which is also a popular misconception. In Shelley's original book, the doctor had no lab assistant. He only appeared in the first films.'

Bliss pursed his lips. 'I bow to your greater knowledge. How do you know that, by the way?'

'I read.'

'Mary Shelley?'

'You sound surprised.'

'That you can read at all, yes. That you know Mary Shelley blows my mind.'

Parkinson offered up a mock kiss. 'Speaking of blowing your mind, can one of my girls be of service to you today, Inspector?'

'How about you, Nicola? You ever turn yourself out these days? Some mutton for the young lambs going to slaughter.'

This time she laughed. Harshened by habits including cigarettes and alcohol, it sounded as if it got caught up between her ribs. 'Only on special occasions. For special people. You never know – your own Chief Constable might be one of them.'

'That would surprise me. The way I hear it, he'd be happier with Fritz or Igor.'

Behind them, Chandler puffed out her exasperation. 'Will you two put a lid on it, please? Jimmy, do us both a favour and ask her what you came here to ask. This place makes me feel itchy.'

'You can get a cream for that, DS Chandler,' Parkinson said. 'I hear it stops all types of irritating cu–'

'I think my colleague is right, Nicola. We haven't got all day to bandy words around with the likes of you. As pleasant a thought as that might be.'

Parkinson summoned her son into the room. When he joined them, he was accompanied by a young blonde woman; they looked so similar, Bliss guessed they were siblings. He thought back to his encounter with the landlord, and Beaumont's description of the woman who'd been in charge of the three men cleaning out the victim's flat.

Parkinson had been casually swivelling from side to side in her chair behind the oak desk. Now she stopped and leaned forward, clasping her hands together and resting them in her lap. 'Now the gang's all here, ask away. I'm not saying you'll like the two-word response, but I won't stop you trying.'

Bliss put away his thought about the young blonde behind him. 'Your cooperation is all I ask, Nicola. You know the score otherwise. In fact, if you're straight with me, we can get this over with in double quick time.'

She batted her eyelashes at him. 'I reckon everything you do is over in double quick time. You don't look built for stamina. Not to worry. I'm all yours, Inspector. Have your way with me.'

Bliss snorted. 'Not in this or any other lifetime. Tell me, Nicola: over the past few months, has your agency given any specific warning to your girls not to try going independent?'

She leaned back, pondering the question for a few seconds, and examined her nails before replying. 'They already know that would be a terrible mistake. We tell them precisely who they work for and with. Indies are not welcome, and those who stray are cut off.'

'In what way do you mean?'

'Don't go getting your knickers in a twist, Inspector. When I say they are cut off, I mean they get slung out of their flats and they lose our services and protection. They're on their own.'

There was that grin of hers again. Bliss wanted to slap it off her face. He had a mental image of a cartoon he'd once seen in which Daffy Duck was dealt a right-hander, resulting in his bill circling his head several times. He wondered if he could generate enough energy to do that with Parkinson's smug grin.

'Are they also on the receiving end of a clump or two as they're being thrown out?' he asked.

She shrugged. 'I'm never there, so I wouldn't know. If they get mouthy then our people might get handy. But we are talking about just a bit of a hiding. Nothing more than that.'

'And there were no recent, precise warnings? Possibly that matters could be taken further if any of them persist?'

'Our girls don't get the opportunity to persist. There's no "three strikes and you're out" bollocks here. If we find out they're doing business on the side, they're gone. End of. Simples.'

'And does it still happen anyway?' Chandler asked.

'Occasionally. But not with your victim, if that's what you're trying to suggest. I asked around. She knew the score and never gave us any cause to suspect she might be playing away from home. Sadly, some of these girls ain't got the brains they were born with.'

'Maybe that's because some of them are little more than children.'

Parkinson's mouth formed an 'O'. She put a hand to her chest and feigned shock. 'Detective Sergeant Chandler, whatever do you mean? All our girls are of age. They are also free to come and go as they please. If they stay, all we ask is that they abide by the rules. Most choose to stay. Those that don't… fuck 'em. Easily replaced.'

'What, another container coming in from some port, Nicola?'

'I have no idea what you mean. If you're referring to the ordeal you're putting poor Mr Drake through, I think you'll find he'll be free soon enough to explain the error of your ways to your face.'

'What kind of woman are you?' Chandler barely managed to whisper. She turned to glance at Troy and the blonde, standing quietly in the corner of the room. 'What kind of mother?'

But the likes of Parkinson thrived on such hostility. 'The kind of woman men want to fuck and women want to change places with, love. Don't sneer down your nose at me, you rabid twunt! I live the life I choose. Nobody forces me to do anything I don't want to do. I realise you think you're better than me, DS Chandler, but yours is one sad, lonely tart's opinion that I couldn't give a flying fuck about.'

Bliss put himself between the two women, hoping to take the sting out of the situation. 'You stick to your story, Nicola. You ignore the fact that young girls were and probably still are being trafficked into this country so's they can have their bodies sold for them on a daily basis by scum like you. If you think that makes you special somehow, I reckon that confirms everything we've always thought about you. But now you've insulted my partner here, I've decided I'm done being nice to you.'

Parkinson rose to her feet and folded her arms slowly and deliberately. 'Is that right? And what exactly does that mean?'

'How many girls do you have here at the moment?'

Smirk. 'No comment.'

'No problem. I'll make a call. After which I'll hang around until some of my fellow police officers arrive in one of those bright yellow and blue motors. They will inspect every inch of this place, and they will interview every person caught inside the building. I'm not sure on what grounds yet, but I'll think of something before your brief arrives. And when they're done, they might even spend some time parked up outside. That'll be your business done for the day, Nicola. Oh, and I'll order the same thing for tomorrow, and the next day, and the next...'

'All right, all right. I get the picture. How about I apologise?'

'Stick your apology,' Bliss snapped back. 'Most of the time I can choke down what goes on here, because I don't even think about you or your sordid little enterprise when I don't have to. People like you are the shit on my shoe. But every so often I feel the need to wipe that shit off. So now you and I have a problem.'

Parkinson did not appear in the least bit perturbed. 'Are you sure that's how you want this to go? Mr Drake might be banged up, but he still has a big reach. He won't like you coming for him a second time, Inspector.'

'That sounded like a threat.' He turned to look at Chandler. 'Did that sound like a threat to you, Detective Sergeant?'

'It did,' she replied quickly.

'I don't make threats,' Parkinson said. 'All I'm doing is telling you how it is.'

Bliss sniffed. Looked her up and down. He could see how she might attract men looking for MILFs, though she was growing ever closer to being a GILF. To him, however, she was pure poison in subhuman form. 'I don't care. Besides, it's Detective *Sergeant* Bliss to you these days, Nicola. And the reason I'm a DS at the moment is because I've about reached the point where I don't give a damn any more. My thirty-year detective's pension is secure enough, so now I'm that man you were always taught to fear: the one who literally has fuck all to lose.'

'I'll advise Mr Drake accordingly.' She brushed back a strand of hair and glared at him, spite leaking from her eyes.

'Good. And you're on notice as well, love. If I have a problem with him, I have a problem with you. You and this place. You and the agencies you're involved with. Pretty soon, things turn around and it's you who becomes the problem, and therefore the reason for Drake's problems. I know you're not scared of me, Nicola. But consider what he might be willing to do to pull a big ugly thorn out of his side.'

Parkinson licked her lips. She could not disguise the shudder that rippled through her body. She swallowed and said, 'Now who's the one making threats?'

Bliss's smile froze in place. 'Wrong. Because, like you said: I'm only telling you how it is.'

The room fell silent. He glanced over his shoulder. Troy Parkinson's tight stare was so steely it might have cut him in two. Bliss lifted his head. 'What, you have nothing to say? You not going to leap in to defend your mummy? Is that because you're shitting yourself, or because you know everything I said is true?'

'He doesn't involve himself in my business,' Nicola said sharply, striding quickly around the desk. A raised finger pointed directly at Bliss. 'And he's learned to say fuck all to the likes of you. He's just here to witness what's said and done in this room; that's it. You leave him out of this.'

Bliss continued his lingering appraisal of her son. 'That right, Troy? You're just another pulse in the room? Observing? You proud of her, are you? Proud of the way she exploits young girls? Proud of good old Mum who has sexual slaves on the go night and day?'

'I said leave him be!'

This time the woman's voice was a shrill cry. Bliss turned to rest his gaze on her once more. She had taken a step closer to him. In response, Chandler had taken a step closer to her. 'Touched a nerve there, have I, Nicola? Troy's a mummy's boy, is he? Is that why he's hanging around lately? I mean, if he has bugger all to do with the business, I have to wonder why he's available to stand there like a spare dick at an orgy listening to you trying to defend yourself and what you are.'

Those pouty lips of hers were thinned and almost white with rage. 'I think it's time you left.'

'Don't worry, we're going. Before the sickness in the air here seeps into our bones.' Bliss turned to leave, then paused and said, 'By the way, do you fancy telling me who stepped in to fill the void when your boss got banged up? I've just realised I might have been talking to the monkey when I should've gone to the organ grinder.'

Parkinson responded with a laugh, which in turn caused her to cough: a hacking, wheezing sound. When she'd recovered, she said, 'Jesus! You really are bloody old, aren't you? Almost as ancient as those sayings of yours.'

Bliss angled his head. 'Is it you, Nicola? We know Drake kept his family out of it, and for good reason. So they needed someone expendable to shepherd the sheep. A figurehead to play at being the boss. Perhaps that person is you.'

Arms refolded, the woman's fingers began to tap against her own ribs. 'You never know. And you never will. You got lucky before; Mr Drake is not about to let that happen again.'

'Yeah. I think it is you. I can see all that ambition burning in those haggard old eyes of yours.'

'You don't know what you're talking about. You haven't got a fucking clue, you useless fucking pig!'

Bliss tutted. 'That's no way to talk to an officer of the law. I'd threaten to drag you to the nick in cuffs, only I suspect you'd enjoy it too much.'

'That's your problem, filth. You have no idea what enjoyment is these days. I bet you haven't truly enjoyed yourself since you lost that pig wife of yours – Hazel, was it? Way I hear it, she was murdered by the bloke she was fucking… that had to hurt. I do hope so. I hope it hurts you every time you take a breath.'

Bliss did not rise to the provocation. She had tried a similar tack before, and it hadn't worked then, either. She was little more than a virus, and his many confrontations with her had led to him building up an immunity against her particularly virulent strain. Instead he grinned. 'Nice try. You're deflecting. I can tell. I struck a nerve when I mentioned you running the show these days. I know it's you, Nicola. I didn't before, but I do now.'

'Prove it.' The demand emerged in a loud snarl.

Bliss nodded and continued on his way out of the door. 'I might do that. Either way… we'll be seeing you.'

FIFTEEN

THE EVENING BRIEFING DISSOLVED into a mood of vocal enthusiasm. Bliss took the opportunity to inform the team about the conversation he'd had with DS Bishop earlier in the day, by which point everybody with something to report had already said their piece.

DC Hunt, who had attended the post mortem with Phil Gratton, revealed little more than they had already surmised for themselves: death by manual strangulation, with clear indications of fingers being placed around their victim's neck, the thumbs pressing into her throat. Evidence of petechial haemorrhaging had also been noted in her eyes. Time of death had been narrowed down: Nancy Drinkwater confirmed the victim had been dead for no longer than eight hours by the time she was found. That set TOD at no earlier than 2.30am on Tuesday.

Further investigation had been carried out into their victim's background. No birth records or National Insurance number were found. Checks with the NHS had also come back negative. Immigration revealed no record of a Majidah Rassooli having entered the country, even on a student visa. She had not applied for asylum status, either. Her presence in the UK was about as illegal as it got, and had almost certainly arisen against her will. This confirmation immediately brought Bliss's attention back to Lewis Drake.

There were other traffickers – plenty of them, in fact. But this poor girl being on the books of one of Drake's escort agencies was no coincidence, to Bliss's mind. They'd brought her into the country having either abducted her themselves or paid a pittance for her. After cleaning her up and feeding her a few decent warm meals, she was put to work for them. That was her life when she was murdered.

Bliss mentioned this when it came to his turn. He said it as much for Glen Ashton's sake as anything, believing he'd be reporting back to DI Kennedy later that same evening. 'Penny and I will continue to work together with ERSOU to gather as much information as we can, but we do have to accept and understand how limited our scope will be. While none of us are dismissing the lone punter as killer theory entirely, I suggest the clean-up of her flat afterwards is key… I think Penny and I met Parkinson's daughter, by the way. What's interesting about her is that she matches the description Beaumont gave us of the young blonde who was running the show that day.'

Bishop was keen to pursue that angle, and decided it would be good to establish communication between all parties during that entire period. 'Where are we on our victim's phone?' he asked.

'Phones, plural,' Ansari reminded him. 'So… the number attached to the web page we believe to have been controlled by one of two agencies comes back to a batch purchased for cash roughly two years ago. Twenty of them were bought at King's Cross station, all on the EE network, all prepaid pay-as-you-go. None of them, as far as we can tell, are still using the SIM card they came with. The other phone is much more interesting. A Wilcy Fox device, bought on eBay, SIM free. That has to be her own phone, the one she used for her private clients. We've submitted a RIPA request to cover both devices.'

'Didn't we find a few Wiley Fox mobiles using EncroChat earlier in the year?' DC Gratton asked. 'Mainly by that drugs gang we helped bust.'

'You're bang on,' Bliss told him. 'But we're not seeing any connection between the two.'

A Netherlands-based encrypted phone system, used mainly by organised crime gangs, had been hacked, exposed and brought down following a lengthy police investigation. It was widely believed that a coalition of anarchist groups was already hard at work developing a replacement solution.

'Have somebody find out the name of Parkinson's daughter, please,' Bishop said, turning back to Ansari. 'When you have the details, add her phone and Troy's to the list. I want to know what this bunch have been up to. If they've been in communication with Majidah Rassooli, I want to know about it.'

It was good work, but they all knew how long it could take for the phone company to come through with the data. Bliss was keen to get out of the building to clear his head – but before the briefing broke up, he made sure everybody knew that Bishop was too nice a bloke to insist on being regarded as the unit's leader under such trying circumstances. Nevertheless, Bliss demanded, they should do so from that point on; Bishop was their boss unless DCI Warburton was present.

'Temporary or not,' Bliss concluded, 'Bish deserves the respect he has earned. This team has a great reputation for keeping things relatively relaxed. I know the top brass hate that, but it suits us. So I'm no longer the boss. I'm Jimmy unless formality is required. If so, it's plain old DS Bliss.'

Their DCI wanted an update afterwards, having been attending a course in Huntingdon for most of the day, so she invited

Bliss, Bishop and Chandler for a drink. As usual, she left it to Bliss to decide where they should go.

Its stone-built structure swaddled with ivy, the Botolph Arms had originally been built as two fairly large and grand separate dwellings. They had remained that way for over two centuries before being converted into a pub. Set back from the main road in pleasant grounds, the Botolph was regarded as a local family pub, its interior warm and inviting. Warburton bought them each a drink before settling down to the day's final business.

'I wanted you all here because Bish is going to have to rely on you two quite heavily in the coming days,' she said. 'I was collared by DCS Feeley as I made my way out of Hinchingbrooke; his opposite number in central Cambridge had been in touch. Apparently, Inspector Kennedy remains keen to see this case back under his wing. I have a feeling that unless this Lewis Drake angle can be confirmed within the next forty-eight hours, it'll be taken from us. Jimmy, where are we on that score?'

Bliss took a long pull of his Old Brewery ale, decided it was all right, and had another. When he replied, his tone reflected his sombre mood. 'In truth, I'm not confident. As I mentioned at the briefing, I don't regard the murder as the work of a private punter. But this eastern European agency is a possibility we can't ignore. Majidah turned out for both of them, it seems. Without further details, we can't know which of them was responsible for bringing her over here. That's about the only thing stopping me going harder at Drake's business.'

'Plus, there's the possibility that this other agency is also run by Drake's OCG,' Chandler said. 'It's been buried deeper and seemingly with no UK contact base.'

'And the NCA?' Warburton asked. 'Organised crime gangs are their bread and butter. How much use has Ashton been?'

'He's done okay,' Bliss said reluctantly. 'All that he can do, in fact. Time is the key element here: we need it, but we don't have it. Whichever way this op leans, I keep coming back to our victim having my card on her. I keep changing my mind about who did what, but if I had to guess, I'd say it was our Somalian girl who gave up hers. I don't know how the two met, nor where, but I think they did. And I think she handed the card over because she was leaving the area and decided Majidah needed it more. The most logical place for us to start trying to run down the connection between them is the home in which our Somalian girl was living before she absconded.'

'But Majidah couldn't have been living there as well, otherwise we'd have her on our system,' Bishop pointed out.

'True. But the two might have met elsewhere and struck up a relationship.'

'It's thin,' Warburton said.

'But quite possibly our only real lead to follow up on, at the moment. However, I think we should run her photo in the local papers and the TV news, asking for anybody who knew her or recognises her from somewhere to come forward. The girl had a life outside of what she did, and somehow we have to find a way to it.'

All eyes turned to their DCI. Hers fell upon Bishop. 'Do you want to take that on, Bish? For reasons we're all familiar with, Jimmy is no longer considered for media briefings. As DI and deputy SIO on this, however, it's something you ought to handle. It'd go down well when the time comes for you to take the step up for real.'

Bishop looked uncomfortable, and Bliss thought he knew why. 'I think Bish might need some clear guidelines as to what his response should be if my demotion comes up. This is our biggest case since then, and I don't see how it won't get a mention.'

'Jimmy's right,' Bishop said. 'I'd want to stonewall them in the event they ask about it, or my reaction to it.'

'We're only talking local media at this stage,' Warburton reminded them. 'The *Telegraph*, *Hunts Post* and *Cambridge News* and possibly the *Independent*. Them plus *Look East*, *Anglia* and *Cambridgeshire Live*.'

'It only takes one question, boss.'

She regarded Bishop for a moment, then nodded. 'Blanket "no comment" on the subject. We'll put you together with our own media staff – they'll settle your nerves. To make it easier, we'll have press releases rather than a briefing for the newspapers, together with the NCA security photo. You'll speak to the TV people only. A media officer will be with you at all times.'

Bliss noticed how reluctant his colleague was. It seemed like another aspect of the job Bishop did not want. That it went hand-in-hand with a promotion to DI was something he would have to accept. It was expected of him, and this would be his first taste of that level of scrutiny.

'Perhaps I should advise Bish how best to deal with the media?' he suggested.

That elicited the laughter he'd hoped to inspire. Bishop's large frame juddered as he chuckled at the thought. Taking advice from Bliss on how to deal with journalists would be like accepting peacekeeping guidance from ISIS.

They called it a night after the one drink, and Chandler drove Bliss home. As she pulled in to his turning, she said, 'Can I ask you something personal?'

He choked back a laugh. 'Since when have I ever been able to stop you? I don't know why you even bother asking.'

'Just to be polite.'

'What is it this time, Pen?'

'I've been thinking about you and… ladies of the night?'

'What d'you mean by that?'

'Well, there was your... relationship with Connie Rawlings during your first posting here, for one thing. Not that I have anything against women like that, nor what they do. But I know you grew attached to her during that investigation, and I've also heard you shutting down negative conversations where others like her are concerned. Now this young woman's murder has clearly affected you, and it makes me wonder what it is about hookers that has you polishing your armour.'

Bliss said nothing immediately. Connie Rawlings had been a witness; she'd also been a prostitute. In a moment of human weakness, animal instinct, and hunger for instant gratification and comfort on both their parts, they had gone to bed together. It was only the one time, and their connection had not contributed to her eventual murder, which occurred because of what she knew about the main victim in a case Bliss was running at the time. Yet somehow the correlation between that memory and another from further back in his past felt like a rapid thrust to the heart with a stiletto blade – or perhaps even a heel.

Chandler must have sensed his immediate discomfort. She put a hand on his arm and told him it was okay, that he should ignore her question and forget she had ever asked it.

But Bliss shook his head, ready to tell his partner something he had never told another living soul. 'I once had a snout who happened to be a prostitute. She fed me information, but she was also a friend. Her name was Elaine. I tried on many occasions to talk her out of being on the game altogether, but she wouldn't hear of it; said it was all she was good for. In her mind, it was either that or knock out some kids and live on the dole for the rest of her life. She always did have a low opinion of herself. In the end, shortly after I made DC, the best I could do was to speak with Vice and help fix her up as an escort with an agency. Get her off the streets, give her some protection. Stability. I like to think I got through to her.'

'So what happened?'

'A couple of days after we last spoke, maybe twenty-four hours before I could have sealed the deal, she got into the wrong car with the wrong man.'

Chandler closed her eyes and screwed up her face. 'Oh, Jimmy. I'm so sorry.'

'It's okay. It's desperately sad, but not one of those things I blame myself for. I did all I could. All that she would allow me to do. Just sheer bad luck and piss-poor timing.'

'Did you get him for it?'

Bliss nodded. 'Some sad loser. Middle-aged man with a wife and kids. It was his first time with a pro. He panicked, convinced himself it was a setup and that he was going to be blackmailed. Told us he couldn't allow his family to know what he'd done.'

'So murder was a better option?'

'Sometimes it is to these twisted fucks.'

'That explains a lot,' Chandler said after a lengthy pause. 'About you, I mean. And somehow it doesn't surprise me in the least.'

'Yeah. Wears you down over time, though, Pen. Maybe one day you reach the point where you become a tiny little nub, and the next you disappear inside yourself altogether.'

'You're beginning to worry me, Jimmy. The way you talk sometimes.'

He laughed and shook his head. 'Don't worry about me. I'm not the kind to do something stupid.'

'You what? You do something stupid at least twice a day.'

'Fair play. But not that stupid. Not what you're thinking.'

Bliss knew his partner didn't want to leave it there, but they had gone as far as he was willing to take matters for one evening. Before exiting her car, he did leave Chandler with one final thought.

'How naïve was I to have ever imagined that placing Elaine in the hands of an escort agency was in any way saving her?'

'You can't know that it wouldn't have done, Jimmy. Plus, it doesn't sound as if you had a great deal of choice in the matter.'

'Perhaps not. But we know how these girls are treated. They're as good as modern-day slaves, with no way out other than down or… or out. I think about what happened to our victim, and yet she was in precisely the situation I was happy to put my friend into.'

'Which we still know is better than walking the streets,' Chandler assured him. 'You did the best you could. Or, at least, you tried to. If she wouldn't quit, it seems to me you at least showed you cared.'

Bliss sighed as he climbed out. Nodded. 'I hope she knew that, Pen. I really do.'

He was surprised to find the house empty; he checked his phone and found he had missed a call from Emily while he was in the pub. He grabbed a bottle of Anchor Steam from the fridge, slid open the door leading to the garden, and stepped back out into the cold night air. It was about time to switch on the pond warming device to keep his koi happy. He drained half his beer before listening to the voicemail Emily had left.

Afterwards, he deleted the message and leaned back against the house, eyes on his fish. A tough day at work on too little sleep had left Emily feeling exhausted, so she was going to go to her own home and crash out there. She'd sounded a little sullen, but that could have been tiredness. They had no permanent arrangement as to when she came over or where she slept, so this was not unusual. The fact of this message coming the day after she inadvertently met one of his exes was not necessarily relevant.

Bliss put on a Guster CD. Their *Lost and Gone Forever* album was his favourite, though he had been promising himself to put together a mixed CD or MP3 collection for the car. First track up was 'What You Wish For', and Bliss felt the pull of the lyrics swarming around inside his head; the lines about getting what you deserve and sweeping secrets under the bed got caught up most of all. They remained with him even when the second track came in. Were the secrets he was keeping about to get him what he deserved? Would Neil Watson prove to be the final nail in the coffin of his career? And perhaps even the wedge that drove him and Emily apart for good?

He was out of Anchor Steam, so had to settle for a bottle of Stella next time around. Emily had made sure he had fresh food in the fridge and cupboards, but he wasn't in the mood to make dinner for himself. He considered calling her, but decided she probably needed the space. He thought that was the real reason she had decided to go home, and wondered what that meant for them both.

When the CD moved on to 'All The Way Up to Heaven', Bliss fastened on the lyrics once more. He regarded himself as an atheist; perhaps even an anti-theist. Certainly he had no time for heaven, the great beyond or the comfort of any light at the end of a tunnel. For Wile E. Coyote, that had only ever become an express train about to mow him down, and Bliss gave the concept no greater weight than a cartoon. But if one day he was eventually proven wrong, he hoped that along with his father and wife he would also find his old friend Elaine there waiting for him.

SIXTEEN

THE MOMENT HE ENTERED the incident room the next morning, Bliss was hailed by Carolyn Miller. He'd picked up a tray of coffees from a roadside vendor close to home; their cardboard container was yielding to the weight, making the task of carrying them more difficult than it needed to be. He set them down on the empty desk next to Miller's, relieved not to have spilled the cups everywhere in the process.

'Help yourself,' he told her. 'There's black or there's white. That's about as fancy as my orders get.'

Miller thanked him and took one marked with a fat W. She seemed a little reticent after summoning him across the room, so Bliss encouraged her to tell him what was on her mind.

'I hope you don't mind me injecting myself into your case, sir,' she said, 'only I noticed something peculiar when I was putting the exhibits away last night. I double-checked as soon as I got in this morning, and felt I had to say something.'

Bliss gave what he hoped passed for a grin, though his early morning attempts were often mistaken for grimaces. 'Well, now you have to tell me, don't you? Can't leave me dangling like that, Carolyn.'

She gave him a grateful nod. 'It might be nothing, but I'd kick myself if I didn't tell you. It's our victim's clothes, sir. They're all wrong.'

Curious, Bliss nodded for her to continue. 'In what way?'

'The sizes, sir. Whenever we have a new major crime, I tend to familiarise myself with the victims – I can't help myself. I've seen the photos of ours in this case, and she was a tiny little thing – much smaller than me. So you see, while the bra might be about right, nothing else is. I'd say our victim is a size six. However, the knickers in evidence are a size ten, the stockings are way too long, and the dress is a fourteen. If she'd been wearing it, you'd have all noticed right away. It's way too big for her, sir. It would swamp her. I don't think the clothes we have are hers.'

Intrigued by this and immediately realising its importance, Bliss asked Miller to open her desk drawer and pull out all the bagged items. When she reached the shoes, Miller paused, running an eye over them. 'I didn't think to check earlier, but these look too big to me as well, sir.'

Bliss grabbed a pair of nitrile gloves from an open box and wriggled his hands into them with some difficulty. When they were pulled tight and he was able to flex his fingers properly, he opened each bag in turn and spread their contents out on a nearby table. Since first stepping inside the forensic tent in the early hours of Wednesday morning, he had been wondering why the clothes had been left in a neat pile close to the body. His mind tumbled through the possibilities, but this did not sit right with any of the scenarios they had considered so far. He began to feel that familiar mixture of excitement and trepidation lodging in his stomach, together with the need to take extra breaths.

According to its label, the dress was sold by Dorothy Perkins. The name sounded familiar to him, so he thought it was probably a high street brand. Bliss asked Carolyn to stand up. When she got to her feet, he held the dress up against her.

'You think the size on the tag is right?' he asked her.

'I'd say so, yes. This could be two whole sizes bigger than me, so I think this is a genuine fourteen.'

Next came the shoes. The brand name looked to have been on the inside heel, but had been worn away. But when he turned the shoe over, he saw on the instep a figure and some lettering. On closer inspection, it was a sticker that had not been peeled off. It told him the shoe was a size seven, made in China from manmade materials.

'We can get an accurate measurement from pathology,' he said. 'But a seven would be pretty big for a girl as petite as our victim, wouldn't you say?'

Carolyn nodded emphatically. 'Absolutely, sir. They also look to be a wide fit, which again would suggest they belonged to somebody much larger. Perhaps the owner of the dress.'

To Miller, the bra still looked as if it could be right. Bliss had no clue. However, as one of the cups had also contained the two business cards tucked away inside the lining, he had to ask searching questions about their find. Until this juncture they'd had no reason to ask whether their victim was the one who had secreted the cards away, but it was now a matter for urgent re-examination.

The exhibits officer had already given her opinion regarding the size of the lacy red crotchless knickers. Bliss had another question. 'The bra and knickers don't match. I don't mean to be indelicate, Carolyn, but… I'm right in saying that's quite common, yes?'

She smiled. Nodded. 'Yes, sir.'

'For a regular woman going about her regular day,' he added, thinking out loud. He recalled the escort agency photographs online. 'But not for an escort about to meet her client. Sorry, I'm rambling. I can't be sure what that tells us.'

So wrapped up in the moment was he that Bliss had failed to notice colleagues drifting into the incident room. Behind him, Chandler cleared her throat and said, 'What have I told you about messing around with ladies' underwear, Jimmy?'

Bliss started, dragged out of wherever his mind had wandered. He turned, saw the team eyeballing him, and gave an embarrassed smile. 'To wait until it's been worn at least half a dozen times without being washed before sniffing it?' he shot back.

Chandler's look was one of disgust. 'At the very least. So, what's on your mind?'

'Sorry about that. I was miles away. Let's begin at the beginning. Starting with handing out these coffees.'

***

Bliss assembled the team, which today included both DCI Warburton and Detective Superintendent Fletcher. He and the DSI exchanged nods as she made her way over to her usual spot at the back of the room. Prior to the slow slicing case, Fletcher had been seeking promotion. She'd missed out on the job at nearby Hinchingbrooke, which would have given her overall responsibility for Peterborough and the teams at Thorpe Wood. Bliss still wondered if his behaviour had cost her that step up, or if she was merely biding her time. He hoped it was the latter; he liked having her in that position, but not if she was stuck there against her will, with him the reason for it.

'We have a surprising turn of events,' he said, kicking off the briefing. 'Due to the eagle eye and great instincts of Carolyn Miller, our exhibits officer for Operation Phoenix, we have another piece of the puzzle. Only trouble is, this one doesn't help us, as far as I can tell. In fact, in some ways it takes us further away from completing the entire picture.'

Bliss went on to explain their findings. 'I know some of you arrived at the tail end of our musings at the time,' he said. 'But it's important that we are all on the same page here. So far we have been working on two main theories: firstly, that our victim, Majidah Rassooli, was murdered for plying her trade on the side; and secondly, that she was strangled to death by a punter. Those were our order of priority in respect of actions so far. I won't argue if anybody suggests we came up with the theories and tried to run the investigation along those lines. Yes, it would be great if we could do things the other way around, but every so often you get something more obvious. This looked like one of those cases.'

'Are you now saying it isn't, sir?' Hunt asked.

'No. Not quite. I'm saying this fresh evidence has thrown a bloody big rusty spanner into the works. We were thinking along the lines that one of the agencies Majidah worked for had discovered she was hooking on the side. Stripping her naked and piling up her clothes didn't sit quite right, but we seldom know all the circumstances. I never liked the alternative theory, of a punter who got out of hand. It felt too contrived, too much work afterwards. The location never quite did it for me, either.'

'Which makes this odd matter of the clothing being the wrong size even more peculiar,' DCI Warburton said.

'Precisely, boss. That would appear not to gel with either scenario. So I'm wondering what we've overlooked.'

'Are you suggesting this operation rolls back on investigating the agencies, DS Bliss?'

'I'm saying I think we have to pause and reflect, boss. Instead of setting aside the pieces that don't fit our hypotheses, let's examine them more closely.'

'Such as?'

Bliss ran a hand over his face and brushed over the tiny scar on his forehead. 'The location, for one. Why would a punter meet her or take her out onto the chalk pits on a chilly autumn evening? It was unseasonably cold and frosty that night, remember. For that matter, why would she go? I'm not overlooking the fact that he could have picked her up in his car, killed her elsewhere and taken her to the pits afterwards. Only, that doesn't tie in with her flat being cleaned out the following day.'

'Which is where the escort agencies come back in,' Bishop said. He was standing alongside Bliss, and had been happy to take a back seat until he had something to offer. 'The location of the dumping ground still doesn't make a lot of sense to us, but her being murdered by her agency bosses is a better fit with everything else, other than the clothing.'

'So the chalk pits remain an anomaly we can't yet explain,' Bliss continued. 'For either scenario. Her body being left naked isn't unusual in itself, but we were puzzled as to why the clothes had been left close by. That was another angle we'd not been able to work out, although to be fair, we haven't yet had the time to focus on it. But in being drawn back to them, I'm finding the whole thing stranger still. The clothes being hers would be one thing, something we'd still have to question. But some or all of them not being hers is bizarre.'

Bishop scratched the back of his head. 'I have to admit, this aspect alone makes me think we've been wrong on both counts so far. It felt staged before – now it feels too staged. And these different sized clothes mean something. I'm with Jimmy. I think we need to take a step back and start looking at this again, from the beginning and from every possible angle. What seemed logical to us from the start still might throw up the answers we're looking for, but I think we need to fill in the missing pieces of this smaller puzzle before we can move onto the larger picture.'

'Where will you begin second time around?' DSI Fletcher asked. She seldom – if ever – spoke at briefings, and her asking a question was rarer still.

Bliss kept quiet. This was Bishop's moment. Time for the big man to step up and take charge of his team.

'I think we start by scrubbing the boards, ma'am,' Bishop said after a slight pause. 'We piece the investigation together again, only this time with greater focus on the clothing. As a team we need to discuss what we think this means.'

'And what does it mean to you?'

Bishop shuffled uneasily from foot to foot and wrapped one meaty fist in his other hand. 'I'd love to have an answer for you, ma'am. But like I said, we're clearing the boards and starting afresh. It would be wrong to throw wild guesses at this new piece of information. We need to put our heads together and thrash out ideas. It's what we do. I've learned that from the best, and it's a process that works.'

'It doesn't appear to have worked for the past couple of days, DS Bishop. Days that are now lost to us.'

Bliss inwardly winced. Fletcher was not giving him an easy ride. It was her way of testing his mettle. He wasn't worried; Bishop had the right stuff.

'That's the way these investigations sometimes go in the early stages, ma'am,' his friend said with conviction. 'We're still gathering information and evidence. Each piece that comes in can cause you to alter course. I'd say the clothing size issue is a significant one, and when something like that happens you have to evaluate it carefully. Taking a step back to reconsider is never a bad thing. It can clear the mind, sharpen focus. Above all, it can correct thinking.'

Fletcher's lips twitched. 'And where does your thinking tell you to start?'

Bishop was ready for her. 'First action will be to run this new information through HOLMES, ma'am. So far we've focussed all our efforts on the victim, which was absolutely the right thing to do. I think from this stage in the proceedings we have to start looking harder at the killer. Because I'm getting the sense that this might not be his first time.'

SEVENTEEN

THE HOME OFFICE LARGE Major Enquiry System had been around for thirty-five years. Now into its second incarnation, the additional features of HOLMES II allowed users working serious crimes to interrogate the database using relatively unstructured queries. In this instance, Bishop had asked for the operator to seek information on similar crimes, using a number of keywords associated with their findings. It wasn't the most reliable of systems, but it usually got the job done.

A uniformed constable by the name of Pickford had been selected for HOLMES duty, and he came rushing over to interrupt the conversation the Major Crimes team were an hour into. He flashed a wad of yellow paper, whose colour told them this was the result of the data search.

'Look at the first page,' he said, barely able to contain his excitement. 'The list of perfect matches.'

Bishop took the printouts from him and set the top page face up on the desk. The others angled themselves to get a clear view.

FEMALE > BETWEEN 17 AND 25
MANUAL STRANGULATION

SEX WORKER
FOUND NAKED
OPEN LAND > SOC OR BODY DUMP
TREE > BODY FOUND BENEATH OR CLOSE TO
CLOTHES > FOUND CLOSE BY
CLOTHES > INCORRECT SIZES FOR VICTIM
BODY DISINFECTED AND WASHED CLEAN POST MORTEM

Bliss recognised the silence that followed: a moment captured in time in which everybody present acknowledged the significance of the find. A seismic step forward in an investigation that warranted celebration, yet at the same time was tinged with apprehension and weighed down by experience and understanding.

He had investigated a number of major crimes during which multiple murders had been committed. The majority were carried out for reasons the investigators were capable of understanding: revenge, jealousy, hatred, or even financial reward or some other inducement. True serial killers, those whose motives were psychological as opposed to rational or emotional, were much rarer. His last one had been his first case after returning to the city. Prior to that, he'd been involved in only one other.

Everything he read on that yellow sheet of paper screamed as loud as any voice, telling him they were confronting a serial. Pausing to take a step back so they could move on had not merely provided the necessary clarity they had sought; it had completely shattered their original line of thinking as if it were as fragile as glass. In its place had stepped forward something monstrous.

The name of Malcolm Thompson continued to burn in Bliss's mind like the dying embers of a bonfire. A man whose psychopathy arose from a mind that had been twisted and tortured out of all recognition first by his equally murderous father, and then by a mother so wicked and callous it was impossible to fathom what dark imaginings she was capable of. His younger victims had all been left alive following their rape ordeals; the older women, he had brutally and ritualistically butchered.

The eerie silence broke as everybody seemed to talk at once. Bliss raised his hands to quieten them all down. His throat felt tight and dry as he spoke. 'Listen up. Those of you who were on Operations Observer and Limestone may think you've already worked serial killings, but you'd be wrong about that. Pavl Savic killed a number of people, but the man was a gun for hire, trained to kill in exchange for money. As for our slow slicing case a short while ago – again, while there were multiple victims, genuine and understandable reasons lay at the root of them. Believe me, this is going to be different. Ask those who worked the Thompson case, if you need some insight. There's a difference, requiring a completely different mindset. These people don't think the way we do. Their process is way out of our scope. But don't worry about it – be thankful. Believe me, it will energise you and have you using different parts of your brain.'

During the ensuing silence as his words sank in, Superintendent Fletcher burst into the room, having earlier returned to her own office. She apologised for interrupting their meeting, but said she had some urgent news for the team.

'Your HOLMES search threw up a red flag,' she said, panting a little. She paused to draw in a deep breath before continuing. 'I took a call from the Yard. Any matches you found were originally entered into the system by them. I'm sure you realise what this means. My opposite number informed me they have three unsolved cases on their hands, all matching this same MO. When the murders appeared to stop, they assumed their man had either died, fled the country, or was perhaps even banged up somewhere. It seems likely that he simply moved out of London and bided his time before selecting his next victim. As you might expect, the Yard are keen to discuss Operation Phoenix with us.'

Peterborough's Major Crimes team was accustomed to working with other units and authority areas. Tighter budgets, fewer staff, and combined computer databases had inevitably led to a more collaborative policing method, which continued to evolve. There was no longer any room for jurisdictional squabbling. Bliss was glad of this, as he had always regarded it as counterproductive. Working recent cases with the Lincolnshire and Wiltshire authorities, in addition to the Met and the City of London police, the team had achieved successful outcomes. In each situation, Thorpe Wood had taken the lead. Bliss suspected that would not be the case this time.

He realised nobody was speaking. When he glanced up, all faces were turned to him. DS Bishop had not taken on the role of responding to the Superintendent's news, and they were both waiting for Bliss to say something.

'Sorry,' he said, flustered. 'I suppose the experience does rest with me. I'm still trying to wrap my head around the shift in momentum. When I came in here this morning, we were going to look for a way in to Lewis Drake's escort business, and now we apparently have a serial on our hands.'

'I reckon it's thrown us all, Jimmy,' Bishop said. 'I worked the Thompson case with you, but I'm not sure I'm ready to lead something of this magnitude.'

Bliss shrugged. 'We all experience our firsts, Bish. Thompson was only my second. I'm happy to stick to you like glue for the rest of the investigation, but I think you're more than able to handle running the op from our end.'

'From our end?' This from Warburton, whose forehead creased quizzically.

Bliss nodded. 'This is going to be the Met's case. In fact, we'll do well to have any involvement at all. Remember, this was only ours because of the Lewis Drake connection. If the Met believe there's nothing to that, they may decide to work it with DI Kennedy in Cambridge instead.'

This gave rise to groans all round. Bliss slapped a smile on his face and hushed them. 'Have a bit of faith, people. I'm not giving up on the link with Drake. This girl was one of his, remember. Our new intel suggests he probably wasn't involved with her murder, but if whoever is running the show on his behalf is looking at their investment being wiped out, they're not going to be happy about it. We need to be prepared for some blowback. Also, our killer has to have targeted Majidah, and for all we know, that could still have happened through the agency. It's doubtful, but neither DI Kennedy nor whoever the Met have running things at their end need to know that.'

Bliss paused, realising why he had felt free to make that statement. 'Which reminds me – anybody know why Glen Ashton isn't here?'

'I think he was going to his ERSOU office first thing, boss,' Phil Gratton offered up. 'Chasing down something more solid than he thought we were coming up with.'

'That's in our favour, then.' Bliss looked to DSI Fletcher. 'Ma'am. I take it the Met officer in charge of their case wants to meet with us? If so, are we going there or are they coming here?'

'That was one of the things I came down here to tell you. They're already on their way.'

Bliss breathed out, his heart thumping behind his ribs. 'More good news. That gives us time to prepare for their visit. I know this goes against the grain, but I don't have a problem with them taking the lead on this. They have three victims to our one, so they must have a lot more intel and evidence to share with us than we have for them. But I'm buggered if I'm going to see us elbowed out of the way only for Cambridge to step in. We've worked this case, not them. It might only have been for a couple of days so far, but those are our man-hours and our sleepless nights. If everyone agrees, I want us to split our efforts: one half of the team works the new information, the other stays on Drake and his seedy little empire.'

'Is that simply a tactic to keep us involved or a genuine avenue to explore?' Fletcher asked.

'It's both, ma'am. I'm not big on coincidences, but I accept they occur. Our victim being one of Drake's girls might well be one of those curious things that happens every now and then. On the other hand, until we've pursued the matter to its logical conclusion we won't know for certain. I think that keeps us in the mix, and might still lead to something we can explore further.'

Fletcher uncrossed her arms and nodded. 'You have a green light from me.' She turned to Warburton. 'Diane?'

The team's DCI gave her own nod. 'I'm happy with that. How about you, Bish?'

He responded without pause for reflection. 'I think it's the perfect strategy.'

'Good. And you'll take point on this?'

Bishop drew himself up to his full height. His barrel of a chest rose and fell. 'Of course,' he said. 'Myself, DC Ansari and DC Gratton will focus our attention on the clothing, the intel we have in from HOLMES, and the killer. I'll put DC Hunt with DS Chandler and DS Bliss to continue working the Lewis Drake angle, together with our victim.'

Hunt groaned theatrically. 'Why am I always the last to be picked or the first to be handed over to the other team? I feel like the fat kid in school at playtime.' Everybody laughed, including

Hunt himself. 'It must be my winning personality,' he said. 'I have too much charisma, and you bosses don't want to be outshone.'

Bishop nodded enthusiastically. 'He's right, you know. Sunglasses on, everyone. John has his disposition set to stun.'

When the resulting laughter died down, Bliss wandered over to Hunt. He patted the DC on the back and said, 'Just for that, the cakes are on you.'

A raucous cheer went up and there were wide smiles all round.

Fletcher pushed herself away from the desk she'd been leaning against. 'Excellent,' she said, seemingly delighted with what she'd seen and heard. 'I'd say Majidah Rassooli is in good hands.'

EIGHTEEN

AVING BEEN TOLD THE Met contingent would make the journey in no less than two hours, Bliss had made excellent use of the time. He first questioned DC Ansari about EE and the apparent code written on the back of the black business card. She had spoken to three different people on the tech side of the company, each of whom was confident it had nothing to do with them.

'John did have a good thought, though,' Ansari said. She glanced across at DC Hunt and nodded for him to continue.

Hunt cleared his throat first. 'My brother was always showing me these games hidden away inside software. Microsoft Excel was a particular favourite. They were known as Easter eggs. I could be entirely wrong, but EE could stand for Easter egg. I say that because the rest of the letters and numbers on the card could easily relate to a spreadsheet. A1 is the first cell reference in every sheet. And I'm guessing if you type Enter into that cell, the Easter egg pops up in cell DP575.'

He looked at Bliss expectantly.

Bliss gave him a blank look in return. 'John, you had me right up to the last bit. Are you saying DP575 could be one of these cell references? I don't think I've ever seen anything more than a Y or Z column.'

Hunt's face broke out into a smile, clearly happy to be on solid ground. 'Oh, yes. You can have over sixteen thousand columns, and more than a million rows. Sir, I could be completely wrong, but I've seen these Easter eggs in action for myself, and this could be one.'

'To what purpose?'

'I have no idea. Usually they're games, inserted by the developers. But in theory it could be anything. Excel '97 had a basic flight simulator hidden away inside it.'

Chandler was shaking her head, not appearing to follow the thread. 'Hold on a minute,' she said. 'You said these Easter egg things were small programs built into the software. How could some code added by a developer – somewhere in America, presumably – possibly have any connection to our case?'

'I was wondering that myself,' Bliss said.

Hunt shook his head. 'Those are official Easter eggs – as you rightly say, built in during the development stage. But as a user you can also create your own Easter eggs using the language of the software itself. They can all be programmed to do certain tasks.'

'So how do we go about finding it?'

'Ah.' His happy expression fell away. 'We'd need to find the right sheet in the right file. Perhaps it's one that has some connection to the escort agency on the card – Dark Desires. An agency which, by the way, we've yet to locate. As far as I can tell, it doesn't even have a website.'

Bliss blew out his cheeks. It was a bright idea, but one that ultimately left them no closer to discovering additional information. He clapped the DC on the arm. 'It's a good thought, John. Possibly inspired. I'm not sure how we tie any of it together, though. Or even if it's associated with our victim. But we have to assume both cards are important somehow. One was clearly on her person so that she could get hold of me if she was in trouble; that didn't work out too well for her. But she also has to have kept this other card tucked away for a reason.'

'Do you want me to stay on it?'

'As far as possible, John, yes. You and Gul are both good at running down this sort of thing. But let's say you're right about this Easter egg stuff. To find the spreadsheet, I think we first have to find a website for this Dark Desires place.'

Ansari looked doubtful.

'What is it, Gul?' Bliss asked. You think otherwise?'

'I can't know for sure, sir – none of us can at the moment. But if there's no obvious website to be found – and so far there isn't – maybe it's not findable using standard measures. Dark Desires might exist only on the dark web.' She nodded excitedly. 'That might be it, sir. And if that's the case, it could work the exact opposite way to how you thought. It could be that the Easter egg leads to the website, not the other way around.'

Bliss didn't know enough about the dark and often lawless realms of the web to feel particularly confident, so he asked Ansari for a quick primer. She explained how sites on the dark web could not be reached using a standard search engine like Google. They were designed and configured specifically to work outside of the domain name system, and without DNS the search engines were unable to find these hidden addresses. If names existed at all, they were usually identifiable as a string of random letters and numbers. Otherwise the sites could be found only if you knew their precise IP address.

Bliss stopped her there. 'Bear with me, Gul. Believe it or not, I came into the job around the same time as computers did, but I'm strictly a user and not an enthusiast. I use the tool in front of me for the job in hand, and have no interest otherwise.'

'I get that. I have no interest in koi fish.' She smiled at him and he returned one. 'Sir, all you need to understand is that these websites are hidden away. To get to them, you either need to know the exact address or use a specific piece of software. TOR is the most popular, but even that's not adequate for the deepest, darkest web. For those sites you have to know the address in full, because you can't search for it.'

'TOR?' Bliss spread his hands as if completely lost.

'It's a specially designed browser called The Onion Router that not only helps to conceal your IP address, and therefore your identity while browsing, but also provides access to the lower reaches of the dark web.'

'And you think this Easter egg thing avoids all that and provides direct access to this Dark Desires site. Or, at least, there's a chance it could do?'

'It's pure guesswork on my part. But if John is right about the Easter egg, then yes.'

'But educated guesswork?'

'Yes, sir.'

Bliss nodded, though he still did not fully appreciate the complexities. 'That'll do for me. Keep at it, you two. Meanwhile, I think Pen and I will pay the delightful Nicola yet another visit. I'm sure she'll be thrilled to see us again. Good work, Gul. You too, John.'

His rank allowed him the freedom to ask, instruct, or order a constable, yet doing so with Ansari and Hunt while not being their overall boss felt strange. Two months into his probation, and it was starting to wear him down rather than improve matters. He left the pair to it and went to find Chandler.

***

Bliss and Chandler visited Parkinson for a third time in as many days. To Bliss's way of thinking, silences spoke volumes, while words were often telling, but for him there was nothing quite like staring into a person's eyes when you mentioned something unexpected. Eyes never lie; they either say nothing or they tell the truth. Experience told Bliss this, and it had seldom failed him.

Following their usual exchange of unpleasantries, Parkinson immediately went on the defensive. 'This is harassment,' she insisted. 'Our solicitors will hear about it.'

Bliss grinned. The accusation was becoming something of a theme. 'Wind your scrawny neck in, Nicola. We're here to ask a single question, that's all.'

'Just the one? You promise? Because I have legitimate business to attend to, and your presence here is starting to fuck me right off.'

'I give you my word,' Bliss said, hand raised as if swearing on the Bible.

He took the ensuing silence as tacit agreement, and went straight for the jugular. 'Tell me about Dark Desires, Nicola.'

'You tell me!' she snapped at him. 'I bet you've got a few of your own.'

Parkinson had immediately got to her feet when he and Chandler entered the room, and had remained standing. He stared directly into her eyes, and in them he saw the flicker he'd hoped for. His instincts had been right; if the website was lurking on the dark web, as Ansari had suggested, there was no doubt in his mind that it was owned by the Lewis Drake organisation. Even if Nicola herself had nothing to do with the site or what it offered, she was at the very least aware of its existence.

'The Dark Desires website, Nicola. What's your involvement?'

'Never heard of it.'

'Oh, come on. You can do better than that. A woman like you, with your reputation? I'd be surprised if you didn't own a piece of the action, but even if it's a rival outfit you must know all about it.'

'And I just told you otherwise. Please don't call me a liar.'

Parkinson's expression had completely altered, and her voice had turned low and threatening. Neither her son nor her daughter were anywhere to be seen on this occasion, but Igor was there and his massive presence seemed to fill the room. Bliss had made himself aware of the man's position at all times, and he checked again after Parkinson's attitude hardened. He saw through her as if she were transparent, but he also knew she would not budge. As for Igor, he seemed unmoved by anything he had heard so far.

'Nicola, please don't take me for a complete fool,' Bliss said. 'Maybe you don't own or run the site – that's fair enough, though I do think it has something to do with Drake – but I won't call you a liar if you don't mug me off. I know you've heard of Dark Desires. It's obvious by your reaction. So why not tell me what you do know? That's all I'm asking.'

For the briefest of moments, he thought he might have won her over. But eventually she pointed towards the door. 'See yourselves out, Detectives. And, fair warning: if you come back again, my associate here might not be so accommodating.'

***

The Met sent two men. Detective Superintendent Cliff Hammersley and Detective Chief Inspector Shaun Attwood both wore navy suits, crisp white shirts and blue ties, though that was where any resemblance between them ended. Hammersley was of mixed race, average height with an upright stance, and Bliss put him somewhere in his fifties. His whiter shade of pale DCI had to stoop when he entered the meeting room, and had the clean-cut, round-cheeked face of a child, making it impossible to estimate his age.

By the time they arrived at Thorpe Wood, DSI Fletcher had already gathered together Warburton, Bishop, Chandler, and Bliss around the table. Having driven over from Bedford, Glen Ashton sat with them. It gave the home team the advantage in terms of numbers, but it was more than that: these were the investigators currently running the show. It was important to let the Met officers see that for themselves.

His fleeting visit into the heart of darkness played on Bliss's mind as the meeting with the Met detectives began following a rapid exchange of greetings and introductions. In front of each person seated around the large table was a lever arch folder of information compiled over the past ninety minutes. It contained details obtained from the Met, as well as those provided by Thorpe Wood and Cambridge.

It was only when DSI Hammersley pulled out a pair of reading glasses that Bliss remembered his own. He'd been carrying them around for a few weeks, forgetting they were in his jacket pocket. This was not a file he could take away with him and read at his leisure, so he quietly took out his own spectacles and slipped them on.

'Operation Challenge has been running for two months,' Hammersley began, his own folder still closed. 'During that time we've investigated three murders so similar to your own that we must consider them to have been committed by the same hands. I confess we did not identify the pattern until victim number three, but I think the reasons for that will become apparent. In your pack you should have a full set of notes, photographs, witness accounts, pathology reports, and of course the case file as it stands. There's also a map identifying the location of each body dump. Any questions before we start looking through this material?'

Bliss had one. He removed his glasses before speaking. Nobody seemed to notice. 'Sir, you mentioned the "body dump" with confidence. We've been uncertain about this specific element. Lividity patterns clearly tell us our victim was moved after she was killed, but we've not been able to rule out the possibility that she was strangled close to where she was found at the chalk pits.'

Hammersley nodded. 'DS Bliss, right? Yes, we have that confidence because we know something you do not – something it took us a while to bring into the puzzle. You see, we are reasonably confident that each of our three victims was held for between ten and fourteen days prior to being murdered.'

The information came as a complete surprise, but Bliss was already seeing how their own case conformed to that pattern. Majidah Rassooli's landlord had mentioned something about his tenant not being seen for a while. Nicola Parkinson had also confirmed that the young girl had not worked for them in many days.

'That makes sense of some of the information we have,' he said. 'I suspect that's exactly what happened in our case, too.'

'And yet it leaves us with a considerable gap to fill,' Hammersley continued. 'We'd established that victims two and three both had to have been taken within twenty-four hours of the previous kill. But there's a much longer gap between our last victim and your first: a good few weeks. The question is, did he kill in the meantime, and are there other victims' bodies yet to be discovered?'

'And if so, where?' Bliss said.

'What do you mean by that, Sergeant Bliss?' DCI Attwood asked. Bliss was impressed at how easily his boyish face became stern. Narrowing his deep-set eyes gave the man a menacing appearance.

'I mean we shouldn't automatically assume that what we initially thought of as our first victim is actually our second, third or fourth. If there are other victims, they could be your fourth, fifth or sixth.'

The two Met officers exchanged glances, and DSI Hammersley took up the conversation. 'That's actually something we've considered at length. In fact, we've thought of little else since our man appeared to go quiet. We were counting the days in the end, because we were getting nowhere finding him. Forensically he's pretty clean, although we have fibres and soil samples and perhaps even shoeprint casts. Not a single witness, though. That alone tells us how careful he is, how much planning goes into what he does. So, yes, it's entirely possible that we've missed other murders in London.'

'Although it's highly unlikely,' Attwood added sharply. 'Mainly because of the MO; he leaves the victims where they can be found. It's unlikely that this could have happened again inside the Metropolitan area without us being aware of it. Cliff and I discussed this very point on the drive up, and we think it's much more likely that he struck elsewhere. Until today you thought your own victim was a one-off, and it's quite possible that another area thought the exact same thing. We're having checks run in neighbouring counties first, before spreading the enquiry nationwide.'

'Presumably they will have had about as much luck as we both have in finding evidence that might lead to our killer,' Superintendent Fletcher said. 'So while other murders would explain the void between the known victims, they're unlikely to take our investigation any further.'

'Will any of this pooled knowledge?' Bishop asked. He looked around the table. 'I think we can agree a connection has been established. But the Met's nothing, added to our own nothing, surely still leaves us with nothing.'

'And there's always the possibility of the gap between victims being explained by something else entirely,' Chandler said. 'A short stay in hospital. Being held on remand. Even murderers take holidays. Or he might simply have been lying low.'

'True. But at least we can check into remand prisoners between specific dates, which is something.'

This elicited nods of agreement. But Bliss was keen to jump in. 'I think the boss is right. At the moment we still have nothing to work with. However, my personal baseline in such investigations is to find the anomalies. We're talking four murders that we know of, with the presumption of more. Even if he planned to the nth degree, it's unlikely he could have executed all those plans to the same fine margins. Perhaps our answer lies somewhere in those minute differences.'

'How about the clothes?' Chandler said. 'I'd like to know what the original investigators made of the clothing that was left with the bodies.'

Attwood responded to that. 'At the first crime scene, we found a mixture of clothing belonging to the victim and clothing belonging to a woman or women unknown to us. Subsequently, items we believe to have been worn by previous victims were added to the mix.'

'So the unidentified clothing might belong to a single woman?'

'Yes.'

'Had it been worn? Were you able to tell?'

The Met DCI nodded. 'Yes, it had been. And those unidentified items were all approximately the same size, which is why we believe they could have belonged to one woman. It's all there in your folders. Right down to each individual item and their designations.'

'But what you're saying is we're looking at one item from your first victim being left at the second crime scene. Another at the third, together with an item from victim number two.'

'Yes, it is.'

'So if the unknown clothing did all belong to the same woman, she might well be one of the anomalies DS Bliss mentioned. She may even be the real first victim.'

'That's a nice idea,' Hammersley said. 'We had already considered the possibility of there being a first victim yet to be discovered. However, we'd not thought about it specifically in terms of identifying anomalies. It would be relatively easy to add a further heading to the existing case files.'

'And we are ready and willing to offer you all the help you need,' Superintendent Fletcher said. 'DCI Warburton is our SIO on Phoenix, and her team are obviously already deeply involved, so they are primed to go.'

Hammersley cleared his throat. Cheeks pinched, he leaned forward and said, 'It's been decided by those above my pay scale that this is to be your case. You have the most recent victim, while our own trail has grown cold. Plus, we've mostly moved on to new investigations and it was felt we'd be better off focussing fully on those. Ostensibly, we're here to hand over, and of course anything you need to know that you can't find in these files or on the digital versions being sent to you today, please give us a bell and we'll gladly provide it for you.'

Bliss was astonished. The Met did not let go of investigations lightly, especially those involving murder. He was about to probe further when he was suddenly struck by a terrible realisation.

'Hold on a moment,' he said. 'I think we skipped over something pretty important. Your records tell you our man takes a new victim within a day of murdering and dumping the last, correct?'

Hammersley nodded. 'That's right.'

Bliss felt his shoulders slump. When he spoke, his voice was low and troubled. 'In that case, if he's back and following his previous routine, he may well have already struck again.'

NINETEEN

NINETEEN-YEAR-OLD ABBI TURNER HAD considered herself streetwise until the man calling himself Des Knowles entered her life. He'd played her so easily that not only had she been blind to his intentions, but she would never have guessed it of him in a million years. An apparently shy, timid soul, he came across as a decent human being who lacked the confidence to approach women naturally. In retrospect, his had to be one of the oldest tricks imaginable. And still she had fallen for it.

As an upscale escort working for a downscale agency, Abbi was never entirely sure how her organised dates were going to turn out. Some men hired her because they were genuinely lonely and wanted a companion for the evening; others paid for a dating experience they knew would ultimately end up in a bedroom if they were willing to ask and pay extra. The majority skipped everything but the sex.

Des Knowles had taken her through each stage, cautious at first but seeming to grow in confidence every time they met. Initially anxious and edgy, their first encounter lasted less than an hour at a club before nerves got the better of him. Their second ended in a similar fashion, though it lasted twice as long. Finally they reached the stage where he brought up the issue of sex and paid her the extra in cash, after which they ended up in bed. He was surprisingly skilled and attentive to her needs, and although it had been a long time since a man had satisfied her, she had enjoyed the experience. Eventually they became comfortable enough that he would simply arrive on her doorstep and they would spend the night together without the need for a date.

Having accepted him as a regular, Abbi spoke to Des about cutting out the middle man. Their time together would be exactly the same, she explained, only at half the cost. She recalled him expressing his discomfort, fearing they might get caught avoiding the agency fees.

'I'm allowed a life of my own,' she'd assured him; she now regretted every word. 'That includes a sex life. They don't need to know if money happens to change hands.'

With some reluctance on his part that she had come to understand was a complete masquerade, this became their new arrangement. Then one evening, upon his arrival at her flat, Des appeared to be as nervous and distracted as he had been on their first date. She asked him what was wrong. At first he refused to talk about it. She asked again, and he shook his head, saying he couldn't face discussing it. Eventually she coaxed it out of him, and he spoke as if ashamed.

'I never imagined we would reach this point,' he mumbled, wringing his hands. He still could not bring himself to look at her. 'I've never spent this much time with one woman before. Never felt as relaxed with somebody the way I do with you. I think I've always been afraid of coming this far, you see.'

'Tell me,' Abbi had said. 'You can say anything you like to me. You know that, Des.'

Looking back, she could not be certain what her intention had been. She liked him. She enjoyed his company and their time together, which wasn't always spent between the sheets. But even now she couldn't honestly describe her motivation.

'You're going to think me dirty. Repugnant,' he said, still unable to meet her eyes.

For a moment she said nothing, but eventually she found the right words. 'Des, I'm going to be honest with you. I don't spend time with you for the money. I mean, I still need to earn a living this way, but when I'm with you… I know I could do that because I want to, and I enjoy it. In fact, I'd quite like to see how that goes. It could be our new arrangement, if you like. But you have to remember that I am what I am and I do what I do.'

'I understand that, Abbi. Of course I do. But I don't think of you that way.'

'Which is nice. I like that about us. But not everybody is as kind as you. Some men are harsh. Some men want things others might describe as dirty. Even repugnant. Your words, not mine. But what I'm telling you is that I'm fine with that. Nothing should be out of bounds between us, provided we're both in agreement. If you want to take things to a whole new level, I'm game as long as it's also something I want to be a part of.'

She had imagined his preferences might involve scat or golden showers; those, she did find repugnant, and would have refused had he asked. But if they were of interest to him, Des made no mention of it. Instead, what he considered 'dirty' was merely erotic asphyxiation – at least, up to a point. Unlike most people whose tastes embraced this particular peccadillo, he had no desire to be choked, but rather to be the one carrying out the choking during the moment of climax.

Abbi recalled her immediate response all too well: 'For a moment I thought you were going to suggest something truly awful. Choking is fine, Des. Honestly, it gets requested more often than you might realise. Usually I'm the one with my hands around their throat, but it goes both ways. We do have to establish some ground rules first, though.'

If she had been concentrating or at all wary, Abbi might have taken more notice of the glint in his eyes at that precise moment. But she was genuinely relieved that he didn't want her to lie beneath him while he pissed or shat all over her. She could tell him from experience that neither was particularly pleasurable, and the scat games were disgusting beyond belief. Income was income, and those freaks paid good money to get off over her, but that stuff was something she refused to even consider unless the financial reward was substantial.

What she thought Des wanted was to put his hands around her throat and squeeze, to stem her flow of oxygen as he came inside her. A demonstration of his dominion over her, allowing him to break free of his crippling shyness. But not if he had to pay for it, and only if she agreed to it. Despite her tender age, there were not many sexual experiences she had yet to take part in, and she had encountered many types of deviant along the way. What Des was asking of her was nothing, relatively speaking.

Or so she had thought.

When she came to after that first time, Abbi realised she must have been drugged. Enough to make her fully compliant, to enable him to remove her from her flat and bring her elsewhere; a narcotic sufficient to render her unconscious, leaving her with no memory of what took place from the time her eyelids grew heavy until the moment they fluttered open again.

Returning to consciousness naked and trapped inside a room about a dozen feet square, she had no way of knowing how many days had passed since. The only furnishing was a thin mattress laid on the rough concrete floor, a duvet providing meagre covering for both warmth and modesty. The room was windowless, brick-built and solid. A wall light encased in a metal cage provided feeble illumination from a bulb dulled by a thick crust of grime. When it was not switched on, she could barely see her hands in front of her face.

A routine, of sorts, had since been established. Every so often Des entered the room, tore the duvet from her grasp, led her outside, barefoot, along a short, narrow corridor and into some kind of caged wet room in which he hosed her down. The water was seldom warm, and often brutally cold. He gave Abbi no soap, no shampoo. He ordered her to scrub herself down from head to toe with a nylon-bristled brush which hung from a hook by the coil of hose. She was allowed no deodorant, no moisturiser, no makeup, nor even a toothbrush. Other than being allowed occasional use of the toilet facilities adjacent to the wet room, she hadn't been permitted to go anywhere else. At no point since her capture had she seen daylight. He fed her greasy bacon rolls, washed down with milky tea. This had become her life.

During the lowest moments of her incarceration, Abbi fought her misery for as long as she had the strength; she hoped that keeping it at bay might also keep her sane. But as time passed in fearful solitude, and her mind chipped away at already fragile defences, the fissures expanded and tears began to leak through. As swiftly as the trickle became a torrent, so the torrent turned into huge convulsing sobs, causing her bones to ache.

Weeping forced her to confront every one of the demons clawing their way through her soul. Sure, she was clean at the moment, but the needle had already won its skirmish with her. Hardly a day went by that Abbi did not miss it, but the difference was she no longer craved the high. Her drug of choice had initially released her from a nightmare – at least, that's how it had felt at the time. In the clean period since, she had come to realise that all she had fought to escape from was normality: a clingy sister who adored her so fiercely that she demanded too much attention, and devoted parents whose 'savagely brutal dictatorship' was in fact nothing more than a mother and father wanting the best both for and from their elder daughter. Hers had not been a life of beatings and abuse, yet for reasons she was unable to fathom, their love had choked the life from her, to the point where she needed to escape its clutches in order to breathe.

What followed had been the true misery.

Until she'd met Des Knowles, whom she had truly believed was capable of leading her back out towards the light.

The last time he'd visited, his demeanour was very different. Since taking her and locking her away in the room, he'd barely spoken to her at all; his face had been a set mask of determination, as if he were on a mission that needed completing. This time, however, she'd seen something approaching the man she had grown to know and have feelings for. Abbi decided to have one last stab at re-establishing communication between them.

'Why are you doing this to me, Des?'

At first it seemed as if he would ignore her desperate pleas. But he looked down at her as she sat on the mattress and his face softened. 'I need to break you,' he told her. 'Completely. I must make you fully compliant.'

'I don't understand,' she said, warm tears stinging her eyes. 'I always did everything you wanted of me.'

'Everything but the one thing I really need.'

'Which is? I'll do anything, Des. Whatever it takes. Whatever you need. All you have to do is name it.'

He nodded. 'I know. And that's the problem. You'll do it willingly, which is not how it's supposed to be now I have you here. Because for me to make this right, I have to break your spirit. I have to make you fear me. Hate me, even.'

'But why? I don't understand.' Abbi reached up towards him. The duvet slipped from her body, revealing her naked form in its entirety. She gave herself to him willingly.

He slapped her hands away. 'Of course you don't. How could you? The truth is, I have to make you desperate, to want to do anything to escape. To do anything you can to get away from here. From me. It's that fight, that desperate struggle, that makes it all worthwhile.'

Abbi wept, her features strained. 'I don't know what you mean, Des. Please tell me. Make me understand. Why is this happening to me?'

He leaned forward. In that instant, his eyes went cold and flat, as if all life had fled from them in a single blink. He ran his fingers through her hair and said, 'Because next time somebody puts their hands around your throat, I need you to fear for your life. To resist them, to fight them off for real. As if your life depended on it. Because next time, it will be for real. Next time, you will be fighting for your life.'

TWENTY

ONLY THE MAJOR CRIMES Unit team, Detective Superintendent Fletcher, and Glen Ashton remained in the room. Hammersley and Attwood had stuck around for a further ninety minutes, discussing every facet of their own investigation and offering comments on the efforts of Cambridge and Thorpe Wood to date. By the time that stage of the meeting broke up and the two Met detectives took their leave, they were all in full agreement that everything that could have been done had been done.

'What was that all about?' Bliss said, looking around at familiar faces once more.

'We got lucky, I'd say,' Fletcher replied. 'Though the dubious look on your face tells me you're about to suggest otherwise, Jimmy.'

'I'm sorry, ma'am, but I'm sceptical at the very least. I realise they're short-staffed and burdened by case overload, but that's not the Met I know. What's more, Hammersley couldn't have been more reluctant if he'd tried. He virtually said as much – that the decision had been taken out of his hands by somebody further up the chain. The question is: why?'

'Are you implying they know something we don't know, something they haven't mentioned?'

'I can't put my finger on it. But the Met don't pass off investigations that readily. And to do so by packaging up all their own case files and having two senior officers traipse up here to hand them over is unheard of in my experience.'

'Perhaps they live in more enlightened times since their move, Sergeant.'

Bliss gave a gentle snort of derision. 'I'm sure that's how they love to describe themselves, ma'am. Great PR. But I'm not having any of it. They were too quick and too willing. Eager, almost. But not the two men actually leading the investigation; neither of them were happy about it.'

'Would you like me to call my opposite number and ask him directly?'

'Do you think it would do any good? Is he likely to tell you if there's an elephant in the room we can't yet see?'

Fletcher took his point. 'If you're right, why would they drop it in our laps?'

'It's what you do with a mess,' Bishop offered. 'Maybe they've seen their own people finding no joy working on three separate cases that are all connected. Perhaps they sent their own people to dig a bit deeper into what we have, to find out if we've managed to take it any further than they could. When I made the point about adding their nothing to our nothing and getting nothing, maybe that was the moment DSI Hammersley decided to hand over the poisoned chalice.'

Fletcher closed her eyes and sucked in a deep lungful of air. She let it loose slowly and said, 'You're saying we've been had. The Met saw this case as a lemon and were happy to give it up.'

'Their senior leadership, yes,' Bliss insisted. 'I could tell by the look in Hammersley's eyes that he wanted his team to finish what they'd started. But I'm guessing he swallowed his pride because he was instructed to do so if we had nothing new to offer.'

'Which, if you think about it, tells us a great deal,' Chandler said. 'We've had this case for five minutes compared to them. With all their resources and reputation, they have little viable evidence, no suspects, no witnesses, not a great deal of forensics. Clearly, the Met don't see any way of bringing this case to a satisfactory conclusion without at least one more victim ending up naked in a field somewhere.'

'Penny's right,' Bishop said, picking up on the thread. 'We've been chasing a false trail. They can see that, but they've also seen that we have nothing more to go on than they ever did. The Met think this case is a loser that will become nothing more than a gruelling media ordeal for whoever has it.'

'Which begs the question: why did it not go that way for them?'

All faces turned to Glen Ashton, who had been sitting at the table in silence the whole time. Bliss had assumed the ERSOU man was sulking, or at least reluctant to speak up, but he recognised the significance of what was being suggested.

'Glen's not wrong,' he said. 'We didn't know about these other murders. We weren't aware there was a serial out there. There's only one possible reason for that: the Met never admitted to it.'

Warburton was intrigued, and shuffled in her chair. 'How could that possibly happen?'

'Their three murders were spread out between three separate boroughs across London. That gave them the opportunity to put a lid on it. There's no way the press wouldn't eventually have figured out something was going on, so the Met struck some kind of deal with them.'

'What kind of arrangement are we talking about?'

Shrugging, Bliss said, 'I'm not sure, boss. Perhaps they offered the media an inducement provided they agreed not to broadcast their speculations. We've seen it happen in the early stages of other murder investigations in major cities. They convince the media that revealing the story will cost more lives. The press have been stung that way before, so they don't want to become the new story, having caused further loss of life.'

'Okay, okay,' Fletcher said, rapping a hand on the table and bringing the meeting back to order. 'Whatever their intentions, the Met have left us to run with this. What I'd like to know are your ideas for taking the investigation in the right direction.'

Once again it was Bishop who stepped up; Bliss was proud of his colleague and friend. 'Ma'am, we are confident that both the jogger who discovered Majidah Rassooli's body and the dog walker who saw him doing so are not involved. We could do our own interviews, but I'm happy with the statements provided by Cambridge.'

'And the post mortem results?'

'Provided us with nothing we didn't already have, other than confirming how she died and when. I was reading the PM report when our Met officers arrived. As we already knew, there's evidence of our victim and the previous victims being scrubbed with some mixture of disinfectant, after which they were washed down with detergent. If our girl was raped prior to her murder, any evidence of that has been washed away. As a forensic countermeasure it's overkill, but it's effective. Nancy Drinkwater was unable to say either way whether Majidah had taken part in sexual activity immediately prior to her death; however, there was no tearing and no bruising suggestive of rape.'

'Other forensics?'

'Fibres obtained from clothing and the body are still being examined and tested, but assuming the Met's own unit missed nothing, I don't expect us to have anything worthwhile to report, either.'

Fletcher chewed on her lip before responding. 'So we have four victims, that we know of. All four were sex workers of some description, between the ages of seventeen and twenty-four. Each of them went missing for between a week and ten days prior to being murdered. Chances are they were all strangled to death somewhere other than where their bodies were dumped. And all were left naked, out in the open, next to a pile of clothing.'

'Under or close to a tree,' Bliss added. 'That aspect also feels like part of his signature, to me.'

'There appears to be no racial element,' DCI Warburton said. 'We have young women from vastly different backgrounds here.'

Fletcher nodded, but raised a hand. 'This is all very well, but all I'm hearing is what we have and where we are as things stand. What I want to know is the direction we are heading in. What's your next move?'

'We have a clear strategy with two different paths,' Bishop told her. 'As you're aware, our initial focus fell upon Lewis Drake's little empire – the part that relies on escort agencies and other forms of prostitution. Admittedly, this was when we thought we were dealing with a single victim, because she was flagged as being one of his agency escorts. It was an obvious way to go.'

'And now?' Fletcher prompted.

'We see no reason to give up entirely on that area of focus. While it appears likely that Drake's organisation had nothing to do with Majidah's murder, they remain the people who were closest to her before her abduction. It's certainly possible that her killer was one of her clients. The Met were keen to look into that angle, and although they were unable to pinpoint a single client connected to each of the earlier victims, it remained an open and valid line of enquiry.'

'I agree. What else, DS Bishop?'

'We've divided the squad into two separate units. DI – DS Bliss, together with ERSOU in the form of Investigator Ashton, is looking into the Drake side of things. In addition, we can't rule out the two business cards found in our victim's bra – well, in what we believe to be hers, at least. Jimmy himself mentioned anomalies earlier, and this is a significant one. So he and his group are running with that, also.'

'And you and your team?'

'We were originally going to follow up on the possibility of the murder being committed by a random punter. Now we know that's not the case, we'll shift across to looking at possibilities other than clients – so, in this case, men who have something against sex workers. Something so deep they'd be willing to kill them for it. We're also concentrating our efforts on the clothing and the HOLMES data.'

'If my reading of this is correct,' Fletcher said, 'we don't have a great deal to go on.'

With the attention still on Bishop, he gave a single nod and a long sigh. His shoulders sank as if deflating. 'We don't,' he admitted. 'Other than letting us know we have a serial on our hands, nothing we have from the Met is of help, as far as I can tell. That means our own investigation is still only two days old. For a bog-standard murder that would be a long time, and we'd expect to have a suspect in our sights at this stage. This case is anything but, though, and we should keep in mind that the Met team had no success in two months or more.'

'How is it that we have so little by way of CCTV evidence?' Fletcher asked.

'More by judgement than luck, I'd say,' Chandler offered. 'Since the start of this operation we've been asking ourselves why the chalk pits. We still don't have an answer to that question, but what we do know is that there's not a huge amount of CCTV in the area. There's a note in the Met's case file suggesting they hit a similar barrier. Add to that the fact that we have no idea where the victims were taken from, and only a vague idea of when, and you can start to see why it's been so difficult.'

'Clearly. But can we try to pin some of that down? Check CCTV close to our victim's home on the days when we think she might have been taken?'

'Yes, ma'am. But there's very little to pinpoint, and that has to be by design.'

'Speaking of pinpointing, where are we on the phones?'

Glen Ashton raised a finger. 'I ran an eye over the case file to see how far the Met got with that, Superintendent. As with our victim, no phones were found with the bodies, and none have surfaced since. They appear to go dark at the approximate time these girls are believed to have gone missing. The Met traced the records of each device, which provided them with an approximate location of the phone the last time it was used; actually, the last time the relevant SIM cards were used. They were thorough, so they also traced the IEMI number of all three devices, and achieved the same end results.'

'None of which took them any further, correct?'

'Correct.'

'And where are we with obtaining data for our own victim?'

Bishop was up to speed with that aspect of the op. He explained that while he expected authorisation and results first thing Monday morning, the team were not pinning any hopes on the data being of any significant help. He went on to say that the results from devices belonging to the Parkinson family were due around the same time, providing information that might allow the team to ascertain their proximity to Majidah Rassooli in the hours leading up to her own phone going dark.

'Very well.' DSI Fletcher pushed back in her chair, signifying an end to the meeting. 'Identifying when her phone stopped pinging masts will give us a better idea of when she was most likely taken, and that will help us narrow down the CCTV reviews. But that's for next week. We have the weekend upon us. Usually I'd have no issue allowing for overtime in a case like this. My reluctance to do so here should be obvious. My question being, Bish: what is even a full team likely to achieve over the weekend that we haven't so far and the Met were unable to do in the time they had?'

'There are no obvious potential opportunities for a break-through, ma'am. None that I'm seeing, at least.' He turned to Bliss. 'Jimmy?'

'If you're going to push me for an answer, I'd have to agree,' he said. 'But with great reluctance. My intention is to find out who gave up my business card, and why. Perhaps they saw or heard something; maybe our victim even told them about somebody she feared. We can't know until we've spoken to them, so that's a prime action as far as I'm concerned. Then there's the second business card. Whatever this Dark Desires is, the card mattered enough to Majidah Rassooli to keep it tucked away alongside mine. That tells me it's significant, probably connected, and there-fore of equal interest to me. I also want to rule Lewis Drake and his cronies in or out. Those are all definite avenues to follow, and heavy on physical resources. I'm not due in on Sunday, but I'll be working whether or not there's overtime on offer. If this were my case, I'd be offering overtime, but only to those who want to work their time off – that is, you don't make it compulsory.'

Bishop nodded and glanced back at their superintendent. 'I'm on duty both days, ma'am, so it's easy for me to go along with that. Your call as always, but I think Jimmy has a point.'

Without further pause, Fletcher got to her feet and snatched up her binder. 'That's how we'll play it. I will attend Monday morning's briefing. I'm not on duty over the weekend, but I am available should you need to contact me. Let's hope it's a pro-ductive couple of days.'

As the door swung closed behind the DSI, Warburton also stood. 'Let's see if we can make the rest of today count before we call it quits.'

Ashton rubbed his hands together. 'I can't believe it,' he said, beaming. 'A juicy serial to get stuck into. That'll be good for the old CV.'

Bliss regarded him with narrowed eyes. 'I just this second realised I owe you an apology, Glen,' he said.

'You do? Why's that?'

'Because prior to your last remark, I thought you were only acting like a prick. Now I see you actually are one.'

The big man lost the wide grin. 'I didn't mean anything by it. I've never worked a serial before, that's all.'

'Yeah, well, take it from me, they're not all they're cracked up to be. There's no fucking glamour, if that's what you think. At the end of the day some poor sods still lose their lives.'

'Forget it, Jimmy,' Warburton told him. 'I'm sure Glen didn't intend to sound as crass and opportunistic as he did. Tell me, do we have anything new to work with?'

Chandler nodded. 'Jimmy asked for info on Nicola Parkinson's daughter. John Hunt messaged me to confirm that we have added her mobile and her brother's to our data request. He's also carried out a full PNC check, but there are no outstanding warrants on either of them.'

'And what's the daughter's involvement?' This time Warburton looked directly at Bliss.

He explained about her being a possible match for the woman seen at the flat by their victim's landlord. 'Which reminds me. The landlord, Beaumont, was supposed to have come in today. Any news on that?'

'Phil Gratton also messaged me,' Chandler confirmed. 'Beaumont's statement is in the case file.'

Bliss nodded. 'Good. It might be worth finding a photo of the daughter and showing it to him. He claims to have spoken to a young blonde; there's a chance it's her.'

'You think we'll get that lucky?' Warburton asked.

'It's a long shot…' he admitted. 'But maybe not. If Drake's organisation is connected, or perhaps someone in his organisation is, then why not Parkinson? And if she has something to do with it, why not her kids?' Bliss dipped his head in Chandler's direction. 'Is the daughter known to us, Pen?'

Nodding, Chandler said, 'Like mother, like daughter. Not for tomming or running a knocking shop, I hasten to add – but she did get a pull for carrying a blade, and she also glassed a girl in a nightclub. She's on a suspended.'

'What's her name?'

'Wilma.'

Bliss chuckled. 'Really? I was always more of a Betty man myself.'

'Me too,' Bishop interjected. 'Always had the impression she was far too much woman for Barney to handle.'

Warburton put back her head and groaned. 'Ugh, men. Debating the qualities of cartoon characters? Really?'

Bliss feigned outrage. 'Betty was hot! For a Stone Age woman, that is. Wilma was more like… well, Penny.'

'Oi!' Chandler's hand flicked out to slap him, but he jerked away in time.

'Let's hope we can progress further than the bloody Flintstones,' Warburton said as she headed for the exit. 'Otherwise, I'll see some or all of you here tomorrow at some point, I'm sure. Let's aim for a nine o'clock start, shall we?'

The others responded as one. Bliss found Bishop looking at him, brow creased. 'Neither of them said anything about a media briefing,' he muttered.

'That's because they have nothing to add,' Bliss told him. He followed it up with a grin. 'Take that as a vote of confidence, Bish. You heard what the Met had to say, you heard the subsequent conversations. They have faith in you to work with media relations and come up with a statement.'

Bishop blew out a long breath. 'I had no idea it could be this tense.'

Bliss winked at him. 'You could always do what I did.'

'Yeah. And what was that?'

'Blow it so badly they never ask you to do it again.'

Bishop coughed up a dry laugh. 'Let's call that Plan B, shall we?'

Bliss joined in. 'You'll learn,' he said softly. 'You'll learn.'

TWENTY-ONE

Acknowledging the change in operational status of Phoenix, plus the commitment to putting in some time over the weekend, Bliss took himself out onto the stairway landing to call Emily. She wasn't out on location, so answered immediately.

'You sound rested,' he said after a few seconds of catching up. 'A night on your own seems to have done you some good.'

'Actually, it did. I got a few things done around the house, had a nice long soak in the bath and an early night. How about you?'

'Oh, you know. Same as you, really: did some housework, relaxed in a nice warm soup of my own dead skin, and off to the land of nod before ten.'

'Of course. That's so you.'

'I know. Completely predictable.'

'Hmm. My guess is you made do with some toast or cereal, washed down with several beers. Then you sat up until the early hours mulling over your new case – if you even went to bed at all.'

She was closer than he liked to admit, so he quickly got them off the topic. 'I don't know if you had any plans for later, but if you fancied getting together, tonight might be a good idea; I'll pretty much be on duty all over the weekend. This murder case has shifted up a gear or two today, and I could be called out at any time even when I do make it home.'

'In effect, then, if I don't see you tonight, I probably won't until Monday at the earliest?'

'That's about the size of it. You know how it goes.'

A pause. Something he had become used to in their conversations of late.

'Jimmy, I'm not sure what to do. Cards on the table: if we do get together tonight, I think I'm probably going to want to discuss us. I realise you'd rather stick needles in your own eyeballs than do that, and to be honest with you I'm a little anxious about it myself. Perhaps it's better left until we've both had a chance to think about our current situation some more.'

Bliss's initial reaction was to pounce on the way out she had given him – but he saw the flaw in her argument and had to mention it. 'We can do that if it suits you best,' he said. 'But Em, you know better than that. If I'm working all weekend, my mind is going to be wrapped up in the case. I could lie and tell you my every waking thought will be about us, but you know me. I probably won't think about it again until we see each other on Monday or Tuesday. That's no slight against you or our relationship. It's the harsh reality of the situation. Is there any chance of us getting together tonight but not talking about anything meaningful?'

'You mean we can spend the entire night together provided we don't address the elephant in the room?'

'Hey, I know I've nothing to be ashamed of equipment-wise, but comparing me to an elephant is probably exaggerating. A bit.'

Emily didn't laugh. 'There you go,' she said, her voice flat. 'Deflecting again. Right on cue.'

Bliss knew he was – not that he liked her pointing it out. It sounded so cold and clinical when she said it. She had always analysed their relationship more logically than he had. He preferred to go with the flow, allowing things to take their natural course; he had been wondering for some time if things between the two of them had run theirs.

'I do want to see you,' he told her sincerely. 'You have to believe that. I enjoy spending time with you. But I don't want to waste it *talking* about us when we could be getting on with *being* us.'

'Oh, Jimmy. You see, this is where the compromise aspect of a relationship kicks in. You want one thing, I want another. And when it comes to this specific topic – when I want to talk about what we have and where we're going – so far I'm the one who's always had to make that compromise.'

'Really? Is that what you think?'

'No, it's not what I think; it's the truth of the matter. So I leave it until the next time. And next time I leave it until the next… and so on. So what I'm thinking is, we have to see if you are capable of bending when I most need you to. To sacrifice what you want, to give me a single night during which we discuss all the things I feel we need to get out into the open.'

It suddenly felt extremely hot out on the landing. Bliss sucked in some air. His head began to swirl, and he blinked rapidly, looking to stabilise himself. The reaction came as a result of the rush of sudden pressure Emily had applied. He breathed out deeply. And again. He did not want to take this conversation any further – he was starting to wish he hadn't called at all – but here he was. As he told others on many occasions, things are as they are, not as we might like them to be. He had to deal with it.

'Fine,' he breathed. 'I don't know what time I'll be home, but come over whenever you can. It sounds as if you think this talk we're about to have is long overdue.'

'And you don't?'

'We've been seeing each other for two months. That's not a lot of time, especially if you tot up the actual number of hours we've spent together.'

'Isn't that part of the problem? The lack of quality time we get together?'

'I didn't think so. Clearly I'm wrong.'

When Bliss was finished with the call, he placed another.

Sandra Bannister answered on the third ring. 'I was wondering if you'd contact me,' she said. 'Let me guess: you don't have anything for me, but you'd like me to dig out some information on your behalf.'

Bliss smiled. 'Why do you think so little of me?'

'I've spent time with you. Isn't that all the answer you need?'

'And yet you get far more from me than I should give.'

'True. Which is why I put up with your requests. What is it this time?'

'Off the record, never to appear in print even as a casual mention?'

'Ooh, sounds serious. Okay. But I'll hold back if I think somebody else might beat me to the punch. Have to protect my leverage.'

'Naturally. In that case, when you ran your features on Lewis Drake, did you ever get wind of anything he might be up to on the dark web?' Bliss deliberately withheld any specific mention of Dark Desires.

'Not that I recall. I'll check my notes and our archives, but I can't say it rings a bell. It's possibly not something we considered at the time, so we wouldn't have pried. Are you still investigating him, Jimmy?'

'Should I not be? I want that twisted bastard for murder, and there's no way I'm going to allow him to win his appeal, either.'

Bannister chuckled. 'Sounds like fighting talk. I'll expect some fireworks. Tell me, what's this dark web thing all about?'

Bliss couldn't fault her for at least trying. 'I'll keep that to myself for the time being.'

'Spoilsport. Does it have anything to do with your strangling victim?'

Sometimes he forgot how sharp an investigator she was; the reporter would have made a decent detective. 'Let's say we're keeping an open mind.'

'Did she work for one of his agencies?'

Even Bliss was surprised at how quickly Bannister had pieced that together. 'Acting DI Bishop will update you all during his media briefing later. What I will tell you, if you promise me you'll dig into Drake and any possible dark web connection, is that…'

'What? Why the pause?'

'I need to hear that promise.'

'Okay, okay. I'll look into it and get back to you.'

'Thanks. All right. Sandra, be prepared for this to explode. It's far bigger than we expected. As usual, I'll make sure you hear about it first. There may be some aspects I'm unable to reveal, but I'll give you everything I can by way of a head start.'

The journalist was more than happy with that, and promised to start looking into Lewis Drake's operation immediately. Bliss tapped the phone against his forehead. His use of a newspaper reporter as an unofficial researcher could never be officially sanctioned, but within the job everybody knew the police and the media worked together in small one-to-one cells. Investigating officers relied on journalists to feel their way into areas that were protected against official police intrusion, while ambitious – or even merely enthusiastic – reporters trusted police sources to feed them news prior to it being broken nationally.

His mind swiftly flipped back to Emily. He wasn't ready for the conversation she wanted to have. It was difficult enough for him to be emotionally attached when working mundane or slow-moving cases, but something like this series of murders sucked him into a vacuum and would not spit him out again until it was over. He allowed no time for himself, let alone others, during such critical investigations. But he knew that ultimately, no matter how long they talked or where they took it, the answer boiled down to one thing: his feelings.

Bliss sighed, pocketed his phone and turned back towards the corridor. Somewhere inside his head he knew there was a spool of thought that insisted he wanted to spend the rest of his life with Emily. Yet somehow, his heart continued to be completely unaware of this commitment.

TWENTY-TWO

B EFORE LEAVING HQ, BLISS pulled up a case file whose number was indelibly imprinted on his memory. He navigated the folders on the system before opening the one containing victim images. Having eventually located the individual whose photograph he needed, he ran off six hard copies.

Fifteen minutes later, he pulled his pool car off Mayors Walk in Westwood and into the large parking area of a house set thirty paces off the main road. He switched off the engine and turned in his seat. From the inside pocket of his jacket he pulled out two of the photos he'd printed. 'Ready for some grunt work?' he said to DC Hunt and Glen Ashton.

Hunt was a decent copper who put in his time and worked hard without complaint – other than when he was sent on post mortem duty. He lacked ambition and was seldom proactive, but Bliss nonetheless considered him an asset to the team because he followed orders and never shirked a duty. He'd anticipated an objection from Ashton, though, and he got it.

'You expect me to go door to door?'

Bliss sighed. 'What are you, Glen, some kind of Bongo?'

In the front passenger seat, DS Chandler sniggered.

Ashton's forehead rippled. 'What the bloody hell is a Bongo when it's at home?'

Bliss grinned. 'It's an acronym we use to describe a lazy cop: books on, never goes out.'

The investigator grunted. 'Well, that's not me. I do my fair share – you can ask anybody I work with. But not this sort of crap.'

'Why not? You think you're above doing a bit of legwork?'

'Would you have done it when you worked for the NCA?'

Bliss turned further around to face the big man who seemed to fill the entire rear seat of the Mondeo, squeezing the slighter form of Hunt into the far corner. 'First of all, Glen, I put the time in on the streets when I wore the uniform. Second of all, yes: I would have knocked on doors while I was with the NCA. In fact, I did, on several occasions. Pal, if you think being an investigator for ERSOU makes you something special, your career with the agency will be much shorter than you ever imagined. Most of the men and women I worked with there are dedicated, enthusiastic professionals. They'll spot you coming a mile off if you're anything less.'

He held out the photos. 'Her name is Haweeo Salat. This is our runaway Somalian kid – one of those we rescued from the container. She preferred to call herself Primrose. Pen and I are going to have a chat with the couple who run this place. Primrose lived here for almost six months, so they know her better than anyone. But she could have had friends or been known to any of the neighbours. So, yes, Glen, I want you and John to go out there and ask questions. I want to know where this girl fled to when she ran away. I also want to know who her closest friends were.'

Ashton responded with a surly shrug of compliance. DC Hunt could barely conceal the smirk thinning his lips. 'Come on, Glen,' he said. 'Get down and dirty with us mere plebs.'

For the best part of a decade, Eamonn and Dottie Wilkey had run the halfway house for young and single asylum seekers who were awaiting legal formalities and judgements. A cheerful couple in their late fifties, they led Bliss and Chandler into the vast kitchen, and Eamonn set about making them a hot drink each. The two detectives pulled out chairs at a huge dining table made from reclaimed and treated railway sleepers, which was laid out for twelve people.

'I take it you're full as per usual,' Bliss said, indicating the place settings.

'And then some,' Dottie replied, rolling her eyes. 'I only wish we could take more. We're only allowed eight at a time, even though we could probably move things around and squeeze in another couple.'

Bliss did a quick recount. 'Eight? There's a dozen places set.'

'We always set a couple of spares in case friends drop by.'

'You mentioned something about Primrose at the front door,' Eamonn said, pulling mugs from their hooks and setting them down on the counter next to the bubbling kettle. 'I remember you, Inspector Bliss. You popped in on the day Prim came to us. You asked about her, made sure she was settling in okay.'

Bliss nodded. 'I felt sorry for the poor kid. She'd been separated so quickly from the other girls. Mainly because certain elements of her story had come across as weaker than others to the officials she met.'

'Yes, she told us all about it,' Dottie said, turning away from the tea and coffee jars to look at him. 'Prim was not one of life's great talkers, even though her English was pretty good. She seemed overawed by everything here, which only made her shyness that much worse.'

'But she made friends, yes?' Chandler asked, notepad flipped open on the table, pen tapping against it.

'After a fashion. Excuse me for asking, but are you able to tell us what she's done wrong? I know she ran away from us here, but I simply refuse to believe that girl was capable of breaking the law.'

'She broke the law when she ran away,' Bliss reminded her. 'But that's not why we're here. In fact, we have no idea where she went, nor what she's up to. I can assure you, Mr and Mrs Wilkey, if we track down Primrose and manage to speak with her as a consequence of anything said here in this room, that's as far as it will go. All we want is some information. Her immigration status is of no concern to us or our investigation.'

'Perhaps we can help,' Eamonn said.

Bliss waited until the Wilkeys brought the mugs over and joined them at the table. 'I'm hoping that's the case. But we'd also like to talk to anybody she was close to. Close enough to share secrets with, that is.'

'There were a couple of girls Prim was friendly with. A young man, too. But as you know, this is a transitory home for these people. Six months is about all they get, at best. Either they move on because they've been successful and are being settled elsewhere, or they get carted off to a more formal holding area prior to deportation.'

'So you're saying the people she may have been close to have long gone?'

'Yes. And we never learn their ultimate destination. Occasionally some of them will write or drop us an e-mail, or maybe comment on our Facebook page. But I don't recall any contact from the three I mentioned since they left us.'

Bliss had not expected this to be easy. 'All right. So, let's see if either of you can help. As you're probably aware, Primrose was one of five young girls rescued from a shipping container, having been trafficked to the UK. The thing is, I gave each of them a business card so they could get hold of me if they ever landed in any trouble. One of those cards has turned up in the possession of someone other than one of the five girls. We've since tracked down three of them; another willingly went back to her home country, so finding out if she left her card behind is going to be almost impossible. We're hoping to speak with Primrose or anybody who might have known she intended to run away, because there's every chance it was she who passed her card on to another young girl.'

The Wilkeys looked at each other. Nothing other than a shared confusion passed between them, as far as Bliss could see. When Eamonn slowly shook his head, Bliss thought it was genuine. 'She definitely didn't mention any of that to us,' he said. 'My wife and I have obviously chatted about what happened many times since Prim ran away. Whether you believe it or not, Inspector Bliss, neither of us saw it coming. It was a huge shock when we found her things missing and her room empty that morning. Yet… at the same time, I think we both understood.'

'You mean she was scared of having her appeal for asylum rejected.'

'She was. We weren't allowed to sit in on any of her interviews with the authorities, but Prim was shaken after every one of them. She told us they kept badgering her about the reason why she left Somalia, insisting she must have done so willingly in order to improve her life prospects here in Britain. Well, you met her. Did she come across as that kind of person to you?'

'No,' Bliss said, recalling the timid girl he had spent some time with immediately after her rescue. 'But we can never truly know a person. Not deep down. Like you, my impression of her was of someone reserved and meek, but a young girl who was also determined to make a go of things in this new world she found herself in. I suspect she came into contact with other Somalians who gave her a way out – most likely down to London to settle into a community in which she could disappear.'

Nodding furiously, Dottie Wilkey set down her own mug and wiped away a stray tear. 'Prim was a sweetheart. Never gave us a moment of concern. She was polite, helped out around the house, and above all she was kind. We would have missed her however she'd left us, but it did hurt that she chose to go without saying goodbye.'

'I suspect she thought she might not be able to leave you both if she did that. I imagine it was the only way she *could* leave.'

Eamonn reached out a hand and gently squeezed his wife's fingers. 'I'm sorry we couldn't be of more help. In terms of friends, Prim never had many. But she did talk about somebody she'd met in town one day who'd also been trafficked. I remember her coming home and telling us about this young woman, and thanking God that she had been rescued from that life before it had even started.'

'Did she say what kind of life she meant?' Chandler asked, beating Bliss to it.

'No. Not really. We got the impression she was referring to the things we sometimes see on the TV, where girls are trafficked into the country and used as… slave labour, in various ways.'

'Did she happen to tell you this girl's name?'

Dottie's brow furrowed. 'It might have been Sara. I seem to remember Prim saying she was originally from Croatia.'

Bliss sucked on his bottom lip. It sounded as if the girl had used her real name, not the name she was known by if she did indeed work for an agency. 'Are you quite certain? No other name? No surname, or perhaps a nickname?'

The woman shook her head. 'I'm sorry. I can't even be sure it was Sara.'

'That's okay. It might still be helpful. Thank you.' He turned to her husband. 'Mr Wilkey? Anything jog your memory here?'

Eamonn's shake of the head was firm. 'It was Dottie who told me about it. That's not something Prim would have felt comfortable discussing with me.'

Bliss felt his initial excitement deflating like a punctured tyre. He managed to raise a feeble smile. 'I understand. We'll see if that leads us anywhere.'

The two detectives finished off their drinks before thanking the couple and leaving the house. It was a large property, clean and tastefully furnished; Bliss imagined the pair provided a warm and inviting home for their charges. He was grateful to them, because he knew how much girls like Primrose needed that kind of stability in their lives.

'Where now?' Chandler asked him as they settled back into the car.

'It's not much to go on. I doubt the name will get us very far, but we could ask Marta Lsenko. Even if she doesn't know the girl, she might be able to ask around for us, given they probably move in the same circles.'

'That's a good idea. I was thinking we could have someone go through the adverts. It's not much, but how many Croatians can there be in the city?'

'More than you imagine. But the majority will have come across when the borders opened up, looking to find work. Legit rather than trafficked.'

'Probably worthy of following up on, I'd say.'

Bliss agreed. 'Even if John and Glen come up empty-handed, at least we have a name to work with. Primrose might be gone for good, but she may well have left enough of herself behind to help us out.'

TWENTY-THREE

HUNT AND ASHTON HAD discovered nothing of interest, although they both mentioned the antipathy shown by many neighbours towards the halfway house.

'I had a lot of people talking to me about boats out at sea or creating more camps to house them,' DC Hunt said as they drove back to Thorpe Wood.

'Same here,' Ashton said. 'Some people reckoned their presence keeps the house prices in the neighbourhood artificially low. Not that anyone was being racist, of course...'

'That halfway house is literally a stone's throw from some of the most expensive property in the entire city,' Chandler said. 'Westwood Park Road is one of the best addresses you can have in Peterborough, and the surrounding streets are full of people who think living close by gives them an air of superiority.'

Bliss glanced across at her. 'Ouch! Sounds as if you speak from experience, Pen.'

Chandler casually hiked a shoulder. 'I dated a lad from this area. Only went to his place a couple of times, but his mother virtually ran around after me with a dustpan and brush as if the skin I shed was tainted. His father spoke down to me. That was the first example of mansplaining I came across, I think, only it was probably more like poorsplaining.'

'Wealthy people make me sick,' Hunt said, and to Bliss the flat statement came across as bitter. 'Walking around with their noses in the air, thinking they're so much better than those of us who actually do the work.'

Bliss eyed him in the rear-view mirror. 'They're not all like that, John. Just like us cops are not all racist thugs in need of defunding. I've met a good many wealthy people who are thoroughly decent, in the same way that I've met many people living in poverty who are complete arseholes.'

Hunt stared out of the window and made no comment. Bliss had never been able to work the man out. His colleague seemed to have a chip on his shoulder about everyone and everything. A man with a permanent grudge and an attitude bordering on the paranoid. He could be good fun during after-shift drinks, and although he seldom did more than he was asked, he did at least have a diligent approach to his job. You didn't have to be liked to be respected. Bliss knew something about that himself, which is why he'd always make room for John Hunt.

After dropping their two colleagues off at HQ to wade through the adverts and agencies in search of Croatian girls, Bliss and Chandler headed out to Serpentine Lake. Before leaving Mayors Walk, Bliss had called Marta Lsenko's number. She was free, but despite the inclement weather had insisted on meeting outdoors. When Bliss parked up, they spotted Lsenko sitting on a nearby bench. Daylight was fading rapidly around them, and lights began to spring into life as the evening approached.

The three walked while they talked, a fine drizzle settling over them. The young woman wore a full-length grey coat, with a teal scarf wrapped around her neck and pulled up tight against her throat. Both Bliss and Chandler had the top buttons of their jackets fastened, hands thrust deep into pockets. Little clouds of breath preceded them along the paved pathway.

Initially, Lsenko was dismissive; not aggressively so, but she wasn't one for small talk and simply couldn't think of who they might mean when they mentioned Sara. The girl came across as brusque even when she didn't mean to be. Chandler urged her to think longer and harder, reminding her that it could be important.

'If she and Haweeo became close, she must have been an approachable sort. You remember Haweeo, Marta?'

'Of course. How could I not?' Lsenko seemed affronted by the question. 'She call herself Primrose. You spend time like that with a person, you never forget their name or their face.'

'I can only imagine. Look, we think Primrose gave her card to our murder victim. If that's the case, she must have thought the girl needed it more than she did herself. We're hoping that this Sara might know the circumstances, that Primrose might have told her about it before she left the city.'

'Primrose gave away her card?' Lsenko's voice was a mixture of disbelief and awe, as if a priceless treasure had been spurned.

'We don't know that for sure. Lilit Petrosian opted to be repatriated. But although for that reason alone she's the most likely of all of you to have given her card to another girl, we don't see how she was ever in a position to do so while she was still here in the city. Lilit was driven from our station to London without ever mixing with anyone other than yourselves and us. The card ended up in Cambridge in the clothing of a girl from Peterborough. That's why we're focussing on Primrose and her friend, Sara.'

They all came to a halt when Lsenko stopped walking. She stood for a moment looking at the ground, scuffed at the same spot with her boot heel.

'You know us, Marta,' Bliss said softly, sensing the young woman's hesitation. 'We're not looking to hurt anyone – other than those who deserve it. If you know something, anything at all, please tell us. If this Sara is an illegal, I promise you her information will go no further than us. All we want is a conversation.'

The moment Lsenko looked up again, Bliss knew she had something to tell them. She gave a long sigh before speaking. 'I do know this girl. Sara. I also know Primrose from other than container.'

'You two met up after you were separated?'

A nod. 'I know Sara. Sara know Primrose. We had coffee at Costa in Queensgate by escalator.'

'Okay,' Chandler said, giving her a wide smile. 'That's good. It's nice that you were still in each other's lives. Do you know why Primrose left, and why she gave the card away?'

Bliss could tell the young woman was still uncertain. 'Marta, I think you know how important this is. I promise you none of it will splash back on you or your friend Sara, and we are not going to chase down Primrose. I hope you believe me.'

'I do. Yes, of course. You and Penny.'

'In that case, please, tell us what you know.'

'I worry what you will think of me.'

Lsenko's pale features trembled from more than the cold and fine rain. Bliss took a half step closer, shaking his head. 'You need never concern yourself with that. Penny and I know what you had to live through. We don't judge you, Marta. You fought to stay alive, so you earned the right to choose how you live that life.'

Before hc even finished speaking, her face crumpled and tears began streaming down both cheeks. She pawed them away carelessly. 'I want to be more than I am. But I want the things I never had before. Back home. What I do is not easy for me as a woman, but is easier for me as a person. You understand?'

Bliss didn't quite, but he nodded anyway.

'Sara… she do worse things. I have sex with men for money. But I do nothing… I think you say… degrading. Just sex. Sara, she… do much worse. She have friend who do things Sara refuse to talk about. I think she call her Amber.'

'Could it be Autumn?' Chandler said. The moment she spoke, she winced and mouthed a 'sorry' to Bliss for interrupting the flow of their conversation. But Lsenko was nodding and smiling, agreeing on the name.

'Did Primrose give her card to Sara so that she could pass it on to Autumn?' Bliss asked. 'Did she think Autumn might need help from me?'

'Yes. Sara tell me she worry about her friend. Say she do dangerous things. Terrible things. Sara want her to stop. Prim come to me later, she say she is leaving because she not want to go back to Somalia. We speak about you, and we talk about card. Prim say she have no need of it where she is going.'

Bliss was keen to learn more about the card and what Autumn did that was so wrong her friend believed she needed protection. But he also wanted to put Lsenko at her ease. 'Did Primrose tell anybody where she was headed? Have you heard from her since she left?'

The girl shook her head. 'No. She think it better if I do not know.'

'Are you sure? Like I said, I have no intention of searching for her. But it'd be nice to know that she is well and getting on okay.'

'I know. I trust you, as Prim did. But she would not tell me where she go. Just that she would be with her own people in community that will accept her.'

Bliss nodded and said, 'Then that's all we can wish for. I hope she's happy. So, we have to go back to Sara. Do you know how to reach her?'

'No. I see her from time to time. This is all.'

'Okay. How did she know Autumn?'

'They work together sometimes. You know, when men want two women. They also do the… dangerous things. The things I will not do.'

'Do you know who Sara worked for? Which agency?'

Lsenko nodded. 'Is private. Secret. You not find on internet very easy. Only when you have correct way in.'

'You're talking about a dark website,' Chandler said. 'Is it called Dark Desires, Marta? Is that the one?'

Lsenko's face scrunched up in horror. 'You know this? You know about black card?'

'We do. We told you our victim had Jimmy's business card hidden in her underwear, yes? Well, she also had a black card with her. It had some kind of code written on the back of it in gold pen. Do you know anything about that?'

'I do not write this,' Lsenko replied, putting a gloved hand to her chest. 'I do not work with black card people.'

'No, I'm not saying you are. But Sara does. She must know how it works. Perhaps she told you enough that you can provide us with more information.'

'All I know is what she tell me one time. This Dark Desires is for men and women who want more than sex. It is sex for them, but not for me or you or Jimmy, I am sure. They need girl willing to do things I would never do. Some dirty, filthy… ugly. Some dangerous. Make me scared. Too scared.'

'And the card? How does the system work, Marta?'

'You call number. You say what it is you want. You must prove who you are first, then get sent – what is called? – file. You prove more, you pay, you get sent way to enter. Once inside, you find girls who do these things.'

Bliss was trying to follow Lsenko's broken and uncertain English, but having a good idea where it was headed made life so much easier for him. 'So if this is me and I want something…

out of the ordinary, I call Dark Desires. I provide my details. Presumably somebody checks me out, after which they send me a spreadsheet file. I pay for the service, I provide even more information about myself. If they are satisfied, they send me a password into the sheet, plus whatever needs to be entered into it. I do that, up pops the link and away I go. Into the dark web.'

Nodding throughout, Lsenko also continued to glance around; fearful they might be observed, Bliss guessed. 'Marta,' he said, 'this is important. Do you know what it was that Sara's friend Autumn offered the people who used this service? Did Sara ever mention it to you?'

'Yes. Sara was not ashamed. She say Autumn was, but still she did the work. I don't like to say. It scare me to even think about it.'

Bliss understood. 'That's okay. Let me tell you what I think it was. You just nod or shake your head.'

'I can do that for you and Penny.'

'No, not for us. For your friend Sara, and her friend Autumn. Okay?'

'Okay.' This time she raised a smile, and Bliss was glad of it.

'Was it choking, Marta? Was that what Autumn offered her clients? It's called erotic asphyxiation, but you probably know it as choking.'

Lsenko's face screwed up again as she let out a loud sob. A fresh torrent of tears streamed from her eyes. 'Yes,' she said through her misery. 'Yes.'

TWENTY-FOUR

B LISS WAS CONSCIOUS OF how hard the team had worked since the discovery of the body at the chalk pits. Fatigue had to be setting in. Ahead of the evening briefing, during which the entire team were due to catch up with the day's events, he had a word with Bishop. With most – if not all – of the team expected back the following day and quite possibly for the entire weekend, he suggested they cut out the briefing altogether and send everyone home early.

Bishop had understood, even agreed, but he had another take on it. 'I keep coming back to our killer's MO. If he does have another girl out there somewhere, I hate to think of her spending one second more in his company than she has to.'

'You're not the only one taking that into consideration, Bish. But you know this team; you think Penny, Gul, or even Phil are going to go home tonight and not spend much of their free time mulling it over? My point is, we've hardly stopped to breathe, and as exhaustion creeps in, so mistakes get made. It's not only better for the case, it's an issue of wellbeing. We're asking people to give up their own time to come in over the weekend. Uniforms, too. Let them know you're aware of this by telling them all to bugger off home now. It'll do them the power of good – and you, in their eyes.'

Bliss knew his colleague's heart was in the right place. They couldn't know for certain that another girl had been abducted, however likely it seemed, and he didn't expect any of the team to have a restful night. But he had driven his colleagues hard in the past, and experience told him that releasing the valve a little allowed the pressure to dissipate gradually rather than exploding in a single eruption.

Always ready to listen to and accept advice, Bishop weighed up the options and went with Bliss's suggestion. The relief on the faces of the team was palpable.

Before leaving work, Bliss put in a call to Sandra Bannister. She didn't pick up, but he neglected to leave a message. He and Chandler walked out to the car park together. 'You got time for a quick one?' she asked.

Bliss chuckled. There was a time when his response would have been automatic and obvious. Chandler caught on quickly. 'No, I don't mean that, you dirty old sod! That's never been on the table.'

'It doesn't have to be on the table, Pen. Over a desk will do.'

'Smartarse. All right: it's never been on offer, and it never will be to the likes of you.'

'That's fair enough. Though once again I feel it's only proper for me to remind you who put their lips on mine that night a few years back and almost snogged the air out of my lungs?'

'We were pissed, Jimmy. You could have been DCI Edwards, for all I knew.'

'Now *that* I would pay good money to see.'

'Yeah, well you make the most of that memory. It's never going to happen again.'

He remembered it well. Another of their brief flirtations. He had never been certain how far either of them had been willing to take it, but he suspected that at one time their shared loneliness might have thrown open a door lying slightly ajar. He was glad it had never gone past the point of no return. Chandler was his best friend, and nothing was worth ruining that relationship.

'All right,' he said. 'But no, as much as I'm loath to refuse the offer of a quick pint with you, I have fences to mend at home.'

'Ah. You and Em all set for a showdown, is that it?'

'Not my choice. Although I think I passed some sort of test.'

'You did? Tell me more.'

'She said she'd come over provided we could talk about us. You can imagine how that went down with me. My first reaction was to try and put it off, but she was insistent: either we got into it or she wouldn't come. She mentioned compromise or some such nonsense.'

'And you broke first?' Chandler's eyes glinted. 'I'm impressed, Jimmy. That's a massive step.'

'Yeah, but into what? I hate the whole idea of it. When I'm with someone, I don't want to waste time having conversations like that. I want to enjoy the moment, not sully it with a shitload of soul-searching. Think about it; have you ever known a discussion like that to go well?'

'It is what mature, loving couples do from time to time.'

'Really? I mean, I remember having chats like that with Hazel – we spoke about where we were going, getting our own place, marriage, family – so yes, I'm not unfamiliar with the concept. But we were young, our focus was on spending the rest of our lives together and how that would all pan out.'

The lines on Chandler's forehead grew deeper. 'Then why are you surprised that Emily wants to have similar conversations with you? I know you went into this relationship reluctantly, but you're a good couple of months into it now. You and Hazel were young and thought you had your whole lives together, stretching out far into the distance. You and Em are moving towards the other end of the same scale; believe me, Jimmy, she's wondering if she's going to grow old alone or with someone else by her side. And she's asking herself if that person could be you.'

Dusk was deepening, approaching full darkness. It felt like a metaphor for life. His life. Emily's. He raised his hands. 'Okay, I understand the importance of the discussion I'm about to have. But why now, when I'm deep into a case and my mind is wrapped up in that? Surely we could have put it off for a few days, maybe a week or so?'

Chandler shook her head as if dealing with a simpleton. 'Oh, Jimmy. Think about what you said from her perspective. When aren't you deep into a case? And on the rare occasions you're not fully immersed, you're resting, overcoming the fatigue from your illness. There's never a good time to have that conversation with you, is there? It looks to me as if she has decided enough is enough. Talk or walk, my friend. Talk or walk.'

Bliss had already chosen to talk. And when he arrived home, that's precisely what he did. She asked him to sit and listen while he put away a bottle of San Miguel, but instead of listening, he began their conversation.

'Emily, I realise we got this second chance and that at the time it felt like fate had taken a hand. Well, fate and the crafty mind of Penny Chandler.' They exchanged warm, knowing smiles. 'But in all honesty, I don't think you're getting what you need from me. And if you aren't getting that at the moment, it's right for you to question whether you ever will. My truthful answer is that I don't know if I can ever be the man you want me to be, for us to have the kind of close relationship you want us to have. But I'm also aware that my saying I don't know is of no use to you.'

Emily was soft on the outside, but she had a steely core. A stoical, intelligent woman, she had little time for tears or tantrums. She felt things deeply, but she also recognised the way things were. If she lacked the ability to change a situation, or compel it to be changed, she could live with the repercussions. Bliss knew this about her, and understood he was incapable of breaking her.

They sat together on the new three-seater sofa, his one concession to having another person sharing his home – even on a non-permanent basis. Emily sat with her knees pulled up to her chest, her head resting on his shoulder. As they talked, her hand idly brushed his arm.

'I want to love you more than I already do, Jimmy,' she said. 'But so far I've been unable to let myself fall all the way; it's a matter of self-preservation. So yes, I've been guilty of holding back.'

Bliss released a long breath. 'I think I was aware of that. Though I'm not great at picking up signals when it comes to this sort of thing.'

Rolling her eyes, Emily said, 'That's an understatement. But there's no blame here. The thing is, while I may be holding back for fear of getting my heart broken, I don't believe you are. I think this is it for you. This is all you're willing to give at this moment in your life – maybe even all you are capable of giving. I don't know if the missing piece is whatever you're still holding onto with Hazel, if it's your commitment to the job, or perhaps a combination of the two. It might be me – that you can't make that commitment to me. All I do know is that I never get all of you, Jimmy. And I don't see a point at which I ever will.'

He wrapped his arm around her shoulder, pulling her closer. 'In my defence, I never promised you otherwise.'

'I know. And please don't get me wrong. I'm not angry with you. I didn't expect more from you, either, but I suppose I did hope for it. For a sign, at least. A sign that you had it in you to put all that you are into what we have together. But I came into this with my eyes wide open, which is why I have no regrets.'

'So because you think it can't move any further forward, it has to be over? Is that what you're saying?'

'No. It's not that at all.'

'Then what is it, Emily? I'm lost here. You have to help me understand.'

Nuzzling him, her fingers moving with his, she gave a gentle sigh and said, 'In some ways it has nothing to do with you and me. But at the same time, perhaps it has everything to do with you and me. The fact is, I worry about you. I *am* worried about you. This rage you have inside you towards Neil Watson... it's as if you have a death wish. Not your *actual* death, but the death of your career and your happiness. Jimmy, you're walking such a fine line with your probation, you're approaching the final couple of years in the job – a job you're extremely fortunate to still be out there doing – and yet you're happy to risk everything because you think someone got away with committing a terrible crime.'

Bliss swallowed, digesting her disapproval and finding it hard to stomach. 'And you think that makes me wrong?'

'Yes. Not in how you feel about what happened or towards him. Of course not; the thought of what he did to that child makes me feel physically sick. But at times you're such a hypocrite, Jimmy. You love going around telling people that things are what they are, not what we want them to be. But you think you don't have to live by those rules yourself. Of course it's wrong if that man did murder his stepson and got away with it. It's horrendous. And I'm angry at the lack of justice. But why is it only you who doesn't seem to be willing to accept that you can't always get the result you want? It wasn't even your case.'

'That's hardly the point,' Bliss said, flushing as he defended himself. 'Whose case it was is irrelevant to the eventual outcome.

The boy is still dead, and that murdering deviant is walking around on our streets as if he owns the place. He should be banged up.'

'And only Jimmy Bliss can put him there.'

'That's not what I'm saying. But I do appear to be the only one trying to do it now that the trial is over.'

'Isn't that just one of those things that are as they are?'

He snorted and shook his head. 'Okay. You've got me on that one, Em. You win that argument. Yes, I say one thing and do another. But why does any of that have to affect me and you? Why is it getting in the middle of us?'

'Because it's a symptom of a man who has no intention of changing his ways, irrespective of what it costs him.'

'You mean the job? I should give a stuff about the job. All it's ever done is shit on me from a bloody great height.'

'And that was never your fault? You never played a role in your own downfall? And besides, it's not only the job we're talking about. Your reaction to this man is unreasonable – in fact, I'd go so far as to say it's irresponsible. You're goading him. You want him to slip up, to show everybody what he's truly like.'

'Where's the problem in that?'

'Because if you push him too far, who do you think he'll take it out on? The next time you stand in front of him, maybe it'll be you he beats to a pulp. Maybe you'll be the one he murders. And worst of all, Jimmy… you don't even appear to care if that's the way things go. You'll just die with a wide grin on your face, knowing you got your man.'

Bliss flapped a hand and turned his head away. 'You're being dramatic.'

Emily broke away from his embrace and sat forward. She reached out, pulled his hand back down and clutched it in her own once more. 'Am I?' she asked him, tears glistening in the corners of her eyes. 'Am I really? I don't believe that's the case, Jimmy. I don't know if this has something to do with what happened to Mia, or whether it's a culmination of everything you've experienced in your adult life. Maybe it's even the fact that you see yourself being out of this way of life all too soon. I'm not sure if even you know. But you are on a downward spiral, and though you have me and Penny and your mother all eager to help pull you out, nothing seems to reach you.'

The muscles in his face became taut, his jaw clenched. He felt heat rise from his throat to his face. He could almost feel his eyes withdraw into their sockets. This was not something he wanted to hear. No matter how close to the bone, for him this was no mere conversation; this was his life. Emily and those she had mentioned were special to him, important in every conceivable way, but he was done with being moulded. That had ended a long time ago. He was not the man Emily wanted him to be, nor the one Hazel had ever imagined he could become – but eventually you had to accept who you were rather than the person you might have been. Or the one others wanted you to be.

Living the way he did came at a price, and once again it was asking him to pay out. And he knew he would. He'd forego whatever comfort he and Emily could have drawn from each other in future years if it meant he could still put people like Neil Watson in prison. In the same way that he'd sacrifice a more restful, peaceful lifestyle if he could nail the man who had strangled the life out of at least four young women.

That was who he was. It was who he would always be.

It was the one thing Jimmy Bliss was certain of.

TWENTY-FIVE

BLISS WAS RUNNING ON a combustible cocktail of adrenaline and anger. With Emily having left soon after their conversation faltered, he knew he ought to stay at home, spend the night in his recliner, listening to music and drowning his sorrows in alcohol. It was the tried and trusted method of blocking out emotional pain, and it had worked well in the past. But this time he felt beyond that, and knew precisely where to go to pick a fight.

SheDevils was located in the city centre, opposite Peterborough's main marketplace. If you had a penchant for shelling out on overpriced booze and watching young women cavort on stage wearing little and sometimes nothing, with private dances highly encouraged, SheDevils was the place for you. It wasn't the kind of establishment Bliss would usually want to be found anywhere near, but Neil Watson worked the entrance as a doorman. When Bliss cruised by, he made sure the bulked-up man was aware of his presence before he swung the car around and pulled up in a vacant slot further along the road.

Watson threw several hard stares Bliss's way, all to no effect. This went on for fifteen minutes. Then, right on cue, he broke away from his equally brawny partner, crossed the road and headed towards the parked pool car. With mounting excitement coursing through his bloodstream, Bliss watched the irate man approaching. The sensible thing would have been to drive away, having successfully slipped beneath the man's skin enough to prompt a reaction; on another night, he might well have done so. On this particular night, however, he was not quite himself. Instead of powering off, he got out of the car to confront the clearly furious doorman.

'Okay, you prick!' Watson snarled, teeth virtually meshed together like an enamel cage. 'I've had about all I'm willing to take from you. I'm calling my solicitor. Right now.'

Bliss regarded him casually, as nonchalant as he could manage. 'Please do. It's a free country, or so I am told.'

'He'll take you to the cleaners, Bliss. This is harassment!' Watson spat the last word, spittle fleeing his lips as if it had been trapped against its will.

'You think? I was merely sitting here pondering my day, wondering whether to pop in for a drink. You're the one who crossed the street to confront me, not the other way around.'

Watson took a step closer, glaring and prodding the air in front of him. 'Because you're following me.'

'So you allege. I say that's not the case.'

'So what are you doing here? Outside my place of work?'

'This is where you work? I had no idea. I was just out for a drive. Feeling a bit restless.'

'Yeah? Then why aren't you still driving?'

'I got tired. You know what they say about pulling over when you get tired.'

'And you happened to feel tired here?'

'It does look that way. Believe me, it's pure coincidence. We've all got to be somewhere, right?'

Another step. Another jab with the pointing finger. 'You're talking out of your arse, and my solicitor will tear you a new one. That's if I don't do it myself.' Watson looked around. The street was quiet, pavements empty. 'Nobody would blame me if I did. Believe me, I'm so fucking tempted.'

Bliss took a beat or two to settle himself. How far did he want to take this? And to what purpose? Perhaps this was the moment he had been building towards. He eased out a long breath, a fine mist briefly lying between them. 'You think because you have thirty years on me and you pump your body full of steroids that you'd kick my arse? That kind of complacency can be dangerous.'

'You reckon?'

'I do. Besides, I don't think you have it in you. I reckon you're only brave when it comes to hitting women and children.'

'I did all right against your mate. Or didn't that wanker you had following me tell you about the pasting I gave him?'

'Yeah, he told me. Told me it was no big deal, either. Reckons you're a bit soft. You suckered him, otherwise things would have gone the other way. Like I said, women and children are more your mark.'

Watson's shoulders tensed. His fingers flexed. He was teetering on the edge, and Bliss was glad of it. He recalled Emily accusing him of goading the man, and had known all along that she was right.

The finger came up one more time. 'You need to get the fuck out of here, old-timer. And I mean right this second. If you don't, I'll have you. I swear I will. You come at me as a man and not a cop, and I'll beat the shit out of you.'

The sensible thing remained for Bliss to get back into his car and drive away; any victory Watson took from it would be a hollow one. Only he wanted to see how far this bully would go. The man had an inch on him as well as three decades and a few kilos of heavy muscle, but Bliss could tell he was no brawler.

The man didn't set himself right. His stance was weak, leaving him vulnerable.

Watson would expect him to back off, so instead Bliss moved in close. His opponent would need to put distance between the two of them if he intended to take a proper swing. Bliss realised he'd left himself open should the doorman decide to use brute strength rather than throw a punch, but he believed in his assessment of the man. If he was wrong… it didn't bear thinking about.

'I'm right here, Neil,' he said. 'Still in your face. And you know what? I'm enjoying myself. You were right. I am harassing you, and nobody is going to say I didn't deserve whatever you decide to dish out. You have all the advantages, but I'll still let you take the first shot.'

Bliss knew his Sun Tzu; these were the perfect circumstances to wait, allow his enemy to move first. If he'd read Watson correctly, the man would opt instead to make a lame excuse and walk away – provided he hadn't taken a recent hit of his drug of choice, in which case Bliss would be screwed.

Watson's hands clenched. He shifted from foot to foot, but still his feet were too close together and in line with each other. If he went for it and Bliss slipped the punch, which would be slow and predictable, he'd immediately become unbalanced and topple forward. That would hand the advantage to Bliss, and he had only a split second to decide how far he wanted to go. In his current mood, the thought of taking it to extremes did not deter him. He thought Watson would back off, but a large part of him wanted it to go the other way.

Unlike his opponent, Bliss had slipped naturally into the right position to both repel an attack and respond swiftly with his own. His last fight had ended up a panting, wheezing mess on a muddy embankment; he was out of shape and had the stamina for probably no more than a minute of the kind of physical exertion trading blows with somebody entailed. Even if he won, he'd almost certainly break knuckles, tear ligaments and pull muscles. And yet still he egged Watson on.

'Come on, big man,' he said. 'If you need some encouragement, pretend I'm a small kid you can batter to death. We both know that's more your style.'

Anger erupted in Watson's eyes, but rapidly diminished. He had managed to reel in the momentary outrage, and Bliss assumed the man had come to his senses. Even if he had the heart to tackle Bliss, his was a no-win situation. Whatever the provocation, attacking a police officer would forever condemn him and land him in the kind of trouble he'd thus far managed to avoid.

'You haven't heard the last of me,' Watson muttered softly. 'I do you out here in the open and that's me finished. But keep both eyes open in the shadows from now on, Bliss. And one eye open when you sleep.'

Empty threats. Bliss had heard it all before, and he knew the difference between a meaningless gesture and genuine intent. He planted a wide grin on his face and got back into his car. As he drove past Watson he winked and gave the man a wave, the further insult not necessary but nonetheless satisfying. Applying pressure was the sole intention of this campaign Bliss had decided to wage against the man.

As he turned the corner he caught sight of two women exiting the club through a set of double doors. He recognised both. He pulled up by the kerb and powered down the passenger window. 'Fancy seeing you two here,' he said. 'You want a lift home?'

Marta Lsenko said she was only walking her friend to the taxi rank, and from there she was headed to O'Neill's bar and restaurant to meet somebody. A somewhat sheepish-looking Yeva Savchuk accepted his offer. Bliss asked for her address, and was surprised to hear she lived out in Cardea, a relatively new collection of privately built homes.

'You have your own place?' he asked.

'A one-bedroom house. Is small, but clean and warm.'

'You've done well for yourself. I'm happy for you.'

'Thank you. I work hard. But I would be nothing if not for you and your colleagues. If you are looking for me to thank you, I am happy to do this.'

Bliss turned his head to look at her. 'What? No, Yeva – that's not what I want at all. I want nothing from you. I'm giving you a lift home, that's all.'

The girl's face turned crimson and she let her chin drop. He could tell she had not wanted to make the offer, and she certainly would not have been happy to thank him in the way she'd implied. He understood her impulse, however. Such was the nature of young girls whose fate had come close to living that kind of life on a permanent basis.

'I was surprised to see you with Marta,' he said quickly, hoping to shake them both off the subject. 'And coming out of a place like that. Do you mind if I ask you what you were both doing there?'

'I do not mind. I told you I will not do what Marta does. But I do have second job. I dance at club. Not lap dance, you understand. Nor full strip. I dance pole, I earn good tip money. I don't dance for men or do other things for money. You understand difference?'

'I do.' Bliss nodded. It seemed important to her.

'I do this because I enjoy exercise and atmosphere, not because I have to. Not like Marta. She need to earn living this way.'

'I get it. But I didn't think you and Marta were close.'

'We see each other at club only. We are friends, but not close. What we went through, we went through together. You don't forget such things. You don't forget the journey or the people you make journey with. We share something. A different kind of friend.'

Bliss felt an overwhelming sympathy for both girls. All of them, in fact. The five they had rescued, the one who had escaped only to lose her life so brutally at the hands of Lewis Drake's men. Not forgetting all those who had come before and since. The trafficking of people followed by indentured slavery had gone on seemingly since there had been people around to exploit. That it still existed, with all the money, technological advances and united police forces spread across the world trying to prevent it, was an abomination to him. Such people were enslaved against their will, and often they were still in chains of one form or another. Across the decades this seemed to have largely been forgotten.

'I don't suppose you've ever come across a young Croatian woman by the name of Sara, have you?' he asked her, on the off-chance. 'Marta knows her, but says she doesn't know how to contact her. I wondered if you knew the girl and how I might get in touch.'

Savchuk looked across at him, and Bliss knew before she spoke that his night had not been in vain after all. 'Why? She do something bad?'

He shook his head. 'No. Not that I know of, at least. The thing is, Yeva, she might have information for us about the young girl I told you about – our victim. There's also the possibility that she may be in danger. If she were to meet with the wrong man… she could be another victim.'

'You know who victim is?'

'We do. We believe she was called Majidah Rassooli. Also known as Autumn, or sometimes Honey or Larmina. Do any of those names mean anything to you?'

Shaking her head, Savchuk began to tear up. 'No. I don't know these names. I know Sara because she was friend to Primrose – you know Haweeo?'

'Yes. We're aware the two were close. We think Primrose might be the one who gave up her card. She may have given it to Sara, or she might have known Majidah and handed it over to her directly. In truth, I don't know how much Sara will be able to help us, but I would like to speak to her about it. And warn her off… if she'll listen.'

'Warn her?'

'Yes. She might well be in danger.'

'How? What kind of danger? From who?'

'I can't tell you everything I know, Yeva. It's confidential, you understand? But if Sara is connected to our victim in a specific way – and it sounds to me as if she might be – then she is at risk. I'm not exaggerating. It's the kind of risk that can cost a girl her life.'

After several long seconds, Savchuk finally relented. 'I think I know how to speak with Sara. You let me meet. I persuade her to talk to you. You and Penny, I think. Sara will feel more comfortable with Penny there. I tell her you are good people, that I am here because of you. She will speak with you, I think.'

Bliss wanted to push harder, but he knew he had to handle this young woman more delicately. It was against her nature to trust, and encouraging somebody else to do the same would be a massive deal to her. It would take all she had to give.

'Thank you,' he said. 'Please try for me. We'll meet her wherever suits her best, whenever it suits her most. Just me and Pen. We want nothing more from her than to talk. But please do warn her we think there is a man out there who is dangerous, so the sooner she speaks with us the better.'

TWENTY-SIX

BLISS TREATED CHANDLER TO breakfast the following morning; he met her at the Holiday Inn, which served a delicious eggs Benedict. He had no idea if their hollandaise sauce was made by the chef or bought from a supermarket, but it was tasty. After they were done eating, he told his companion about the conversation he'd had with Emily the previous night.

'I can't believe it,' she said, slumping back in her chair. 'So that's it? You two are finished?'

'As a couple? Yes. As friends? I hope not.'

'So it's not salvageable? At all?'

'I think the crux of the matter, Pen, is that we both decided there was nothing *to* salvage.'

'So after you had your talk, she just upped and left?'

Bliss gave a wistful smile. 'Yes and no. That was the odd thing about the whole experience. She left, I went out for a drive. When I got back home, she was there again. Waiting for me in her car, not wanting to use her key. I made us a drink and we talked some more, though we mostly seemed to go around in circles. She ended up staying. She came up to bed with me. We didn't… nothing happened. She lay in my arms, her back to me, until we fell asleep. She went off first. When I woke up just after five, she'd already left.'

'Did she leave a note?'

'She did. You know Emily.'

'What did it say?'

'What if it was personal?'

'Oh, just tell me, you tosspot!'

Bliss smiled at her impatience. 'She said she loved me. That she probably always would. But she also said that no matter how we feel about each other, we want different things from life. She was glad we'd been honest enough to talk about whether we could make it as a couple, and that neither of us is to blame that we don't have it in us to succeed. She wished me love and happiness in the future, and hoped I wished the same for her.'

Chandler put a hand to her chest. 'Aw, really? That's so... so...'

'So Emily. I know. She uses few words, but they say everything.'

'What brought all this on, Jimmy? Did you see it coming?'

'I did. And as usual it's mostly my doing. But I'd rather not discuss it right now.'

'Okay. I understand. I'll call her later, see how she's doing. Probably get more sense out of her, too. How are you? How do you feel about it all?'

'I'm torn. Part of me thinks I ought to wallow, another part of me is grateful for the time she and I had together but accepts it simply ran its course. And most of me realises I have an investigation to run.'

'Not any more you don't. It's Bish's investigation. Remember?'

He nodded. 'Of course. But still our investigation to work. My head is too much in the game to think outside it. Maybe that's why my conversation with Emily went so pear-shaped.'

'You can't blame it on that. Whatever your issues, it didn't go wrong because your mind was suddenly elsewhere.'

'It didn't?'

Chandler raised her eyebrows. 'No. It went wrong because your heart wasn't there. Not enough of it, at least.'

'And you know this based on what I just told you? You're a better detective than I give you credit for.'

'That's true. But I know because I'm a woman, not because I'm a pretty shit-hot detective.'

'Are you claiming to be pretty and shit-hot, or pretty shit-hot?'

'The first one, of course. You had to ask?'

Bliss let out a long sigh. 'Ah, I don't know what I'm doing any more, Pen. The moment I take a step forward, I'm taking another back again. I'm going nowhere fast, but I don't seem to be able to slow down enough to make proper decisions. There's never enough time in the day.'

Chandler winced. 'I feel responsible somehow. I forced the relationship with Emily on you at a time when you weren't prepared.'

'No, it's not your fault. I said it was mostly my fault, but in truth I agree with Em when she says nobody is to blame. You're right to say I wasn't ready. I always knew what we had together suited me more than it did her. I thought it might last longer than a couple of months, but if you think about it, it's the most time we've ever spent together despite knowing each other for fifteen years. We put an awful lot of faith in what we had at the beginning, hoping to resurrect it somehow. She was both married and widowed during those intervening years, whereas I… I'd hardly moved on at all.'

'Not in the way she needed you to, perhaps. You're a different man in many other ways, Jimmy. And though I won't say you're stuck in the past when it comes to your personal life, neither have you moved on a great deal; I probably should have realised.

I think I was hoping you'd finally found someone. You and Em felt like the perfect couple.'

Bliss nodded. 'I know what you mean. Thing is, I've got maybe twenty to twenty-five years left, and most of that is going to be spent not working. You know better than most what the job means to me, so when I thought about the future I realised I hadn't yet reached the point where I could see Emily as being part of it right to the end. She saw it differently. And she didn't have any confidence in me ever to reach that stage.'

'Is she wrong?' Chandler asked. 'Because if she is, it's not too late.'

'I honestly don't know,' he admitted. 'But it is for the best. I think it tells us everything we need to know when I say I'm not even remotely sad about it.'

'Tell your face that, then.'

Bliss raised a fist. 'You want a mouthful of teeth?' It was a line from an old Steve Martin and John Candy film. It always made them chuckle. Chandler gave him a playful punch on the arm, and they moved on.

***

Encountering virtually the entire team in the major incident room came as no surprise to Bliss; only John Hunt had failed to show, which also came as no surprise. He immediately informed the team about the discovery of their potential new lead, Sara, and described his subsequent conversation with Yeva Savchuk. He did not linger on where or how they'd run into each other, instead explaining that he had spotted her on the street in town with Marta Lsenko and had offered them a lift home.

'Marta was meeting somebody at O'Neill's, but Yeva accepted my offer. She's living over in Cardea. It gave the two of us a chance to chat. I mentioned Sara, and thankfully Yeva not only knows her but is willing to contact her on our behalf. She's going to try to set up a meeting.'

'To what end?' Bishop asked. 'You think she's likely to tell us more than we already know?'

'Marta gave us plenty of colour; what she described was horrific. But to hear it first-hand rather than through a third party might make all the difference in how we assess our approach. Also, in addition to my fears that her next such encounter might be with our killer, there's also the distinct possibility that they've already met. Our man might well see these women a few times before he acts. If he becomes a regular, they're bound to let their guard down around him.'

'What if he already has her?' Chandler said in a low voice. 'After all, if he follows his previous pattern, we can be confident he's taken somebody. There's every chance it could be her.'

Bliss dipped his head. The thought had already occurred to him. 'It's possible. Hopefully we'll know one way or another come Monday, or possibly even sooner. But there is another reason why Sara might be useful to us: she might be able to give us some names. Other girls who allow choking. Perhaps even a girl who's not been seen for a few days.'

'Sounds like a plan,' Bishop said. 'You can handle that with Pen. In the meantime, where are we with this Dark Desires website? Any closer to knowing where it operates and who runs it?'

Ansari had been sitting, but now got to her feet. 'I've been in contact with our tech people at Hinchingbrooke. I've also spoken to a guy Glen Ashton put me onto at the NCA. They both said they'll do what they can when they can, but no promises. They have heavy workloads of their own, and this is a tough ask.'

'Because it's hidden?'

'Yes.'

'Could we try using the black card?' Bliss suggested. 'I think we know what to expect. We could talk to county, ask to borrow an undercover legend. Use it to pose as a potential client. We know our way in if we can get our hands on the spreadsheet; perhaps one of our tech people can find a way deeper. Even if it proves to be a dead end, we will have established communication. Tech support or the NCA might be able to trace the other end of that contact stream.'

Bishop nodded immediately. 'The boss is in. I'll have a word with her and ask for authorisation. We may need Superintendent Fletcher to step up on our behalf, because I think we'd require an entirely clean legend for this to work. Clearly the people running Dark Desires have their heads screwed on. They must vet potential clients as forensically as we would. We know their tech can be high end, so we have to assume the people running it use those skills to ensure nobody slips through the cracks.'

'You mentioned the NCA… Any idea why Ashton isn't with us today?' Bliss wasn't sure why, but he had expected more of the investigator.

'None. Perhaps he's happy with his involvement so far.'

'All the same, he needs to be advised as to where we are. I don't want him doing his own thing and getting in our way.'

'I'll notify him,' DC Gratton offered. 'I'll give him a buzz first, and if I get voicemail I'll leave a message telling him to check his e-mail. I'll send him all of our updates at the same time as I do the case log.'

Bishop nodded. 'Cheers, Phil. Ask him to run anything he has by us before he acts on it. Remember, there's a good chance this is all being fed back to DI Kennedy in Cambridge.'

Bliss clicked his fingers. 'Wasn't I supposed to be doing that? A daily report? Completely slipped my mind.'

Chandler chuckled. 'Of course it did, Jimmy. Of course it did.'

He spread his hands. 'We can't all be perfect. Anyway, fuck him.'

'Any other loose ends we can tie up at the moment?' Bishop called out, clapping his hands together to draw his team's attention. 'Anything on phones, CCTV, this clean-up crew who went to our victim's flat? Please tell me we have some movement here?'

The response was muted. Mobile phone data had been promised for Monday; Ansari and Gratton were due to work on CCTV feeds; nobody had anything on the clean-up crew. Uniform had visited Tim Beaumont to show him Wilma Parkinson's DVLA photo, but the landlord had claimed not to recognise her as the woman he'd spoken to.

'What d'you think, Jimmy?' Bishop asked. 'Is Beaumont worth another chat? Have him in here this time, apply a bit more pressure?'

Bliss shrugged. 'You were there, Bish; your guess is as good as mine. Personally, I think we got everything from him. But if you want him pulled, I'm happy to have another crack at the bloke. I'm assuming it won't be under caution.'

'Not at this stage, no. I agree – I don't think he held anything back. He was a bit slippery and trying to cover his arse, but there's probably nothing else there beyond dodgy business practices.'

'Nothing out of the ordinary in Rassooli's financials, either,' Chandler said. 'Plenty of regular cash payments, but no large sums in or out other than her monthly rent. And no movement at all in two weeks. Another dead end, sorry to say.'

'What was her final transaction?' Bliss asked.

Chandler riffled through some notes. 'Shopping at Tesco.'

'Local?'

'Yes. Serpentine Green.'

'Okay. I suppose that at least adds to the timeline we have for her. Shame it's not more.'

'I do have one new item,' DC Ansari said. 'It doesn't actually take us any further, but it could yet lead to an opening somewhere down the line. Yesterday I took photos of the labels on our victim's clothing and had Constable Maynard chase up the retailers or manufacturers to see if they were able to narrow the items down to particular batches. My hope is that if we're able to get that far, we might also be able to trace the purchases themselves. A tough ask, and Maynard was unable to obtain any firm answers as of yesterday evening. However, I looked at the Met's package of intel to see what they had on items of clothing; to their credit, they'd done the exact same thing. What they got back was a mixture of results, but surprisingly positive in terms of tracking the items down. Some were confirmed as having been purchased by the first three victims. But here's the truly interesting aspect: each of the items listed as not belonging to any of the known victims was paid for with cash.'

'That's good work, Gul,' Bishop said. 'So the obvious next question is: where were they bought?'

Ansari smiled. 'North London. A Matalan in Wood Green.'

Silence reigned for a few seconds as the team took in this new information. Bliss quickly ran through the different permutations before realising the opening this created. He looked across at Ansari. 'Gul. It seems to me that if the Met were able to identify the store and the cash payments, they were also able to follow through to time and date. Time and date allied to in-store security cameras surely gives us footage of the customer in question.'

Ansari was already nodding. 'Correct. But this brings us back to the part where I said it takes us no further – yet. The person caught on camera paying for the clothes is a woman. What role she has – if any – is unknown, and so is she. The Met were far too late to trace the cash, so there was no possibility of obtaining prints. The purchases were made almost a year prior to the first murder. The woman could be connected to our killer, or she might even be a victim we've yet to discover. But the unidentified piece of clothing found next to Majidah wasn't purchased at the same time. So, what I'm hoping is that it was bought elsewhere, perhaps even here in Peterborough. If so, it might give us a better lead.'

Bliss huffed in frustration. So close, but no cigar. Ansari had done good work, as had the Met, but while their efforts had forced open another thread for the investigation to follow, it had ultimately unravelled. If they could not identify the woman who purchased the clothing from Matalan, they had no way of tying that loose end off.

Thirty minutes after Bishop had thanked everybody and brought the briefing to a close, Bliss took a call from Superintendent Fletcher. The pleasure of his company was requested, only her actual words were: 'Get your arse up to my office!'

Every time he entered the third floor, Bliss was reminded of his previous encounters with the upper echelons of the police service. They had not always gone as well as he had liked, but in Marion Fletcher he had found a superintendent who almost always put the job in hand ahead of her personal ambitions. At most places of work, people tended to hate their bosses; that was the natural order of things, and the service was no better and no worse in that respect. But he had come to like and admire the DSI, and was already feeling disappointed that he had clearly upset her again. Enough to have her come into the station on her day off.

Dressed casually in blue jeans and a maroon hooded sweatshirt, Fletcher was staring out of her office window when he entered. In the reflection he saw stern features, and his heart sank a little deeper.

She turned, thumbs hooked into her pockets. 'I've had my opposite number over at Cambridge central on the phone to me, Jimmy,' she said. 'Do you have the vaguest notion why?'

He puffed out his lips, but decided a shrug might be too much. 'Not really, ma'am. Are they looking for a progress report, because I'm pretty sure that went out last night?'

Fletcher regarded him for an uncomfortably long time before replying. 'Let's start again, shall we, Sergeant? Assume I've asked that same question for the first time. Your response would be…?'

Bliss felt himself slump on the spot. 'All right. I confess I've not yet got around to updating DI Kennedy. As the Americans like to say, "my bad". Thing is, ma'am, it's not as if they don't know what's going on. Glen Ashton is filling them in on a daily basis, I suspect.'

'Suspect or know?'

'Obviously I can't know for sure. However, you'd have to be a fool not to realise what's going on. I understand my reporting back to the DI was one of the conditions of us being allowed to run with this case, but as having Ashton thrust upon us was also a part of that deal, you have to assume he's telling them everything.'

'So we're relying on suspecting and assuming, are we? Not good enough, Jimmy. Not good enough by a long way. You and I both know it was the possible link to Drake that swung things in our favour. With that connection looking increasingly unlikely, I don't know how much longer I can fend them off.'

'With respect, ma'am, we don't know how likely or unlikely it is. We have a strong lead to a dark website which might still prove to be owned by Drake's organisation. And we have the Met's blessing to continue with their own case. In my opinion, we have more than enough to keep Operation Phoenix running.'

Fletcher gave a resigned sigh. 'Then it's a good job I said as much and got Cambridge to back off. Not down, but off. That means they are still sniffing around in the background, so tread carefully. And please do DI Kennedy the small courtesy of at least calling him.'

'I will, ma'am. You can trust me on that.'

'Really. I can trust you, can I? Why, then, am I hearing today about a complaint being made about you by a member of the public?'

Bliss became instantly wary. It was not the time to tiptoe around pretending he had no idea what this was about; it was time to get out in front of it. 'If this is about Neil Watson, I can explain.'

'I have no doubt about that. I'm sure you will if I order you to. And perhaps some of what you tell me will even be the truth. But here's the thing, Jimmy: as of next Friday, I am on annual leave for two whole weeks. While you're all here freezing your private parts off, I'll be sunning myself on a beach in Barbados. What that means is, I won't be here tinkering with budgets or pulling together crime stats or, heaven forbid, managing crimes. More importantly in your case, Jimmy, I won't be here to protect you from yourself. So while I can make this complaint go away, I won't – I'll simply set it aside until I return. Meanwhile, I don't think I wish to be burdened by the precise details of whatever vendetta you're pursuing this week.'

Bliss blew out some air. 'Understood, boss.'

'But you should not regard that as permission to get your kicks in before midnight on Friday, either.'

'As if I would.'

Fletcher's gaze turned icy. 'We both know damned well you would. Jimmy, learn your bloody lesson for once and stay away from the man. I don't know everything you have going on with Watson, but I can tell it's not going away easily. That said, I'm ordering you to make it easier – on everybody, but especially you. If you ignore my instruction, it will be DCS Feeley you'll be dealing with and not me. I think we both know what that means.'

'And meanwhile Watson walks around as if he doesn't have blood on his hands. Literally. I'm sure you at least looked into him before you called me up here. You know what he did. What he's capable of.'

'I do. Which suggests he'll screw up again. His kind always do.'

'The trouble is, ma'am, when his kind screw up again they usually leave a dead body in their wake.'

'That's not what I meant, and you know it.' Fletcher's volume and tone distorted upwards.

'I know what you meant. You meant he'll step out of line again and someone will do the right thing this time and report him to us before his violence becomes extreme. But we both also know the reality is more likely to be that things will end up where they did before. He's killed one kid already, and – '

'Allegedly. You keep forgetting that part.'

Bliss threw his hands in the air. 'He did it. If you've even glanced at the relevant case file, ma'am, you know he did it every bit as much as I do. He beat that poor boy to death, and the mother was so terrified of him that she thought she'd be better off inside than out here with him. You know she's already been got to by her fellow prisoners? Boiling hot water all over her throat and chest. That, to her, is preferable to a life with Watson.'

Fletcher shifted her stance a little, tilting her head. 'And yet legally – which is still what counts, no matter how any of us feels about it – Neil Watson is guilty of nothing. In fact, you're closer to being charged than he is. So far he's made a complaint about you stalking him, claiming harassment. Right at this moment, I don't want to know the details, Jimmy. And not only because I'm looking forward to my holibobs, nor because I don't care what happens to you. I don't want to know the details because I fear that if I did, I'd have to turn you in to the DCS myself.'

Bliss nodded, calming himself. 'I appreciate that. Thank you, ma'am.'

'For what?'

'For giving me the opportunity to clear up my own mess.'

'What mess? I know nothing about any mess; I told you, I'm the three wise monkeys rolled into one where this is concerned. You deal with it. And if you make a mess of it, you know what to expect. No thanks from a grateful public. No handshakes all round from a proud employer. Neither I nor DCI Warburton will be able to save you this time. You'll be on your own.'

He gave a humourless smile. 'That's starting to have a familiar ring about it,' he said.

'Just you make sure you don't bring anyone else down with you, Jimmy.'

Bliss shook his head. 'Not a chance. I'll get Operation Phoenix done with first, ma'am. Me and the team as a unit. Anything else is mine and mine alone.'

TWENTY-SEVEN

AFTER A TIME, ABBI came to realise she was close to a river or a wide drain. Locked away inside her cell, she couldn't hear a thing emanating from the outside world. But during those infrequent occasions when Des opened up to drop her food off or collect her rubbish, or when she was allowed to visit the toilet or forced to endure the drenching and scrubbing, she picked up the odd noise drifting in on the cool breeze.

The gentle rush of flowing water was the sound that reached her most frequently. She thought its fluctuating strength might have something to do with the tide. Every so often a dog barked in the distance. On two occasions she caught the guttural grind of a large diesel engine, and immediately thought of a tractor or harvester.

Her initial thoughts were of her immediate surroundings prior to being drugged by Des. There was the river Nene, of course, but the gurgling she occasionally heard did not remind her of a river whose flow she knew so well. She frequented the drainage ditches and waterways out in the Fens less often, but they were ubiquitous. Abbi knew from her father, a keen observer of the tri-county flatlands, that draining of the Fens dated back to Roman times, though it began in earnest only in the early 1600s. Even so, between the rivers and the drains, there were hundreds of miles of waterways spread across the area.

Not that this knowledge did her much good under the circumstances. She had no idea how long she had been unconscious, and therefore had no way of knowing for certain in which direction her captor had driven. She might not even be in the same county, though the close proximity of mechanical farming equipment suggested a rural location. She was inclined to think that Des would not have wanted to drive far from the city, so hope remained that she was still relatively close to home.

But there was not much solace in that possibility. Even if she had known precisely where she was being kept, it would have counted for nothing. After all, she was unable to contact anybody to inform them. The real question was much more simple: had anybody missed her enough to report her unexplained and unplanned absence?

The thought caused Abbi to surrender to melancholy. How had she ended up here? How had things gone so badly wrong with her parents that she would rather sell her body than return to the home in which she was raised? They had not treated her poorly; that much she could admit. It wasn't as if her father had ever travelled the short distance along the landing from his bedroom to hers – a story she had heard often from other girls. He had only ever treated her kindly, with compassion and love. Her mother's personality was more reserved, and if there was harshness to be found, it certainly came from her. But even these outbursts were tempered with understanding. That, and a simple desire to raise a child properly.

The absence of sexual abuse and parental negligence aside, she had never been physically mistreated, either. Her father worked hard, and her mother kept a clean home and always put a hot evening meal on the table in addition to running her own small arts and crafts business. So much for leaving home to find independence, Abbi thought miserably. For the past couple of years she had submitted to being sexually victimised with great frequency and no tenderness – and that lifestyle choice had ultimately led her into the clutches of a man like Des and a place like this. What she would give for the warmth of her centrally heated home, her mother's cooking and baking… even her father's absurd, unfunny sense of humour. Together her parents had given her a great start in life, and this was what she had done with it.

Finished with sobbing, shame burning her cheeks, Abbi stretched herself out on the vile mattress to ease away the tension in her muscles. Moments later she curled up into a ball. She pulled the duvet tight around her neck and tucked her feet up to envelop them. The room was not quite as cold as it had been on the first couple of nights, but neither was there any reprieve from the air's corrosive touch.

The one thing that had surprised her about the situation she found herself in was that Des had not touched her sexually since her incarceration. She had come to understand the immense high some people got from being strangled – oxygen deprivation created a unique euphoria, and when coupled with orgasm it delivered a sensation unlike any other. But choking someone else out while obtaining that same sexual rush was a completely different thing altogether. She could only imagine the added excitement came from a sense of having control over life and death in that instant.

In truth, from the moment she first realised the terrible situation she was in, Abbi had assumed the worst: that Des would take their choking game further and further, leaving her closer each time to unconsciousness and, eventually, worse. That he had subsequently treated her more like an animal had left her confused, but equally wary. Because if Des had no intention of continuing with his peculiar form of lust, what exactly was the purpose of keeping her locked up like this?

About to close her eyes in a bid to snatch some much-needed sleep, Abbi heard a key scuff in the lock. She jammed her eyes tight shut and turned her head away as the door groaned open.

'There she is,' Des said. 'She's as good as broken in. Your money buys you an hour. But remember, I have others waiting, so leave her in good condition.'

Abbi's heart skipped several beats. She bit into her lip, deep enough to feel the warm flow of blood in the curve between her mouth and chin.

'Don't worry about it,' came a voice she did not recognise. 'I'm experienced. No safe word, right?'

'Of course not. Where's the fun in that?'

Abbi felt her entire body become rigid, her flesh both crawling and tightening at the same time. She choked down a groan, perhaps even a cry of terror. Pain rippled across the muscles in her stomach, pulsing like a living creature trapped beneath the skin.

'Good. She won't need one. I'll take her close to the edge and pull her right back again.'

'You'd better,' Des said flatly. 'You snuff her on the first attempt and it'll cost you big.'

Still lying on the filthy mattress, Abbi's stomach clenched again as she stifled the scream that threatened to erupt from the very centre of her being.

TWENTY-EIGHT

A T LUNCHTIME, BLISS NIPPED out to buy fish and chips for everyone. Netherton Fisheries served up some of the best in the city,
and had the advantage of being only a short drive from HQ. It
was something he did occasionally when the team put in extra
hours, and despite not being their boss anymore he insisted on
paying when Bishop offered to step up instead. It inflicted some
serious damage to his debit card, but keeping the troops happy
was worth every penny.

While he was waiting for the food order, Bliss popped outside to make a call. Kennedy was not exactly overwhelmed with
enthusiasm, but he at least listened graciously as Bliss reeled off
a summary of where the investigation was and where he hoped
to lead it.

'Shame I had to wait until now for an update,' the Cambridge
DI said curtly.

Bliss sighed into his phone. 'To tell the truth, I didn't appreciate you and Ashton treating me like a mug after calling me out
to the chalk pits. It was amateurish, and I admit I've responded
in kind.'

After a moment, Kennedy said, 'Yeah, I'll give you that one. It was Glen's play and I let him run with it. It was stupid of me. I hold my hands up, okay. Neither of us treated you with the respect you deserve.'

It was a fulsome apology as far as Bliss was concerned. He promised to keep the DI in the loop going forward.

Bliss and the team ate in the canteen so as to keep the air in the incident room as fresh as possible, sharing bottles of Coke and 7-Up between them. Back at their desks thirty minutes later, DC Ansari had begun filling them in on tech support progress when Bliss took a call from Yeva Savchuk. Sara had agreed to meet with them at Yeva's house. She was already there but would be gone again in an hour. If they still wanted to speak with her it was now or never. Bliss did not hesitate. He told Bishop about the call, and less than fifteen minutes later, he and Chandler pulled up outside Savchuk's front door.

The house was small but tastefully furnished. High-end electronics, expensive sofas with plump cushions, dark wood tables and bookshelves. The girl had a flair for décor, and an eye for nice things. The Croatian girl was slender with wavy brown hair that reached down almost to her waist. Big eyes and high cheekbones dominated a face too stern to be truly beautiful. A slightly crooked nose lent her some character. She wore a pale blue leisure suit beneath a fluorescent pink Superdry hoodie. Each ear supported half a dozen rings, and a single stud pierced her nose.

The two young women sat side by side on a large sofa, leaving Bliss and Chandler to take the two matching armchairs opposite. A small coffee table stood between them, a glass chess set and board sitting squarely in its centre. Sara fidgeted constantly, looking ill at ease, her eyes cast downwards while she played with her hair.

Bliss coughed once into his fist to draw her attention before speaking. 'I understand Yeva has already filled you in as to where our interests lie.'

She shifted her shoulders; a vague, uncommitted gesture.

'We believe your help could be important, Sara. For two reasons: firstly, it's possible that your own life could soon be in danger. Secondly, it's equally possible that you may know somebody who is already under serious threat.'

'This is to do with chokers, yes?' Her voice was much deeper than Bliss had imagined, a rough smoker's edge to it. He glanced down at her fingers, saw tell-tale nicotine stains surrounding shiny nails studded with jewels.

Bliss nodded, relaxing his features. 'It is. And please understand that neither of us are here to pass judgement on what you do. It's of no concern to us, other than it perhaps putting you in the sights of a man who enjoys killing by manual strangulation. You can tell us anything. Believe me, there's not much we haven't heard. You won't shock us.'

Sara nodded as if this was acceptable to her, but her eyes flitted between them still, anxious and uncertain. 'I tell you this, you do not tell my employer, no?'

Chandler slid forward and leaned in. 'Absolutely not. All we want from you is information. We will discuss it with our colleagues, but nobody from the outside. As DS Bliss mentioned, it's not of interest to us in that way. You're perfectly safe with us, Sara. And whatever you tell us is safe with us, too.'

'Okay. Ask me and I tell you if I can.'

Bliss leaned back, indicating to Chandler that he was happy for her to continue. 'We might occasionally have to ask you something awkward,' she said. 'Something you may find a little embarrassing. But please don't worry about it. We have some initial questions, but these tend to expand in a wider direction that's dictated by your responses. So let's get going, and please tell us if you need something explaining or if you'd like to take a break.' She smiled. 'Okay. I'll begin by asking you if you know of any other girls who offer the same erotic asphyxiation act who haven't been around for the past few days – say, since Tuesday or Wednesday. Anyone come to mind?'

Sitting upright and on the edge of her cushion, Sara extended a finger and tapped it against her pouting lips. Her eyes narrowed as she gave the question some consideration. They tightened further still when she spoke. 'I can't be sure, but this is possible, yes. We girls who meet such men have WhatsApp group. On phone, you understand?'

Both detectives nodded. Bliss said, 'Yes, of course. I assume you exchange information about the men you meet, and that way you can warn others if there's somebody out there whose behaviour is suspect?'

Sara nodded furiously. 'Yes. This. I do not know of man who others think badly of, except the ones who smell or are gross in other ways. But I have not seen WhatsApp from one girl in a few days. Her name is Abbi.'

Bliss felt a flutter in his chest, a spark chasing through his bloodstream. 'Do you know this girl outside of the WhatsApp group, Sara? Have you met? Do you know where she lives?'

Disappointingly, the girl shook her head this time. 'No. She do what I do, but we do not meet. I know from group that she is not like many of us – she is not from other country. She is called Abbi Turner. She is from here.'

'You mean the UK?'

'Yes. But here, also. Peterborough.'

'So it's your understanding that this Abbi Turner is a local girl, born and raised here in the city?'

'Yes. This is what she tell us. Not many like her. Most like me and Yeva.'

Bliss glanced across at Chandler. Her eyes widened and she nodded. Bliss thought about his next question. 'Sara, this is extremely important. Did Abbi mention anything about a man who recently struck her as being… not quite right? Perhaps a man who got too rough, or wanted to go too far? Maybe a man who didn't immediately respond to the safe word?'

'No.' The girl seemed certain. 'Like us all, she not happy doing this, but she say little about client. One man she quite like. She tell us he is gentleman.'

Chandler was immediately alert to this. 'Did she happen to mention his name?'

'No names. We use no names unless men are bad.'

Bliss understood why his partner had been interested. It fitted their limited profile for the killer to first ingratiate himself with one girl in particular, lulling them into a false sense of security before striking. He decided to push a little further. 'Sara, I know you say you don't use names inside the group. But it's possible that Abbi knew one or two of the other girls better than you. Perhaps they were friends. They might know who this man is. Would you ask them for us? Ask your WhatsApp group if any of them know Abbi well. And if so, whether they have seen or heard from her in the past few days. Also, if she ever told them the name or any other details relating to this client she liked.'

For the first time since they had initially made the girl feel comfortable, she started to look uncertain and anxious once again. Bliss could imagine why, and he tried to set her mind at ease. 'We don't want to involve them if we can possibly help it, Sara. Just as we have no interest in what you do for a living, we have no interest in them, either. Not in any way that will get you in trouble with us. But we do care about you as people. Yeva here has already vouched for us, and you can trust us as you trust her.'

Yeva bobbed her head and turned to her friend. 'Believe them, Sara. They do not wish to hurt any of us. Only to protect.'

Sara took a long breath. 'I will send message. I will ask. You want I do this now?'

Bliss smiled. 'If you don't mind. The sooner we know, the sooner we can respond. But please do tell them this is urgent. The man we are after – the man who killed another girl earlier in the week – may be stalking Abbi. He may even already have her. Tell them the more they are honest with us, the better our chances of finding her alive and well.'

Without another word, Sara slipped her phone from her pocket and began thumbing in a message. While she did so, Bliss switched his attention. 'Thank you for this, Yeva. It may be nothing, but if not, then your swift action might help Abbi.'

Chandler got to her feet and looked down at him. 'How about I step into the kitchen and give Gul a bell? I'll ask her to start a search for Abbi. Check our records, NCA's database, the electoral roll, social media. We could get an early hit.'

'Good,' Bliss replied with a nod. 'You do that. Might as well get the ball rolling while we're waiting.'

Sara was already finished. She gave Bliss a dubious look. 'We wait now, yes?'

'Do they usually respond quickly?'

'If they are not busy. Some work over weekend, others not. We get some answers soon, I think.'

Bliss regarded her more closely. What he had first taken to be a smooth complexion, he now noticed owed much to heavy makeup. Her cheeks and chin were pitted with acne scars, possibly due to having started wearing cheap makeup from an early age and sharing it with others. She looked to be around nineteen or twenty, but her eyes were much older.

'Sara,' he said gently. 'You know how Yeva and I met. I understand why some girls feel as if they have no way out of what they are doing. That they must allow themselves to be used or they may find themselves on the street, or worse. Is that why you do it? Are you forced into it by those who brought you here?'

Her big eyes blinked and she shifted uneasily in her seat. 'I not talk about them. You tell Yeva I not have to talk about them.'

'I did. And I meant it. You don't have to. I'm simply trying to understand. You see, if I could, I would rescue you all. I'd make sure that the men who did this to you can never hurt you again, but I know that's impossible. I've been fighting it one way or another for the past thirty years or more, and it's as bad today as it ever was. All I can do is try to help the girls who cross my path. Please know this, Sara: if you're ever in trouble with these people, if you don't know who to turn to in a crisis, you can always call us. Penny and I work out of Thorpe Wood police station. Ask for either of us. Okay?'

Sara's face lit up and she became someone else altogether. 'Thank you for this. Yeva trusts you. Now I do, too.' Her phone pinged twice, and she glanced down at the screen. 'Nothing to help so far.'

'That's fine. It perhaps only takes one girl to turn things around for us. Also, you mentioned how Abbi spoke of a client she liked – I assume he was fairly regular and she got to know him over time. How about you? Do you have any regulars who have perhaps tried to befriend you, not simply do what they need to do and leave? I ask because I wouldn't be surprised to find that this man we're after sees more than one girl at a time.'

Again she seemed to stare far off into the distance as she took herself out of the moment to consider his question. Finally she shook her head. 'I cannot think of such a man. I do have regular clients, and we get to know each other a little more. You see man only for one hour, you have no time to understand him. You see man for one hour a week for many weeks, you learn things.'

'But you can't think of anyone who claims to be looking for a longer-term relationship? Somebody who says they want more than whatever it is you do for them currently?'

'No. I think not.'

Chandler came back into the room. She remained standing. 'Wheels are in motion. Anything back from the WhatsApp group yet?'

Obligingly, Sara's phone pinged to announce another incoming message. This time Bliss saw her eyes widen. She frowned and read the message again before turning her attention back to them.

'A friend say she know Abbi. They talk. Abbi tell her about a man who became private client. They still do as he asks, but he pay her and not agency. Abbi mention him often and have fondness for him. She think he want to be her boyfriend. She think maybe she want that, too.'

Bliss nodded eagerly, feeling his pulse rate increase. 'That sounds like precisely the kind of man we'd be interested in. Did this friend mention the last time she spoke to or saw Abbi?'

'Yes. She say Monday. She try calling her since but only get told to leave message. She is worried.'

'Understandably so. I have to be honest and say that I am, too. Please ask your friend if she will speak to us.'

Sara started pressing buttons immediately. Less than ten seconds passed before she got a reply. 'She does not wish to. But if you ask me question, I ask her and she will answer if she can.'

Bliss was a little frustrated, but he understood the other girl's reluctance. He doubted if Sara would have spoken to them willingly had Yeva not vouched for them. It was a vetting process he was willing to go through again, but he worried about the time it would take. 'Okay,' he said. 'Please ask her if Abbi ever mentioned this man's name.'

'We don't use name. I told you this.'

'I understand. But if this man was becoming more than a client to Abbi, she might have mentioned it to someone she considered to be a close friend.'

Sara accepted this with a shrug and once again sent out a message. There was no immediate response. Sara typed something else and hit send. They waited a further twenty seconds before the next ping. This time the message was from another member of the group, telling Sara she did not know Abbi. The next message was the reply they'd been waiting for.

'She says Abbi once spoke his first name only. She call him Des. That is all.'

Bliss bit into his lip. It was something, but nowhere near enough; nothing that would help find either him or her, that was for sure. Knowing his name might help further down the road, however, so Bliss buttoned up his frustration and smiled at the young Croat. 'Please thank her for us. Please ask her to think about it some more, and if anything else occurs to her, to contact you or the station. She needn't give a name – just ask for DS Bliss or DS Chandler.'

As her thumbs became a blur once again, Bliss rose. He smiled at Yeva, who had given up her time and her home to them. 'We appreciate this,' he said. 'As I hope you have come to understand, you mustn't ever be afraid to call us. Whatever the reason. That card counts as long as I still breathe.'

Sara was done and on her feet. Chandler tenderly rubbed the young girl's arm and told her not to worry, but also to take care and be cautious. 'Please watch your back – be careful – at all times. This Des person might be a friendly punter and not our man at all, and you need to be wary of any clients coming to you for their choking fix.'

'I will be careful. Thank you.'

'No, thank you,' Bliss said. He shook her hand, smiling as he did so. 'This has been extremely helpful. Take care of yourself, and please do pass on any relevant responses you get from your group.'

Out on the street, they stood in the drizzle for a moment, Bliss's face turned to a leaden sky that looked almost low enough to touch. 'Why do we live in a world of such opposites, Pen?' he asked.

'I'm not sure I know what you mean.'

'Well, on the one hand you have these lovely, sweet young girls who are pleasant and warm and considerate. On the other you have the sleazy reptiles who use and abuse them.'

'That's human beings for you, Jimmy. The best and the worst of us get to share the same space.'

His face creased into an ugly snarl. 'I'd like to crush the pricks who take advantage of these kids.'

'Not to mention the bastards who force them into it in the first place,' Chandler said, walking around to the passenger side of the car.

'Which brings me back to Lewis Drake. What if Dark Desires is his, Pen? What if he's ultimately responsible for putting Majidah Rassooli and the man who murdered her in the same space?'

'If that's the case, we'll find evidence for it. We could try making a case for joint enterprise.'

Bliss shook his head. 'No, he's too far removed from it, especially as things stand. But I want him to pay. He has to pay.'

Even as he said the words, he knew his plea was little more than wasted breath, twisting away from him in a coiled exhalation that disappeared as quickly as all hope.

TWENTY-NINE

FOLLOWING A COUPLE OF after-work drinks with the team, Bliss spent Saturday night in limbo. His head ached with the weight of the investigation. The thought of another young girl – whether Abbi Turner or someone else – already being in the clutches of such a vile monster churned his stomach. A case like this one offered so many opportunities for the investigation team to feel completely useless, and this was one of them.

Earlier in the day he'd thought they had made a valuable breakthrough. DC Ansari had come up with a possible address for Turner, having plotted her profile by taking snippets of social media information and tying them in with their own personal data search facilities. They'd not found Turner at the home in question, but a neighbour had pointed them in the direction of her family. Unfortunately, this brought them to another dead end, with neither parent having seen or heard from Abbi in more than a year. Chandler had poked a card through Abbi's letterbox, asking her to call as soon as she saw the note, insisting she was not in trouble.

Bliss strongly believed otherwise. He had a terrible feeling that Abbi would soon become their next victim.

Having the girl's photo on the whiteboard added to his despair. Putting a face to the name meant he would see her whenever he closed his eyes, at which point he would dwell upon all she might be enduring. He knew she might have run away or taken herself off on holiday, choosing not to update any of her social media or contact those close to her in any other way. But he wasn't feeling it. It didn't sit right with him. This was not a girl who went five days without keeping in touch – not by choice.

A rapid exchange of calls between Chandler, Yeva and Sara, plus more than a little gentle persuasion, eventually also gave the team Abbi's personal mobile number. It could not be pinged, suggesting it was either switched off or had been made inoperative by removal of the battery, SIM card, or both. Ansari compiled yet another RIPA request, requiring access to not only text messages, voicemails and image galleries, but also the mapping provided by its GPS movements prior to going offline.

The team were also frustrated by delays in obtaining permission to use an undercover legend. Their request was caught up in the bureaucracy of official channels, and they all knew that meant it was being wrapped in layers of red tape and undergoing all manner of checks requiring signatures of authority. Bishop had eventually called a halt for the day late in the afternoon, and subsequently bought the first round in the Woodman.

Later on, Jimmy took advantage of a night alone by calling his mother in Ireland, conversations with whom latterly had led him to suspect her memory might be on the wane. He also enjoyed a long chat with Molly, a suspect and witness from a previous investigation who had somehow found herself able to pick the rusted locks on the solid steel gates guarding his heart.

Around eight-thirty, Bliss tried taking his mind off the case by watching streamed repeats of *Better Call Saul*. He'd previously enjoyed the way the series interwove characters and events from its predecessor, *Breaking Bad*, into its storyline, but this time found his mind drifting after only ten minutes.

This particular investigation was unusual. Cases most often split themselves into two categories: those that gave up their secrets rapidly, leading to early arrests, and those whose lethargic pace led the investigation team into labyrinths from which there was no escape. The difference this time lay in the fact that they were consistently obtaining leads, but none of them had so far prised open the operation enough to provide that single pearl of an answer they needed most. Whatever it was – a piece of CCTV, some DNA, a verbal slip, a witness statement, or a chance occurrence – it had not yet happened. Bliss's irritation with that stasis only increased his inability to settle.

He played some music, but nothing improved his mood. He went for a drive, but the cobwebs fluttering in his mind remained. On his return, a couple of hits from a new bottle of fourteen-year-old Tullamore Dew loosened him up, but had no effect on his overall outlook. He was in a funk. Shortly after midnight he took his acoustic guitar out of its case and began to strum softly. Bliss soon realised how soft and stiff his fingers had become through lack of practice; the strings hurt like hell, especially the thinner unwound top three. He played through the pain for an hour, remembering the chord sequences to a number of songs. By the time he was done, two of the fingertips on his left hand had been sliced open and he had to wipe blood from the fretboard. He was thrilled to do so.

Sunday came and went at a crawl. Bliss nipped into HQ, but only DCs Gratton and Ansari were in the squad room. Neither had an update for him, so he took himself off to the city-centre community hall where PC Griffin taught boxing to kids deemed to be at risk of falling foul of the system. Keeping himself tucked out of the way, Bliss first went through an old familiar stretching routine. With heat still in his muscles, he worked a thirty-five-kilo punch bag, which provided good resistance. Afterwards he went through a series of strength exercises: sit-ups, push-ups, crunches and burpees. He eschewed the skipping rope, figuring he had no need to improve his footwork speed or agility in order to train others. Instead he warmed down on the speed bag, bobbing and weaving in between strokes. Sweat cooled on him quickly, and although he was leaving a shower for when he got home, he did towel himself down before getting changed.

As he was leaving he met PC Griffin, on his way in. The two men smiled at each other, but instead of saying hello, Griffin pointed a finger and said, '*Tore Down House*.'

Bliss shook his head. 'Too easy. Scott Henderson.'

'With…?'

'Thelma Houston, of course.'

'Damn! Thought I'd have you with that one.'

Griffin had learned of Bliss's musical tastes, in particular his love of blues and guitarists. The young constable fancied himself as something of a connoisseur, and the two often challenged each other's knowledge.

'I'll make it easier on you, Barry,' Bliss said. 'Song title and album name.'

Griffin steeled himself. 'Hit me.'

'"Waves", from *Erotic Cakes*.' The moment he finished speaking, Bliss knew he had his man. The deep frown and near panic in his opponent's eyes told a story of their own.

After a full twenty seconds, Griffin's shoulders sagged. 'No,' he said, shaking his head ruefully. 'I don't know it.'

'Check it out. You'll love it. Guthrie Govan.'

'You know I'm going to go deeper next time, Jimmy? That's four on the spin you've won.'

Bliss shrugged. 'Some of us have what it takes, pal. Others…
they have to run to catch up with my casual dude stroll.' He
winked, waved and said his goodbyes. 'See you Wednesday, Barry.
Don't be late.'

'"Any Major Dude"!' Griffin called out.

'Don't embarrass yourself, man. Steely Dan, off the *Pretzel
Logic* album.' His grin grew wider at the parting shot.

The workout was more exercise than he had taken in a long
time, so Bliss thought he had earned an early dinner at the Wind-
mill. As usual he sat with his back to the wall, allowing him to
survey the entire bar. By the time he was finished he could already
feel his muscles growing tight, and knew he was going to ache
like a bastard in the morning. In his youth he'd often take an ice
bath after a particularly rigorous workout, but there was no way
he could face one of those again. When he pulled up outside his
house a short while later, he was both surprised and delighted to
see the old labrador that had taken to loitering close by.

He still had no idea who the dog belonged to. Having originally thought the animal was a stray, and assumed when it
stopped coming around that it had possibly wandered off to die
alone, Bliss had been thrilled to see it turn up again a few weeks
ago. Since then it had been a regular visitor, and he left food and
water out beneath the porch by his front door every evening.

Throughout the afternoon and evening, his thoughts flitted
between the separate strands of the investigation, to the point
where he was unable to focus on any of them. Determined to
clear his head, Bliss ploughed through several albums and CDs.
He'd recently bought some remastered Badfinger music, although
whenever he played their songs he became melancholy at the
thought of their tragic history. Lynyrd Skynyrd had the same
effect on him. When he started thinking about it, and realised
how many of his favourite musicians had been taken over the

past few years, his melancholy slid downhill towards the full-blown blues. Bliss stirred himself out of the trough by putting his mind to the investigation once more. This time, he had a spark of inspiration.

It took three phone calls in which he had to survive irritation and a certain amount of animosity at having disturbed people on their day off, but eventually Bliss got what he needed. Afterwards he sent a text to Bishop, explaining why neither he nor Chandler would be at HQ until the following afternoon, before calling Penny herself to give her the news.

THIRTY

THE VAST THAMESMEAD SITE included both HMP Thameside and HMP YOI/Isis in addition to the infamous Belmarsh prison. The three-storey yellow-brick entrance to the latter presented a grim exterior, either side of which ran an equally austere perimeter wall. Behind its bland concrete facade stood several individual pods, each enclosed within its own concrete wall for added security. To access the main prison, most visitors had to negotiate fifteen gated doors after first having their fingerprints scanned. Bliss and Chandler enjoyed the benefit of being escorted via a different route, though they were eventually subjected to their own security checks, including meeting the biometric challenge.

From the main building they entered the high-security unit. In its small reception area, beneath a bank of CCTV cameras, they each removed their shoes and put their belongings through an x-ray scanning machine. They stepped through a metal detector, after which both were thoroughly searched, right down to the linings of their clothes, the soles of their feet and inside their mouths.

Chandler shunned the offer of a separate room in which to submit to her search, having been warned the process would require an extra member of staff and so slow them down. Instead she opted to undergo it in the main area, wearing only her underwear. Bliss could almost feel his partner's eyes boring into him, daring him to take a peek. He resisted for as long as he could before finally turning to face her. He gave a wink of approval, accompanied by a low whistle. Chandler had turned forty but clearly took care of herself. Her long legs were shapely and firm, stomach taut, small breasts defiantly perky.

Bliss sucked his stomach in as she glared back at him, arms now folded across her chest. He was in decent condition for his age but could no longer deny the paunch he'd developed. He thought his partner might offer an opinion about his own choice of underwear, mocking his jockey shorts with their jade-coloured floral pattern. Instead, she dropped her own barely repressed irritation and returned the whistle and objectifying appraisal.

'See what you could have had,' he called over, indicating his own body with a sweep of his hand. 'You're going to be thinking of me next time you're with Shrek, aren't you?'

Unable to help herself, Chandler cackled. She placed both hands on her hips. 'You get a load of this, old man: your one and only chance to ogle at this fine specimen of womanhood. I bet it's been a long time since you've laid eyes on anything this firm.'

He had to laugh. 'I'll tell Emily you said that.'

A poked tongue was her only retort this time.

A red gate barred the way beyond the reception security area, and they waited at least five minutes while additional checks were carried out. Beyond the gate they had to pass through a further four doors, no more than two of which were ever open at the same time. On the first of two floors, the second room on the eastern spur was a designated legal team area. No cameras or listening devices were allowed within its cramped rectangular space, though the panic strip was prominent around the width of all four walls.

A guard accompanied them through each separate section of the prison; at no point did they lay eyes on any of the prisoners. As soon as they entered the room in which they were due to meet with Lewis Drake, the guard spoke into his two-way radio and gave the okay.

'I guess you've seen it all in your time, eh?' Bliss said to the guard, a stout, muscular man who looked to be in his late forties. 'The real dregs of humanity are kept in here.'

'We've also had the likes of Assange and Archer,' the guard said, offering a shrug that suggested it was all in a day's work. 'Not here in the HSU, of course. Behind these walls we've had men like Ian Huntley, Charles Bronson, even Ronnie Biggs. Huntley walked around with a target on his back, what with him being a nonce… IRA men were all the rage for a while; now it's Islamists. I'm on the last year of my spell in this unit, and I couldn't honestly tell you who was the worst. Your man Drake, though – he's a real piece of work. Slippery bastard, so watch yourselves. One minute he's charming you, the next he's frothing at the mouth, wanting to tear your arms off.'

Bliss glanced at the table bolted to the floor and affixed against one wall. The steel loops used to restrain the prisoners looked impervious to even the most violent of rages. 'Thanks for the tip,' he said. 'But we know Drake well enough.'

'Oh, so you've bumped up against him before?'

'Yeah. We arrested him. We are why he's in here.'

The guard's response was immediate. 'I'm glad you mentioned that. It might well up his aggressiveness. He was in one of our other Cat A blocks originally, but his violent outbursts became impossible to manage. He's a genuine escape risk as well, so the

HSU is the best place for him. Odd thing is, since day one he's refused all requests for visitors.'

'We're the first?' Chandler said, her surprise evident.

'Other than his legal team. Don't know how you managed it, either, at such short notice.'

'Friends in low places,' Bliss told him.

The guard chuckled. 'Yeah. I guessed it was something like that. Well, you're welcome to him. Just one thing, and I don't mean to come across as sexist or anything, but you need to be prepared for him, DS Chandler. The man has been banged up in one prison or another for more than two years, and despite his appeal he knows he's never walking out of here. That's something to keep in mind at all times. The only women he's laid eyes on since he's been away have been guards. But they don't count for much, because I don't think he even regards them as human, let alone women. It's good that you've chosen to wear trousers, and I'd advise you to keep your jacket fastened. If you have to look directly at him, make sure you break eye contact often. Anything else and he'll see it as interest on your part. He won't be able to reach you, but he has a foul mouth and he'll be looking to get a rise out of you.'

Chandler arched her eyebrows. 'Thank you. I dare say I've heard worse. The day one of our more charming clients back home in Peterborough told me how much he'd like to cut my throat, wash my face in acid, set light to me, and then fuck my still-smouldering corpse, was a particular highlight.'

'Bloody hell,' the guard said, his voice no more than a stunned whisper.

'That was one of her better first dates,' Bliss said.

The three laughed; it was preferable to showing their anxiety. Chains or not, the thought of being trapped inside a room with somebody as psychotic as Lewis Drake was enough to set anyone's pulse racing.

The door opened, squealing theatrically on its hinges. A moment later, wearing a yellow T-shirt and standard maroon jogging bottoms, in stepped the man himself – all five-eight and barely twelve stone of him. Even with a freshly shaved head and contact lenses having replaced his glasses, Drake was not an imposing figure.

His reputation for explosions of vicious and untamed violence, however, preceded him. Even without having interviewed him previously, Bliss would recognise this man for what he was: monstrous, and entirely lacking in either morals or conscience.

THIRTY-ONE

THE LOOK OF TWISTED amusement on Drake's face was worthy of a photograph, to be used in a training exercise at a later date. Even after the prisoner managed to get a grip on his emotions, Bliss still detected a faint twitch of the lips and a pulsing tic beneath the man's left eye. Drake's legal team had informed him of the interview request, and against their advice he had chosen to go ahead without representation. Having those responsible for his incarceration in such close proximity once again appeared to be giving him some kind of perverse thrill. After giving Bliss no more than a cursory glance, his eyes alighted on Chandler and remained there while he sat and had his cuffed hands chained to the steel loops on the table. The guard who had brought him to the room remained standing by the door.

Bliss sat upright, swallowing down his earlier unease. 'Hello, Lewis. I'm sure you remember us, but for the record, I'm DS Bliss; this is my colleague, DS Chandler. We'd like a chat with you.'

The prisoner didn't so much as blink, nor did he look Bliss's way. 'Is that right? Well, I suggest you leave me and Sergeant Chandler here all alone for ten minutes while we get reacquainted.'

'Most men only last two minutes with me, Lewis,' Chandler said. 'I'm that good. I reckon you'd need no more than thirty seconds. At best.'

Drake leaned forward across the table, seemingly unruffled. Light bounced off the thin film of sweat covering his head. 'You think it's wise to disrespect a man like me?'

Chandler grinned. 'Why not? I helped put you in here, after all. Besides, what are you going to do from there?'

This time it was Drake's turn to smile. He wore a relatively new set of false teeth, and Bliss wondered if he'd lost his own in some random act of violence. 'You think my reach extends only as far as these chains?' Drake rattled the cuffs on his wrists for emphasis. 'That would be a big mistake.'

Chandler opened her mouth to respond, but Bliss caught her attention and gave an almost imperceptible shake of the head. He understood her motivation: proving she would not be cowed by such a man. But he needed her not to take it too far. He wanted information from Drake. Also, the prisoner was not wrong about his influence outside of this prison.

'I think any talk of respect is premature,' Bliss said. 'That has to be earned. And it cuts both ways. So, are you happy for us to continue?'

The corners of Drake's mouth curled upwards as if drawn into a smile by an invisible string. 'I'm never exactly happy when I'm in the same room as the filth, but I'm up for it, yeah. I can handle you pair of arseholes, that's for sure.'

Bliss eyeballed him. The gamble of forcing Drake into a corner seemed to have paid off, the man's ego taking charge as he'd intended. The voice was raspier than he remembered it, and he wondered if that was due to lack of use. But he was talking, and Bliss hoped that would continue. Moreover, he needed to make sure the man remained in the room long enough to listen.

'Good. We'd like to talk to you about one of your old businesses, Lewis. And let me make it perfectly clear that we don't expect you to rat out any of your family or friends or even those workers you don't give a toss about. If you don't believe me, or you suspect we're trying to take you for a fool, let me ask my questions, after which you can choose to answer them or not. How does that sound?'

After a moment that seemed to last an eternity, Drake's narrow shoulders rose and fell. Still he did not avert his gaze, his eyes fixed steadily on Chandler, who had remembered the advice not to try matching the stare.

'Excellent,' Bliss said, adjusting himself to get a little more comfortable. The tension in the room was palpable. 'I'm going to begin by reading out a few names. When I'm done, I'd like you to tell me what your current connection to them is. That sound okay, Lewis?'

'Just get the fuck on with it. I haven't got all day.'

'Somewhere else to be?'

This drew the man's gaze. His eyes formed tight slits. 'Yeah. Chess club. And *Pointless* is on the telly later.'

Nodding, Bliss read the names printed on a sheet of paper he'd taken from his breast pocket. 'EZEscorts. Galaxy Escort Agency. Glamour Pussy Escorts. Dark Desires.'

Only the last provoked a reaction. It came and went in an instant, and you had to be looking for it – which Bliss was. What he saw bothered him enormously.

'What's in this for me?' Drake asked, stretching out his legs. 'I'm not sure what you hope to get out of it, but I'm bloody certain there's fuck all reason for me to say anything to you.'

'I'd say that depends on how cooperative and useful you are, Lewis. Even in this unit you're allowed certain privileges. I can have a word in the right ear to ask about extending one or two of those for you.'

He had Drake's attention. Being in jail stripped a man of so many things, and high-security units like this one took away even more. Gaining something significant in exchange for giving up so little was an offer worth considering. Bliss thought of sweetening the pot, but instead opted to go another way. Drake might not believe him if he offered too much in one go, but honesty was a currency all prisoners understood.

'I'm making no promises. You need to understand that. But if you open up to me, I will do what I can.'

Drake's chest expanded as if he'd plumbed himself in to an air pump. He held the breath for a moment before releasing it in one long sigh. 'All of those except the last one are familiar to me. They were my agencies. Legit businesses, I'd remind you. Various members of my organisation run them for me in my absence. But you already knew that, so why ask?'

'Let's call it a test. To see how upfront you'd be. Banged-up villains aren't usually the most trustworthy of people, Lewis. And the ones who murder young women by slipping them into drums of acid tend to be stone-cold liars.'

Drake sat back and went to fold his arms, the chains pulling tight against the steel loops. Anger erupted like a rash across his face, but he quelled it swiftly and soon relaxed again.

Bliss was surprised by the man's strength of will. 'What about Dark Desires?' he prompted.

'I don't know nothing about them. Never heard of them.'

'Are you sure, Lewis? See, that contradicts what we've been told. Our understanding is that Dark Desires is one of yours, only even more seedy and repulsive. And perhaps the most secretive.'

'I don't have a clue what you're talking about. What is it, even?'

Bliss had been leading up to this since spotting Drake's initial reaction to the name. If he was wrong, he would be handing Drake the advantage; if he was right, he might be adding fuel to an already raging fire.

'It's another agency, Lewis. Only with this one you get to pick girls for the most vile and dangerous acts you can possibly think of. Real degrading, abhorrent stuff.'

Drake shook his head. 'Nah, I don't have nothing to do with shit like that.'

'Of course not. You're such a humanitarian,' Chandler muttered.

Drake spun his head. 'Stay the fuck out of this, darling, or jump at shadows the rest of your natural.'

'And here I was thinking this was going so well,' Bliss said, keeping his cool. 'No need for threats, Lewis. You may not care for my colleague's remark, but she's not wrong to sneer, is she? You're a despicable man who wouldn't turn his nose up at anything, however unsavoury or sordid, if it meant buying another beach house in sunny Florida.'

Drake laughed, his head bucking backwards. 'You know how many fucks I give what you think of me?'

'I'm guessing that would be none.'

'Well, aren't you a clever copper? Brightest of the bunch, are we? I'm guessing DS Chandler there is for eye candy. I can see why, mind. I'd do her – at a push. I mean, she is getting on a bit.'

Chandler acted amused. 'You'd have to be the last man on earth, and I'd have to be dying. And I'd still put up a good fight rather than endure one touch from you.'

'I'm sure part of that can be arranged, darling.' Drake chuckled, not rattled at all by any part of their conversation. The sick bastard was enjoying himself. Worst of all, Bliss believed him when he said he knew nothing about Dark Desires. Even so, he had one last move.

'Let's say we take your word, Lewis, and Dark Desires is not yours. Why do you think we are hearing otherwise?'

'How should I know? Maybe it's Fuck With A Copper Week. Oh no, wait a minute. That's every week, yeah?'

Bliss remained impassive. 'Nice one. You got us there, Lewis. But you know what I'm wondering?' It was time to follow up on that initial reaction he'd seen in the man's eyes.

'No. And I don't give a fuck, either.'

'I'm wondering if somebody inside your organisation is running Dark Desires without your knowledge. From what I hear, the punters visiting that site pay a lot of money to get their jollies. It's an extremely lucrative part of the enterprise, Lewis. A shitload of money coming in, and apparently you're not seeing a single penny of it. That can't be right, can it?'

This time Bliss knew he'd struck a blow. Again it showed in the man's troubled features, but his entire body also went rigid. Drake stuck his chin out and both nostrils flared.

'What's up, Lewis? You not liking the idea of someone pulling a stroke like that behind your back? Have to say it surprises me. Looks like you're not the big-time Charlie you thought you were.'

'Is this for real?' Drake managed to say through a mouth that was virtually clamped shut. 'Or are you pair of wankers winding me up?'

'Why else would we be here? We came here thinking you might be able to give us some specific information about a Dark Desires client. Turns out you weren't even aware of its existence. Didn't take much time to cut you out of the loop, did it?'

Drake said nothing for a good twenty seconds. Eventually he jabbed his head in the direction of the door. 'On your way now, Pinky and Perky. If I can think of a way you pair of useless shits can scratch my back, I'll consider scratching yours. Might take me a day or two, though. So off you trot. I'm missing chess club.'

Finished with the interview, Bliss kept his eyes fastened on Drake until the man flinched and narrowed his own gaze. 'Just so's we're clear,' Bliss said in a low voice. 'That shot you took at my colleague about her jumping at shadows the rest of her life had better be bravado on your part.'

Drake smirked. 'Yeah? And why's that?'

'Because she happens to be more of a lunatic than I am. If it were me, I'd have the authorities punish you for that threat by taking away some of those privileges we spoke about earlier – whereas my sergeant here has her own unique style and substance. She has a way of creating her own shadows. The world outside is a vast place, Lewis, but that's not the case in here. In here, you can be got to. In here, every shadow is a potential threat.'

The man made no reply. He faced Bliss for a long time, before shifting his focus. 'Let's call it quits, eh?' he said. 'No need for either of us to hold a grudge, is there, darling?'

'I don't hold grudges, Lewis,' Chandler said, getting to her feet as Bliss also rose. 'I get even. Usually long before I have anything to get even about.'

'You're a hard-arse, eh?'

Chandler's eyebrows arched then fell. 'Pray you never have to find out.'

***

Mobile phones were not allowed inside the prison, so when Bliss retrieved his and switched it back on, a series of text messages and voicemails came in. As he and his partner walked across the car park, he selected one from Bishop and listened carefully to what his colleague had to say. When he was finished he turned to Chandler, a wide smile illuminating his face.

'We got the go-ahead to use the undercover legend. It's already in play. Bish used the card – and the legend held up, because he got back the spreadsheet and the directions. It worked a treat. He said typing Enter into the A1 cell ran something that brought up a link in that buried cell further down the sheet. The password came in another separate e-mail, and they're in.'

'How bad is it? Did he say?'

'No. Just that we were in and work had already begun on monitoring.'

'Perhaps this was a wasted trip.'

Bliss was undeterred. 'Maybe. But you saw how Drake reacted. I'm confident he knows nothing about the site, which I wouldn't have known if we'd not come. I'm equally certain we now have him wondering if he's been cut out of a money-making machine being run by somebody inside his outfit. Believe me, after what he heard from us, Lewis Drake is going to do some digging of his own. All of which means our visit might still bear fruit.'

'I wouldn't want to be in the shoes of whoever is doing this on the side. What he lacks in size and stature, he more than makes up for in viciousness and lack of scruples. You still reckon it's Parkinson?'

'She'd be my prime suspect, yes. Nicola has a unique position inside the organisation, and few people know that business better than her. I wouldn't be surprised to find her son and daughter involved, either.'

Chandler was listening to him, but checking her own phone at the same time. 'This isn't so good,' she said, still reading a text. 'Yeva heard back from Sara. Somebody else in the WhatsApp group confirms Abbi Turner has been off the grid since Wednesday.'

He cursed and turned his face to the rain that had begun falling from a sky swollen with malicious intent. As they had suspected, it was looking like their killer had already abducted his new victim. Bliss had been prepared for this moment since first hearing from the Met about the other murders, but now he and the entire team had to face one clear truth: they were up against the clock, and a young woman's life expectancy was ticking down with each second that elapsed.

THIRTY-TWO

B Y THE TIME BLISS and Chandler arrived back in the city, both DC Ansari and Glen Ashton had news about the investigation. Bishop was not in the incident room, so it was Ansari who updated them while wincing at the taste of her vending machine hot chocolate.

'With ERSOU's assistance, we've been monitoring traffic coming in and out of the Dark Desires website since we first located it. There's a whole technical explanation for what we're doing and why we're currently waiting for further results. Do you want to hear it?'

'Is it possible to tell us in layman's terms?' Bliss asked. 'I'd be okay with all the geek speak, but you know how slow on the uptake Pen can be at times.' He received an elbow nudge from Chandler for his troubles.

Ansari gave a knowing smile. 'I'll do my best. A full technical explanation would involve telling you all about up and down data streams, IP traffic, proxy servers, private networks, public domain, and virtual private networks. Am I right in thinking you aren't interested in any of that?'

'Absolutely. After all, I'm getting on a bit, and Pen is as thick as a plank.' That earned him a second nudge aimed at the ribs, which he managed to avoid. The less-than-nimble movement resulted in several muscles complaining with sharp jabs of pain, leaving him groaning and wishing he'd taken the elbow instead.

'You all right, boss?' Ansari said.

Bliss winced and stretched his limbs. 'Yeah. Just ache a bit.'

Chandler snorted and chuckled. 'Don't worry about him, Gul. He's playing the martyr here, but he banged on about it all bloody morning on the drive down to London. Only one thing worse than man flu, apparently, and that's man ache.'

Bliss shook his head. 'Don't ever become as cynical and unsympathetic as her, Gul. Heart like stone, this one. Go on with what you were telling us.'

'All right, let me think how best to describe it more simply… Okay.' Ansari walked over to the closest whiteboard and began drawing on it with a blue marker pen. She outlined a rectangle on the left side of the board and another in the centre. In the first she wrote an L and in the second she wrote DD. She then took a step back and tapped the first shape with the marker. 'Let's say this is your laptop. This here in the middle is the web server on which the Dark Desires website resides. If you go online and access a site in the usual way, the security protocols at the other end can see your laptop's network address – its IP number.'

'That much I'm aware of. So does it work the other way around? Can my laptop see the Dark Desires IP address?'

'Not the server itself, no – not easily, anyhow. But if it was a standard site with a domain, you would at least be able to see the external address it shows to the public. For instance, what website do you visit most often?'

'Besides Pornhub, Jimmy,' Chandler said.

Bliss ignored her. 'I suppose that would be the Chelsea website.'

Ansari nodded and took out her phone. Seconds later, after a dazzling display of thumb-typing, she said, 'Okay. So when I ping the website name, the IP address comes back as 151.101.2.133. That isn't the IP of the domain server, rather the public-facing one assigned to them. But because it's part of the domain name system, we can at least get that far.'

'Which presumably provides a starting point for your tech wizards to dig deeper?'

'Precisely. That said, in our case we're dealing with the dark web, remember? No domains. No domains means no lookup facility. And the Dark Desires server won't be connecting directly to the internet in the usual manner; it will have layers of protection which ultimately broadcast a completely different IP to the outside world.'

Bliss exhaled softly. 'All right. So its own security measures effectively disguise the address of the source.'

'That's it in a nutshell.'

'So, for example, if its address was 1.1.1.1, the security stuff might tell us it was 2.2.2.2 instead.'

'Bang on.'

Bliss thought about the logistics and the definitions of the example given. 'But whoever updates the website with new information or removes the old won't be working on the server itself, will they?'

'Almost certainly not. More likely a computer terminal or laptop.'

'So are they likely to also have all this same level of protection?'

'That's a great question, but impossible to answer, I'm afraid, until we know what device or devices are being used. See, an organisation will probably have its own private network – so if you use one of its devices, it'll be directed through the same route out onto the internet. If that's the case, it becomes even more secure, because its private network is hidden from anyone or anything outside the organisation.'

Bliss thought about Lewis Drake, his operation and the people who worked for him. If you were going to run Dark Desires without either him or his other employees being aware, it was unlikely that you would do so from within the operation's own organisational framework.

'What if the source isn't inside the organisation's private network? Is the server still likely to have that level of protection?'

'The server will still be protected in the same way,' Glen Ashton said, jumping in for the first time. 'It's standard protocol these days to place a server behind a proxy and a VPN. Only a real amateur would fail to protect such a valuable and private resource.'

'Fair enough. But how about the device they're using to update it?'

Ashton nodded. 'Now we're getting down to the real nitty-gritty. We have to assume it's still protected with a VPN – or possibly even several of them – but most likely not inside a private network as well. However, it's far more likely that the person doing the updates uses a suitably secure laptop, tablet, or home PC. Possibly even their phone.'

Bliss's technical knowledge was limited, but he was capable of following the logic of it. 'So if I'm getting this right, you've reached the point where your software is attempting to breach the security on both the server and the device connecting to it?'

'Yes. And we got there because we were eventually able to establish a pattern. It's to do with that upstream and downstream IP traffic Gul mentioned before. We can tell which devices are being used to look at data and even download data, but more importantly in this instance, which ones upload data. There is always some back and forth, up and down, but a greater preponderance of one will tell us who is doing what. We've managed to identify both – now we wait while the software does its job and finds its way through the security.'

Bliss tried to keep the pieces flowing in order to see how it might all come together to produce the information they needed. Meanwhile, Chandler sought her own clarification. 'Let me see if I've wrapped my head around it: you'll eventually be able to identify the exact computer this mostly upstream traffic comes from?'

The face Ansari pulled before responding suggested Chandler was close but not quite there. 'Provided they're not going through a local network, yes. If they are, we'll hit another wall. We can tunnel under it, but doing so would be illegal. In truth, what we're doing could already be construed as an illegal act, but at least it's one we can argue about afterwards.'

'So the best we could hope for in those circumstances is to contact the organisation concerned and ask them to track it down and tell us.'

'That's correct. Which, in this case, they will obviously refuse to do.'

Chandler glanced across at Ashton. 'So what can the NCA do about that, Glen? Issue a warrant and threaten to close them down if they don't comply?'

Ashton considered the question before replying. 'It's a legal quagmire. If we can prove they are functioning as an organised crime outfit, if we can prove trafficking... the onus is on us to provide evidence to the CPS that the organisation is operating illegally. If we do that, then we can seize it all and analyse it at our leisure. But that also depends on who owns the hardware and where they're based, and reaching that point will be hugely time-consuming. I'd say the best chance we have is that some of the traffic is coming from a device with mid-level security that we can breach. If whoever is doing the updating does it from a home laptop, we'll benefit from the domino effect. It'll mean we can find their provider. If we find their provider, we can find their router. If we find their router, we find them.'

Bliss put this together with what he and Chandler had discussed on their way back from London. If Dark Desires was being run by Drake's people without his knowledge, then in all likelihood it would not be receiving the technical security privileges of that operation. For all he knew, it was a one-man band using a home laptop – or a one-woman band using hers.

It quickly became clear that they had two main leads: get to their killer directly through the girls he used, or via the website from which he sourced them.

'Gul,' he said, 'what if I were to suggest that the person running Dark Desires might well have a function inside Lewis Drake's organisation, but be operating the site without his knowledge or consent?'

Ansari drained the last dregs of her hot chocolate before saying, 'That scenario provides us with our best chance of tracking them.'

It was precisely the reply Bliss had hoped to hear.

Bishop entered the room at that moment, deep in discussion with DC Hunt. Bliss had been waiting for him to return to the incident room before announcing the outcome of the visit to Belmarsh. It was evident from the first sentence that Bishop had not informed the rest of the team about the trip.

'Is it everything they say it is security-wise?' Hunt wanted to know.

Bliss nodded. 'And more. Mind you, they did allow me to leave with personal photos taken on my phone.'

'Of what?'

'DS Chandler standing around in her underwear.'

He heard a gasp beside him. Felt the sting of a slap on his fore-arm. He chuckled. 'If anyone would like a copy, let me know. I'm thinking of starting a WhatsApp group, so you can apply there.'

'At least I still look fit, old man,' Chandler said disdainfully. 'My belly isn't sagging, unlike somebody's I could mention.'

'True. But gravity is taking its toll on your boobs, you have to admit.'

'Whatever. You still got a thrill copping a free peek.'

'You're a woman. You were standing there in your underwear. Of course I'm going to look.' Bliss glanced around the room, searching for support.

'Stick me on your list, boss,' Hunt said, raising a hand.

Ashton followed suit. 'I'll have some of that, too.'

Chandler clapped her hands together. 'This is all very sweet and charming and more than a little pervy, but can we please get back to business? For your information, our phones were confiscated upon arrival, so our esteemed colleague Detective *Sergeant* Bliss is a lying gobshite.'

Bliss held up both hands. 'It's a fair cop. But the image of Pen in her bra and knickers is indelibly imprinted on my mind's eye, so if anybody would like me to describe it in minute detail, see me afterwards.'

This provoked more laughter. Chandler ignored it. 'We're basically waiting for the ERSOU techs to spit out some answers, but we have no idea how long that wait might be. In the mean-time, there's every chance that Abbi Turner is being held by a madman even as we speak. Does anyone have any bright ideas how we can move forward on that?'

His partner's question echoed the turmoil rampaging inside Bliss's head. He found himself going back and forth and meeting insurmountable barriers at every turn. They were waiting for the system, waiting for Drake to contact them with a name. The latter did not fill Bliss with confidence; Drake was more likely to take things into his own hands than he was to work with the police. Meanwhile, the girl he believed to be their next victim was potentially being subjected to any number of unspeakable horrors. It seemed to him that if Abbi Turner was that person, getting to know her better should be their next move.

He suggested as much, and this received a ripple of enthusiasm. 'But how?' Bishop asked, putting voice to the most obvious question.

Chandler was the first to respond. 'We could obtain a warrant to search her flat. The address we have for her is bound to be her own home rather than her work-based accommodation. I'm not sure what we'd find there, but it's a good place to start.'

'How about her profile on the dark website?' Bliss asked.

Bishop shook his head. 'It works in a completely different way. It provides only a central mobile number. All communications are routed through there.'

'We could scan the other sites for her, though,' Hunt said. 'We have her photo. Gul and Glen can have a go at tracking her to other sites if DI Burton is busy. They'll hopefully offer up a number and location. If it's different to the one we have, we know it's for clients only and that the one we have is the one she calls home.'

'Sounds like a plan.' Bishop looked to DC Gratton. 'Phil. Start working up the warrant. Use the address we have – we can always amend it later on if we need to.'

Bliss was shaking his head. He had an empty feeling in his stomach. 'We're reaching and hoping. I hate it when a case deteriorates to this point. Five days in, so much information flowing through our hands. Yet not only are we no closer to catching this bastard, but he's already secured his next victim.'

'But it's still progress,' Bishop argued. 'On Wednesday we thought we had one murdered sex worker on our hands. Today we know we're after a serial, we know how he acquires his victims, and we also have the name and address of his next victim.'

'I agree. That's why I mentioned the flow of information. But where are we still? Scratching our heads, playing catch-up. Yes, we've clearly made good progress; I'm not denying that at all. It's the details we're short of, and with no obvious way of obtaining them quickly.'

'Patience and diligence, Jimmy. Patience and diligence.'

Bliss dipped his head and smiled. 'Hitting me with my own words, eh? Low blow, Bish. Low blow.'

Bishop chuckled. 'But clearly they made an impact. I remember you telling me there were three assets we needed most of all when an investigation reached this stage. Patience to wait for a break without becoming disillusioned. Diligence to ensure we don't miss that break when it presents itself to us.'

'I'm happy you took it in and have found it useful. But do you recall the third item on the list? I didn't mention it to you at the time, but added it at a later date.'

Bishop shook his head.

'Luck,' Bliss said. 'When the strands of a case get tied up in knots and you feel as if you're getting nowhere, it's often a stroke of luck that gives you the break you waited for patiently and worked towards diligently.'

'Of course. If I remember correctly, I argued against including it.'

'You did. You said the first two were down to us, whereas the third was out of our hands. That luck should never be considered alongside what we brought to the table.'

'And I still believe that to be true.' Bishop sniffed and stood upright. 'I won't sit by and wait for fortune to decide our case.'

Bliss wagged a finger at him. 'And like I said back then: you're missing the point. You don't wait for a lucky break; you work twice as hard to force it out into the open. Afterwards you can look back and admire all the hard work that went into a successful investigation, but in my experience you should never rule out a stroke of good fortune turning things your way when you least expect it.'

THIRTY-THREE

THE TEAM HAD COMMANDEERED a section of the canteen and were sitting together enjoying their lunch. Ansari and Hunt both ate food they had brought in from home, while the others each tucked into an all-day full English. Fuel was important; Bliss always recommended to others that they take regular pit-stops, while forgetting to do so himself more often than not. Investigations had a habit of stopping all the clocks for him, turning his world inside out to the point where he'd barely know what day it was, let alone what time.

Having the unit together without the need to discuss ongoing caseloads was good for morale, and Bliss was pleased to see DS Bishop continuing the tradition. After-work drinks were a great way of blowing off steam, but people had home lives to get on with, too. Food and drink mixed with laughter midway through a shift was fast becoming the only point in the working day they all looked forward to.

Inevitably, the conversation turned once again to Belmarsh and the various merits or otherwise of the semi-naked Bliss and Chandler. The pair swapped insults, but when she claimed to still be as 'fit as fuck', Bliss had reluctantly agreed. 'She'd make the

Thorpe Wood swimsuit calendar if we did one,' he announced to the table in general, with an appreciative nod. 'I mean, she's no Christina Hendrix, but she has nothing to be ashamed of.'

Chandler gave a mock shudder. 'Ooh, such glowing compliments. Be still my beating heart.'

'Give me another crack at that in a year and I won't have to suck my gut in,' Bliss said, laughing. 'I'm going to start helping Barry Griffin with his boxing coaching – hopefully we'll get a bunch of kids in shape and give them some direction and self-respect. I realised I needed to do that myself if I wasn't going to come off as a complete berk. That's why I had that workout yesterday, only it almost killed me. Every muscle in my body ached like a bugger this morning. It took me ten minutes to get out of bed.'

'Growing old is a bastard,' Bishop said. 'But it beats the alternative.'

There was no arguing with that. Meanwhile, Chandler was grinning at Bliss. Finally she said, 'Poor you, with your man ache. But to prove my heart isn't as hard as you suggested earlier, I'm going to do you a favour. A friend of mine is a physio who also gives deep tissue massages for a living. Thirty minutes with her and you'll feel right as rain. If you like, I'll give her a bell to see if she can slot you in later. She does lots of sporty types when they have muscle issues.'

Bliss thought about it. He hadn't had a massage since his fighting days, but he could still remember how loose he'd felt afterwards, the tension kneaded out of his muscles by strong fingers. He agreed and nodded his thanks.

The conversation turned to a recent TV series featuring UK police; as usual, the team picked holes in the procedures that had been portrayed. Just as Bliss finished eating and had shoved his plate to one side, his personal phone rang. He took the call outside on the stairway.

'Good to hear from you, Teddy,' he said. 'How are you doing?' He still felt guilty over the beating Barr had received from Neil Watson, and had been wondering how to help the man out.

'Better than I ought to be. Either I recover more quickly than I thought I did, or Watson's punches and kicks were less brutal than they felt at the time. Anyway, no real damage done. Superficial cuts and bruises. I'm out and recuperating.'

'That's good to hear. Makes me feel a bit better.'

'Yeah, you and me both. But it's not why I'm calling. I thought I'd let you know that your man is currently having a drink with a lowlife by the name of George Moss.'

This took Bliss by surprise, and he was immediately concerned. 'You're still on Watson? Bloody hell, Teddy. I didn't expect you to carry on following him, mate.'

'Oh, this is for me, Jimmy. Before, it was business and I was on the clock. Now it's personal.'

'You watch yourself. One more hiding like that and you might not walk away from it.'

'I was careless before. I'm on my game this time. So, Moss… what d'you reckon?'

'I reckon I'm interested. He's the piece of filth who gave Watson his alibi for the night that poor kid took his final beating.'

'That's the fella. You have to wonder why they're meeting at this precise moment.'

Bliss gave it a moment to consider the implication. 'Could be nothing more than a friendly drink – they are mates, after all. On the other hand, Watson might be feeling the pressure and warning his pal.'

'You've not spoken to Moss yet, have you, Jimmy?'

'I've not had that pleasure. No fixed abode, last I checked, so I couldn't track him down.'

'You in a position to take a break? If you get down here sharpish we could take one each when they leave.'

Bliss thought about it. He badly wanted to nail Watson. But his immediate allegiance was to Phoenix, four murder victims, and Abbi Turner. 'I can't, Teddy. I'm about to finish my break, and we've got a real arseache of a case on. Where are you?'

'I'm back in my motor, parked up close to the Yard of Ale on Oundle Road. The pair of them have been inside for a little over twenty minutes.'

'I know the place. I wonder if it's a regular haunt. Teddy, you were following Watson. Did you see Moss go inside or was he already in there?'

'Watson arrived first and hung about outside. When Moss showed up a few minutes later, they went in together.'

'So it was a prearranged meet. Did you happen to notice how Moss got there? Did he drive or is he on Shanks's?'

'He walked, as far as I could tell – though I suppose he could have driven and parked out of sight around the back.'

Bliss's mind stirred through all of the possibilities. 'Let's hope it's the former, because that might mean he lives close by. Mate, I'm sorry I can't get away. You're on your own time, and I know your beef is with Watson. You do what you need to do.'

'Fair enough. But what would you like me to do, Jimmy? You want me to follow Moss?'

'I'd love to know where he's kipping down. As much as I've enjoyed my little chats with Neil Watson, it'd be good to give Moss a go to test how loyal he is to his mate.'

Barr seemed pleased. 'Consider it done. I do want to give Watson a taste of his own, but I'm not strong enough yet. I can see how it would help knowing where to find Moss, so leave it to me.'

'You sure?'

'Yeah, no worries.'

'Cheers. And Teddy... take care, mate.'

Bliss took a deep breath as he ended the call. He gazed out of the stairway window; the dull and dreary day cast a pall across the entire city. He felt it creep through the glass pane to envelop him. Rain was on the way, and as he thought about the phone call a chill ripped through his body. Barr was a decent man, and probably feeling embarrassed at getting caught unawares by the likes of Watson. He sought revenge, but he also understood the longer game. Giving Watson a hiding could wait. Snapping the cuffs on and putting him where he belonged was still the ultimate goal. Bliss knew he could trust Barr to do the right thing.

As he climbed the stairs up to the second floor and rain began to tap against the window, his phone went off again – this time a text. He was intrigued to see Sara's name pop up on the screen; he hadn't expected to hear from her directly at all, let alone so soon.

The message contained two words, in urgent capital letters: CALL ME.

Bliss pulled up the number and dialled immediately. 'Sara? Thank you for your message. It's DS Bliss. Do you have something for me?'

'Yes. I think I have something to help you.'

'Good. Take your time and tell me everything.'

'I hear from another WhatsApp friend. She know Abbi well. She say she has not heard from Abbi, and Abbi is not answering phone. This we knew already, yes? But when I ask about man Abbi sees often, she tell me Abbi has new boyfriend. He is first client, then boyfriend. Abbi tell her this man is kind to her. He want them to be together.'

Bliss licked his lips, felt the keen nudge of anticipation. 'Did she mention a name, Sara? Is this the Des from before? The same man?'

'Yes. But the reason I call is she tell friend one thing I think will help. The man has… I cannot remember word for this, but he has place that take care of dogs.'

'You mean a vet? A veterinarian?

'No. Not this. He take care of dogs when owners go away, yes?'

'He runs a kennel?'

'Yes! That is it. A kennel. She know nothing more than this. But it helps, yes?'

Bliss felt elation tug at his insides. If the man had not been lying to Abbi and either ran or worked at a kennel, the scope of their impossible search had narrowed considerably.

'It's a massive help, Sara,' he said. 'Thank you so much for letting me know.'

'You find Abbi now, yes?'

'We'll do our best. Just know that what you've told me might be all the difference we needed.'

This time when he tucked his phone away, Bliss ran up the stairs; his muscles protested, but he didn't care. This was the best news he'd had since first laying eyes on Majidah Rassooli's cold, dead body on the frosty chalk pits of Cambridge.

THIRTY-FOUR

H OWEVER UNCONNECTED THEY MIGHT eventually prove to be, breaks in a case often came along together like a fleet of London buses. Bliss had barely finished telling his colleagues about his conversation with Sara when first Glen Ashton and then Chandler received their own rewarding updates.

The NCA investigator gave a loud cry of triumph and jumped to his feet. 'Yes!' he cried, slamming two balled fists on the surface of the desk he'd vacated. 'We found the source of our dark website – and the device uploading data to it!'

All heads turned his way. His beaming face shone with excitement. Gone was the naïve posture of previous days; in its place was a man secure in the knowledge that he had earned a reward for a job well done.

'It's a specialist provider called Zen. Our traces bypassed every VPN and proxy and found their way to the source router. I'm about to begin the process of compelling the company to give us the details of the account owner.'

This prompted cheers, backslapping and wide grins all round. 'Great job, Glen,' Bishop said. 'You too, Gul. You've both worked really well together, and this is terrific news.'

'I've just taken an interesting call, too,' Chandler said. 'I think the rub of the green is finally shifting our way. A CHIS of mine informed me there's talk of a hit being taken out on Nicola Parkinson. If it came from Drake – and I think that's more than likely – he seems to have gone outside his own organisation for once. Clearly he doesn't know who to trust these days. What's more, that bitch must have caught wind of it, because she's had it on her toes and is nowhere to be found.'

'So for once in his life Drake was telling us the truth,' Bliss said. 'He genuinely had no idea about Dark Desires. Since our visit he must have put the word out and discovered it was Parkinson raking in the money without cutting him in.'

Chandler failed to stem the grin spreading across her face. 'Karma works quickly these days. I wouldn't want to be in her skanky shoes, with that mad bastard wanting her head on a pike.'

Bliss shrugged. 'She deserves everything she gets. I've half a mind to forget we ever heard about it and let natural justice take its course.'

DCI Warburton had been working alongside her team, and now she stepped forward to offer her own view. 'In the short time I've been at Thorpe Wood, I've had the misfortune to encounter that odious creature on only two occasions. I don't think I've felt genuinely clean since. I'm inclined to agree with you, Jimmy, except for one thing: collateral damage. If we could guarantee it was that bitch Parkinson being taken out in some dark alley with no one else around, I'd say we have more important matters to focus on than saving her scrawny arse. But these things can get messy, and I'd hate to think that innocent bystanders might get caught up in a bloodbath.'

Bliss nodded. He'd not been entirely serious himself, and neither he nor any member of his team would turn their backs on a murder threat simply because they disliked the intended victim.

It was a perfectly natural instinct to think of someone like Nicola Parkinson as surplus to requirements in respect of the human race. But, despicable or not, she was currently a citizen in need of their protection. That thought led him to another.

'Did your snout mention anyone else on Drake's shit list?' he asked Chandler.

She shook her head, but lines deepened on her forehead. 'No. Are you thinking about her son and daughter?'

'Yeah. Because even if they're not involved – and I'm willing to bet my house on both of them being in it up to their horrible necks – they could be snatched up to be used as leverage once whoever has the contract finds out Nicola has done a runner.'

Bishop reacted before Bliss could turn to him. He jabbed a finger at Ansari. 'Make sure this Zen broadband provider knows who to get hold of and how. Then I want you to locate the home address for Parkinson and her offspring and get yourself over there right away. Take Glen and Phil with you. Also, let's have uniform taking the doors off all their known knocking shops. We have to find all three of them before anybody else does.' He switched his attention. 'Jimmy, Pen – you want to look into these kennels? I can tell you from experience there are a good twenty or more in the area, and most are in places you might consider ideal if you were going to abduct young women and keep them under lock and key for a couple of weeks. John and I can help you with them.'

'Just a thought, boss,' Ansari said, piping up. 'A number of those kennels may be either temporarily closed or have gone out of business altogether in recent times. If you run a Google search, they usually say whether they're open or not.'

'It's a good thought. We can start with the ones that are closed, because nobody's going to be keeping someone against their will at a functioning one.'

Bliss couldn't help but wonder if they were missing something that would help narrow their search further, but agreed with Bishop: splitting the team covered both emergency situations. He cared about his task more than the other – in that he'd not spare a second thought for Nicola Parkinson's plight. In his opinion, whatever lay in store for her was long overdue.

Chandler had already pulled up a view of the kennels in the wider Peterborough area. Eighteen red droplets freckled the map like blood spatter. Shaking her head, she looked up and said, 'Good for them, bad for us. This lot seem to have made it through. But we're looking as far north as Deeping, to the west around Elton, and on the other side we're looking at Coates and Turves.'

'We don't know how much time we have,' Bliss said, looking up at Bishop. 'But it's going to take us the rest of today to hit this lot. We need traffic and uniform on it with us.'

Bishop nodded immediately. 'Absolutely. I'm sure our favourite DCI's charms will do the trick there.'

Warburton rolled her eyes. 'Why is it always me?'

'You have the rank, boss. I'm only acting. Plus, like I said, you've got the charm. And you're going to need it when people kick off about budgets.'

'Hmm. I'll let that go this time, Bish. But we may need to have words later. Perhaps a nice new training course for you to attend.'

Bishop groaned but laughed it off. He turned back to Chandler. 'We'd best start divvying some of these up. I'm thinking we take the kennels closest to HQ, leave the others to uniform and traffic. Sound good?'

'Yes, boss. On closer inspection, four of the eighteen appear to be for cats only, even though they feature in the search for kennels. I say we leave them out altogether. That leaves us with fourteen. We could take eight, leave the remaining six for other teams.'

'Okay. I'll take four with John, you and Jimmy visit the other four.'

It took Chandler a further ten minutes to select the most appropriate location groupings to cut down on the driving time between them. She typed the lists up and printed off hard copies. Not content with that, she sent a list of kennel names and their postal codes to each member of the team, together with a list of who each one was assigned to, selecting a generic name for each of two teams they hoped to pull from other units. This way everybody not only had their own tasks on their phone, but also knew where everyone else was assigned in case of trouble and calls to assist.

Bliss sat back and took it all in from the sidelines. He'd endured two months of this so far. Having been both responsible for the unit and accountable to the more senior ranks, he currently felt like a spare part. By this stage he'd usually be barking out instructions of his own, making snap decisions, allocating actions to personnel. He'd feel the deep grind of the job in his bones. More, he'd feel the weight of it settle upon him. Irrespective of his current position, he continued to feel all of these things. The subsequent welling of frustration was intense, because he lacked the influence to lead.

Not that Bishop was failing. So far, his missteps could be counted on the fingers of one hand and wouldn't require the thumb. He was doing the job Bliss knew him capable of, proving himself worthy of the permanent promotion he deserved should he wish to go forward with his career ambitions.

'You're missing it, aren't you?' a voice said, snapping him out of his silent contemplation. Diane Warburton was smiling at him. 'I know a little of how you feel, Jimmy. Each shift up the ladder leaves you a little bit more detached from the daily grind. Until one day you realise they don't need you any more. Bit like kids, really. They rely on you for everything for so long, but bit by bit they pull away.'

'Independence,' Bliss said, nodding. 'We all crave it, but we never think about the people we become independent from. It's tougher than I'd anticipated.'

'You're a third of the way through, Jimmy. These next four months will flash by.'

'But to what end?'

'Keep your nose clean and this will be your unit once again.'

'Perhaps. The cynic in me wonders if that will actually happen.'

'It may not if you don't let go of your nocturnal activities.'

Bliss's eyes widened. 'Marion Fletcher told you about Neil Watson?'

'Of course. Why wouldn't she? That's how the chain of command works.'

'I take it you don't approve?'

Warburton took a deep breath, compiling her response. 'I feel the same way about Watson as I do that awful Parkinson woman: if they get their comeuppance, I'm not going to lose any sleep. But in his case, not if the cost is losing you, too.'

'That's nice of you to say so, boss. You want to keep some eye candy around, don't you?'

She laughed. 'How well you know me. Look, Jimmy, I can't tell you I don't understand your inclinations, because I do. The DSI showed me the case file, and the investigative notes make it abundantly clear that Neil Watson had been systematically beating that child prior to his eventual and wholly predictable and preventable death. Whether he administered the final blows, perhaps we'll never know. But he's equally responsible, if not more so than the woman currently doing time for that poor lad's murder. I'd like to see him off the streets. But you do realise that if you step too far out of line, it's not only your job at risk – it's your freedom?'

Nodding, Bliss swallowed and spread his hands. 'I'm not about to do anything ridiculously stupid, boss… Moderately, at worst. My aim at the moment is to force him to lose his patience with me. If I get him in a roid rage at the right time, he might even tell me everything. I genuinely think he'd like to boast about it, because he certainly doesn't feel any shame or remorse. Quite the opposite, if you ask me. At the very least he'll end up attacking me if I keep pushing his buttons, and that'll earn him some time behind bars. And I'll be a frequent visitor, one who's happy to spread rumours about him to some of the genuine hard bastards in there.'

Warburton fired a look of genuine concern at him. 'And if it goes the other way – if he has you for harassment – he walks, and you are kicked out of this job. You have to ask yourself if he's worth it, Jimmy.'

'With all due respect, boss,' Bliss said, 'Neil Watson might not be worth it, but the child he murdered certainly is.'

THIRTY-FIVE

B LISS MUST HAVE KNOWN more frustrating afternoons, but it was hard to bring one to mind as he left Thorpe Wood later that day. The vast majority of kennels were open and in business. This made them less than ideal locations in which to keep under lock and key an unwilling young woman who was probably being subjected to sexual abuse on a regular basis. Having the kennel staff, dogs, and in some cases their owners on site was hardly beneficial to the search teams, either, but the job had to be done nonetheless. Only two sites initially refused them entry without warrant, and Bishop had been unfortunate enough to cop them both. They had eventually agreed after he pointed out how much more thorough a warranted search might be, potentially requiring the complete closure of the site.

Of the three businesses that were no longer operational, Bliss and Chandler had one on their short list. It was out in Eye, close to the quarry. The site backed on to Cat's Water drain, a narrow river that wound its way from the industrial area of Fengate all the way round and across to Thorney on the north-west fringe of the city's boundary. In addition to the kennel blocks and the main office building, the property also contained living accommodation in the form of a large bungalow. Bliss had been pleased to see two cars parked outside.

The owners proved to be a delightful elderly couple. Their story was symptomatic of the time and social conditions in which they lived. Stoical, they had accepted their fate and closed down the business in the face of huge competition and a meagre profit that dwindled with each passing year. The less people travelled, the less they needed to board their pets; it was a simple enough equation, with no room for diversification. The couple were happy enough for the two detectives to search away, even tossing Bliss the keys and asking him to pop them back through the letterbox when they were done.

'It's still the best break we have at the moment,' Bishop insisted when they all assembled in the incident room shortly before 5.00pm. 'We need to widen the search. Perhaps get other areas involved and looking on our behalf.'

Bliss understood his colleague's line of thinking – but the trouble was, none of them knew precisely how far that search area might extend, nor in which direction. The dumping of their first victim's body at the chalk pits suggested the holding area might be as far south as Cambridge. A lot of acreage stood between the two cities. It felt like an impossible task. But Bishop was right not to show his anxiety. Bliss wouldn't have, either.

Data had started coming in from mobile providers. There was plenty of it, and it would take a while to collate into some kind of order. Warburton, Bishop and Bliss discussed the relative importance of what they had and what was to come. Their first request had been related to their victim's presumed business phone, and the three decided they had progressed beyond the point where its data would be of use to them in finding Abbi Turner. Their initial goal, that of finding out why Majidah Rassooli had been killed and by whom, was no longer the Phoenix priority; what they were after now was anything that might lead them to the man Turner had been seeing recently. For that, they needed her phone data, which had not yet arrived and was unlikely to be ready for assessment until the following day.

Bliss was the first to venture his thoughts on the matter. 'I'm not convinced we'll find what we're looking for. People can be dumb, which is often the reason we catch them. They make stupid mistakes when they commit crimes. But we're not talking about criminals here. These girls share information the way they share their fears. Yes, you could argue that if they are willing to branch out on their own, they're probably dense enough to make stupid mistakes, like having incriminating text conversations on their phones. But do any of us genuinely believe we'll find something from this Des bloke on Turner's phone?'

'You said criminals could be dumb,' Bishop countered.

'And I'm not saying he's not. I'm saying I doubt she is. Keeping incriminating evidence on a phone she's already not supposed to have would be foolish in the extreme.'

'So why did we have Gul beg for the data?' Warburton asked.

'Because we still need to go through the motions. And yes, I suppose there is still a remote possibility of us finding something useful. But we've moved on since making the initial request, the parameters have changed, and to me it's more likely to be Nicola Parkinson's phones that give us something solid.'

'And when do we expect to have that data in?'

'First thing tomorrow, with a bit of luck and a following wind.'

Bishop was of the opinion that they'd be better off recharging their batteries while those with the right amount of technical savvy went about the business of sorting the data into neat packages of relevant information. Warburton agreed. Both looked to Bliss, who nodded.

After Warburton called it a night, Bliss rejected requests to join the others for a drink. He had plans, he told them. He just didn't reveal what they were.

Chandler had come up trumps. Her friend, Trish, worked for a company based in a unit in Orton Longueville. They specialised in exercise and physical therapy, part of which included specialist massage techniques. Bliss sat in a chair outside her designated room for fifteen minutes while she treated her final scheduled client of the day. When it was his turn, he shook Trish's hand and thanked her for extending her working day on his behalf. She looked to be about the same age as Chandler, and wore what looked like white scrubs beneath a white jacket, her hair up and held in place with an array of claw-like clips.

'Penny told me it was an emergency,' she explained with a warm smile.

'I think she exaggerated. I ache and I'm a bit sore, but I'd hardly describe it as a crisis.'

Trish shook her head. The smile broadened. 'Oh, no. Penny said the emergency was her need not to hear you whingeing and whining anymore.'

Bliss laughed. Typical. 'Again, she exaggerates. So, how do we do this?'

Trish asked him a few pointed questions about his general health and fitness and made a few notes in her diary as well as on a sheet of unlined A4 paper. Eventually she nodded. 'Sounds to me as if the areas we need to work on most are your arms, shoulders and legs. If you're happy for me to go ahead, I'll leave the room for a couple of minutes while you strip down to your underwear. There's a fresh towel on the massage table that you can wrap around you for modesty.'

Five minutes later, Bliss was face down looking through a hole in the table while Trish got to work on him. Powerful fingers kneaded his muscles, from his wrists up along the arms. She had just moved from his biceps to his shoulders when he asked how she came to know Chandler.

'I run exercise classes as well as doing this,' she told him. 'Penny comes as often as she can make it – usually on a Thursday night, when we have later sessions running. We got on well and we've been friends for the past couple of years. Actually, she mentioned you to me before. Said you were instrumental in putting her back in touch with her daughter.'

'I did what I could. Other people did the hard graft.' Bliss grunted the last word as her fingers found a tender spot. In truth, he was enjoying the sensation a lot more than he would ever admit to Chandler afterwards. Outside of work, he hated to accept her good ideas, but this had been one of her better efforts. The pain provoked by massaging sore muscles quickly evaporated, the restorative natural chemicals released into his bloodstream helping along the stretching and softening of fibre and tissue.

By the time Trish had finished with his calves, Bliss was becoming drowsy. Yet at the same time he felt exhilarated, soothed by the skilful masseuse. He knew he was experiencing a mild case of euphoria, and it felt wonderful. He owed Chandler a drink.

'Okay,' Trish said eventually, walking around to the head of the table. 'If you can just turn yourself over and lie still for a few minutes, I'll prepare the oils for the next stage.'

Bliss didn't want to move, but started easing his body up from its prone position. 'Fair enough. What is the next stage?'

She smiled at him and gave a slow wink. 'It's okay, Inspector. There's no need to say the actual words. I've seen enough police officers in my time to know you won't. But, hey, nobody comes here for just a massage. You relax. I'll finish you off nice and slowly.'

Bliss's eyes sprang wide open. Something raspy started buzzing in his ears. Did she mean what he thought she meant? If she did, he had to put a stop to it. But if she didn't, how insulted would she be? Her being Chandler's friend only added to the pressure.

'When you say… finish me off… what does that entail, Trish?' He winced at the feeble uncertainty he could hear in his voice.

'Oh, you want details, do you? Well, it's down to you. It's a freebie because of what you did to help Penny. But just because it's free doesn't mean it has to be a quickie. If all you want is a happy ending, I can give you that – but if you want more, I'm game.'

Bliss pulled himself up onto his forearms. He swivelled himself around until he was sitting on the padded table, thankful for the towel bunched up around his waist. He kept his head down, desperate not to meet the woman's eyes. 'Thank you so much for the massage,' he said. 'You were excellent, and I feel great. But I think we can leave it there.'

'Oh, come on. There's no need to be shy, Inspector. As I mentioned, you wouldn't be the first policeman I've pleasured.'

He groaned and began levering himself off the table to his feet. Which was the exact moment the door flew open behind him. 'Detective Sergeant Bliss!' a female voice said. 'What on earth is going on here? This is a room for legitimate massage therapy, not a knocking shop!'

Bliss turned to look back over his shoulder. 'You bloody monster!' he cried. 'I'll pay you back for this, Penny Chandler. You see if I don't.'

She was already cracking up. 'You should see your face. I wish I had a mirror – better still, a camera. Hold on, let me get my phone out.'

'Don't you dare. You've done me up like a kipper, you rotten cowbag. What if I'd gone through with it?'

Convulsed with laughter, Chandler pulled both hands to her stomach. Beside her, Trish was doubled up, laughing so hard she appeared to be in pain. The pair were unable to say or do anything else for a full minute. By the time they got their breath back, both complained of needing to pee.

By that time, Bliss had closed his eyes and put his head in his hands. He'd been entirely had – set up by Chandler in a way he'd never dreamed possible. He wanted to laugh. He wanted to cry. But one thing he knew for sure: he would never, ever live this moment down.

THIRTY-SIX

THE VOICEMAIL MESSAGE HE'D received from Edward Barr interested Bliss enormously. Teddy had followed George Moss from the Yard of Ale pub as planned. The man started walking towards the railway bridge, but had then nipped down an alleyway between a shop and a house. Wary of being caught out a second time, Barr had hung back, emerging onto the street at the far end in time to see his quarry disappear into the cream and grey housing block on the other side of the road. As he'd walked slowly along by the garages opposite, he spotted Moss appearing from a staircase doorway. The man headed along the external landing and eventually used a key to open the third door on the right.

Subsequent investigation revealed the flat's tenant was one Christine Bell. Further searches listed Bell and Moss as having been foster children in the same local authority home. The information had taken a fair bit of digging out, Barr claimed – more spadework than the police would have been willing to do in their casual searches for a man whose reputation suggested only mild – if frequent – form.

Following a swift pint with Chandler and Trish, during which time he took the sly digs and occasional renewed howls of laughter with good grace, Bliss called Barr as he climbed into his car. 'I got your message. You still on him, Teddy?' he asked.

'I hung around for a few minutes, but started sticking out. I didn't want to risk blowing it. I thought him using his own key swung it as being the place he crashes in. If he ain't there when you drop by, he will be later.'

'I'm going to pay him a visit shortly.'

'You want backup?'

Bliss smiled to himself. 'You recovered, have you, Teddy?'

'Well… no.'

'There's your answer, then.'

He briefly thought of involving Chandler, even if only to make her aware of his whereabouts and the situation he had become embroiled in, should things turn ugly and become worse than that. He decided not to, for two viable reasons: first, Chandler would nag him to step away and allow matters to take their natural course; second, when he refused to do so, she would insist on accompanying him. That was a risk he was unwilling to take, because he didn't know this particular journey's destination.

Minutes after speaking with Barr, Bliss was knocking on the door to Christine Bell's home. It was she who answered. Although not recognising the man who stood on her doorstep, she did seem to realise he was not about to try selling her a new set of windows or spread the word of God. She asked who he was with deep suspicion in both her tone and her stance.

'I'm the man you need to invite inside without making a fuss or continuing to question me,' Bliss said, having decided not to show his warrant card ID. 'I need a chat with George. I'd prefer to do so quietly, but I can go the other way if you force me to.'

Bell's glare was defiant, but he could tell she wasn't about to do anything stupid. He eased off the hard-edged approach. 'Look, all I want is a word. Nothing more than that.'

With a sigh of disapproval, she stood to one side, but made sure to first call out a warning to Moss. When Bliss walked into the living room at the far end of the hallway, it was like stepping into an oven. The night was cold, but the radiators in here must have been at their highest setting. Bliss's attention was immediately drawn to the man on his feet in the centre of the room, one hand holding a bottle of beer like a cosh.

'Put it down, George,' Bliss said, shaking his head slowly and deliberately. 'That's not the way you want this to go, believe me. I'm not even here about you. I want to talk to you about Neil Watson.'

The penny dropped and relief flooded the man's eyes. All tension left his body. He was not a big man, but tall and rangy, and in relaxing he lost some of his presence. He tossed the bottle onto the sofa behind him. 'You're police, yeah?'

'For the time being, I'm not telling you who or what I am, George. Let's say I'm a concerned citizen.'

'Yeah, right. I know one when I see one.'

Undaunted, Bliss moved on. 'Whatever. I'm not interested in what you think or don't think. My only interest in you is your association with a child-killer.'

Bell gasped. She looked from Bliss to Moss and back again, pawing at a gold crucifix on a chain around her neck. 'What?'

'I take it George hasn't told you about his mate, Neil Watson?'

'I know him. He's been here a few times in recent weeks. What's all this about him being a child-killer?'

'Don't listen to him, Chris,' Moss said, shaking a hand defensively. 'The filth are trying to fit Neil up. He was shacked up with some kid's mother, and she murdered the kid. Not Neil. She's even doing time for it.'

'Yes, and for his crime,' Bliss insisted. 'So go on with your story, George. Tell Christine here why Neil is not also behind bars.'

Moss peered down his nose contemptuously. 'What, you mean because the kid's mum confessed? You mean that reason?'

Bliss took a step closer. Close enough to see the film of sweat on the man's thin moustache. 'You know I don't. Watson is not doing time for murder, or even GBH, because he had an alibi. Isn't that right, George?'

'George?' Bell's voice was soft, unsure of herself as her gaze shifted to Moss. 'What's he on about? What is all this?'

Moss said nothing. He breathed heavily, his frame having become rigid once more. Bliss had sensed the man's earlier relief when he'd realised the stranger in the living room was only a cop, but he was becoming agitated all over again. It caused Bliss to wonder who he'd been expecting – and what the result of that visit might have been.

'I don't think he'll come straight out with it,' Bliss said to Bell, capturing her attention. She was no taller than five foot in her slippered feet, hair unwashed and unkempt. Her clothes looked clean, at least, if creased and leached of colour. The fingers of one hand continued to toy with the chain at her throat.

'No? Why's that?' she asked defiantly.

'Probably because you'll know a lie when you hear one. So allow me. Your friend George here was Neil Watson's alibi the night that poor child got beaten to death. Even if his story were true, Watson's to blame because the death was known to be cumulative. You know what that means? It means the poor little mite was beaten on a regular basis, and the ongoing effect of those beatings created weaknesses in the boy's skull. That's awful enough, I'm sure you'd agree. But the fact is, I don't believe George's story. I don't believe he was with Neil Watson that night. I believe he's covering for him – for the kind of man who would beat a child so often that the poor little sod had physical damage and old breaks too numerous to count.'

'That's not possible,' Bell said. She shook her head fiercely. 'I know from having my own son, Charlie. You go to emergency with any cut or break and they're on you, always suspecting the worst.'

Bliss nodded. 'That's often the case, yes. But it's the follow-up that counts. Social care teams are always overstretched, and cases get away. Some kids fall through the cracks because their parents are plausible and the case workers are exhausted. One such child fell victim to Neil Watson and his rage.'

Bell's face flushed and glistened. 'You don't know that. You can't. Otherwise he'd be locked away as well.'

'There's knowing, Christine, and there's proving. It wasn't my operation, but I know it as if it were after reading through the case file and talking to the investigating officers. They went after him for doling out the fatal blows on that night. Then along comes George Moss, says Watson was at his place at the time. That was in Huntingdon, not too far away from where Watson lived with the woman and her son. But according to Mr Alibi here, he and Watson were together from early evening until long after that little boy succumbed to his final hiding. The moment the investigators could no longer push that angle, the case for proving Watson's involvement over time also fell apart. Especially after the kid's mother coughed to the lot, absolving Watson of any and all responsibility.'

'There you go, then!' Moss cried, a hand tossed carelessly in the air. 'What more do you people need? She says he never hurt the kid, not once. Then she says she laid into her son that night while Neil was with me. You wanted to bang him up, and when you fucked up you decided to try to fit him up instead. Don't listen to him, Chris. You'll only ever hear lies from his sort.'

Bliss wiped a hand across his face; it came back slick. 'Christ, it's hot enough to boil a monkey's arse in here. Listen to me,

George. Whether I'm with the police or not really isn't the point. Why did you lie for him that night, and why did you meet him for a drink today?'

'What?' Bell turned, hands on hips, her face rapidly turning crimson. 'You told me you were at work all day!'

'Yeah, well, I stopped off on my way home to see Neil. What of it?'

'You didn't tell me, is what. You made it seem like you came straight home.'

'What the fuck does it matter? I met him. We had a couple of pints. Big fucking deal!'

'Why today?' Bliss wanted to know. 'Why did you need to see him today?'

'I don't see how that's any of your business. In fact, I don't even know why you're still here. You're the filth. You ain't got no right to be here. So why don't you fuck right off?'

Bliss took a breath. Calmed himself. 'On the contrary, George. I have every right to be here. It was Miss Bell who invited me in. This is her home. Her name on the rent book.'

Anger creasing his features, Moss turned to Bell, a desperate look in his eyes. 'Tell him, Chris. Tell him to go fuck himself and leave us alone.'

She swallowed a couple of times, blinking as if she was having trouble seeing him clearly for the first time. Bliss noticed tears in her eyes and knew he'd got through. Eventually she shook her head. 'No. No, I don't think I will, George. I think I want to know more.'

'Why? Because this prick says so?'

'No. Because I'm not sure if I believe you.'

For a moment, Bliss thought Moss might launch himself at her. Tensing, he readied himself to get between them if needed. But he decided it would be safer to remove her from the equation. 'Miss

Bell,' he said, keeping a watchful eye on Moss. 'You mentioned a child earlier. Is he with you? Here in the flat?'

'No. He's at my mum's.'

'Close by?'

'Yeah, not far.'

'Good. Then you can do us all a favour. We need to take some of the tension out of this situation – plus, I need to speak freely with George. Take yourself off to your mum's place. Spend an hour or so there while me and George get to know one another better.'

'Chris… take no notice of this bloke.' Moss looked terrified, his voice high and pleading. 'You stick around. I want a witness.'

But Christine Bell seemed to realise something was not quite right; it was as if she instinctively knew there was more to this story. And Bliss could tell she wanted no part of it, no matter who or what Moss was to her.

Less than five minutes later, the two of them were alone together. Moss had collapsed into an armchair the moment Bell closed the front door behind her, as if doing so might somehow prevent what was about to happen.

Bliss remained on his feet. He stepped closer until he was looming over the frightened figure. 'I don't know what kind of man you were before you agreed to alibi Watson,' he said in a hushed voice. 'I don't know what kind of man you've become since. But I do know what kind of man you can be, George.'

'Yeah? What's that?'

'A better one. A smarter one. The kind of man who finally tells the truth. Because I think that truth has been weighing on you. See, I reckon Watson wanted to meet with you today to find out if he could still rely on you. He's in trouble, George. Starting to feel the pressure I'm applying. He needs to make sure your story remains the same and will hold up to further scrutiny.'

'And it will. Because it's the truth.'

'So you say. Fair enough. But you know, there are two things wrong with that.' Bliss paused, waiting for Moss's eyes to find and hold his own. 'First, if Watson is starting to get anxious, he might suspect you'll fold completely once the necessary weight is applied. I don't reckon he's a man to take things on trust, George. Sooner or later, he'll come to the conclusion that you're a problem he needs to deal with.

'Second, there's me. See, whatever you may think I am, whatever you may think I do, right now it's just me standing here in front of you. But Neil Watson will have his own way of dealing with you. I can't imagine it'll be painless, and I can only assume it will be fatal. Me? I'm not that generous, and I'm considerably more in control of my temper. I can make pain last a bloody long time when I put my mind to it, George. I can keep it up for hours. Days, if necessary. I'll hold back on making it fatal, and all you'll know is that continuous agony. But there's an easy way to prevent either of those eventualities from happening.'

'Yeah? How's that?'

'You tell me the truth.'

'I can't do that. You know I can't.'

Bliss nodded. Smiled. Then narrowed his gaze. 'I know you can't. Of course I do. But I also know you will, eventually. If you want to endure the suffering I'll put you through first, let's get on with it. I'm game.'

'You can't do that. You're a copper. I know you are. There's no way you can threaten me like that and get away with it.'

'I can not only make the threat, George – I can also follow up on it. You know why? Because I'm not stupid enough to get caught. Christine doesn't know who I am. If we're both gone by the time she gets back, she won't know we left together, nor where you are.'

'I'll tell everyone after you let me go.'

Bliss lowered his voice. 'Oh, George. Who said anything about letting you go?' He smiled. 'On the other hand, you can save all that shit and tell me everything I need to know right now.'

'What kind of choice is that?' Moss asked, throwing up his hands.

Bliss shrugged. 'No choice at all, George. But either way, you'd better tell me how this is going to go, because it's getting late, I'm tired, I need a drink, and I've had fuck all to eat. That combination makes me even more irritable than usual. So… what's it going to be? I can manage another hour. Can you?'

THIRTY-SEVEN

B LISS AWOKE TO A grey morning and a sky that looked as forlorn as he felt. Low, dark clouds ploughed weary furrows across the sky, looking eager to unleash their cargo. It felt to him as if a couple of them detached to hover above his head while he took a shower. As he soaped away the last remaining residues of a restless night, he contemplated a couple of conversations he'd had the previous evening.

The first was with Bishop, who himself had received a call from DC Ansari. The search for the Parkinson family remained ongoing; there had been no sign of either Nicola or her children. Tracking their financial movements was the next stage, but authorisation could not be obtained until the morning.

'Any word on who the contracted hit was placed with?' Bliss had asked.

'None. We'd only be speculating at this stage, what with Drake having gone outside his own organisation. I had Glen check the NCA system for Drake's personal finances, which they've been monitoring since we first brought him in. No sign of him directing money anywhere over the past twenty-four hours.'

'We have to assume he has cash squirrelled away somewhere, then. And somebody he trusts with access to it whenever only cash will do. We need to think hard about who that might be and come up with a name.'

'I agree,' Bishop said. 'I don't know of any hitman who wouldn't demand at least half up front. Money is going to change hands soon, that's for sure.'

'And when it does, we need to be prepared. Any joy with tracking down the Dark Desires server?'

'Do we even need it now? The hope was it'd tell us who was running the show, but I think we all agree it was Nicola Parkinson and her vermin brood.'

Bliss nodded, though he knew Bishop could not see it. 'True. On the other hand, knowing its precise location may lead us to an address we don't have listed for her or the Drake empire. A fresh address gives us renewed hope of finding something concrete. If we let ourselves get too carried away with the chase, we might forget to pick up the evidence wherever it can be found.'

'Of course. You're absolutely right. I'll get on it first thing in the morning.'

Up next was Chandler; for some reason she hadn't been able to turn in for the night without rubbing more salt into his wounds. 'Did it at least help with your aches and pains?' she asked after she'd finished laughing.

'Actually, it did. Very much so. I felt so loose afterwards, though it's all starting to tighten up again. Trish is good at what she does.'

'She said you were a good sport. She's glad you didn't whip your towel off and tell her to spread the oil thickly.'

Bliss put his head back. The memory left a huge smile on his face. 'So am I. That would have been a sight for sore eyes, if you'd burst into the room at that point.'

'Oh, believe me, the sore eyes would've come afterwards. I'd have poked them out with a stick.'

They'd laughed together for a while longer, before turning to Phoenix. They discussed the case for twenty minutes without getting any further, before saying goodnight.

As he got dressed, Bliss's thoughts drifted back to George Moss. The man was every bit as vulnerable as he'd assumed, caving in at the mere thought of suffering the kind of pain Bliss had described. Fearing the repercussions, he'd demanded protection. Bliss assured him of it, though he had no intention of going out of his way to provide any once they had the man's new statement in evidence.

'I… I gave N… Neil an alibi,' Moss had stuttered. His voice cracked and dry, he seemed broken by the admission. 'He turned up unexpectedly that night at the place where I was living. He was all pumped up and red in the face. Actually, he looked bloody terrified.'

'And what exactly did he say to you?' Bliss had asked.

'He told me he'd given the kid a hiding from time to time, that it was what good male role models did to make sure kids had discipline later on in life – plus it forced the kid to do as he was told there and then. He said he'd been at home all evening taking care of the little brat while the boy's mother was off gallivanting with her trampy friends – his words, not mine.'

At that point Moss had broken off from his story, looking across at Bliss as if seeking some kind of acknowledgement that the difference between him and Watson was plain to see. Bliss had nodded for him to continue, which Moss did after clearing his throat.

'Anyway, it turned out that the boy hadn't eaten all night. Neil had assumed the kid's mother had fed him before she went out, but she'd left it for him to do. When the two of them started arguing, the boy butted in, and Neil lost it. Completely. He told me it felt like someone else's hands and feet laying into the poor little sod, until he noticed the blood all over his own clothes, and felt it on his face. He warned his other half not to say a word to anyone about him being there. Said he threatened her, but he didn't go into details about it.'

'So you knew he'd snapped and killed the boy, and still you covered for him,' Bliss had said in disgust. 'Perjured yourself for him, knowing he was a child-killer.'

'Yeah.' Moss had not been able to meet his eyes. 'But not because we were mates – it was never about that. Any other friend and I wouldn't have done it.'

'Then why?'

After a moment, he managed to look up. 'Because I was shit scared. That's the truth of the matter. Neil terrifies me when he goes off on one, and I had no intention of being on the end of it.'

Bliss shuddered at the memory, and at the image currently playing on a loop inside his head. Hearing this new version of events, it felt almost as if he had been there with Watson. If he closed his eyes, he could see the heavily muscled lunatic, eyes wide with rage, foam spilling from his lips. Slapping, punching, kicking the defenceless little boy. And later picking up the lad's cricket bat…

How must that have looked through the kid's eyes?

How must it have felt?

Bliss quelled his mounting fury before setting off for work. He also placed a call to an office at Hinchingbrooke HQ.

'DS Nicholls.'

'Harvey, it's Jimmy Bliss.' The man's real name was Paul, but where was the fun in that?

'Hiya, Jimmy. What can I do for you this dull morning?'

'I was wondering if we could meet around lunchtime today. Say half-twelve?'

'I can do that unless I'm called out, of course. What's up?'

'It's about Neil Watson.'

Silence. Then, 'I was afraid you were going to say that. You weren't able to let it go, were you?'

'No. And it's not a matter of me second-guessing your case against him, Harvey. You did nothing wrong. He pulled a fast one, and it had the desired effect. But I may have opened the door for you.'

'And we need to discuss it in private, I'm assuming?'

'We do. I didn't exactly go through the proper channels to obtain the information I have.'

'Of course not. Why would you?'

'Don't be like that. I know I went behind your back, but it had to be done. For my own peace of mind, if nothing else. You want what I have or not?'

'If it helps nail that sick fucker – absolutely.'

'Good man.'

They agreed upon a meeting point before Bliss disconnected – not only from the call, but from that particular investigation. A more pressing case awaited him at Thorpe Wood, and for one poor young woman each minute that passed had to feel like a lifetime.

The rain was holding off when he stepped outside the front door, but he could smell it in the air and feel it settle beneath his skin. The old labrador lay nestled close by, so Bliss quickly went back indoors to fetch a dish of water and a few crumbled-up treats for his relatively new pal.

He took his first call of the day as he settled behind the wheel of his car. It was from Sandra Bannister.

'If you're calling to give me a bollocking, save your breath,' he said. 'I apologise. I should have come back to you sooner.'

'You're damn right about that! Have you seen the front-page story the *Express* is running with today?'

He hadn't, but immediately felt familiar hooks of anger and frustration raking at him. 'I'm guessing it's about the serial we appear to have inherited?'

'What the… what's going on, Jimmy? You have something this big, and you leave me out in the cold? Why am I only finding out after some gleeful prick who wants my job sends me a web link?'

'I've not seen the article, Sandra. But it's a leak, not a plant. We didn't want this out there.'

'Are you sure about that? I know how you people operate, remember?'

'I'm certain. There's no way this is good for us or our investigation.'

Bannister paused. They'd built up a fair amount of trust over time, and he hoped she'd realise he was telling her the truth. 'Fair enough. But why am I only learning about it for the first time now?'

'I've said I'm sorry, and I am. I did call you; you didn't answer and I decided not to leave a message. I forgot to call back, but it didn't seem urgent. When I saw your name pop up, I thought you were getting back to me for an update. I genuinely had no idea this was going on.'

'None of which helps, to be perfectly honest with you, Jimmy. My editors expect me to be on the leading edge of activity at Thorpe Wood. I'm being asked how I could have missed something of this magnitude.'

Bliss began to feel the initial stirrings of irritation. He measured his tone when he next spoke, but added some flint to it. 'Sandra, I'm not your paid source. You and I have an arrangement.

We help each other out as and when it suits. This is a rapidly developing case, and I haven't had much time to think about your feelings – or your job, for that matter. I called to update you, and would have done so had you answered. Don't make more of this than it already is.'

He could almost see her look of fury flare up and diminish as she realised he was right. His mind was in overdrive and his thoughts turned to what she hadn't yet mentioned.

'This scoop you're angry about,' he said. 'It mentions a potential serial killer, yes? Three murders in London, and the same killer responsible for our victim over at the chalk pits. Is that as far as the story goes?'

'Yes. Why? Are you saying there's more to it?'

He could tell by what had not been said so far that only a part of the story had been unearthed – so the leak was probably out of Cambridge, possibly the Met. This was a version missing salient new facts. 'Sandra, if I tell you something off the record and assure you that I promise to come to you with the full story the moment we break the case, will that pacify you?'

'I suppose it depends on what you tell me.'

Bliss stiffened. 'Don't push it. You want it or not? It makes no difference to me, because I'm not asking for your help this time.'

'But you did. You have. You asked me about Lewis Drake and this dark web business he might be running.'

'Yeah, well, we're beyond that, don't you think?'

After a moment she said, 'I'm sorry. I was angry. I still am. But if you didn't know, then you didn't know.'

'Good. And I swear I didn't. But here's the thing the leak wouldn't have mentioned, Sandra: our killer has already taken his next victim.'

THIRTY-EIGHT

THE FIRST THING BLISS did when he reached HQ was to pull
Bishop to one side for a confidential chat. Standing inside his
old office once again felt peculiar; he was now the outsider occu-
pying another man's territory. Yet one glance at the wall put his
mind at ease and pinned a smile upon his face.

'You rescued it from what should have been its final resting
place, then?' he said.

DS Bishop followed his gaze. Nodded. 'That Pissed-ometer is
part of the furniture in this office, Jimmy. It's a bit more battered
than it was before, but the wall looked too bare without it.'

The cardboard arrow indicated a mood part way between
'steaming' and 'furious', but for once it was out of kilter with how
Bliss truly felt. Bishop must have guessed his train of thought.

'It only went back up first thing this morning,' he explained.
'Nobody has had time to adjust it yet.'

Bliss regarded him closely. 'Do you know who does it?'

Bishop gave him a quizzical look. 'You mean you don't?'

'No. Not a clue.'

'Good. Let's keep it that way. So, what did you want with me?'

'First of all, let me say I don't want to take the piss; I won't use my previous rank and our relative positions to take advantage. That said, I would like an extended lunch break today. I have a personal issue to take care of. I'm thinking of getting away by midday, back again by one-thirty, perhaps two o'clock.'

Bishop's frown formed a fearsome collection of lines and bulges on his forehead. 'Jimmy, your temporary demotion hasn't made you a different person. Why would you ever imagine I'd think you were pulling a fast one? I know you. If you need the time, take it.'

'Thanks. If something breaks, the case is still my priority. I'll drop my plans, you know that.'

'Of course. It didn't need to be said. Please, do what you have to do. If I see your name on the whiteboard, I'll know you're here. If I don't, I'll call you if something pops.'

Bliss was grateful to him. He'd expected nothing less, but he'd owed Bishop the courtesy.

Moments later, with the team gathered together, they knuckled down to the briefing. It was DCI Warburton who stood front and centre on this occasion. She felt it was time to reaffirm her position as SIO, to make it clear how the investigation was being perceived from the top, and to also discuss the news leak.

'I can't begin to tell you how angry I am that it's come to this,' she said, both angular cheeks inflamed. 'I'm not going to pretend that none of us consider journalists to be valuable sources of intelligence – nor to imagine that the currency used to obtain access is anything other than case information. But I hope everybody in this room agrees this new leak is a step too far. The one chink of light is that the degree of information released suggests the source is not a member of this unit. If this daily rag had been aware of our interest in Abbi Turner's disappearance in connection with Phoenix, I have no doubt they would have released those details at the same time. So the leak almost certainly came from somebody close enough to have known about the jump to serial killer status, yet sufficiently distanced to be unaware of our probable abduction. Believe me when I tell you I am personally going to hunt this source down and plug the leak with my boot.'

'What difference do you think it will make to the case?' Chandler asked. 'Are we under greater pressure because of it?'

Warburton nodded. 'Superintendent Fletcher is – as am I. My hope is that's where it ends. I'm certainly not going to add to your burden. You run the case as if this news is not splashed all over the front page. You can't allow it to influence your thinking.'

'I'm sure I speak for us all when I say we appreciate that, boss,' Bliss said, looking around the room. 'Not every DCI would be so composed. Nor willing to stand strong with us, for that matter.'

Warburton stared at him in surprise for a second or two, then chuckled. 'I've never taken you for a brown nose before, Jimmy. But please do remove it from my backside before I attempt to sit down.'

This drew some laughter, and Bliss took it well. 'Yeah, yeah. All I'm saying is thank you for supporting us and keeping the politics out of the room.'

'I will for as long as I can. Obviously, the fact that the Met had this and handed it over to us is both a poisoned chalice and a challenge. Nobody above the rank of Superintendent relishes the prospect of us having to work in the public eye, and of course their first thoughts are for self-preservation. But you're fortunate enough to have Detective Superintendent Fletcher as your lightning rod. So, we move onwards and hopefully upwards. Let's update the room with overnight details.'

It took no more than twenty minutes to make everybody aware of any new information. There wasn't a great deal to add to the previous day's tally: they were stalled in tracking down suspect kennel providers, had found no trace of the Parkinsons, there was still no word on who had contracted the hit job from Lewis Drake, and nor did they yet have the required data from the Dark Desires server location. Bishop refused to be bowed, however.

'Our priorities are clear,' he said. 'We have to find another way to trace the man in Abbi Turner's life. We monitor any and all financial movements relating to all three members of the Parkinson family. Plus, we dig deeper into their backgrounds to see if we can work out where they might have run to. I want you all to contact every CHIS on your books. Spread the word to every colleague out there. We're offering good deals for anybody who gives us the name of the hitman Drake hired. And it's only a matter of time before we've secured the location of that bloody server – not that I have the foggiest idea how it will help us.'

'All knowledge is power,' DC Ansari said, nodding to herself.

'Of course.' Bishop smiled, arching his eyebrows. 'Is that one of my sayings?'

Following a short peal of laughter, Ansari replied, 'I think it's Francis Bacon.'

'The guy from *Footloose*?'

This time the laughter emerged as a ripping snort. 'That's Kevin Bacon, boss. Francis Bacon was a philosopher.'

Bishop shrugged. 'I'm guessing it doesn't matter. I take your point, though. As an even wiser philosopher once said' – here he paused to glance at Bliss – 'we don't know what we don't know until we know it.'

'I don't think that was Jimmy, boss. Wasn't it…' Her voice trailed off as she noticed Bliss shaking his head.

He didn't think it served any useful purpose to set Bishop straight at this stage; he had uttered the phrase once, but had taken it from the former US Defence Secretary Donald Rumsfeld.

However, it did flush out a stray thought. There was something he had intended to do, but had been sidetracked by having to visit the kennels. He struggled to bring it back to the forefront of his mind. He was sure it was somehow connected to their hunt for Abbi Turner's probable abductor. He'd missed something, and it nagged at him like a toothache. He knew if he spun the wheels long enough it would come to him, and as Bishop concluded the briefing, it did.

Bliss made his way over to Bishop, motioning for Chandler to join him. 'I forgot something,' he said. 'Yesterday I had it in mind for us to take a look at Abbi Turner's gaff. To see if there was anything there that might provide us with insight about this man she was seeing. Later on the thing with the kennels came up and that became our priority, so the home search completely slipped my mind.'

Bishop was already nodding. 'Yes. Go. Take the door off its hinges – I'll authorise that immediately because intelligence says she's missing, possibly the next victim of our killer. Meanwhile, I'll work with Phil on those bloody awful Parkinsons and this hitman. John and Gul can tag along with Glen in focussing on the server location. Sound good to you?'

'You're the boss, boss.'

'Yes. But does that plan sound okay?'

'It does, Bish.' He offered his colleague a sympathetic tap on the arm. 'Don't worry yourself into a coronary. You're doing a great job.'

Bishop swallowed and licked his lips. 'Perhaps. But I'll tell you this for nothing: it doesn't half make me want to be a plain old DS again.'

Bliss pondered his friend's words as he and Chandler headed over to Turner's home. He recalled his first step up into the role of Inspector. The day before, his old boss had taken him to one side and spoken at length about the job and the differences Bliss was about to encounter.

'You always think you're ready, Jimmy. You have the experience. You have the know-how. You've studied and you've passed your exams. If you're lucky, you've been mentored well, and you have a clear idea about the way you're going to handle things differently; we all do. But soon enough, along comes that first major case. Now, in addition to your own responsibilities, you're also responsible for the work of every other officer in the team. Not only that, you're accountable. For the case. For them. For everything. And even though you haven't changed as a person, you're now an entirely different species in the eyes of people you were working in tandem with only the day before. All of a sudden you're on the other side of the desk – effectively, you're management. And you put all of those things together, old son, and it… well, it makes all the difference in the world.'

And it had. The effect was immediate, and life was never quite the same again. Olly Bishop was getting a taste of what Bliss had experienced all those years ago – only these days the responsibility and accountability went even deeper. He'd seen it in his friend's desperate eyes, heard it in the cracked voice.

'What are you thinking about?' Chandler asked. 'I can smell the gears burning from here.'

It took a while for Bliss to respond, but when he did his voice was imbued with defiance. 'I need to clear my head when it comes to our original case, but I'm not going to do that until I know Abbi Turner is safe and this madman is tucked away in a cell.'

Chandler turned her head away and forced out a long, steady sigh. 'I don't have a good feeling about this one, Jimmy. His MO suggests he keeps the girls for between seven and ten days. We're a week in, give or take. I can't help feeling this might be the one we can't turn around in time.'

'I can't say I disagree.'

'You think we might find something at her place?'

Bliss gave the question a moment of thought. 'What I think is this: if she fell for this man, if he meant something to her, the one place we're most likely to find evidence of that is in her home.'

THIRTY-NINE

AN AREA OF CUL-DE-SACS and uniform semi-detached homes with plots of lawn to the front, Ravensthorpe had been built on the site of the old RAF Westwood base ahead of the new townships being developed in the late seventies. Abbi Turner lived in a shared ownership house. A representative from the housing association landlords met them at the property. Bliss had been perfectly willing to take the front door off its hinges as instructed, but a well-placed phone call from Chandler had secured entry for them.

The first thing Bliss noticed was how clean the place was. It smelled fresh, too. It was one of the main differences he'd noticed between the escort type sex workers, whose livelihoods relied on their abstinence from both drugs and an excess of alcohol, and those who worked the streets or knocking shops and snorted or injected their way through life. In the homes of the latter, you needed to double-glove and were glad of a mask. These girls with the classier gigs worked hard at staying clean in every way.

He preferred to search specific areas in tandem with his partner, so the pair got to work upstairs. Of the two main rooms, Abbi appeared to use one to sleep in and the other as a walk-in dressing room and wardrobe. Before touching anything or carrying out his search, Bliss first stood on the threshold to Abbi's bedroom. Something clicked into place that ought to have occurred to him before. He turned to look at his partner, annoyed with himself for having wasted time.

'Pen, give Bish a bell, would you? Tell him we need a couple of CSIs out here and a bagging team. If this bloke Abbi was partial to ever came here, his hair, prints and DNA could be all over the place. We'll continue our search, after which they can follow up forensically.'

While Chandler made the call, Bliss worried about the slip. First he'd forgotten about searching the property, and then he'd failed to extend that action to the crime scene investigators. Both lapses were perhaps understandable given the rapidly changing circumstances, and he'd recovered from them. But they caused a twinge of anxiety in his chest, all the same.

The examination of the upstairs area proved fruitless. It told them Abbi Turner was a young woman with taste and more than a little sophistication. Her chest of drawers and bedside cabinets contained paraphernalia connected with her work, along with erotic lingerie. Bliss pulled the drawers out of their runners and flipped them over; people often taped items on the underside in an effort to conceal them. He discovered nothing.

If her dressing table was anything to go by, Abbi liked makeup, perfume and jewellery. Much of the latter was of the costume variety, but in a box mercifully free from a spinning ballerina or the tinkling sound that usually accompanied one, he also noted a few relatively expensive items. She preferred white gold, silver or platinum to yellow gold, and in a Tiffany box he found a simple bangle. To Bliss's untrained eye, it looked like the real deal.

Beneath the bed they found only a thin layer of dust; behind the chest of drawers, more of the same. Simple and elegant, the furnishings suggested a young woman whose income matched her taste and keen eye. Bliss found himself becoming impressed with Abbi, which prompted a fresh squirt of adrenaline. The natural urge was to search quickly, but much could be missed if you gave in to that inclination.

The spare room holding the majority of the girl's clothes gave up no obvious clues. Bliss was no *Vogue* reader, but he had always been able to spot quality. Amongst her daily wear items and the more formal and suggestive clothing, he identified simple knee-length skirts and blouses made from good fabrics. Each piece told him a little more about her.

'Nice clobber,' he said to Chandler. 'I bet she wears it well, too. The right hairstyle and scent to match any occasion.'

His partner agreed. 'If these aren't knock-offs, our Abbi is not only a girl of refined tastes – she has the bank account to match.'

'Where are we on her phones?'

'Last I heard, data was starting to come through. Plenty of messages stacking up in her voicemail, but no outgoing texts or calls since last Wednesday.'

Bliss had one final look around the room. 'This place was her escape,' he said. 'When she was here, she was just a woman who enjoyed fine things and could forget all about her miserable recent past.'

'And much of her not-so-enjoyable present as well, I imagine.'

He nodded, saddened by the thought of the young woman's lifestyle outside this house. 'Perhaps a bleak future, too. But at least she did get some respite here; not all of them do.'

Before heading downstairs, they carried out a cursory check of the bathroom and toilet. If he had been hoping to see two toothbrushes, Bliss was disappointed. No shaving bag, aftershave or male deodorant, either. No sign at all so far that a man had come anywhere close to sharing Abbi's life.

There were only two main rooms downstairs as well. The kitchen yielded nothing of significance, and as they exited it, Bliss had the sinking sensation that the search of Abbi Turner's home was not going to take them any further in their investigation. He barely said a word as they sifted through the living room. He noticed a chessboard laid out on a stout rectangular side table. Unlike Yeva Savchuk's, the set was wooden. A game looked to be in progress; he wondered if they'd catch a break and find their killer's prints on any of the pieces. He'd make sure the CSI team paid close attention to it when they arrived.

When he and Chandler had entered the house, Bliss had no real idea of what he hoped to find. A brochure or leaflet, perhaps, advertising the kennels their man might have a connection with. One drawer in every home – most often in the kitchen – usually contained such items. Chandler had found Abbi's and tipped its contents out on the small circular dining table. The two of them ferreted around, but came across nothing useful.

Chandler went through a wall calendar looking for names. She found seven, but each was female. She made a note of them anyway. Bliss found an address book. It mostly contained details scrawled on Post-it notes. After finding two numbers associated with male names, he called DC Hunt to ask him to run the numbers and when he got hits, put them through a PNC check.

They were halfway through their living room inspection when Hunt called with answers. The name Ian came back to a hairdresser who worked from home, while Jakub was a Polish national who provided a handyman service.

'I called both men once I knew who and what they were and had checked their records,' Hunt told Bliss. 'Ian did our girl's hair once every six weeks. Last time was a month ago. Jakub built some cabinets for her.'

Bliss had spotted the shelves. Built from limed white oak,

they had a cabinet-maker's finish about them. Perfect joints, no screws; the work of a craftsman. He admired them more closely as he went through Abbi's small collection of Blu-Rays and CDs. In his experience, people often hid letters and notes between book covers, but as there were no books to be found he thought perhaps he might stumble upon something tucked between the various cases. Once again, he completed his search with nothing to show for it.

Chandler had completed her own exploration of the soft furnishings and the coffee table drawers. Groaning a little as she stood upright, she turned to him and shook her head. 'Forensics might come up with something – but whatever it is, it won't be obvious. I have to think the reason we've found nothing is because there's nothing here to find.'

'That's what bothers me. No computer, laptop, tablet, or even a games console. Don't you find that odd?'

'Not really. These days people have everything they need on their phones. Plus, whatever she had could have been stolen.'

Frustrated, Bliss let go a deep sigh. 'I thought we might find what we needed here. No idea what it might have been, but I felt sure we'd find some indication that this man actually existed.'

'You think he might not?'

'He could be nothing more than a fantasy. Plenty of girls who do what Abbi does for a living yearn for that one man who will take them away from it all. Perhaps that's all he was. Somebody who lived only in her imagination.'

Chandler let out a sudden groan and cursed. 'I forgot to do the bins in the kitchen. We'll leave the main ones outside to CSI. You never know, though. The recycling bin might hold something for us.'

Alone in the living room, Bliss walked across and stood on the threshold. He surveyed the entire room section by section, seeking something out of place – an item you had to stand back from in order to fully appreciate its significance. His eyes moved beyond the chessboard and a moment later hesitated. He glanced back. Had his attention been snagged? If so, by what? He moved a couple of steps closer. The game looked to be no more than eight or nine moves old. One piece captured by each player. No discernible pattern that he could see, though he was hardly a player of distinction. He moved in for a closer inspection.

The pieces themselves and the board appeared to be made from ebonised mahogany and sycamore. A nice-looking set. Bliss struggled to see what his mind had clearly latched on to. Thirty-two chessmen. Four bishops, four knights, four rooks, two queens and two kings. Sixteen pawns. Equal numbers in the ebony-tinted mahogany and sycamore. Except…

The white king was not made from sycamore at all. Neither did its styling match the other king. It was close in both colouring and shape, but Bliss could tell it was not part of the set. It did not match. Remembering its position on the board, he picked up the piece, then did the same with the black king. The latter was a good deal heavier. Indeed, the fake one felt almost hollow.

Puzzled, Bliss brought the item up to his face for closer inspection. He blinked a couple of times. Took out his reading glasses and squinted at it, rolling it over between his fingers. That was when he noticed the crack running around the neck of the piece, and a moment later he realised it was not a crack at all but an engineered join. Holding the base firmly, he pulled on the top of the king and it popped off in his hands.

The king was not a chess piece at all; or at least, if it was, its appearance was one of disguise. Because in removing the cap, Bliss had exposed its true identity. The chess piece was, in fact, a USB stick.

FORTY

IMPATIENT TO DISCOVER MORE, Bliss had fetched his backpack from the boot of the car. From its largest zipped pouch he withdrew his spare laptop and powered it up. He and Chandler sat at the tiny dining table, trawling through the contents of the chess USB stick.

'I bet you anything you like most of this is also in the cloud somewhere, synced from her phone automatically,' Chandler said as Bliss scrolled down a list of folders.

'I'll take that bet.'

'You would. Old people like you and young people like Abbi think differently. It's second nature for them to let their technology do the heavy lifting.'

Bliss nodded, ignoring the jibe about his age. 'I know all that. But you're forgetting who probably has her phone. He would've wiped the storage clean.'

Chandler sucked on her lip. 'Of course. But I bet it's backed up, so we might still be able to retrieve it.'

'He probably deleted that as well. The provider may have back-ups themselves, but if the more recent files were only removed last week, I'm betting they're gone for good.'

'Well, I wouldn't want to rely on data retention rules, so let's hope she kept everything on here.'

'Let's hope.'

Bliss saw nothing obvious in the list of folders, and so navigated back to the top of the list and opened up the first. With his partner looking over his shoulder and remarking on the content as they waded through the stored data, they had reached one labelled *Misc* before they struck gold.

The third image was the first to also feature a man. It looked like a selfie, taken by Abbi. She wore a full-lipped pout. The man was smiling, but had a hand raised to partially obscure his face. The next one seemed to have caught the same man unawares. This time he was sitting in Abbi's living room. Above average height and build, with thick dark hair; if this was Des, he looked like an everyman. His lips curved upwards into a smile, but the rest of his face told Bliss the response was not genuine. The man's eyes, in particular, were narrowed in concern.

'What does this one say to you?' Bliss said.

Chandler bent forward to study the picture. 'I'd say he's not as happy as he might first appear.'

'My thought exactly. I wonder if Abbi noticed it.'

'You think this could be him?'

'Candid shots, here in her home. He's not a client. Not at the moment this was taken, anyhow.'

Chandler leaned on Bliss's shoulder. 'There are no clients at all so far, I've noticed. No people other than Abbi herself.'

'That's to be expected. Would you allow yourself to be photographed if you were about to carry out some sordid act on a young girl?'

'True enough. So why did he?'

Bliss started clicking through the rest of the images in the folder. 'Because by this stage he's moved on from being her client.

He's something else to her now, and he has to play along. If he's pretending to be her boyfriend in order to lull her, take himself off the books so nobody knows they're seeing each other, he can't react negatively if she takes the odd snap of the two of them together. Besides, he knows he's about to have full access to her phone and all of its data.'

Bliss scrolled back a couple of shots. He made the image larger and centred it over the man's chest. 'Can you make out what that says?'

Chandler leaned in closer, forcing Bliss to move his head out of the way. 'No,' she said. 'It breaks up more the further you zoom in.'

Bliss resized smaller and squinted. The man wore an olive-green fleece. On the left-hand side of the chest was some writing over what appeared to be a small image. The whole thing looked like a logo of some description, but the poor quality made it indistinct.

'You think Gul might be able to do something with it?' he said.

'Absolutely. Our tech guys taught her well.'

Bliss had never been a fan of hope, but he began to feel its grip, a tightening claw swelling his chest. He nodded absently, as if to himself. 'I think this is our man,' he said. 'I reckon this is Des. And if that's the case, then that logo might be the stroke of luck we were looking for.'

***

Upon their return to the incident room at Thorpe Wood, Bliss immediately took a call from Belmarsh. He was desperate to reveal their breakthrough to the team, but was equally intrigued to find out why he was being contacted by the prison. Lewis Drake's solicitor explained to him that they were being joined in a conference call by the deputy governor. This was in response to DS Bishop's earlier conversation with prison staff concerning

Lewis Drake's contact with the outside world, following the visit by Bliss and Chandler.

Drake's solicitor announced herself as Geraldine Murray. She wasted no time informing Bliss of her concerns regarding the interview having taken place without Lewis Drake having the benefit of legal representation. She was hardly pacified when he reminded her that not only had her client agreed, but also her office had been informed prior to the prison offering its own approval. Even so, Murray moved on to assure him that Drake had neither taken nor received any phone calls since the interview.

'How certain can you be that he had no use of a mobile phone?' Bliss asked.

'I object to the implication!' Murray snapped. 'My client understands this would be a breach of his conditions.'

'I'm sure he does. But my question was to the deputy governor, not you, Mrs Murray.'

Simon Price had been DG for five years. That was all Bliss knew about the man, but he hoped he would be honest as opposed to being an arse-coverer. 'I understand what you're getting at, Detective Sergeant,' Price said, 'and under normal circumstances I don't think I could speak with any genuine conviction. However, as Mrs Murray is well aware, her client was in a state of frenzy following the interview yesterday morning. So much so that when he demanded to make a phone call and was denied immediate access, he became unhinged. As such, Mr Drake has been in isolation ever since.'

Bliss took a breath. He knew what the follow-up question had to be, though he hated having to ask it. 'That only means he's had no contact with fellow prisoners, sir. How about prison officers?'

'I'm way ahead of you. First of all, let me say that in this secure unit, Mr Drake only ever comes into contact with our most experienced, most trusted officers. Even so, I've personally spoken to the two who have communicated with him since his isolation. They insist there is no possibility of Drake having made a call himself. Nor has he had the opportunity to pass along a message for somebody else to make a call on his behalf. He's had no external access of any kind.'

'You can guarantee that?' Bliss prompted.

'Insofar as I am able to guarantee anything. I trust my staff, DS Bliss.'

Almost before the DG had finished speaking, Geraldine Murray pounced. 'Now that we've established my client's situation, Detective Sergeant Bliss, would you please inform me as to why this is so important to you at this time?'

He gave a wide smile of satisfaction. 'You know, I don't believe I will, Mrs Murray.'

'I beg your pardon? Is this the way you choose to behave after you've received our full cooperation?'

'Your cooperation came at your own insistence. My job here was to establish whether Lewis Drake had communicated with anybody on the outside since my colleague and I spoke with him. Any cooperation you speak of has come from Mr Price and the staff at HMP Belmarsh rather than yourself.'

'In which case, I demand to know why.'

'You can demand all you like. It changes nothing.'

'Then I demand to speak to a superior officer. Immediately.'

'You'll find quite a few of those in the armed forces, Mrs Murray. If you'd like to speak with a *senior* officer, however, please do call Thorpe Wood police station. I'm sure they'll be delighted to avoid – sorry – take your call.'

Bliss thanked the DG for taking part, was solicitous in saying his goodbyes, but by the end was glad to be off the phone. He looked around for DS Bishop, but he was nowhere to be seen.

'Gul!' he called out. 'Do you know where the boss is?'

Ansari looked up from her computer keyboard, smiled and raised her eyebrows. 'Which one?'

'Bish.'

'He's meeting with the DCI. What's up, Jimmy?'

Bliss walked over and leaned on one of the new Perspex screens that separated the work pods. He relayed the content of the call he'd taken. 'What do you think it means?' he asked. 'Perhaps Drake didn't put out this hit on Nicola Parkinson after all.'

'Maybe. But from what you say, we've still got to at least consider the possibility.'

Gratton was sitting close by and had been listening in. 'Who else would?' he asked. 'And why? Lewis Drake had good reason. Who else is losing out by Parkinson and her kids making a killing from this website?'

Bliss frowned. It was a good question. If Drake wasn't in the frame, it wasn't immediately obvious to him who else fitted. He put a couple of fingertips to his forehead, an ache having formed above his left eye. When he looked up again, his gaze fell upon Ansari once more. 'Have you seen Glen? Is he with the boss and the DCI?'

She shook her head. 'No. He said he was stepping out to make a couple of calls. We were working on the location of the Dark Desires server. I have to say I wasn't at my most enthusiastic at the time. We were all agreed it was for evidentiary reasons only, not something that was going to break the case wide open. But now I think about it, Glen was much the same for a good thirty minutes or so, muttering to himself in that disgruntled way of his. Then he went silent on me, for which I was thankful. Moments later he said something beneath his breath, got up and walked away. I've only just noticed he's not come back.'

'He's probably pissed off at having all his hard work being shifted down our list of priorities,' Hunt said. 'Maybe he's moaning to the DI over at Cambridge about how he's being given all the shitty work.'

'I hope that's all it is.'

'What do you mean by that, Gul?' Bliss asked.

'I'm just reminding you all that Glen is NCA. If he found something, came across a piece of information that might be useful, do we know for sure he wouldn't take it to them first and leave us to find out about it later?'

Gratton was already on his feet and heading for the door. 'I'll check the stairway and the canteen,' he said. 'If he's on the blower to someone, I'll see what I can pick up.'

'You think he'd do the dirty on us?' Bliss asked Hunt and Ansari.

The pair of them looked on as their colleague left the room. Hunt thought about the question, and gave a slow nod. 'I think he might. And to be honest, I don't know that I'd blame him.'

FORTY-ONE

WARBURTON AND BISHOP ENTERED the room just as a tense situation had begun to escalate. DCs Hunt and Ansari stood virtually toe to toe, their faces flushed and eyes lit from within.

'You've been whining about the same thing for the past ten minutes, John, and I'm sick of it,' Ansari said, her voice loud and rising in pitch with every word. 'I don't want to hear another word about how badly we supposedly treated Glen Ashton.'

'It's an opinion,' Hunt replied, leaning forward. 'And I'm entitled to it every bit as much as you're entitled to yours.'

'The difference is, I'm not spouting mine for the sake of it. I'm only reacting to you complaining all the bloody time.'

'And why shouldn't I? You might be happy working alongside somebody while he's getting shafted, Gul, but I'm not. He got a rough deal, and you know it.'

The disagreement might have ended there – just two stressed colleagues seething at one another before deciding to walk away – but that was the moment when DC Gratton entered the fray. He took Hunt's side.

'We pushed him out into the fringes on everything,' he claimed, drawing a supportive nod from Hunt. 'I know he came in here with a superior attitude, but once he buckled down he was only ever useful to the investigation. He found himself stuck on nothing jobs with us time and time again. So, no, I wouldn't blame him, either, if he's taken fresh information to his own people back at ERSOU.'

Bliss kept his thoughts to himself, allowing Bishop to step in to defuse the situation. 'Is that how you two regard the actions I gave you both?' he demanded, looking from Hunt to Gratton and back again. 'John, you're the more experienced, so you can go first. Is that how you feel about the task of locating that server?'

Hunt stood his ground. He was not one for confrontation, but this time he looked as if he was about to dig his heels in. 'If I'm being honest, yes: it felt like a nothing job at this stage. I realise we have to cover every aspect, and gaining evidence along the way is vital. However, with everything else that was going on I thought it was a job we could delay until we'd at least identified our man.'

'I see.' Bishop cleared his throat, buying time. 'It didn't occur to you that one of the reasons why I decided to keep you on it was because the Parkinsons might pull the plug at any moment? And I do mean literally. Down the server, switch it off, physically remove it from its current location, destroy the contents of its hard drives.'

Hunt stared back at Bishop. His defiance wavered only momentarily.

'We don't know for sure that it has anything to do with the Parkinsons.'

'Then for argument's sake, let's say it is them. My argument still stands.'

'Surely between us and the NCA we've collected enough data to establish precisely what that server's role was.'

'Raw data, yes. Traffic flowing in and out, yes. Conclusive evidence…? I'm sure the CPS will tell us in due course, once we've submitted our MG forms. But think how much happier we'd all be if we had the physical server in our possession, John… Phil. And then think how much happier still we'd be if we were lucky enough to collar the Parkinsons attempting to strip down that same server. While it's still running, we can continue to both monitor and record it. We can tell if data is being deleted – and let's assume it will be, ahead of any physical switching off. You two may see that job as plain old dull police work; me, I see it as a vital part of the overall job. A job that had to be done, requiring trustworthy people to do it. I chose you two and Glen Ashton. Not glamorous, I grant you. But potentially critical. I'm sorry you don't see it that way.'

Bishop allowed his disappointment in the two DCs to sink in before turning away and nodding in Bliss's direction. 'What have you got for us, Jimmy?'

'Our man's photo, possibly. We think so, at least.' He explained the circumstances of their find, their search through the folders and the image files themselves. He took the plastic evidence bag containing the chess piece from his pocket and lobbed it underhand to DC Ansari. 'There's a photo on there showing the man wearing a fleece. On the fleece is what we think could be a logo. Can't make it out, though. I was hoping Gul could find us a rabbit hiding somewhere inside the hat.'

'I'll get to work on it immediately,' Ansari said, swivelling in her chair, prising open the bag as she turned.

'Look in the Miscellaneous folder. There's only one image of the man in his fleece.'

'What other dramas have we missed?' DCI Warburton asked, perhaps hoping to take the pressure down a notch or two with some levity.

Bliss responded first. 'I took an interesting call from Belmarsh. The deputy governor himself confidently insisted Drake did not have any external communication or even any internal communication that could have been passed on. Evidently, our visit left him angry enough to draw an isolation stretch.'

'How's that possible? A contract being put out on Nicola Parkinson within hours of you visiting Drake can't be a coincidence.'

'That's precisely what I was thinking. The DG has to have it wrong. Why else would…' Bliss paused, his train of thought deviating. He saw it then. Saw how they'd been had. 'The devious cow,' he whispered.

'Jimmy?' Bishop squinted at him.

'The DG is right. Drake didn't order a hit on Parkinson.'

'So who did?'

'Nobody.'

The room fell into silence for a few seconds, before Chandler said, 'You want to elaborate on that?'

He nodded. 'If we're right, and Nicola Parkinson has been running Drake's operation in his absence, there has to be a communication pathway between the two of them. He didn't contact her after we met with him – he did it before we arrived. He wanted to find out why we were driving down there to speak with him, so he contacted her. I'm betting the idea of us being in the same room as him scared her half to death.'

'Of course,' Chandler said. 'She had to know we'd be talking to him about this case, that we'd mention Dark Desires and her, possibly even in the same breath.'

Bliss went on. 'She made sure word reached the streets about a contract being taken out on her, which she later used as an excuse to have it on her toes. We're sitting here thinking she and her brood went into hiding because they were scared of being hit, when all the time they're on the run from us – and Drake, ultimately.'

It all slotted together perfectly. Bliss knew it did. And so did everyone else in the room. The team reunited in that moment, disagreements forgotten. They discussed it at length, dissecting the theory and finding no reason not to take it forward as a genuine hypothesis. It was as good as any other, and better than most. Bishop called for hush and waited for the room to fall silent once more before speaking to the team as a whole.

'If Jimmy is right – and I think he probably is – it changes only one component of the case: we no longer have to put resources into tracing a contract killer, or attempting to link it back to Lewis Drake. The fact is, for whatever reason, the Parkinsons are still gone and we don't know where or how to find them. We have to double our efforts, hammer every CHIS harder still, because somebody out there has to know where they went, or at least be able to give us some ideas. Agreed?'

A general murmur of acceptance rippled around the room. Bliss nodded along with them. 'But leaving them and that aspect of Phoenix aside, finding Abbi Turner remains our prime objective. I'm of the opinion that we commit most of our remaining resources to her. I seriously don't believe the Parkinsons can help us with that side of things; accessing that bloody server might, though. We can't know what's on there, but if there's even the slightest chance of our man's details being on that machine or in its data in the cloud or wherever, we need to find it.'

Although some faces turned to Bishop, it was Warburton who stepped into the spotlight. 'In terms of policy, I remain SIO. Given Bish's unique position, the decision to make him my deputy provided him with the opportunity to experience a senior investigative role for the first time. As such, I've allowed him to run with it, keeping my supervision to a minimum and mostly in the background. I trust each of you will join me in congratulating him on a job well done so far. I listened closely to everything both he and Jimmy had to say, and I can genuinely tell you all that I would not change a single thing. Please, everyone, do continue. Let's have these bastards.'

Satisfied that Bishop had command of both the investigation and the room, Bliss took the opportunity to cut out. His task was no emergency, but it was still something he had to take care of. As he took the stairs down to the ground floor, he heard footsteps in the stairwell above him. He was out in the car park by the time his pursuer caught up.

'Where are you off to, Pen?' he asked, curious as to why Chandler was leaving at the same time as him.

'I have no idea. You tell me.'

'What?'

'Diane told me I should keep an eye on you. She implied there was a chance you might be working off the books, and suggested I become your shadow.'

Bliss blinked and moistened his lips. 'No offence, but that's not going to happen,' he said adamantly. 'This is one you have to stay out of.'

'Which tells me there's something *to* stay out of. So of course I'm not about to do any such thing.' Chandler crossed her arms and stared at him.

'Pen, I'm ordering you to return to the unit.'

'You *can't* order me. You're not my DI at the moment. I can flap two fingers at you all day long and there's bugger all you can do about it. But Diane is my DCI, and her order was firm and clear.'

He shook his head again. 'This is not something you want to be involved with. We can tell her you stuck to me like glue if you want, but that's not how we're going to do things.'

He walked across to his car, but when he got in, Chandler slid into the passenger seat alongside him. Looking straight ahead she said, 'This is happening, Jimmy. Deal with it. Whatever it is, I'm along for the ride.'

***

The pair shared a booth with Detective Sergeant Paul Nicholls in a coffee bar at Huntingdon railway station, literally opposite the Hinchingbrooke Cambridgeshire Constabulary HQ in which Nicholls worked. He was already sipping a coffee when they got there. The man looked wary upon seeing Chandler with Bliss, but seemingly neither irritated nor angered by the topic of the conversation they were about to have. Bliss bought himself a Coke and his partner a still water before settling in.

'Tell me how this became your problem,' Nicholls said, savouring his latte.

Bliss was ready and responded without pause. 'The moment Watson came to live on my manor, he became my problem.'

'Not if he didn't do anything wrong.'

'Something we both know is not true.'

'Something we both *suspect* is not true, Jimmy.'

'If you say so. I know better; you do, too. That might be the official line, but you, your entire team, the CPS… you all know he killed that poor kid.'

'Prove it.' Nicholls shoved his drink to one side and folded his arms. 'Because that was the task I had.'

Bliss noted the resentment. He would have felt the same way had another detective followed up on one of his cases and insinuated himself into it long after it had been closed. 'Like I told you before, this is nothing against you or the way you ran your investigation. You didn't have the evidence I have. It's that simple.'

'Then tell me. Fire away, Jimmy. Let's have the great DI Bliss show me what I missed and where we at Hinchingbrooke went wrong.'

Bliss swallowed half his drink before responding. 'There you go again. Get over yourself, Harvey. You didn't miss it. And it's "the great *DS* Bliss" if you want to be entirely accurate. Look,

George Moss alibied Watson. That meant you had to draw back and attempt to charge Watson with having contributed to the boy's fragile condition.'

'Yeah. We argued that his constant beatings had left the kid with a skull weakness. CPS told us we had no case. Not one they were prepared to lose, given the mother had already admitted to everything and claimed Watson never touched her son. That alone tainted any clinical observations.'

'Right. So you know it's him, but justice gives you the finger. Only, how much of that changes if George Moss admits he and Watson never spent that evening and night together? What if he says Watson put him up to it, having turned up at his place in a manic state, his hands and clothes covered in blood?'

Nicholls put a hand to his mouth before slowly stroking his chin. 'Has he made a statement to this effect?'

Bliss shook his head. 'Not yet. He wants assurances that I can't give him. He needs you to protect him from the time he makes his statement until the time Watson gets found guilty. Without that, he sticks to his original story.'

'I can do that. What made him change his mind?'

'Persuasion.'

Nicholls grinned and raised his eyebrows. 'Of the gentle variety?'

'Is there any other kind?' Bliss said.

The man's face brightened, but swiftly became bemused. 'How the bloody hell did you do this, Jimmy? How did you even find him to begin with?'

'I have my ways. It's immaterial to the case, because I have nothing to do with it. None of it came from me. That's how this plays out: I give you his address, you pull him. You give him what he needs, he gives you what you want.'

'He'll stand up in court?'

Bliss nodded. 'He will. I have him thinking of Watson as a man he wants out of his life before Watson begins to think of him in the same way. But don't hang about, Harvey. Scoop him up while he's still nervy. I don't want him to do a runner.'

After a moment, Nicholls said, 'This won't all fall apart on me, will it, Jimmy?'

'How d'you mean?'

'I mean if he screams coercion.'

Bliss scratched at the scar on his forehead. He had a quick look around to make sure they couldn't be overheard, but the place was far from heaving. 'George Moss is a stain on humanity's arse. If he says I leaned on him, he may well be telling the truth. But nobody has to believe him. Anyway, he's guilty of providing a false alibi; if I coerced that out of him, so be it. The main thing is, any statement he provides to you will be under the watchful eye and ear of a duty solicitor. My name needn't even crop up. Moss is fully aware of what's at stake, Harvey. All you have to do is walk him through it.'

Nicholls chewed on his lip for a moment, then glanced at Chandler. 'And what's your involvement here, Penny? I realise we don't know each other well, but this doesn't seem like the kind of thing you'd be a party to.'

'Jimmy gave me the details on the drive over. So far, that and this conversation is the extent of my knowledge. The way I see it, neither he nor I are here. That leaves you and this Moss character to work out your own story. Seems to me it's a win-win for you.'

Nodding and turning back to Bliss, Nicholls said, 'So why exactly are you handing this to me on a plate? Why not bring them both in yourself?'

Bliss did not have to consider his answer for long. 'Because I know what a kick in the balls this case must have been for you and your team, Harvey. Hard to swallow when they turn out the way this one did. Kind of case that does things to your mind, keeps you up at night. Maybe even breaks you over time. There are less altruistic reasons why it's probably best for me to steer well clear, but ultimately I'm giving it to you because you deserve it. Hopefully it'll be one less ghost to follow you around.'

Nicholls sat back in the cheap padded bench seat and blew out his cheeks. 'I don't know what to say, Jimmy.'

Bliss was okay with that. 'Then say nothing. Just listen while I tell you where to find him, and the precise details of the deal he and I struck. Your lot can pull him and take it from there. Seeing Watson nailed will be all the thanks I need.'

'You think Moss backing off his alibi will be enough?'

Bliss grinned, having saved the best for last. 'You remember I told you Moss's revised story? About how Watson had turned up at his place that night of the murder, his clothes smothered in blood?'

'Yeah. That's still only hearsay from a man who's already lied to the court.'

'True. But keep your eyes on the prize, Harvey. The clothes. Watson had Moss destroy them. Only… something must have told Moss that one day he might need some leverage of his own.'

Nicholls stared at him, eyes wide and disbelieving. 'You don't mean…'

'Yes, I do. Not only did Moss not destroy them – he didn't even get rid of them. They've been tucked away inside a vacuum-sealed bag, which is currently wrapped in a duvet and stored in his airing cupboard. I know, because I've seen them.'

'And the blood on them isn't going to be only his, either.'

Bliss shook his head. 'Not a chance,' he said.

FORTY-TWO

O N THE FIRST THREE occasions that he put her to work, the man she knew as Des dragged her from what she had come to regard as her prison cell and led her out into the daylight, across a broken stone courtyard populated by weeds, to a rectangular static mobile home. Each time, he first paused to slip a leather collar around her neck; this was attached to a sturdy chain lead with a leather strap festooned with metal studs at the end. Although he did not force her to walk on all fours like the animal he was treating her as, humiliation burned her cheeks all the same. Once inside the prefabricated home, he brought her into a room so small the double bed inside almost filled it.

What she glimpsed of the rest of the house appeared clean and tidy – as Des himself had always been. Yet this room reeked, a foul stench of dirt and squalor combined with stale sweat and something sweet and cloying. It made her gag and recoil. As he slipped the lead off that first time, Des cupped her chin in one of his big hands. Gone from his gaze was any pretence of affection, or even lust. Instead he regarded her with pure disdain.

'Behave,' he said. 'You do that and I might throw you a treat when you're done.'

Abbi no longer asked him why he was doing this to her. She'd long accepted his mute disinterest on that subject. All she could do was continue to berate herself as she wandered the dank corridors of her own mind. How had she missed the lack of humanity in those eyes? How had she failed to realise who and what this man truly was? What he was capable of?

On that first day after she had come around, she guessed he must have taken her so that he could later have her by force – and to do so whenever he pleased now that she was being held prisoner. Compliance seemingly no longer fulfilled his baser needs. The desire for control was a part of it; that much was apparent. But she had never once imagined his darker reason for the abduction until that first encounter in the tiny bedroom, where the man she had seen earlier in her dark cell waited for her on the bed.

The man who raped her that day, and the two who followed, choking her as they carried out their sordid and despicable act, seemed to also get off on her being treated like an animal. Kept locked away inside a brick cage, having to wear a collar when she was removed from it, the lead hooked up to her so casually, as if she had become Des's pet. Her master taking her for a walk, the culmination of which delivered her into the hands of others of his kind.

Abbi dwelt on this after each humiliation. It was hard to imagine anything more degrading for a human being. Any remaining morsel of self-respect she might have had prior to her abduction had been drained away by each subsequent encounter with the lead – more so than the rape and the choking. They were at least acts with which she was familiar; the dregs of human experience, perhaps, but human for all that. All she felt after those first three men was an emptiness inside that she knew would never be filled again.

But the fourth man didn't want the animal show in the bedroom; instead, he took her while she remained in the bricks-and-mortar pen, on the thin mattress, cold air trapped inside the thick walls. He'd also been the roughest so far. The previous three had demonstrated their experience, understanding precisely how far they could take her into the warm oblivion, using only their hands to regulate her destiny.

The other was nearly her last.

The curious euphoria once again overcame her fear and hostility. But then his hands shifted and the choking became strangulation. Abbi felt panic kick in, the rush of dizziness caused by asphyxiation a dangerous sign her body fought against. He had bound her hands together behind her back, and although she struggled by shifting her body weight and thrusting her head in all directions, he was too strong for her efforts to make any difference.

This is it. You knew the risks, Abbi. This man doesn't know where to draw the line. He won't stop until he comes. By which time it will be too late.

Yet by some miracle, he reached orgasm before she passed out. She coughed and spluttered her way back, a dense, fuzzy feeling inside her head. Pinpoints of light glimmered in her eyes. Abbi sucked in the air around her as if it were her last breath, filling her lungs with life. By the time he rolled off and shoved her to one side, she was sobbing and gasping and continuing to splutter.

The man eventually adjusted his clothing and got to his feet. He stood over her, leering and sweating, droplets slipping from his hairline and splashing down upon her bare flesh. Each wet splat felt like a lick of fire. 'How was it for you?' he said. He put back his head and giggled like a child. Moments later he let himself out and slammed the door closed behind him, sealing her once more inside what had almost become her tomb.

Des returned ten minutes after escorting the man from the premises. He stood in the doorway and snapped his fingers. 'Time to scrub yourself clean, you filthy little whore,' he said. 'Let's get you ready for your next owner.'

And my last, Abbi thought bitterly as she struggled to her feet. *By whatever means possible.*

FORTY-THREE

Bliss took the call he'd been hoping for before he made it back to Thorpe Wood. It was Bishop telling him that DC Ansari had managed to manipulate the image of the man caught in Abbi Turner's digital photograph. The logo featured two dogs standing side by side, staring off into the distance like a couple of catalogue models. The text beneath the design read: Bevill's Leam Kennels.

'Is that a place or some unfortunate sod's name?' Bliss asked. You never could tell these days.

'It's a waterway out in the Fens. The kennels are at Ponders-bridge. The place closed down in March and hasn't opened back up again since.'

'You on your way?'

'We're headed out the door as we speak.'

'We'll meet you there. I'm steaming up the A1. I can cut off through Holme and Ramsey St Mary's.'

'Hold on, the DCI just said something… oh, she says if you get there first, don't do anything stupid.'

'As if. Did the name of the kennels give us the name of our suspect?'

'Yes. Positive ID. Man by the name of Des Knowles is listed as the owner of Bevill's Leam Kennels, a business handed down to him by his grandfather. We pulled up his driving licence details and the photo on there matches the shots Abbi took. Few years older, few pounds heavier. But it's him, Jimmy. We have him.'

Bliss took the Sawtry turnoff, which would allow him to cut back over the road he had exited and run alongside it until he reached Glatton Lane. 'Did you hear from Glen?'

Bishop said nothing for a few seconds. 'Sorry. Just piling into the motor. You asked about Glen?'

'Yes. Did he show up? Call in?'

'We eventually received a call, yeah. Turns out he did precisely what we thought he had done. Located the server, called in a couple of his ERSOU mates, and they went in mob-handed.'

'Did he learn nothing working alongside us?'

'You just don't like the fact he got there ahead of us. Tell me you wouldn't have done the same in his shoes.'

Bliss ignored him. 'Who or what did he find?'

'Tiny office space in a block out by the power station. Annual lease. Server cabinet. Two physical servers. A laptop. All hooked up to a power backup and a broadband feed.'

'But I'm guessing nobody was there when they went in.'

'You guess right. The office is leased by an offshore company with no obvious connection to Lewis Drake so far as we can tell.'

'How about to Parkinson?'

'That's a different matter entirely. There we might just have a link.'

Bliss clenched a fist. 'Yes! I knew that horrible bitch had something to do with it.'

His elation was short-lived. 'Not quite, Jimmy,' Bishop said. 'The bank transfers we're seeing point to Troy Parkinson, not his mother.'

Bliss cursed, turning over this fresh information. Could Nicola have pushed everything through her son's finances without him knowing? Or perhaps as a silent partner? Anything was possible, not that it mattered right now.

'I suppose Glen and his ERSOU BFFs are stripping out the kit as we speak.'

'Yes.' Bishop sounded less sanguine this time. 'And making a real song and dance about it, too.'

'He'll learn eventually.'

'What, that you don't shout about it until you know precisely what you have and how it all comes together?'

Bliss grunted. 'That, and the fact that you should try not to antagonise people along the way. Especially the Thorpe Wood Major Crimes Unit. Still no sign of the Parkinson clan, I assume?'

'No. But we're working the streets as hard as we can. In their line of business, you always end up offending somebody. We're bound to get word sooner or later, Jimmy. All ports and border control have been notified, so if they run, they won't be going far.'

Bliss wasn't so sure. 'I was wondering if dear old Lewis Drake might have an idea where to find them. That slippery old fuck used to keep close tabs on his people. Stands to reason he'd be even more paranoid now he's banged up in Belmarsh.'

'I'll put a call in,' Bishop said. 'He might be willing to talk. Especially as we can officially tie the Parkinsons in with Dark Desires.'

'Worth a try. See you soon.'

Bliss cut the call before his acting boss could issue another warning. Bishop had sent Chandler the address and post code, which she was busy entering into the SatNav. He concentrated on driving the narrow roads, all long and straight once he'd pushed past Holme; same again when he turned left towards Ponders-bridge. Behind his stoic mask, he was annoyed by Glen Ashton's move, but that would have to wait. Olly Bishop's jibe stung a little

– he liked to think he was a bit more of a team player than that. He couldn't recall putting the NCA or his own ambitions ahead of the local teams he worked with up and down the country during his long stint with the agency. He always understood he and his fellow investigators were there to assist, bringing their specialist knowledge to investigations involving organised crime.

Ahead of the bridge spanning Bevill's Leam, Bliss noticed a road on his offside that ran alongside the drainage waterway. The SatNav was busy getting confused, so he ignored it. He looked for a road sign, and spotted it squatting behind a metal railing. There was nothing approaching the bridge from the opposite direction, so he barely touched the brake as he threw the pool car to the right. The back end fishtailed a little, but he was able to correct it easily enough.

'Let's get there in one piece, Jimmy,' Chandler pleaded. As was her habit, she had one hand clutching her seat belt.

Bliss allowed a faint smile to touch his lips. 'It's been a long time since you complained about my driving. I'd almost come to miss it.'

'Yes, well, sadly I appear to be the only one who remembers what happened to the last two motors you owned.'

He gave her that. One hoisted from a lake, the next written off after some necessary reckless driving and ramming other vehicles in a traffic jam. Since when, he'd settled for pool cars.

Glassmoor Bank seemed to stretch for miles into the distance, deep into the Fens. To their left the water ran swiftly, its grey colour matching that of the sky above. Along the grassy verge on the opposite side of the road ran a line of overhead cables. The road deserted, Bliss stuck to its centre where there was no camber. He hurtled past a small bungalow, an obvious new build on redeveloped land. Mounds of building sand and pallets of cement remained in the driveway beyond the low red-brick wall out front. Bliss touched eighty before slowing as another crop of buildings came up fast, fronted by a line of trees and wild hedgerow.

Easing off the accelerator, he slowed to a crawl, trying to spot a sign. He realised it might have been removed following the collapse of the business, but he could make nothing out through the treeline. As he reached the entrance he leaned forward to peer into and along the dirt driveway. The first thing he noticed was a low, cladded mobile home. Further along the track, and barely jutting out as if reluctant to peek, lay a single-storey building with heavy wire mesh panels.

'That's a kennel.' Excitement swept through his veins. He glanced at Chandler, who nodded back at him.

They were here.

And now that they were, Bliss also knew in his heart this was where Abbi Turner was being held.

FORTY-FOUR

WHEN SHE WAS TOLD to remain where she was rather than being dragged across to the mobile home, Abbi Turner realised the man she thought of as The Strangler must have returned. He had most likely slipped away to withdraw some extra cash from the closest ATM, or perhaps retrieve it from a stash he kept at home. Either way, Abbi recognised him as soon as he stepped inside, and immediately she drew back against the wall.

'Not him!' she cried out, shaking her head wildly. Her eyes implored Des to listen to her desperate appeals. 'Please, not him. He doesn't choke and release. He strangles! He digs his thumbs in. He almost killed me last time.'

Des turned to face the other man, eyebrows raised. 'Is that right?' Without waiting for a response, he merely nodded and chuckled, slapping the man on the back. 'Well, you know what the price is for that. If I have to replace her, you'll owe me big time. Not to mention helping me dispose of the body.'

His matter-of-fact voice chilled Abbi more than the thought of what was about to happen to her. This man she'd considered a friend – a man she'd even imagined might be the one – was nothing more than a callous freak who kept her locked away for others to abuse. He was no better than the criminals who pimped out their whores across the city while leaving them strung out and relying on their tormentors to keep them in their next fix. In fact, he was worse. Those men never showed an ounce of humanity. He had. And he'd fooled her completely with his act.

The man who had paid for her time walked over. He yanked away the crumpled duvet and licked his lips at the sight of her naked body. 'Open wide, sweetheart,' he said in a sing-song voice. Then he flexed one hand against the other, cracked his knuckles, and got down to it.

***

Bliss pulled over onto the muddy verge. He went to open the door, but Chandler put out a hand to stop him.

'What are you thinking?' she said. 'Bish and the team are on their way.'

'I want to have a shufty,' he said defensively. 'Get a sense of the place.'

'This is me you're talking to.'

'Pen, he could be doing something to her as we speak. We don't know if she has hours, minutes or seconds left. We can't wait. Let's at least take a look, see what we have.'

Chandler relented and slipped out of the car as quietly as he did. Keeping to the grass as much as possible, the pair loped back towards the entrance and the mobile home, sticking to the side of the path where there was little hard dirt or gravel to shift and give notice of their approach. A break in the hedgerow revealed a wide open space in which sat a blue van and a motorbike. Bliss noticed he was shielded from the mobile home by more thick bushes. He raised a hand telling Chandler to stay where she was, before dashing across to the van to lay a hand on its bonnet.

Cold.

He scuttled over to the motorbike and did the same on its engine case cover. This time he had to pull his hand away sharply. He crouched down, wondering whether the bike belonged to Des Knowles or to a visitor. The presence of somebody else added an unknown factor to Bliss's simple equation. With the element of surprise, he'd back himself and Chandler over one man, but add another body into the mix and all bets were off. He took a breath and crabbed his way around the line of hedgerow towards the mobile home. He beckoned Chandler to join him, before turning to study their way ahead.

Between their cover and the home itself lay open ground. It was only five or six paces, but it was more than enough if Knowles or his visitor happened to be looking out of a window in that particular direction at the time. Too great a warning, that much was certain. Bliss calmed himself, taking deep breaths. His sense of unease was not about saving his own skin – or Chandler's, for that matter. Abbi Turner was here, and she was in trouble. He didn't know how he could be certain, only that he was.

One more deep breath. He popped his head out from behind the hedge and took in what he could before pulling back behind his cover. The home ran lengthways from where he squatted. It was gabled at both ends, its cream exterior weathered and stained. A set of boarded steps led up to the front door at the end closest to Bliss. To its left a single window, frosted glass. He was at an angle to the windows running along the side of the property, limiting his exposure. It was a risk, but less of one than it could have been. Beyond the home lay the kennels, whose chain-link fencing emitted mournful groans as it shifted in the breeze. A chill settled in around him, and he felt the first few drops of moisture in the air.

'You stay here,' he whispered over his shoulder. 'Keep an eye out, just in case I'm spotted. Don't show yourself unless it's absolutely necessary.'

'Are you kidding me?' He felt a puff of air in his ear and could tell it was imbued with anger. 'I'm not skulking around here while you go and do all the dirty work.'

This time he turned to face her. 'Pen, that's not what I meant. I need you out here covering my arse. Give me a few minutes, watch my back. When the others get here, show them which way I've gone. If it turns to shit, then come and get me by all means, but I reckon it's better that we both don't walk out there into the unknown.'

Bliss didn't wait for her to respond; he knew it would only lead to further disagreement, for which they had no time. Instead, he moved. After sidling around the hedge, he crouch-ran over to the steps. He stood in limbo with one foot on the first tread, listening for some response to the groan of wood that had betrayed him. It felt like his own heartbeat might announce his presence, so loud was its pulse in his ears. But he heard no rapid movement inside to suggest he had been either spotted or overheard. Encouraged, he eased up the steps. Wrapping his fingers around the door handle, he gradually levered it downwards. It moved silently, and when he leaned in the door opened with a gentle sigh.

He peered into the home's living room. A man sat alone in an armchair, both feet raised up on an upholstered stool, watching some panel show with an open can of beer in his hand. The chair he was in faced away from Bliss, who took the opportunity to move away from him to check the two bedrooms and the galley kitchen. Abbi was not here, but she had to be close by. The motorbike had recently been used, but that did not mean it belonged to Des Knowles. In that instant, his fear for Abbi and his abhorrence at what might be happening to her took over.

***

The man liked his sex rough. He squeezed her breasts so tight the pain made her gasp. His teeth nipped at her flesh, barely less than a bite. He thrust himself in and out of her without drawing any obvious pleasure from the movements. This came as no surprise to Abbi. Men like this one felt little or nothing from the sexual act itself. If not for the asphyxiation, he might go on forever without ejaculating, so desensitised was he to the mere mechanics of copulation.

She had felt that unintentional euphoria on many previous occasions, the biological response to oxygen deprivation acting as a stimulant. It was weird and creepy, but she understood the allure. However, she had never been able to fully comprehend the kind of high the asphyxiators themselves drew from choking others. Certainly it was no biological imperative. No, theirs was a psychological need that only power over life and death could satisfy. And if they timed their climax to perfection, the rapture on their faces was like nothing she had ever seen before.

Keeping her eyes squeezed closed while he sucked on her shoulder and grunted with each thrust, Abbi waited for the moment when he would ease himself up off his elbows, draw himself into a squatting position, drag her back into his groin and shift his hands from her breasts to her throat. When it happened, she tried to let her mind wander as the pressure increased. Back to a time when she felt free and life was still full of so many possibilities.

She had to go back to when she was eleven or twelve. That was when a change came upon her that she was never able to fully appreciate, manage, or overcome. A period during which friends became enemies and vice versa, while her parents reeked of desperation and a lack of unity, allowing her to play each off the other. She had become ugly inside, tormented, with a distorted view of the world and those who inhabited it – especially those to whom she had once been so close. It was as if the moment her body began to transform, her psychological makeup altered to the rhythm of her puberty. A rampant toxicity spilled over into every single aspect of her life, dominating her will and leaving her with no desire to escape its clutches.

Abbi's eyes sprang open when the man's hands shifted again, wresting her out of her stupor. This time his thick fingers wrapped around her neck and his thumbs began digging deep into her throat. Unkempt nails pierced her flesh, drawing thin ribbons of blood. Still he maintained his rhythmic thrusting, in and out, in and out... But as his grip tightened, so his physical grunts became moans of pleasure. His eyes gleamed like distant stars as they had before, only this time instead of pleading with him to stop, Abbi smiled up at him. Then she began to laugh hysterically. And finally she called out, urging him on, begging him to squeeze harder and not to stop until he had drained her lungs.

***

'Where is she?' Bliss demanded for a third time.

At first, Knowles claimed not to know who or what Bliss was talking about. That earned him a backhander across the cheek. When he repeated his denial, Bliss clubbed the man on the bridge of his nose with the meaty part of his fist. Through watering eyes and a mouth puckered in pain, Knowles shook his head from side to side and pleaded with Bliss to let him go.

'I don't know what you want! I don't know what this is about. Honestly!'

Bliss hung a fist before the man's startled eyes, extending a finger to point. 'If you make me ask again, Des, I'm going to fetch a carving knife from your kitchen and I'm going to open up your stomach and let your bowels slop out onto the floor.'

Knowles clamped his lips together, recoiling in terror.

Bliss lowered his face until the two were only inches apart. 'Are you going to make me ask a fourth time? Disembowelment is not as quick a death as it sounds, Des. There will be plenty of time for me to ask you over and over until you finally do tell me. All while you sit there watching the steam rise up from your own innards.'

Knowles leaned to one side and vomited copiously across the floor. He raised a hand in submission. Bliss nodded to himself and stood upright. He grabbed hold of the man and yanked him to his feet. 'Lead the way,' he said, using the sole of his shoe to prod Knowles towards the doorway. 'And don't be stupid, Des. You warn whoever's out there with her, and I'll take my chance finding her after I've ended you.'

Wordlessly, Knowles guided him away from the mobile home, beyond the kennel cages. 'I keep her out of those,' he said, as if it were somehow a kindness. 'She has her own room.'

Bliss said nothing. He shoved Knowles further forward. A light rain had started to fall, and he thought he heard a hissing somewhere away in the distance. Vehicles approaching. Slick rubber on wet tarmac. Close by, water gurgled as it flowed steadily along the drain.

Knowles stopped outside what looked like a brick storeroom and nodded at the door, pointing silently. Bliss snatched up a short run of heavy pipe from the debris that had been left strewn across the yard. He put a finger to his lips and gestured for Knowles to open up. The door squealed ajar, gradually revealing its dreadful contents.

A man on his haunches leaned back against the cold brick wall behind him, chest heaving, sweat leaking from his slick naked body. His mouth hung open, strings of saliva stretching between his lips. His eyes glimmered and dimmed before rolling backwards. At the same time, he let out a low, guttural laugh. 'That was amazing,' he panted, shaking his head in wonder. 'Absolutely fucking amazing.'

Beneath him, Abbi Turner lay motionless on her back. The terribly abused young woman stared at the ceiling in a catatonic trance. At least, that was Bliss's first thought. Only then did he notice the stillness of her pale white breasts. And unlike the cloud of moist air emerging from the mouth of her defiler, around Abbi's face there was nothing at all.

On realising what had become of her, Bliss swung the length of pipe without any thought for the consequences, dropping Des Knowles like a crash test dummy. Then he turned his attention to the still-delirious man on the mattress, and advanced upon him.

FORTY-FIVE

JIMMY BLISS DID NOT cry often, but he did that night. Silent tears, trickling slowly at first before flowing steadily in an unchecked stream of utter misery. The sobs soon followed, exerting pressure on his ribs as each wracking heave threatened to break him in two.

At his own insistence, he'd remained at the scene longer than anyone else apart from the CSI team, who'd be there well into the next day. He was there when Neil Abbott, the forensic crime scene manager, declared the spare bedroom sheets to be 'the Jackson Pollock of the bodily fluids world'. He was there when the piles of women's clothing were found sealed in large plastic boxes in the crawl space beneath the mobile home. He was there when the scrubbing brush was discovered in the kennel compound, human tissue and blood clogged up in its stiff nylon bristles. He was there when gallons of Vetaclean fluid were uncovered and identified as the probable source of the chemical elements found on Majidah Rassooli's body. He left only after Abbi Turner was removed from the scene in a black mortuary vehicle.

Inside the incident room upon his return to Thorpe Wood, the mood was sombre, yet one of renewed enthusiasm for the task ahead. It made no difference to him how often he was assured the squad had done its best. Neither did he care to be reminded how close they had come to rescuing Abbi. Five minutes, five hours, or five days; to Bliss's mind, dead was dead, and no acknowledgement of the vagaries of time and chance would ever change that simple fact. 'Coming close' could never be regarded as a successful outcome. The image of the young woman's lifeless shell replaying across his mind's eye would forever act as a reminder that between life and death there existed only failure.

Yet in the midst of the sorrow and guilt, he somehow managed to embrace the positives with a grim determination that would serve him well in the days to come. Abbi's killer had been caught about as red-handed as it was possible to be; the sick and twisted excuse for a human being in the shape of Des Knowles would also trouble no other women in the coming decades. The failure to save Abbi's life overshadowed these accomplishments entirely as far as Bliss was concerned, yet they were not without merit.

In addition, there was the overarching factor of the investigation to consider: one that would ensure it remained fully active, albeit drastically altered in terms of perception. He and his team had been wrong to initially consider Majidah Rassooli's murder the work of her employers. He and his team, together with the Met investigation, had been wrong to label the murders of four women as the work of a serial killer. Because having seen the horror waiting for him behind that steel door, having arrested the man responsible for strangling Abbi Turner to death, Bliss understood that five young women had died in the exact same way, but each at the hands of a different client; precisely the notion they had been so keen to dismiss from the outset of Operation Phoenix.

Not your traditional client, of course. Not clients of the murder victims themselves. No, this was a different violation altogether, and Bliss understood how and why they had all been fooled by the circumstances.

Currently being held under close guard in hospital, Des Knowles nursed nothing more severe than a concussion, the remnants of the beating Bliss had administered inside the mobile home now the least of the man's concerns. Bishop had been glad of the delay in proceedings. It meant their custody clock would not start ticking down until Knowles was brought to Thorpe Wood for questioning. It was for the best, he'd suggested. Tensions were running high, and a night's sleep would help settle everybody. Their task once they got the man in the room was to not only have him confess his role, but also to obtain the names of the men who'd murdered four other women.

As for Abbi Turner's killer, he'd coughed up pretty much his entire life story in the time it took Hunt and Gratton to drive him back to the nick from Pondersbridge. Whatever high he was on took some time to come down from. By the time a doctor had examined him and declared him well enough to be interviewed, a duty solicitor had attended after initially being advised of the anticipated charges via e-mail. Both Ansari and Hunt had recently received additional training in contemporary interview skills, and Bishop had given them the nod to go ahead.

That the man was in any fit state to be interviewed owed a great deal to Chandler. Having watched her partner marching Knowles towards the kennels, and on towards a small brick structure, she had spotted him pick up the length of pipe. She decided to follow at a distance, keeping one eye on the dwelling, not knowing who else might be inside or how Jimmy might have dealt with them. When she saw Knowles pull open a big steel door, her gaze switched to Bliss and the look of horror that crumpled his face. The moment he swung the pipe, causing Knowles to buckle at the knees and fall face-forward to the ground, she was up and running.

It took her three attempts to talk her partner down.

The man he wanted to lay into remained hunched above his victim, still chattering away as if he had not a care in the world. Each time Bliss raised the steel pipe, Chandler begged him to rethink. She did not approach him, nor did she attempt to wrestle the weapon away from his grasp. Given his incandescent rage, she didn't want to think about how he might react. Her final cry was also her most forceful, and this time it got through to him. His chest rising and falling like bellows, Bliss scowled at the naked man hulking over Abbi Turner's body, before slowly allowing his hand to fall by his side. His fingers unclenched and the pipe clattered to the rutted concrete floor. Bliss staggered once, then turned his attention to the victim.

All of which he had to be reminded of, as Chandler swiftly prepared him for his meeting with senior officers. Brain-fog made him feel woolly and disconnected, but eventually her words seeped through. They had to get their stories straight, to somehow lessen the impact of the violence he had unleashed. Bliss spent the rest of the afternoon and early evening in a haze. When Des Knowles recovered from the blow, he immediately complained about police brutality. Bliss stubbornly claimed self-defence, and although an official enquiry had to be launched, he was not overly bothered by it. He'd not struck Knowles purely out of anger – more to incapacitate the man while he was inside the brick building. He'd pulled the blow; it was hard enough to knock him unconscious, but with no intent to cause any lasting damage.

The sweaty man who had taken Abbi Turner's life and seemed triumphant about it was the truly lucky one. Stepping towards him, the metal pipe still clutched in his right hand, Bliss could not deny the murder in his heart at that precise moment. Nobody would ever need to know the impetus behind it. There was no one else around to bear witness if he made a single blow count. A false claim of self-defence would be left to him and his conscience to overcome, but ultimately he knew who would win that skirmish.

And that was the problem. For all his faults, for all his minor deviations from the rule book, Bliss was no killer. And so the rational side of his nature had taken over. If ever a man deserved such an end, it was surely this sick, perverted rapist and murderer. Removing him from the face of the earth would be doing the planet and its inhabitants a huge favour. Such men gave up the right to expect a humane response to their horrific acts. But while Bliss was happy to play both judge and jury, he refused to also become an executioner.

He barely remembered Chandler arriving and trying to talk him out of it. There had been no need. His arm moved reflexively on a couple of occasions, a primitive instinct prepared to hand out a beating to exact some form of revenge. Instead, and despite knowing in his heart that Abbi was already beyond saving, he attempted to resuscitate her, pumping her chest so fervently the young girl's ribs snapped, at which point Chandler gripped his hands and gently pulled him away. When the rest of his colleagues arrived, they found him holding the limp form of Abbi Turner in his arms, her killer on the ground with his left arm extended and twisted back by Chandler. Ignoring them all, Bliss had wrapped the duvet around the pale naked form on the filthy mattress and pulled her into a close embrace. He held her tight and gently ran his fingers through her hair.

He told her how sorry he was, his voice no more than a whisper.

Sorry for all that she had endured. Sorry for not solving the investigation sooner. Sorry for arriving barely minutes too late.

Sorry.

FORTY-SIX

A<small>T VARIOUS TIMES AHEAD</small> of the interview, different members of the team watched Abbi's killer on a small monitor, his every movement and utterance in the room recorded. A seasonal farm and building labourer by the name of Alex Youngs, he twitched and bit his fingernails while sitting, but preferred to pace the floor, both hands wrapped over the thinning crown of his head. He babbled to himself, a torrent of words strung together into incomprehensible sentences.

A doctor had seen Youngs and adjudged him healthy enough for interview, declaring the obvious high a natural one. The man was left to stew, allowing time for his adrenaline buzz to wear off. Later he spent forty minutes in animated conversation with the duty solicitor before the interview began with the usual introductions and preparation of the recording devices. Detective Constables Hunt and Ansari had used the intervening time to agree upon their mode of attack.

Following the PEACE model of best practice, the planning and preparation stage allowed them to review and assess the available evidence connected to the offence for which he would eventually be charged. This proved to be the first sticking point.

Ansari was of the opinion that a statement from Des Knowles in which he implicated Youngs would be something worth delaying the first interview for. Hunt disagreed, believing their man would fold if they got to him quickly. Ansari caved only after it was suggested that their initial twenty-four hours with Youngs might be over before Knowles was discharged from his hospital bed. While additional time in this case was certain to be granted if they applied for it, they went ahead with the aim of feeding off their own momentum.

After identifying everyone in the room for the digital recording, DC Hunt formally revealed the reasons for detaining Youngs for questioning. The engagement and explanation aspect of the PEACE framework completed, Hunt swiftly moved them on to stage three. This essentially amounted to Hunt and Ansari seeking an understanding of events as related by Youngs, during which they would either ask for clarification or challenge him if they knew any part of his account to be false.

For any detective carrying out a suspect interview in a major crime, this was the moment of genuine tension. Either the man from whom they hoped to elicit answers sat back in his uncomfortable chair and reeled off a composed 'no comment' to every question, or he'd start jabbering and barely be able to contain himself. As Hunt had expected, Alex Youngs was a naïve braggart who couldn't wait to unload.

Des Knowles, he informed them, took advantage of dark web chat rooms to advertise unfettered use of his pets. Abbi Turner had not been Alex's first, he confessed, but he assured everyone in the interview room that when he'd left the previous pet she was alive, though not necessarily well. In answer to Ansari's follow-up question, Youngs said he had no idea what had become of the other girl – only that the next time he communicated with Knowles, the man revealed he had a new pet begging for attention. When shown a photograph of Majidah Rassooli, he smiled and nodded. When prompted to speak up for the benefit of the recording, he nodded again and answered in the affirmative.

'She was a great fuck,' he added. 'Nice, slim neck.'

In response to being asked if he had killed the young woman in the brick shed earlier that day, Youngs became a little coy. He admitted to having carried out his particular fetish – strangling the girl while having sex with her (a sexual act which, he assured them, would become commonplace and accepted in society at some point in the near future). However, he went on to insist that during the act, his conscious awareness had ranged from hearing her begging him to continue, to his eventual release, but with no realisation of her death occurring in between.

At this point, Ansari sought clarification. He had raped the girl, she pointed out. During that rape he had strangled her with his bare hands. When he was finished brutalising her, the young woman was dead. Youngs did not even glance at his solicitor. He told them in a clear, unfaltering manner that what he had described was his own true recollection of events. He had not intended the pet any enduring harm, had certainly not set out to murder it. Events had simply conspired against them both.

'And in this case when you say "pet" you mean "woman",' Hunt said. 'When you say "it" you mean "her".'

Youngs frowned as if he didn't quite understand. 'No,' he said eventually. 'Those are your terms. Not mine. Don't put words in my mouth. To me, when they're locked away or chained up, they're pets. As simple as that.'

'But to be clear, we're talking about a young woman by the name of Abbi Turner. I'm not discounting your preferences, Mr Youngs. I understand that you view these girls as animals and regard them as pets, but before we can move on, we have to establish that we're talking about the same thing. What you thought of as a pet, the rest of us acknowledge as a human being. Yes?'

The nod was grudging at best. 'Yes.'

Closure and evaluation – the completion of the PEACE principles – followed soon afterwards. When Hunt called a halt and informed those present that it was time for a break, but that a second interview was likely ahead of charges being made, Youngs was left to discuss matters with his brief ahead of being taken back to his cell along the corridor known as the Green Mile.

Less than an hour later, following a brief discussion with Warburton, Bishop, Bliss and Chandler – all of whom had watched the interview from another room – the DCI herself made the call to the CPS, who declared themselves delighted with the result. The only debate was whether to charge murder or voluntary manslaughter. The latter was the easier option, and possibly one Young's solicitor could tempt him with for a guilty plea.

'I want murder,' Warburton said bluntly. '"With intent to kill or cause grievous bodily harm" is your weapon for that charge, I suggest. Youngs wrapped his hands around our victim's throat, pressed down with his thumbs, and choked the life out of her. I'm sure he'll claim a loss of control during the sexual act, and I don't doubt he had no intention of killing her from the outset. So no premeditation. But when you strangle somebody, your intention is to cause GBH at a minimum, and you know there is always the possibility of taking it too far.'

The CPS argued the defence was liable to push for involuntary manslaughter due to that loss of control – a considerable step down from murder.   ·

DCI Warburton remained defiant. 'I think you have enough to prove intent on the GBH. If you do, given that intent ultimately led to the victim dying, I believe that gives us our murder. And yes, I know you know that, but I'm letting you know that I do, too. It's what we want. It's the least this man deserves.'

Moments later, she ended the call with a sour look on her face. She was barely able to keep it straight for more than a few seconds, before she punched the air and the room erupted in cheers. With Des Knowles being under guard and on suicide watch in his hospital room overnight, the team hit the Woodman with every intention of not going home until they were all too drunk to walk straight. Hangovers and headaches would take care of themselves the following day.

After cabbing it home, Bliss spent the next few hours sitting in his recliner. No music. No lights in the garden, illuminating its careful design for him to admire. No phone. Not even another drink. Instead he stared up at the ceiling, trying to work out if more could have been done to turn the case around sooner.

In the wider scheme of things, Bliss believed the team might need more than his own sworn statement in order to charge Knowles with every crime they suspected him of having committed. Thankfully, evidence was steadily mounting. He had groomed young women; not for himself, it seemed, but to make money out of their abduction, misery and even murder by turning them out to men whose repugnant desires knew no boundaries. The numerous items of clothing found in containers beneath his home might prove to be enough physical evidence of his connection to them, but Bliss was convinced his team would find whatever was necessary to make a solid case. Knowles did not come across as the type to confess in the way Youngs had, but neither was he a man capable of carrying out his sordid plans without making mistakes along the way. His ownership of the kennels and the wealth of forensic materials discovered there, together with the statement made by Abbi Turner's killer, added all the weight they needed to secure a conviction.

His thoughts drifted back to the clothes. Bliss remained intrigued by the unidentified items, those which did not belong to any of the known victims. It occurred to him that Knowles might well have been in a relationship at one time, the clothes perhaps a legacy of that. Finding out who the woman was and what had become of her might make for another strand of Phoenix.

But what of the other men – those whose hands had stolen the breath of four women, including their chalk pits victim? If any records of communication between these killers and Knowles had ever existed, it seemed unlikely that they still did. Forensic and DNA evidence gathered by the Met had not led them to identify the men responsible. But if Knowles could be persuaded to give up names – assuming he knew them – progress could well be made. Some form of leniency in terms of prosecution might have to be offered to induce him to provide suitable information. After all, the killers had learned of his young captives via a chat room he had set up. Finding these men without Knowles's help would be a tough ask. It was a dispiriting thought, but Bliss believed in the team. If any group of people was capable of pulling this case together, they were.

As usual, the hard work began here. Banging up the people responsible in a holding cell was one thing; sending them to prison with a heavy sentence, quite another. He slowly drew his hands down the length of his face. Feeling old and tired was par for the course these days, but the alcohol swirling around in his bloodstream might keep him pickled for a good while yet.

His thoughts turned to Sandra Bannister. Unsure of what precise details he felt comfortable seeing on the home page of the *Telegraph's* website, he'd already skipped three calls from her. Tomorrow would do. It'd have to. In any case, he was in no condition to discuss Phoenix with any reliability or without emotion.

Thinking about websites sent his mind in the direction of Dark Desires. Glen Ashton had been noticeably absent all afternoon, and Bliss wondered if they'd see the ERSOU man again. If the investigator regarded what he'd done as a minor victory, good luck to him. Tougher times lay ahead.

Yet still Bliss was intrigued. Though their job was to bring an investigation to the point where it could be prosecuted, there was satisfaction to be gained from simply knowing the answer to a puzzle. He'd forgotten to ask if anybody had followed up on his request for Lewis Drake to be spoken to again; that was something he'd have to check on in the morning. It bothered him, though. If Parkinson really had spread the rumour of a contract being taken out on her life, it was a pretty elaborate escape plan. And to what ultimate end? To perhaps deflect attention away from the real reason she and her children had fled? He also wasn't totally convinced by the notion of Nicola having put the entire business in her son's name. Was it genuinely possible for her not to have known about it until recent developments threatened to interrupt the progress of her rising star?

The more he thought about it, the more his headache worsened. He took a couple of cocodamol with some water and staggered up to bed. He'd needed a stress-relieving drink or several after work, and they'd all known going in that they were out on the lash. The consumption of alcohol changed nothing, however; all of their problems would still be there the following morning when they dragged their bleary-eyed selves back into HQ. But the break from the intensity of any investigation was a necessary aside. This one more than most.

As he climbed into bed, Bliss's eyes fell upon the other side of the duvet, which was creaseless. The stark image of Abbi Turner lying cold and still in that desolate bunker cemented itself in his mind. Within moments he was creased double, weeping hot, salty tears, one clenched fist pressed against his mouth. The sobbing and moaning felt as if it lasted hours, though his incapacitation over this young woman he had never known in life lasted only minutes. Perhaps only as long as the difference between her final gasps of life and her ultimate death. Between salvation and damnation.

When he finally came to lay his head on the pillow, Bliss had already started to drift away. But into the darkness he took with him Abbi Turner's final moments, ensuring his deep sleep would not last long.

FORTY-SEVEN

HERE WASN'T A GREAT deal of talk the following morning, but the effort was undeniable. Bliss arrived shortly before eight, and for once he was the last member of the team into the unit. He felt proud of his colleagues and the way they went about their work – yet he had to remind himself this was no longer his team. It was his temporary DI who deserved any congratulations going around.

Bishop pulled everybody into a huddle to begin with. 'We had both a good and a bad day yesterday. Losing a victim we were working so hard to find is devastating, but we have her killer in a cell, and that's all he'll know for many years to come. Her abductor will be checking in with us soon enough, and although he has information we need to draw out, he's another one who won't be tasting free air for a good while. Take the wins, people. You all worked hard to achieve them. As for the loss… what's done is done. The post-Phoenix review will pick the bones out of it, but you have to be content with knowing you did everything you could. That we even came close to being in time was a minor miracle. Let's make sure we do our jobs now and hand the CPS a winner.'

After a stuttering start, things began to move swiftly. Lewis Drake's solicitor phoned and asked to speak with DCI Warburton. She insisted her client had no knowledge of where the Parkinsons might be hiding out, but that he would be sure to pass that information on the moment his own people located them. Bliss scoffed at hearing this. There was no chance of Drake leaving that particular situation alone, and if his crew discovered Nicola and her offspring first, they would never be found again.

Within minutes of that call ending, however, a CHIS provided a possible breakthrough. According to this one-time druggie, now a registered informant, Nicola Parkinson's parents owned a cottage on the Norfolk coast in a place called Mundesley. Bishop decided he couldn't spare any of his team, particularly when they had no idea if the Parkinsons had even fled there. He put in a call to Cromer to ask for a local traffic crew to visit the address, which was nine miles south of their location.

While the team waited to hear back, DCs Hunt and Ansari carried out their second interview with Alex Youngs. Bliss and Chandler observed the early exchanges. The detainee was not the open book he had been the previous day, engaging with his solicitor more often and declining to comment much of the time. His guilt was not in question; a statement in which he had admitted to strangling Abbi Turner had already been logged into evidence, all of which had been captured on the room's audio and visual recording devices. The two detectives were attempting to tie up some loose ends, but the man was having none of it.

'Maybe you should have used that fucking piece of pipe on him after all,' Chandler whispered.

The previous afternoon, Bliss had admitted his initial lust to exact brutal revenge on the man for what he'd done to Turner. He looked across at her and simply shrugged.

'Yeah, I know.' She brushed a sympathetic hand over his upper arm. 'As difficult as it is not to at times, we don't allow ourselves to become like them. But if ever a bloke deserved a hiding…'

Clicking his tongue on his teeth, Bliss said, 'With a bit of luck, Pen, somebody will seek him out inside prison and choose to inflict unimaginable pain on him every hour of every day for as long as he lives. My crushing his head with that length of pipe would not have been anywhere near enough suffering for Mr Youngs.'

Chandler nodded along. 'True. We can only hope.'

'Imagine if someone put the word out about the kind of man they're dealing with.'

She gave him a sideways look. 'That would be wrong of us, DS Bliss.'

The smile he returned was not a humorous one. 'Indeed it would, DS Chandler. But mistakes happen.'

They returned to the incident room immediately upon hearing of Cromer's response to Bishop's request. The traffic crew had indeed found Nicola and her two children at a house overlooking the beach at Mundesley. However, all three related the exact same story: they were hiding from a killer contracted by Lewis Drake. With all three refusing to attend Cromer station for further voluntary interviews, and no reason to arrest them, the attending officers had obtained a clean mobile number for the Thorpe Wood team to use if they wanted to pursue the matter directly.

Which Bliss most certainly did.

'Now what do you want, you persistent old fuck?' she asked by way of a response to his call.

'Dark Desires,' he said. 'I want to know more about it.'

A deep exhalation crackled down the line. 'I told you before, I don't know anything about any site on the dark web. You're wasting your time. And mine.'

Bliss analysed her voice for stressors. He heard only irritation. 'Okay. So tell me, Nicola, do you genuinely believe your old boss has a hit out on you? Is that the truth?'

'Of course it is. Why would I make up some crazy shit like that? Especially when it implicates Lewis Drake, of all people. I'd be bloody mad to do something like that.'

He hadn't thought of it that way before. He understood what she meant, and her denial sounded genuine. Bliss began to wonder if Troy had led his own mother astray, insisting that Drake had taken a hit out on them all. He tried another tack. 'I'm going to send you a series of photos, Nicola.'

'They're not dick pics, are they? I don't think my image software magnifies enough for that.'

'Don't flatter yourself. Call me fussy, but I like my women to be… well, human. No, the photos are from our evidence file. They reveal the details of invoices issued to an offshore company with connections to your son. Your main focus needs to be on what the invoices are for. You'll see there's a good deal of IT equipment, software, plus an office space and some heavy-duty broadband connectivity. Almost as if whoever bought all that kit was running… ooh, let's say a website of some description. Have a look. I'm sending it now.'

He'd already prepared the files and the message. All he had to do was hit send. He did so, and then waited. He heard Parkinson's phone ping. He waited some more. After a few minutes of complete silence, she said in a hard and toneless voice, 'These prove nothing. You could have knocked them up yourself. What am I supposed to say to this shite?'

'I'm gathering additional proof, Nicola. All the evidence we have so far tells us either this is Troy's company or he's at least financially involved in some way. And as we speak, the finest technical minds in the NCA are going through the data stored on those devices. We'll make the case against him. Have no doubt about that.'

Exasperated, Parkinson's voice became shrill. 'What's your game, Bliss? Even if everything you said was true, why would you tell me? Do you not think I'd warn him?'

Bliss huffed. 'Oh, I'm sure you would – even though your own flesh and blood cut you out of a deal that must have made him millions. That has to sting a bit, Nicola. But family is family, I suppose. No matter how much they screw you over. I warn you, though, once we do make our case, we'll find him wherever he goes. He's not getting out of the country any time soon, so that narrows things down a bit for us.'

'So what's your bloody angle? Why call? Why all the questions?'

They had reached the stage at which Bliss had run out of information. From this point on he was reaching, grasping at invisible straws and hoping for something to stray within his desperate clutches.

'It's the young blonde,' he said softly, remembering the irregular thought patterns of recent days.

'What young blonde? What are you banging on about, Bliss? Are you talking about my daughter? You want to drag her into this as well?'

'No, no. I don't think so. Listen to me. The flat our chalk pits victim rented was cleaned out by a group of foreign men and a young blonde. Our witness thought she might be local, but he couldn't tell for sure. Either way, for me that's the piece that doesn't fit. See, as far as we were concerned, Drake or someone working for his organisation – possibly you – had signed off on taking out our victim because she was earning on the side. We assumed the people who cleaned out the flat were working for you, too. Only, that can't be the case if you genuinely had no clue she had her own sideline. And as much as I despise you, Nicola,

I believed you when you told us that. We also know who killed her, and why. But nobody responsible for her death cleared out her flat, either.'

'I'm still not seeing how this has anything to do with me or my family,' Parkinson snapped.

'Me neither. But I'm getting there, so bear with me. Thing is, logic tells me if it wasn't our killer and it had nothing to do with her main employer, there has to be a connection to her sideline.'

'Are you suggesting my boy is involved in her murder?'

'Not really. Because I suspect if he was, either he'd have been there himself for the clean-up, or the blonde girl in question would have been your daughter. If neither of those things are true, I'm missing something. And you might be the person to complete the puzzle for me.'

Parkinson's sudden outburst of laughter bordered on the hysterical. 'What on earth makes you think I'd help the likes of you?'

As reluctant as he was to use the ploy he had in mind, Bliss felt he had no real alternative. 'That's an easy one,' he said. 'Because there's a good chance that your son has also been had over. Tell me – is there a young, slender blonde in his life, Nicola? Someone close? Someone he might have helped get started in her business, without having a clue what it actually entailed?'

The ensuing silence told Bliss his guess had been correct. This was the moment to leave a space for Parkinson herself to figure out the pros and cons, the result of which could only end in his favour. When she eventually replied, her voice sounded hollow and uncertain.

'Troy was seeing a girl a while back. Young, blonde and slim, just like you described. She's not local, though.'

'I can't promise you anything if he's also involved, Nicola. But if you give me a name, I can tell you this much: I won't push for him as a co-conspirator if I truly believe he knew nothing about this sordid business.'

Another pause. For a moment Bliss wondered if he'd lost her. Then he heard her release a long, pent-up breath.

'I'll tell you,' she said. 'Her name is Yeva.'

FORTY-EIGHT

'LAW OF AVERAGES,' BLISS said, meeting Savchuk's stubborn gaze across the table. 'We pulled five of you from the container that day at RAF Wittering. Stands to reason there's no way all of you would prove to be fine, upstanding citizens.'

Bishop had asked Bliss to sit in on the interview with DC Ansari, who would conduct much of it. The feeling was that his connection might make the difference. They sat in what was the largest of the interview rooms, yet four bodies inside that ten-by-twelve space had always felt stifling and uncomfortable. Now it was undeniably claustrophobic, and Bliss was pleased they'd had no need of an appropriate adult as well.

Savchuk's solicitor cleared her throat before responding to his comment. 'You have provided no evidence to suggest that my client is not the fine and upstanding citizen you speak of. Please move on.'

Bliss turned his gaze upon Pru Harrington. No duty solicitor for Yeva Savchuk; Harrington worked for perhaps the best firm of solicitors in the city. She and Bliss had crossed paths before, and they did not like each other.

'See that folder my colleague DC Ansari has placed on the table? It contains all the evidence we need. Your client paints herself as a hard worker for a genuine establishment, yet we know she also used to work as an escort to supplement her salary, and we have witness statements to that effect.' Bliss raised a hand to prevent the solicitor jumping in. 'And before you act all outraged and tell me being an escort is not a crime, it reveals a prior degree of deception and manipulation when talking to us.'

Harrington, dressed in a two-piece trouser suit and looking sharp and elegant, turned her best full-lipped smile on him. 'That wasn't what I was about to say. I was going to make it abundantly clear that unless that folder also happens to contain proof of my client's involvement in this site on the dark web, our time here will be brief.'

Bliss glanced across at Ansari and nodded for her to pick things up. Leaving the folder unopened, the DC took time to gather her thoughts before speaking.

'Your client might think she was clever in hiding her tracks. She had her boyfriend purchase the equipment at the same time as he leased the office space on her behalf. In our opinion, that was simply because she lacked the funds to get the business started. Essentially, she persuaded him to put up the seed money for her little enterprise while allowing her to remain in the background and well away from a paper trail.'

'That sounds to me as if the evidence you have points to my client's ex-boyfriend, not my client. If that's the extent of it, I think we'll be going.' She moved as if to stand, but Bliss slapped a hand on the table, startling all three women in the room.

'Stay where you are,' he snapped. 'Because your client certainly is.'

'I beg your par–'

'Put your arse back in the chair. You're not fooling anyone.'

Ansari jumped back in. 'I'd do as he suggests, if I were you. Because Ms Savchuk is no criminal genius. The thing is, she planned well in getting it all together. Her boyfriend was happy enough to be receiving regular payments to cover the initial outlay and the monthly outgoings. However, your client knew nothing about programming; she had to employ somebody else to do the development work. In addition, the income generated by the site couldn't be funnelled through your client's boyfriend. Far too risky for him, given his association with Lewis Drake's organisation. So instead that money went elsewhere. A traceable elsewhere, as it turns out.'

Ansari sat back, her eyes flitting between the two women seated opposite. Meanwhile, the fingers of her right hand tapped an unconscious rhythm on the folder. Bliss hid a smile; the folder contained a great deal of printed scraps, bulking out the supposed evidence. The team had been extremely busy since Nicola Parkinson had revealed the name of the woman her son had been involved with. What they had managed to discover so far was good enough, but it never did any harm to suggest you had more.

Harrington leaned over to whisper something in Yeva Savchuk's ear. The young woman shook her head brusquely and replied in a soft voice. The solicitor nodded and turned to face the two detectives.

'This programmer you say my client employed – have you spoken with him? He's made a statement?'

Still refusing to open the folder, DC Ansari said, 'Oh, yes. And let me answer what I think your next question will be: we have access to your client's financials, and the trail of money is irrefutable in respect of payments into the website and payments out again, including those being funnelled into offshore accounts belonging to your client.'

'In which case, my client is willing to cooperate, up to a certain point.'

'None of this is my idea,' Savchuk said eagerly, finally raising her eyes from the hands fidgeting together in her lap. 'Troy tell me one day what he want to do, his plans for running a different kind of website in the dark web. But although he say he will pay for things, it must look as if business is mine when it come to the money. He say he will be killed if Mr Drake find out what he is doing. So he pay and I run. He threaten me. If I not do as he ask, I will lose everything.'

Ansari nodded. 'I see. So how did it work, Yeva? Explain the operation to us.'

'You know this already, I think. Is my job to find girls for site, to use black card for to gain entry. My job to do everything. I was like... like slave. No better than if you had never rescued me from container.'

Ansari barely reacted to this obvious appeal for sympathy, while Bliss felt repulsed by it. The DC went on, 'So you admit to running the Dark Desires website and business, and to setting up payments to the offshore accounts in your name?'

'Yes. But I am forced to do this by Troy, you understand.'

'So you keep insisting. But we have only your word for that, Yeva.'

'Are you suggesting my client's word is worth less than that of this Troy Parkinson character?' Pru Harrington hissed.

Ansari calmly met her gaze. 'Not at all. I'm suggesting it's worth no more, Mrs Harrington. I already have a statement from Troy Parkinson; one that describes a different sequence of events, I have to say. I'm doing my due diligence by obtaining information from your client which will hopefully result in a signed statement. Once we have them both, they will be given equal consideration.'

'And is he still in a holding cell, or has he been released on bail? Because that's what I will be seeking for my client.'

'Not that it's any of your business where Troy Parkinson is at the moment,' Bliss interjected, 'but in fact he is being transported here as we speak – and he will be held here until such time as we determine the full extent of the charges against him. I'd remind you that having arrested your client, I fully expect us to be charging her with a number of offences. You can also bank on additional charges to follow if we decide the weight of evidence points more towards your client. And let me be clear with you both: while the actual owner of that awful website might not be directly responsible for the deaths of five young women, the killers' initial access to those women came via that website. As such, I'll be speaking to the CPS about related charges.'

'That is utter nonsense,' Harrington proclaimed. 'Even if you prove my client owned and operated the website, she simply cannot be held responsible for the actions of these men.'

'Your client provided the platform from which a man was able first to use these women for his own sexual gratification, then to abduct them and sell them by the hour to a number of other men, several of whom took their sickening desires too far. Dark desires is what your client promised these men, and dark desires was what they got.'

'There's no way you can prove any of that. You haven't yet substantiated a single thing against my client, and she will be a sympathetic figure in that witness stand when she repeats her tale of being held in sexual slavery and forced to comply with Troy Parkinson's nauseating demands.'

'Are you quite finished grandstanding?' Ansari asked, folding her arms as she leaned back in her chair. 'Please save it for those who might actually be impressed. The media might lap that up when you feed it to them, but a judge and jury will see right through it. As for proof and evidence, we clearly have enough to charge your client. You know the CPS as well as we do. If they are confident, so are we. And in the time it takes to bring this to trial, we'll have gathered more. It seems to me that you have only your client's word going for you. Surely even you can see that won't be nearly enough.'

After a moment of silence, Harrington said, 'What are you looking for here? And what are you offering in return?'

Ansari glanced at Bliss, who nodded and sat back. She then fixed her eyes on Yeva Savchuk. 'If your client stops lying and admits to the allegations, we won't seek others. By that I mean we'll rethink pursuing your client with the intention of linking her business to the murders. I am in no doubt that we will be able to do so. However, as we have one man charged with murder already in custody, and another helping us with our enquiries in the pursuit of other men who committed similar murders, we are confident this investigation will be concluded satisfactorily. If your client cooperates fully and openly, we can tie things together more quickly and completely; that will be enough, as far as we are concerned. However, if she continues to lie and prevents us from bringing matters to a speedy conclusion, we are prepared to go the whole way.'

Bliss nodded again, this time to himself. Gul Ansari had excelled in her time with the Major Crimes Unit, becoming an invaluable member of the team who delivered every single time. Having volunteered to take the training necessary to become a specialist interviewer, she was putting into practice all that she had learned. Tough, shrewd, incisive and instinctive, his colleague also made sure to leave a way out. He took a deep breath to disguise his chest becoming swollen with pride.

'Would you please leave us to deliberate?' Harrington asked.

Ansari got to her feet. 'No. This is an interview room. You can use one of the consulting booths down by the custody desk. If none are available, you can consult in your client's cell.'

'Is that absolutely necessary?'

'Of course. I wouldn't say so otherwise. You get the booth or the cell. Take it or leave it.'

Harrington took it, though when she stood she wore the look of a woman receiving a colonoscopy from Edward Scissorhands.

'I have one more question before you go,' Bliss said. He waited for Savchuk to look at him. 'Yeva, why did you help us? You lied, of course, and there's no denying your complicity. But you also helped prior to your arrest, which suggests you're not an entirely lost cause. I'm guessing you got caught between the proverbial rock and a hard place. What I mean by that is, you eventually realised from everything we discussed that your site on the dark web had in some way led to a few of its users splintering off – that somebody had set up an enterprise of their own. One that had led to murder on several occasions. You then helped us as much as you could without giving away your part in it. You gave up some, you held some back. Would that be fair to say, Yeva?'

Savchuk did not waver this time. 'You are disappointed in me, I know. I am disappointed in myself. This is not what you expect of me. It make me sad. Even so, I will not tell you all that I do. But I will tell you what I do not do. I do not know about murder until you and Penny tell me. I do not know about how it connect to website until I am told. I do not wish for these girls to die. This break my heart. You understand?'

Bliss thought he did. Savchuk retained enough compassion and felt enough culpability to have decided to help the police provided she did not give away her own guilty secret. Yet still something bothered him.

'You say you didn't know until we came to you. But it must have been you who cleared out Majidah Rassooli's flat. How did you know to do that if you didn't know she was dead, Yeva?'

'I do not know this at the time. Majidah… she stop answering phone. She not available when client want her. She lose me money. I think she work for others, so I make sure she no longer have flat to work from. I tell owner to keep deposit, and we will soon bring him another girl to rent flat.'

The landlord had not been straight with them. Tim Beaumont moved immediately to Bliss's mental list of people who owed him. 'Will you answer one more question, Yeva?'

There was no holding back her solicitor on this occasion. 'Detective Sergeant Bliss, I really must protest. My client has already said far more than I have advised her to. You suspended the interview; this is my time. You must back off!'

Bliss continued to look only at Savchuk. He needed an answer to the question circling his mind. 'Yeva?' he said. 'You don't have to answer me, but I have to ask…'

Savchuk nodded, snatching her arm back as Harrington attempted to pull her away. 'If I can, I will.'

'Thank you. You have a good idea what kind of life you might have had if you'd never been abandoned inside that container. You mix with these young women, so you know how some of them have to live. I want to believe that when you decided to run your own website, it wasn't out of pure exploitation or greed. I want to believe you simply took girls who were selling themselves anyway and gave them an easier ride, a better cut – perhaps for some, even a way out. But I need you to tell me I'm not wrong.'

She put her chin down, gave it some thought. Without so much as a glance at her solicitor she said, 'I want a better life. This is true. What I do… is wrong. But you are not wrong about me.'

Bliss closed his eyes and gave a nod of thanks. He heard no deceit in her voice, saw none in her eyes. It wasn't much, but it gave him something to cling to. 'You once told me about your struggle to breathe in that shipping container. How you kept muttering your name over and over. I remember you saying that you'd always cherish the simple, natural act of being able to take that next breath like anybody else.' He offered a sad, reflective smile. 'I suppose you couldn't help but move on to something more rarefied.'

FORTY-NINE

Bliss and Ansari headed back to the incident room. By the doors leading to the stairway, he paused and took the DC to one side.

'You were superb back there, Gul. The right tone at the right time. You provided enough information for them to have to think and react, but not so much that you made it easy for them to respond. With their lies established and on record, you had them where you wanted them. Great stuff. I mean it… hugely impressive.'

'Thank you, boss,' she replied, beaming at him. 'I've been taught by the best. I owe everything to you and the rest of the team.'

Bliss shook his head. 'No. You owe it to your own determination, intelligence and desire to do the right thing. You're a credit to us all. Tell me if I'm overstepping the mark, but have your family come around to what you do?'

'Mum has warmed to it. Not sure my dad ever will. As for my brothers… they refuse to speak about it. Mine is not the kind of job for a good Muslim girl, according to them.'

'That must be hard on you.'

'Not as much as you'd think. Their views are outdated, and so are they. If they choose to live their lives like that, I pity them. I'm proud of the job I do. It has value. It serves the public, and my community is as much a part of that as any other. If they're happy to call the police in an emergency, why shouldn't I be one of those who responds?'

Bliss nodded. 'I'm glad you toughed it out, Gul. I chose you to be a part of this unit because I saw the possibilities, not as part of some diversity protocol – not that I ignore those, but I wanted you to understand why you're here. You earned it. And you'll earn every step on the ladder you choose to make. You're flourishing, and I wanted you to know it was not going unnoticed.'

Ansari thanked him and they moved on. 'I'm sorry about Savchuk, boss,' she said as they climbed the stairs. 'I know you had high hopes for those women we rescued.'

'I'm disappointed. No denying that. But they're human beings with human frailties. Maybe it's me, but she and the likes of Parkinson and Drake are in completely different leagues. I regard her as more naïve than monstrous.'

'I think we'd probably have to ask the women she uses how they feel about that.'

'True. Whatever her reasons, they're the ones being abused on a daily basis. Could be my disappointment clouding my judgement, Gul. She impressed me, that's all. When Pen and I spoke to her first of all, she really did impress me.' He sighed as they reached the second-floor landing. 'Maybe I saw what I wanted to see.'

The incident room was heaving and everybody in it was active. Bliss often told others this was the stage at which the real hard work began. The initial week or two of pursuit would be long forgotten by the time the case went to court. In the meantime it required hundreds of vital hours to ensure the right verdict was achieved. And that was without the assistance provided by criminals themselves, who were so often weakened by time and evidence gathering around them.

While Bliss and Ansari were interviewing Savchuk, Hunt and Chandler had been deep in conversation with Des Knowles. Their initial interview had finished earlier, and the two were discussing their progress with DCI Warburton and Olly Bishop.

'He's being cooperative,' Hunt said, looking pleased with himself. 'Keen to make sure those men who physically carried out the killings go down for the murders themselves. He's going away for a long time if we charge him with joint enterprise, and I think he's reconciled to that, so long as nobody places *his* fingers around the necks of those poor young women for their final strangulation.'

'He's still as guilty as fuck,' Bliss observed, surprised to learn that their suspect had been so forthcoming. 'Even if we don't go for joint enterprise on the murders, he groomed these girls, he abducted them, kept them under lock and key and pimped them out to men, knowing they might end up dead as a result. Did he cough to dumping the bodies?'

'Yep. He helped each of the killers with the disposal, having first disinfected the bodies. He was living in London at the time of the first three murders, running his operation out of a caravan on the fringes of a dodgy travellers' site. He moved up here after his grandfather died, having inherited the kennels. Oh, and he tied up another loose end for us: those unidentified items of clothing belong to a woman he lived with. He told us she upped and walked out on him one day, leaving everything behind. We're tracing her, but it does look as if she's still alive. He reckons he left the clothing to throw us off the scent, and including hers made him feel as if she might also be a victim.'

Rubbing a thumb over the scar on his forehead, Bliss said, 'That's good to know. We'll need her to make a statement about her time with him. Did he say why he chose the chalk pits last time?'

Chandler nodded and spoke up. 'He claims the sites themselves were not particularly relevant, other than in avoiding CCTV wherever possible. When you consider previous dumping grounds, I think that's probably true. He said he'd visited the chalk pits before and remembered that maple tree.'

'So what's his deal there?'

'Nothing special as it turns out; some nonsense about growth, death and rebirth. He thought adding a whole mystical feel to the dump sites might eventually feed the serial killer angle and throw us off track.'

Bliss put his head back and groaned. 'Sounds like a complete nutjob. Is that going to feature as part of his defence? That he's insane?'

'A lot of people believe in a kind of spiritual empathy between humans and trees, Jimmy.'

'True. But they're usually sandal-wearing beardy types.'

'And that's just the women,' Hunt chipped in, laughing at his own joke.

Bliss shrugged, sickened by it all. 'The callous bastard clearly got off on the whole thing. If he'd felt any remorse whatsoever he would've covered them up, not left them out on display.'

The DCI was about to comment when Glen Ashton strolled into the room. His arrival was greeted with a low chorus of boos and blown raspberries, not all of it good humoured. He ignored the jeers and headed straight for the more senior detectives. No air of supcriority this time, but neither was he cowed.

'I realise I'm not flavour of the month around here,' he said, 'but tell me you wouldn't have done the same in my shoes. Any of you? If you'd been given the cold shoulder and all the grunt work?'

Warburton eased herself off the desk on which she had been perched. She pushed back her wavy brown hair and said, 'I'm proud of the way this unit works with others, Glen. I was an outsider myself not so long ago, yet I was welcomed and treated like any other member of the team. Our joint task forces have been collegial, and our relationship with ERSOU in particular has previously been a good one. It gives me no pleasure to say this, but the big difference in your case was your initial attitude. So yes, you probably were treated with a lack of respect. But that's because you didn't even try to earn it.'

He took the rebuke well, his eyes locking with theirs in turn. 'You'll get no argument from me on that score. As DS Bliss pointed out, I was a bit of a prick. But I didn't have that equipment seized out of spite, nor to get one up on this unit. You were busy, I knew I could help, so I took it upon myself to get that part of the job done. I didn't want any squabbles over who did what, either. I realise I went about it the wrong way, but if you're at all interested, I think I have some good news for you.'

'Go on, then,' Bishop growled, eyeing him warily. 'Redeem yourself.'

Ashton nodded. 'I brought myself up to speed with the case file. So far, you've been unable to confirm who the other killers were. Understandable, really. People in that kind of business are hardly likely to concern themselves with genuine names. But this is where ERSOU comes into its own. First of all we drilled deep into Dark Desires, looking at all the men who'd previously requested girls willing to be choked. The site required legitimate identification, so we have a list of authentic names.'

'How does that help to match them against our killers?' Bliss asked. 'The intel is one-sided.'

'Because even Knowles had to have a way of letting these men know he had girls willing to go further for less money. As we already knew, he also used a dark web chat room. In there, the members use fictitious names only, lacking proper ID.'

'Hold on a moment,' Bliss said. 'If the users have fake names, how were you able to pick out Knowles?'

'With him, we were able to work backwards. We began by looking at what he was doing on there in the first place, so were able to look out for the kind of messages he'd be posting. See, the only real secret a dark web user has is their name. What they want or what they offer is usually pretty transparent. In this case, we looked at posts from somebody calling themselves DogOwner, who offered for rent young animals not requiring a slip lead.'

'The fucking evil bastard!' Bishop said. 'A slip lead prevents choking.'

'Precisely. So Knowles was easy to find, but identifying his clients from their user names alone would have been a nightmare.'

Warburton raised her eyebrows. 'Would have been?'

Ashton nodded. 'The type of men who use these boards almost always use several others across the web. ERSOU's proprietary software examines the use of language, to help us build up a profile of these people on the dark web – the algorithm seeks out the same linguistic idiosyncrasies. These men had to have started off with normal agencies, or using one or more of the numerous websites out there matching sexual preferences with the right women. Also, they love a good message board where they can discuss their perversions with others. We have undercover investigators and officers posing as people with similar tastes, which makes it relatively easy to get involved in the discussions.'

'And I'm guessing you got hits,' Warburton said.

'We did. It's not an exact science. But I do have a list for you, containing thirteen possible suspects. We can't narrow that down any further with software alone, but I thought that's where Major Crimes might be interested in taking up the final part of the challenge. I think your team is best placed to whittle it down to find your killers.'

'*Our* killers, Glen,' Bishop told him. He gave a firm nod of appreciation. 'What you did was uncalled for, but you're forgiven.'

'By everyone?' Ashton glanced around, including at Chandler, who had joined them and had been listening for some time.

The silence was electric for a few moments, but Bliss took it upon himself to close the distance between them more than metaphorically. He stepped forward, holding out his hand. 'You have a lot to learn, Glen' he said. 'But so did we all at one stage in our careers. We could probably have dealt with you differently, and I'll take the blame for that. The main thing is, you did right by us in the end. You did right by Operation Phoenix. Which means you also did right by the victims. That earns you a lot of points.'

While Bliss was speaking, Chandler had taken a call. She looked at him when her own conversation ended. 'That was Belmarsh. They can confirm that Drake borrowed a phone and spoke to Nicola Parkinson while we were en route. Seems he asked her if she knew why we were paying him a visit.'

Bliss grimaced. 'Just as we thought: she must have realised we were going to talk to him about Dark Desires, and that once we did he'd be wondering about her.'

'Only we know she didn't have anything to do with it. So why would she do a runner?'

'Guilty by association, maybe. After we spoke to her about it, she must have wondered if somebody else in the organisation was pulling a fast one behind her back. If they were, it was happening on her watch. Perhaps we'll never know if she had any suspicions about her own son. Also, what are the chances she wasn't siphoning off some of the cash that passes through her hands? If Drake was about to get busy digging into the way his organisation was operating, she probably realised she couldn't stand up to that kind of scrutiny.'

Chandler sighed. 'Perhaps we'll get to ask her sometime.'

'What a pleasant thought that is.'

'What d'you reckon will happen with her boy?'

He fired off a look of disgust. 'Who the fuck calls their son Troy these days? I don't know, Pen. He might be as gullible as he's being made out to be. I'm not sure if we have anything on him – not yet, at any rate. Still plenty of time for all that over the coming months while we're putting our case together.'

'What a family, eh?'

'Yeah,' Bliss said, turning away. 'And the real kick in the balls is they might all be innocent this time.'

He caught Bishop's eye and indicated towards the door leading back into the passage. Outside the incident room, Bliss told his colleague he was stepping aside as Phoenix neared the end of its first phase. 'You spoke well earlier, Bish. Now you need to do so again. Pull it all together. Savchuk is going to cough. Gul and I are waiting to hear back from her brief, but she'll go.'

Bishop's face creased into a frown. 'But you were as much a part of this as anyone, Jimmy; more so, if the truth be told. Why won't you be part of the celebration?'

'Because this is your team. You led them. If I'm in the room they'll have one eye on me and may not know how to respond.'

'If this is my team, you're one of my team members. You deserve to be in the room, and you deserve the pint I want to buy you afterwards.'

'I'm still part of your team, Bish. And you can buy me a drink tomorrow night. You get out there and tell them what they need to hear. Besides, I've got something else I need to take care of.'

'One of these days you'll have to tell me what you've been up to on the QT recently.'

Bliss smiled. 'Yeah. One of these days. Probably best kept for when you're not my boss.'

'Acting boss,' Bishop reminded him.

'Perhaps. Anyhow, embrace the victory. Enjoy it. They don't all turn out like this.'

'I'll take the win, but in terms of a victory, it feels quite hollow. Perhaps the list Glen has for us will change that.'

'Then keep them at it. He and Gul worked well together. She understands the language. Between the pair of them I think they can help us track down the men responsible. We find them, we take covert photographs of them, and then we have Knowles confirm ID on them. He'll be as helpful as he can be because he doesn't want any of the actual murders coming back to him.'

Bishop heaved a long sigh. 'Where do these people keep coming from, Jimmy?'

'I have no idea. I think I'd rather we were dealing with a single serial killer than multiple murderers. One sick mind as opposed to five.'

'Yeah. And these were just the men who eventually went too far. The names Knowles gave us during his interview runs into more than a dozen of these fucking perverts. And how about the ones we know nothing about or weren't a match for our purposes?'

Bliss nodded and turned to leave. 'Try not to think about them, Bish. Spend too long considering the numbers and you'll never do the job again. Let's savour the moment before we knuckle down to pull in these other sick fucks.'

'Are you sure you won't stay?' Bishop asked, pleading one last time.

Bliss was certain. Earlier, he had taken a call from DI Nicholls, whose team were set to effect the arrest of Neil Watson. Nicholls had wanted to know if Bliss fancied being there. As if the wildest of horses could keep him away.

'Cheers, but no,' he said to his friend, colleague, and reluctant boss. 'I have one last job to attend to today.'

FIFTY

HAVING WORKED CLOSELY WITH George Moss, DI Nicholls believed the plan he had pieced together ought to work beautifully. Moss would ask Watson to meet him for a drink, dropping a few hints that he was starting to feel the burden of the secret he'd been keeping. The pub in which they met would be filmed and recorded, with everyone in it a member of the team, including the woman behind the bar. Moss's job was to put Watson on the defensive, getting him to talk and to admit to arranging the alibi. They had the man's blood-drenched clothes, but a confession would be a nice addition.

At the appointed time, Moss called Watson to encourage him out for a pint. When he sensed reluctance, he suggested they meet in order to discuss some misgivings Moss had about the alibi he had provided. Watson eventually agreed, and a time was set.

Unfortunately, that was as good as it got.

Bliss was already on his way over to rendezvous with the Hinchingbrooke team when he took a call from an anxious Moss, who was almost gibbering with fear.

'It's blown,' he said. 'Neil is onto me! Now what the fuck am I going to do?'

Bliss spotted a place to pull over so that he could focus on the phone call. 'Hold on, George. Calm down, pal. Explain yourself. What do you mean, it's blown? Why do you say he's onto you?'

'Because he fucking called me back, that's why! He told me something didn't feel right about me asking for a meet-up the way I did. Then he said he wasn't coming, and if he found out I was working with you lot he'd put me in the ground.'

'Shit!' Bliss emptied his lungs, cerebral wheels spinning all the while. 'But it sounds to me as if he only suspects something might be up at the moment, George – there's no way he can know for sure. I'll call DI Nicholls and have him and his people step down so Watson has no way of knowing they were ever there.'

'Oh, terrific. I can't tell you how safe that makes me feel. I'll sleep easy in my bed tonight now, won't I?'

'George, believe me, you're going to be fine. You played your part, and he's never going to find out about it because we'll back off and wait for a better time. Thing is, you have to concentrate. Did it sound to you as if he was going to leg it?'

'He thinks you lot are waiting to slap the cuffs on because I gave him up. Of course he's legging it.'

'All right. Settle yourself down, pal, or you're going to stroke out. Listen to me. This is very important. Do you have any idea where he might go?'

'How the fuck should I know? I'll tell you where he ain't going, shall I? Anywhere I know about.'

Bliss was struggling to steady his own breathing. It was Harvey's arrest, but it was he who had stuck the key into the slot and started winding the mechanism. If Watson got away this would be his failure, too. More than that; if they drove him away now, where might he end up next? And what might he do there that nobody would be prepared for?

'George,' he said. 'Don't panic. I need you to find some backbone. Forget what you think you might know; tell me only what you do know. He's been living in Peterborough for a while. You must have got closer to him over time. Slow your brain down and tell me about the people he pals around with and where I might find them. I know some of the places he might go before getting out of Dodge, but he must have other friends we know little about.'

'I'm telling you, Bliss, he's not hanging around in the city. He's going to scarper. He might... Oh, fuck!'

Bliss felt an instant chill rip through his body. 'What does that mean, George? What have you just thought of?'

'Is our deal still on even if I didn't tell you everything?'

'Not if you lied to us, George. It doesn't work that way.'

'No, I didn't lie. But I didn't tell you something because it didn't occur to me at the time.'

'So tell me now and worry about your own neck afterwards. Otherwise it'll be me you have to fucking run from.'

'Fuck! I thought you didn't need to know. It didn't seem to matter before. Shit!'

Bliss closed his eyes. Teeth barely parted, he said, 'I swear, if you don't tell me right now, George, you're going to need a zip to hold your insides together by the time I'm finished with you.'

'All right. Stop messing with my fucking head. Thing is, there's a woman Neil started seeing. Divorced sort. Lives over at Thorpe Meadows.'

A coldness the like of which Bliss hadn't felt in years crawled between his shoulder blades like a trapped insect. His jaw set so hard he thought it might break. 'Are you sure?' he snapped. 'I mean, are you absolutely certain about this?'

'Yes. One hundred percent.'

Bliss felt his stomach fall away, as if he were trapped in a lift hurtling down its shaft without any brakes. His plan all along had been to enrage Neil Watson to the point where the man lashed out – but it was supposed to be at him. He was the aggressor, the man winding Watson up at every turn. All of the recent intelligence he'd seen insisted Watson had no woman in his life. If it had, he'd never have gone ahead.

Intelligence was wrong, it seemed. Teddy Barr had not discovered the relationship, either. Knowing precisely how the police would think if they knew Watson was seeing another woman, he'd kept it quiet from all but his closest friend.

What have I done? Bliss thought. *Did I wind the man up only to propel him into another act of violence against a woman and…?*

'Tell me she doesn't have children,' he said. 'Please tell me that, at least.'

Moss was silent for a couple of seconds. Then, through a low whimper, Bliss heard the man say, 'I'm sorry. I'm so sorry…'

FIFTY-ONE

THORPE MEADOWS ABUTTED THE city's rowing club and sculpture park, close to the Boathouse pub often frequented by Bliss and his team. Having obtained the address and wrestled a promise out of Moss that he would call Nicholls, Bliss pushed his Mondeo as hard as he could on roads that were wet and treacherous. The moment he brought the car to a screeching halt, he heard a commotion that drew cold dread into his heart.

He climbed out and slammed the door behind him. A vocal gathering of neighbours lurked on the pavement, while others stood on their own balconies. Horror and a peculiar instinctive excitement painted ugly masks upon their faces. Bliss raced up the stairs until he reached the landing on which an affixed plastic card revealed the correct floor. From there he found his way easily, the loud cries, screaming and muffled thuds pulling him in like a tracking beacon.

Bliss had to push his way past the few neighbours who had been brave enough to draw closer to the source of the ruckus, if not intervene to stop it. When he arrived at the door to Poppy Myler's flat, it stood wide open. The din from inside had grown exponentially louder, its source there in its entirety the moment he crossed the threshold.

The passageway was mercifully narrow. If not for that, Bliss estimated he might already be attending a double murder scene. Neil Watson was too broad, too muscular to move easily within the confines of the hall. As it was, his arms flailed, one hand clenched around the thin end of a baseball bat, the other clubbing at a much smaller woman whose bloody face strained every corded vein as she howled and screamed, desperate to maintain her protective stance over a young boy who cowered and wept, snot streaming from his nose and tears spewing from both eyes.

Bliss made a swift calculation and knew immediately what he had to do.

He took two long strides and hurled himself at Watson's wedge of a back, bringing the meaty sides of his two balled fists around in a wide arc to thud into the man's ears. Watson's head was a solid mass, his neck and back and shoulders and arms bulging with power and strength. In his current state, any attack on these areas would be futile; the pumped-up beast was impervious to anything Bliss might have been able to summon up.

But his ears were vulnerable, and the pounding Bliss gave them caused Watson to shriek like a whistling kettle reaching boiling point.

Watson's arm flapped backwards uselessly as he attempted to swat Bliss away. The baseball bat rose and fell against the solid hallway wall, gouging out a large chunk of plasterboard and lodging against it before the rounded wood could cause any damage to flesh and bone. The bat fell to the floor. Bliss used the momentary advantage to strike again, this time one-handed at the nose sticking out from the turned head like the gnomon of a sundial.

Enraged, Watson managed to shuffle around and complete his turn. Facing his opponent, he seethed at having been interrupted. Bliss saw the punch coming from the moment the man's shoulder muscles twitched. But the drawback was laboured and clumsy due to the lack of space. Bliss rolled backwards from the waist. He could easily have avoided the swing altogether, but that was not part of his plan. Instead, as Watson's fist reached the apex of his arm's extension, Bliss met the connection with his head. He reeled back as if it had caused some genuine damage, thrilled to see the man's steroid-fuelled eyes spring wide open in excitement.

This was the beat down Neil Watson had been craving ever since Bliss had first intruded upon his life. This was everything his tormentor deserved, a justifiable punishment for every taunt and jibe and episode of harassment. And that was precisely what Bliss was counting on.

A straight jab with the left followed. Bliss took it on the upper arm. It hurt, but not enough to cause any lingering harm. The main thing was that it allowed him to take another couple of stumbling steps backwards.

In this way, Bliss lured Watson out of the flat and onto the small shared landing. He was peripherally aware of people scattering, fleeing like demonstrators in the face of a mounted police charge. He saved his own energy while Watson expelled his with every grunt and lunge. The blows kept raining in, Bliss deflecting or allowing himself to take the odd one that lacked any genuine momentum and power.

As he'd raced up to the landing, Bliss had noticed that the door leading to the shared external balcony had been propped open with a thin triangle of wood. While Watson hurled abuse at him, losing himself in the anger and fury, Bliss continued to lure the madman away from Poppy Myler and her son. Somewhere nearby, sirens and lights began to occupy the evening air, growing louder, brighter, moving closer, tyres skidding and car doors slamming. The cavalry had arrived. If he could keep Watson at bay for a moment or two longer…

But in his haste, Bliss had grossly miscalculated the size of the balcony, and almost immediately found himself jammed up against its brick and metal railing. As Watson stepped closer, his eyes bulging, nostrils flaring like those of a racehorse, Bliss steadied his stance for the first time and threw his weight behind a right hook. His opponent felt it – as did Bliss, the jolt running all the way up to his elbow. His response was to step in closer still. The two men merged, morphing into thirty-plus stone of bone, muscle, fat, tissue and blood in a single image of almost cartoon-like combat.

***

The stunned crowd looked on as two figures forced themselves up against the balcony railing, vigorously trading blows. A shrill female voice cut through the clamour of raised voices and cries of alarm, cursing and wailing, seeming to grow louder with every passing moment.

The two men swapped shoves and punches, kicks and elbows. Hard, thumping footsteps reverberated along narrow corridors as newcomers to the scene raced up the staircase. Both combatants struck out at will, gouging, using their foreheads, knees, hips, and shoulders as weapons. Anything to both defend against and attack their opponent. Strident voices echoed in the cool breeze that scattered scraps of discarded paper in the air, a blur of motion that captured the imagination, if not the full attention, of those who continued to witness the terrible scene.

Amidst the windmilling limbs and devastating thuds of bone on flesh, further obscenities were exchanged between the rasping gasps of breath that surged into the uncaring night. Only this time they were followed by a forceful rending of cloth on metal, and a sharp cry of terror that died almost as swiftly as it had begun.

And when the mesmerised crowd yelled and gasped in terror as one figure disappeared over the balcony handrail, the other remained on his feet, shuffling unsteadily backwards, no blows left to trade, none now required. Panting and heaving, hands resting on his knees, a huge grin creasing his face, sweat pouring from his hairline, blood smeared across his mouth and cheeks, Neil Watson turned, raised both hands in victory and let out a triumphant roar.

Which was the precise moment that Poppy Myler raced forward to swing the baseball bat that her assailant had only minutes earlier wielded against her.

FIFTY-TWO

'WE'RE GOING TO MISS him around here,' Detective Chief Superintendent Feeley said, gently squeezing Penny Chandler's arm. 'I genuinely mean that. He and I had our differences, but if ever a man had what it took to get the job done...'

He let it go at that.

What else was there to say?

Chandler pulled up the collar of her royal blue coat. Bliss had not wanted black attire, and she had abided by his wishes. People associated the colour black with sombre occasions, and again it had been his wish that this not be treated as such. It was more a celebration of life than a remembrance of death.

One day she might have to come to terms with Jimmy Bliss no longer being around, Chandler thought. But that wasn't going to be today. Nor any day soon. It was only a week since the incident with Neil Watson, but already Bliss's absence had created a hole in her life. There were times when she opened her mouth to speak to him, only to remember he was no longer there and why. It stung. Every single time. He had always claimed to others that she was his rock, yet the truth was she was the one finding herself cast adrift without his stabilising presence. Her world was filled with empty spaces where he ought to be; sometimes Chandler could swear she could see his shadow and feel his breath upon her skin.

'Good to see you again, Pen,' Bliss said, approaching her from the side.

'You too,' she replied, taking a step back to appraise him. 'And kudos on the new whistle and flute. As for pairing blue with dark brown shoes and belt, I can only gaze upon you in awe and wonder.'

He laughed and said, 'First of all, it's just a "whistle". You don't use the whole phrase. Secondly, I'll have you know I'm well known for my sartorial elegance.'

This time her look was quizzical. 'No, you're not. Who advised you?'

'Nobody. This is all my own work.'

'Who advised you?'

Bliss tutted and shook his head. 'Molly. I take it she got it right?'

'Spot on. So, how are you doing, Jimmy?'

'Not so bad. Already going batshit crazy on fucking gardening leave, though.'

Chandler snorted. 'You've had so much gardening leave during your career I bet you could give Alan Titchmarsh a run for his money.'

Laughter shook his whole frame. 'Missing me yet?' he asked.

'No.' She rolled her eyes. 'To be honest with you, the squad room is a lot quieter without your nonsense, coughing and farting.'

'Oi! I don't fart. Never have, never will.'

'Yeah, you and the Queen. You heard the latest on Neil Watson?'

'I hope the fucker's snuffed it.'

'Not quite. But those whacks he got from Poppy Myler did some real damage. Word is he's unlikely to survive. If he does, he may not even register it.'

'Then we can all sleep a little easier.'

'I suppose. How's your noggin, by the way?'

When Bliss had gone over the balcony rail and fallen, he was not alone in being thankful that it was from the first floor. He'd landed on a hedge, but had bounced sideways onto the concrete pathway below. One night in hospital to monitor for signs of concussion was all it had cost him.

Other than his pride.

Those colleagues who witnessed his fall from grace wasted no time in reminding him of it, laughing readily as they described the look on his face as he skipped off the surface of the hedge like a flat stone on water. He still got the occasional headache, but each one reminded him how fortunate he was not to have landed directly on the path.

'Yeah, no problem,' he told her. 'So I lost another few thousand brain cells. I've got plenty to spare.'

'Bollocks have you! I can hear that single one you have left rattling around inside your empty head like a marble in a tin can.'

'And yet I'm still a Mensa candidate compared to you. Look, Pen, I'd love to verbally abuse you and score points all day long, but before the ceremony starts I wanted to talk to you about Poppy. Are we going in to bat for her?'

'Poor choice of words.'

'You know what I mean.'

'My statement attempts to steer it that way, Jimmy, but it's hard to make an argument for self-defence given the time and distance between the blows he struck and her follow-up. But, before you do your nut in, we're solid when it comes to the CPS.

Every indication coming out of here and Hinchingbrooke is that she was still in fear for her life once he got the better of you.'

'Did he fuck get the better of me.'

'Well, he did force you off a first-floor balcony, Jimmy. And the way we hear it from witnesses is he did that only after beating several shades of shit out of you.'

'Well, tell those dozy buggers they're wrong. Has nobody ever heard of tactics? Does "rope-a-dope" mean nothing to you philistines? I had to lead him away from Poppy and her boy. The only way I could do that was to have him think he was getting the better of me.'

'Of course. You keep telling yourself that.'

'I'm serious. I told you this the other day. I bought time and put distance between us and them, giving them time to get away. Soon as I knew I'd done that, I landed a few slaps of my own.'

'Just not the one that has him feeding from a tube, eh?'

He folded his arms. 'Yeah. Well, good luck to her on that. Wish I'd seen it. Sadly, I was upside down on the floor having bounced off a fucking hedge at the time.'

'Fortunately for us all, you landed on your head. Nothing there to damage.'

Bliss gave a resigned shrug. 'I almost fucked up so badly, Pen. I got him so furious with me, which was my intention all along. The only trouble is, I had no idea about Poppy or her kid. He went to them that night intent on taking his anger out on two people who couldn't fight back, two people we had no idea were part of his life.'

'Yeah, and look where that got him. Still, I dread to think what might have happened if you hadn't arrived in time.'

'Like I just said… rope-a-dope. But I got lucky. If he'd damaged either of them, I'd never have been able to live with that.'

'Maybe you'll think twice about taking up a quest on your own in the future.'

Nodding, Bliss said, 'Believe me, I already have. It's forced me to question a number of things.'

They chatted for a few more minutes before he headed off to perform the function he was there to carry out. Moments later he appeared alongside DCS Feeley. The two men exchanged a brief handshake before walking across to the field maple tree whose shadow extended across the spot in which a dead body had been discovered. Its leaves had turned a shade of creamy gold and remained plentiful. In the warm autumn sunlight, even the roughened chalk pits with their terrain of white and green patches lent splendour to the moment.

Detective Chief Superintendent Feeley removed his hat, and to the gathered audience said, 'Not long ago, this area was tainted by the tragic murder of a young woman whose single failing was to assume she could settle here in this country without fear of being mistreated. Today we honour Majidah Rassooli, and hope to reclaim this plot of land as a place to forget the bad and enjoy all that is good once again. Here with me today to share this honour is Detective Sergeant Bliss from the Peterborough Major Crimes Unit, whose idea this entire event was. Please, Sergeant…'

His gaze switched away from the crowd towards the maple, where a single piece of red velvet hung from two tiny hooks threaded into the narrow trunk of the tree. Bliss stepped forward to unhook the covering, revealing a small brass plaque beneath. He read the engraved words one last time, though he knew them by heart. Then, standing to one side, he waited for the thunderous applause to die down.

'Thank you. I'm going to read the inscription aloud,' he said. 'It says: *This plaque is dedicated to Majidah "Autumn" Rassooli and the life she lived against all odds. Henceforth, this exquisite maple will officially be known as "The Autumn Tree".* This is followed by a quote from Emily Brontë that reads: *Every leaf speaks bliss to me, fluttering from the autumn tree.'*

Bliss had to swallow a couple of times before he was able to continue. 'We didn't know Majidah in life, but I hope we served her well in death. My team and I wanted to pay tribute to the young woman for whom we sought justice. And on a personal note, I hope it sends out a message to all who seek to exploit other young women like her. That message was, is, and always will be simply this: nobody should be left in peace to get away with such a crime against humanity, and we will not rest until your calm becomes our storm. Thank you.'

If anything, the applause this time kicked up a notch and endured longer. Bliss lowered his head and stared at the soil beneath his feet. Chandler's hands were sore by the time she finished clapping. Stirring words were one thing, but deeds spoke louder still. And Bliss had spoken so eloquently for them all. Her chest swelled as she looked around at the banks of fellow guests, many of whom were in full uniform.

She exhaled steadily. DCS Feeley might be under the impression that Bliss was not coming back from this latest episode – one way or another. But she knew the man better than anyone other than his mother, and quitting was not in Jimmy Bliss's limited vocabulary. No, Feeley was going to have to think again, because there was fight in that old dog yet.

***

The punch went in hard. A precise jab with the right hand, followed swiftly by an uppercut with the left, then a punishing right hook. Bliss turned to the group of onlookers and said, 'That's how you defeat a static bag.'

PC Griffin laughed, and the ten youngsters standing close by joined in.

Bliss turned to face them. 'But unless you already have them dazed and confused, opponents don't stand still and wait for you to land those punches. When you throw them, you have to prepare to be blocked, and for counter punches coming your way. You have to keep on the move and not stand back to admire the punch you just threw. That's a sure way to get your arse kicked.'

'So you're going to teach us how to punch and how to avoid being hit,' one of the young kids said.

'Barry and I are, yes. But it's not quite that simple. One thing you have to know coming into this is that you will not avoid being hit. You have to learn how to take a punch every bit as much as dishing them out. The art is not only in avoiding them, but also in making those that do land count for less. Your arms are your best friends; better to let them cushion the blows than take them to your chin. But all that is for later. We'll set aside some time for showing you both defence and attack. First of all, you need to know how to train. And I mean train to be fit. Training to fight is an entirely separate thing. Without the fitness, you'll last about a minute, maybe less.'

A loud groan of disappointment went up. Bliss grinned. 'Yes, I know Barry here told you much the same thing when you signed up. Maybe you expected me to tell you something different. Well, think again. The plan is to teach you to be both physically and mentally alert. We'll prepare you for the ring. We'll also prepare you to walk away when you're on the street and somebody wants to show they're better than you. There's no room here for street violence. This is all about those three-minute rounds you spend in the ring against an opponent who has been taught to do to you what you want to do to them. Anybody not up for that, I'd invite you not to attend again. Everybody else: Barry is going to show you some fundamental strength and endurance exercises.'

With the youngsters working out, the two men talked as they observed. 'Thanks for this,' Griffin said. 'I didn't know if you'd make it. Not after everything you went through.'

Bliss's nose crinkled. 'We had a big win. That tends to make you ache less and your cuts and bruises heal quicker. But like you said from the outset, these kids need to see our commitment in order to give theirs.'

'They'd be even more impressed if they knew how much effort we put in at the day job, too. It was a rough couple of weeks, but you must be delighted at how things have gone since.'

'Yeah, there's been some good progress. Knowles and Youngs are on remand locally, four other men were arrested and charged with murder last week. Yeva Savchuk and Troy Parkinson are both out on bail while the CPS decide on their eventual prosecution. We have a long way to go, but I'd say we're on course for a full sweep.'

'Pity you couldn't tie Lewis Drake into any of it.'

'That's the way it goes. But he's not going anywhere anytime soon.'

Bliss felt good as he watched Griffin amble away to put the group through their paces. Things were starting to come together again. He had used his enforced time off to good effect, and mentally was in a better place than he had been in quite some time. He'd even given further thought to following up on the paramedic's flirtations, and decided it was something worth pursuing. Kelly was younger, seemingly enthusiastic about life, and he'd enjoyed their banter on the couple of occasions they'd met. Passing up even a slim opportunity to find happiness was not an additional regret he wanted for his collection.

His sick leave was mandatory and likely to be over within a week or so; in a few months' time he'd be back in his office. Having overcome some major difficulties and changes since his return to the city, the team were functioning well. There was still some daylight between his current circumstances and the date at which compulsory retirement kicked in. Penny was enjoying life to the full and making the most of it. He missed Molly, but had plans to visit her in Torquay over the Christmas break.

The thought reminded him of something. This was the first time in a long while that he had not volunteered to be on the roster over the holidays. In addition to seeing Molly, he was due to spend Christmas Day and Boxing Day in Ireland with his mother. His previous trip over with Chandler had ended up with the pair of them involved in a bizarre investigation, but perhaps on this occasion he'd be enjoying someone else's company.

Time would tell.

A curious sensation crept over Jimmy Bliss.

A feeling of warmth, a kind of energy drawn from it.

He couldn't tell for sure, but he thought it might just be hope.

ACKNOWLEDGEMENTS

First up this time around, I doff my cap in tribute to my four beta readers – Lynda Checkley, Maggie James, Dorothy Laney, and Kath Middleton. Each of you made a valuable contribution and helped to make this a better book than it otherwise would have been. I am truly grateful to you.

The same can be said of my editor, Alison Birch at 'rewritten', who once again did a great job with the edit and made some terrific suggestions and observations while keeping things light.

As ever I am grateful to my Facebook group and ARC readers, and to the bloggers who were generous with their time in agreeing to be part of the online tour for *The Autumn Tree*.

To Nicola Parkinson, who some time ago won the right to have a character named after her: I trust you approve.

Finally, a 'thank you' of course to my readers – your support is always greatly appreciated.

I hope you all like what I did with this one. Some of the scenes made me laugh out loud, some made me sad, some simply made me yearn for more Bliss and company in the future. Not all of you will agree, but as the author, I believe this represents my best work to date. At the very least, I hope you enjoyed the read as much as I enjoyed the write.

Tony
April 2021

Printed in Great Britain
by Amazon